LOVE IN NO MAN'S LAND

Duo Ji Zhuo Ga was born in Changdu, Tibet. She is a photographer, a writer and vice-chair of the Tibet Writers' Association. She now lives in Lhasa.

DUO JI ZHUO GA

LOVE
IN
NO
MAN'S
LAND

Translated by Hallie Treadway

HEAD
of
ZEUS

First published in the UK in 2019 by Head of Zeus Ltd
This paperback edition published in the UK in 2019 by Head of Zeus Ltd

Translated by Hallie Treadway
Edited by Lucy Ridout

A catalogue record for this book is available from
the British Library.

ISBN (PB): 9781786699466
ISBN (E): 9781786699435

Typeset by e-type

Printed and bound in Great Britain by
CPI Group (UK) Ltd, Croydon CR0 4YY

MIX
Paper from
responsible sources
FSC
www.fsc.org   FSC® C020471

Head of Zeus Ltd
First Floor East
5–8 Hardwick Street
London EC1R 4RG

WWW.HEADOFZEUS.COM

LOVE
IN
NO
MAN'S
LAND

Prologue

Cuomu looked radiant. Her multiple tiny plaits were studded with turquoise, she wore four red coral stones on her forehead, and her dark brows gleamed. She had exchanged her fur-lined robe for a light silk dress patterned with pale-blue flowers. He had given it to her last summer when he came back to visit his family, saying that all the women in Lhasa were wearing them.

The dress was useless against the biting cold, quite unsuitable for a herder who spent her days driving yaks and sheep across the plain, but it was beautiful, hugging her figure beguilingly, and as smooth as milk to the touch. It could turn men's hearts as soft as the white clouds above.

Cuomu tingled with anticipation as she stroked the fabric at her waist. He said that when she wore this dress she was as lovely as the celestial maidens on the snow mountain's peak. She wanted to look her prettiest for him. Standing in a moonbeam, dress billowing, silhouetted against the light as she waited for her man, she was a sight to behold.

His leave only ever lasted a month. Thirty days. Thirty sunsets and moonrises – their happiest days. When those days came to an end, Cuomu would lock the dress in her clothes chest, keep her beauty under wraps for another year and begin the long wait for his next homecoming. There was no one else out there in the wilderness worth looking beautiful for, no one else for whom she would endure so many lonely nights.

But this time he wouldn't be going back, that's what he'd said. He would stay home for good. She had put up with their long separations for so many years, and now she would marry him, no matter how much Ama objected. She had been set on marrying him ever since she was a girl, had only ever wanted him.

As she thought about their future together, about how they would never be apart again after today, she was so overcome with happiness that she mixed the sheep and yaks' milk together. The other herder women laughed and teased her, saying she was mad to miss a man so much when he was away.

'You all have men waiting for you at home every day, so of course you don't miss them. I only see my man once a year. How could I not miss him?'

Cuomu straightened up from under the sheep's belly and giggled, the light, clear sound rising to the heavens like a skylark. Like every woman in love, her whole being was filled with the pleasure of it; her face glowed and she wanted to announce her happiness to the world. What did it matter if they weren't yet married? Her heart and body already belonged to him.

He was coming back. He was finally coming back. From now on, her tent would have a man. This was the only thought in Cuomu's head. On star-filled nights, she would no longer need to toss and turn with longing or worry that the men who came dog-driving would force their way into her tent to be with her.

Dog-driving was another term for courting. Every tent had a dog, a mastiff. Whether chained up or free to roam, the dog guarded its territory faithfully, aggressively chasing off intruders. If a man wanted to slip into the tent of a woman he liked under the cover of night, he first had to drive off the family dog. Over time, these night-time liaisons came to be known as 'dog-driving'.

Every young woman with a first tent of her own had a dog to guard her door through the night, alert to the shadows flitting by and whether they belonged to men who were in or out of favour. The dogs loved it when their mistress' suitors tried to appease them with a hunk of mutton or yak meat, and then, with their mistress' tacit approval, the dog would turn a blind eye. They hated it when, as the nightly visits got more serious, their mistresses grew up, made a choice and eventually left them, entering a strange tent and raising a new dog, with no more use for their protection.

Cuomu's dog crouched next to her, the wind gently ruffling his fur in one direction. He gazed intently at the movement of his mistress's hands, her long fingers sliding over the sheep's teats as gracefully as if they were dancing across the strings of a zither. Out there on the grassland, dog and woman made a perfect picture.

After she'd finished milking, Cuomu asked if she could go, then went home to get ready. She untethered the horse she'd prepared, cracked her whip and galloped off along the side of the lake. She was going to meet him. She always rode out to meet him; that was her custom.

She stopped to check her reflection in the lake and adjust her plaits. She'd grown them for him for nine years; nine years' worth of maidenly tresses that now reached her waist. Admiring herself in the water, Cuomu smiled broadly, laughed, spun around and let her long plaits swirl. The grass on the plain had turned brown, plot by plot, then green again, plot by plot, year after year. She'd grown taller and her hair had grown longer, but her heart had not moved on from its first love. She turned, got back on her horse and began to sing his favourite love song:

> *'The stars in the sky*
> *Are like Brother's eyes*
> *Watching Sister's silhouette.*
> *The butter lamps ablaze all night*
> *Cannot see your eyes, Brother,*
> *As they fall inside the tent*
> *To light up Sister's heart.'*

Cuomu's high, clear voice was as expansive as the vast grassland. Every son and daughter of the grassland, brought up in the wind and the rain, could sing of the sun and the moon, of mountains and rivers, of life and love. Their voices soared skywards with the breeze and the clouds, pure and untarnished by even a speck of dust.

As she thought back to his first time home on leave from soldiering, Cuomu's heart churned. She had ridden out to meet him then too. Catching sight of him on the mountain road, it had been as if a pack of wild asses had thundered across her heart. They were running still.

Seeing the distant figure of a woman on horseback, he had frozen momentarily, then cantered over. She had leapt off her horse and flown into his arms. When he kissed her lips, her face was wet with tears. It was as if her heart had suddenly woken from a trance; like a lake in summer, it could not be stilled. Her yearning for him filled the grassland right up to the sky.

She still burnt when she thought of what had followed that first time. He'd lifted her onto his horse and the two of them hurtled across the grassland. As she repeatedly turned to embrace him, the wind howled in their ears, the snow mountain dropped away behind them, and the two young hearts boiled. Reaching a ravine, they had rolled together in the thick grass, he holding her tight, pressing her to him, his gaze intense and unwavering, his rough hands lightly caressing her face. She had stared at him tenderly, stroking his short, bristly hair. In three years he'd got taller, broader and more deeply tanned. He had left the grassland a youth and returned an eagle soaring into the blue.

The snow mountain was behind him. Against its graceful peak, her beloved seemed even more handsome and rugged. Cuomu had laughed lightly. Rolling over again, she'd taken off her thick white leather *chuba* and, smiling, had lain down on top of it, her black hair fanned out around her, setting herself out like a sumptuous feast for the man she loved. He had immediately covered her body with his, their hearts beating as one.

That afternoon at the foot of the snow mountain towering over the vast wilderness, they had composed the opening verses of their passionate love song. The song had lain in their hearts, a beautiful memory, there for replaying. And now at last, after days and months of waiting and watching, they could continue with their music, from today until the end of time.

Lost in her reveries, Cuomu was distracted and failed to see the brown bear with a white circle on its forehead and two cubs by its side. As the bear reared up threateningly in front of her, Cuomu's mind went blank. She had no time to react and no time to calm her frightened horse, which bucked, neighed loudly and threw her to the ground. The horse thundered off, leaving Cuomu defenceless in the grass.

As she rolled, Cuomu drew her knife. Herders didn't usually have to worry about bears on the grassland. Bears generally avoided people, so they rarely came face to face. But if they did encounter each other and the mother bear was with its young, then the battle was on: the bear would launch a ferocious attack to protect them.

The distant memory of a bear cub felled by a gunshot flashed through Cuomu's mind.

Before Cuomu had time to struggle to her feet, the mother bear was already looming over her, roaring. Cuomu rolled to one side and reached back to stab its foreleg. With a snort of pain, the bear lunged at her dress. Dazed, Cuomu rolled again, ripping herself free of the silk dress with her knife. She scrambled up and ran for her life.

Again, a gruesome memory filled her head, of a hole in a bear cub's neck, its blood gurgling out as the clear young eyes slowly shut.

The mother bear howled now, splayed its paws and bounded after her.

How could a woman outrun an angry bear? Cuomu had not run ten metres when the bear caught her in its mouth. With a single snap of its jaws, Cuomu's shoulder shattered with a terrifying crunch. Blood gushed out as if from a spring. Dizzy with agony and shock, Cuomu waved her knife weakly behind her, but struck nothing.

The bear swiped its paw at Cuomu's waist. There was a brittle 'crack', like the snapping in two of a blade of dried grass, and her broken body was tossed to the ground. Still Cuomu yelled and lashed out with her knife, driving it into the bear's shoulder. With a furious roar, the bear retaliated, pawing at her chest and shredding the remnants of her thin dress with its sharp claws. Then it stepped onto her soft stomach.

Beneath the blue sky and its white clouds, the bear's roars echoed across the grassland, reverberating in Cuomu's every vein and nerve-ending.

'Gongzha!' she cried to the heavens. The pitiful sound pierced the clouds, bounced across the wilderness and disappeared between the mountain ridges.

A horse came pounding towards her from afar, dust and chaff swirling in its wake. The man astride it howled despairingly. 'Cuomu!' His cry rang out across the plain. Before he even reached her, his knife flew through the air and buried itself in the bear's foreleg. The bear dropped Cuomu and sprang back. It knew it was no match for this man. It turned tail with a roar and lumbered away with its two cubs.

Gongzha leapt off his horse, with no thought of chasing the bear. He gathered Cuomu in his arms. Her stomach had been ripped open by the bear's paw; her intestines and blood spilt over him. She was dead.

'Cuomu!' Gongzha howled, pressing her rapidly cooling body to his chest. 'I've come back – your man came back. Oh, Cuomu, have you not been counting the days till my return? I'm here now – wake up! Wake up! Wake up and look at me, Cuomu.'

Gongzha cried and cried, his tears falling as heavily as snow in an avalanche.

The weather on the grassland could change in an instant. What had started as a few blades of grass waving in the breeze became a wild storm within minutes, the wind wailing hellishly and hailstones battering the ground, rolling back and forth and giving off a terrifying white light. Sky and earth became one.

Gongzha threw his head back, stared into the heavens and with a long cry shouted, 'Cuomu!' Then he picked up his woman's body and walked deeper and deeper into the gloom. His route was marked in blood. 'Kaguo, I will find you!' he yelled. 'You took my woman's life, and I will take yours!'

Part One

1

The Changtang Plateau lay between the Tanggula and Kailash mountain ranges, 4,500 metres above sea level on the Qinghai–Tibet Plateau. It was the gateway to northern Tibet. Snow peaks were as numerous as trees in a forest and the air was thin, its oxygen content half of that at sea level. Plants cowered close to the ground, their life cycle limited to one hundred days. Known as the Roof of the World, the plateau was hostile to humans. And yet, since ancient times, people had forged routes across it, connecting the highlands beyond the edge of the world to the rest of humanity. The Qinghai–Tibet Railway, the Qinghai–Tibet Highway and the Heichang Highway – these routes across the plateau must have seemed like grand ideas when they were first dreamt up, but actually constructing them proved an immense challenge.

The high, borderless plains were so barren that every living thing had to fight for survival. The land was vast, the people few. People of the plateau were no longer the tough warmongers of old. On the grassland, there were no distinctions between high- and low-class people or rich and poor: the wind and rain battered one person as they did the next. Those who wanted to stay there, who wanted to continue their family line for generations to come, had to adapt and endure, becoming as much a part of the highland environment as a grain of sand or a blade of grass. Despite the forbidding conditions, human activity persisted. War rarely raged in this wild place and its people were neither materialistic nor ambitious. They simply herded yaks and sheep, migrating each season with their livestock, impoverished but free.

Gongzha's family lived on the Changtang Plateau near the shores of Cuoe Lake. A single black tent, which could be relocated with ease, was all that contained them and their hopes and dreams. Today, the adults from the encampment were hunting wild asses and Gongzha was joining them. When most children were still throwing tantrums in their mothers' arms, Gongzha was already trekking through the mountains with his father, Lunzhu. He was the eldest child and Lunzhu had begun instructing him in the essentials of grassland survival as soon as he could, teaching him how to use the shape of a mountain to navigate, how to identify animals by their tracks and droppings, and which part of which animal to aim for if he wanted to kill them with a single shot. Life on the grassland was tough and dangerous, and Lunzhu knew that he could easily have an accident, come to grief in one of the plateau's savage storms, or be mauled by a wild animal. If he were to die, it would be down to Gongzha to look after his mother and siblings.

During the winter, when food for their livestock became scarce, the Cuoe herders always moved their animals down to valley pastures. A couple of days ago, while some of the herders had been at the pasture, getting it ready for the winter, a herd of wild asses had turned up there. They reported this back to the rest of the encampment and it was decided that each family should send a hunter; meat supplies were, after all, running low.

Meat was the staple food of the herders of northern Tibet. *Tsampa*, noodles and rice were fine for snacks or drinking food, but there was no way the men could subsist on that for three meals a day; they wouldn't have the energy to ride and hunt in the wilderness. Life on the plateau required a lot of energy: what flowed in their veins was not just blood but bravery and a determination to survive.

There were already people at the hunting ground when Lunzhu and Gongzha arrived on horseback, Gongzha sitting behind his father. Some of the young men immediately came over to ask Lunzhu's advice. His skills as a hunter were legendary: he'd been on countless hunts, was highly knowledgeable and made good decisions; above all, he had a natural affinity with animals. He always made wise use of his vast experience, and his name, which meant 'Heaven-Made' in Tibetan, reflected that.

'What do you reckon, Lunzhu, which ones should we kill today?' a young man in a lambskin hat asked quietly, rubbing Gongzha's forehead affectionately as he did so.

Lunzhu glanced at the wild asses grazing below. 'How many hunters came out today?'

'Twenty-five. Apart from two tents whose men aren't here, everyone else came.'

'Keep to the old rules: one head per person, and no shooting animals with young.'

'Alright!' the young man replied, then passed on the instruction.

'Aba, why don't we shoot animals with young?' Gongzha gazed up at his father, his eyes wide.

'We need meat now, but we'll also need meat again next year. If we kill the animals with young, what will we do next year? Nature has given us the wild asses to use in times of need: they don't compete with our yaks and sheep for pasture, and we don't even have to look after them. If we run out of food, all we have to do is go out onto the grassland and bring one back. Remember, son, you should never do anything to the point of exhaustion, and that includes hunting. If you do that, you have no room for manoeuvre. Understand?'

Gongzha nodded as if he understood, then scrambled up to sit alongside one of the young men who'd already loaded his gun and was searching for a target.

Production-Team Leader Danzeng came over. He didn't look at Lunzhu, but his words were meant for him. 'We'll go by the old rules and kill two extras for the vultures and wolves.'

Lunzhu nodded.

Danzeng and Lunzhu respected each other, but there was a distance between them. Lunzhu's woman, Dawa, had been

Danzeng's first love. However, circumstances had conspired against him, and the woman he loved had married another man, the man they called the Sniper – Lunzhu. Danzeng would never forget her.

After a big hunt, it was the custom to leave some of the kill for the vultures and wolves. Vultures subsisted primarily on corpses, but in recent years the rains had been regular, few animals or humans had died, and the vultures had gone hungry. The wolves were also hungry: in winter, most animals hid in their dens and it got harder and harder for the wolves to find food; famished, they would attack the herders' livestock. Hunts left behind a strong smell of blood, which drew these carnivores in. Experienced hunters would leave them something to eat at the site of the kill. If the scavengers were full, the men and their livestock would all be a little safer.

'Bala, look! There's a bear over there!' Gongzha was staring at the summit of a distant mountain, from where a brown bear was watching them. 'There's a white ring on its forehead.'

'That's Kaguo, born last year,' his father said. 'The bear cub Dunzhu and his men caught last year was her brother.'

'How do you know?'

'Her parents live on that mountain. I see them every time I go there to catch foxes. When the mother came out for the first time last spring, she had two cubs with her. Kaguo was one of them.'

'How do you know that cub was this one's brother?'

'They both have circles on their foreheads. This one I call Kaguo and the one Dunzhu caught I call Naguo, because its circle wasn't as white as this one's – it had some black in it. You shouldn't assume that all bears look the same – each one is unique and if you observe them carefully, you'll see the differences.'

'Should we kill it, Bala? You can get a lot of money for bear claws!' Gongzha stared at Kaguo, bursting with enthusiasm.

'Certainly not.' Lunzhu gave his son a stern look. 'We're herders, we rely on the grassland to live. Today the grassland gave us all these wild asses, so we have meat to eat. What would we do with all that money? Never forget, Gongzha, that a hunter should not be greedy.'

Gongzha frowned and fell silent. Even though his father was the grassland's top marksman, he had strong principles. He wouldn't kill two animals in the same day. That's to say, if he'd already killed one piece of game that day, no matter what sort of animal he came across next, he wouldn't fire another shot unless he was in danger. As he repeatedly said, if hunters practised self-restraint, there would always be food for them.

Just then, Team Leader Danzeng, who was standing on the highest point, waved his hand and pulled his trigger. A crackle of bullets followed from where the other hunters were hidden. After a moment of shocked hesitation, the wild asses began to bray and flee in all directions. But they were too late to save themselves: any ass that escaped did so only because the hunters had allowed it to.

Gongzha wasn't interested in the wild asses; he was still watching the bear, Kaguo. When he saw how she scampered off at the sound of the gunfire, for some reason he felt a bit sorry for her. The shots weren't loud – they sounded like beans frying – but they scared away all the animals, who instinctively knew their lives were in danger. It was as if the fear of gunfire was lodged deep in their bones. Generation after generation must have instilled in their offspring that the animals on two legs posed the greatest threat; they needed to get as far away from them as possible, because they had guns.

The scent of blood and the sight of their prey crashing to the ground always got the men excited. Perhaps this was also something that had its origins in ancient times and was lodged deep in the bones of humans. When people were in competition with animals for food, a kill was something to be proud of; this had been passed down the generations, so that even when they were not hungry and had no need to hunt, the thirst for blood was still in them. It required only the right conditions for it to burst out. And so, as the men looked at the wild asses on the ground and saw the blood spurting, their pupils dilated with the thrill of it.

Danzeng sent a few people down to do the count. There were exactly twenty-seven: neither too many nor too few.

'These two are really skinny, and this one has a broken leg,' one of the young men yelled back up. 'Who killed them? He's a good shot – got them with single bullets!'

Gongzha knew that the two weakest asses had been killed by his father: two shots, two animals. This was what his father meant by 'survival of the fittest'. Men hunted only out of necessity, and given that they used the lives of animals to sustain their own lives, they were duty bound to treat them with compassion. In the fierce struggle for life, the weakest animals would always be the most vulnerable. Being torn apart by wolves was far worse than being killed with a single clean shot.

Lunzhu slung his gun across his back, took out a pinch of snuff, sneezed, and then said lightly, 'Let's give those two to the vultures and wolves.'

'Yes.' Danzeng nodded and called down to the men. 'Don't take the two skinny ones – leave them for the vultures and wolves.'

The young men began hauling the rest of the kill onto the flatbed carts.

The older hunters lit a pile of incense to thank the Buddha for providing the animals and honour their deaths so they could reincarnate earlier. This was the way of the grassland. Even though they hunted one another, they also depended on one another for survival. If one died out, the others would be lost. Give thanks to the Buddha, give thanks to the grassland, give thanks to every living thing: this was the first lesson Gongzha learnt.

In just a short time, the grassland had been cleared. A light breeze blew and the grass rippled. Save for the stench of blood, it was as if nothing had happened there. As the horses dragged the carts away at a brisk trot, vultures started circling in the blue sky overhead and wolf howls echoed in the distance. The second shift of cleaners began to arrive one by one. After their work was done, the grassland would be pure once more.

2

'Leave your tent at sunrise with the livestock; leave your tent at sunset with a woman.' This line from an old herders' song was an accurate description of men's lives on the grasslands. For herders, the only things of value in their tents were a few pots and pans: the yaks and sheep that gave them their meat roamed out on the grassland and all the clothes they owned hung off their backs. Theft on the grassland was rare; no one would ride a day or two to another tent just to steal some old household goods. Blood was spilt frequently, however, usually when an argument became heated and knives were drawn. If it was just a minor incident, it was soon forgotten. More serious altercations were adjudicated by the elders, and often a sheep or yak would be given in compensation, to stop further revenge being taken.

Most events in the wider world had no effect on life on the plateau, where the Changtang herders carried on as they always had. But the Cultural Revolution was different. In 1966 it roared across the grassland like wildfire. People's respect for religion seemed to disappear overnight. Buddhism lost its air of mystery and herders no longer prostrated themselves fervently before the golden statues of the bodhisattvas or gazed up at them in awe. Temples large and small fell into disrepair. Buddhist monks were stripped of their expensive robes and walked out of their temple halls in everyday clothes, forced to re-adjust to the secular life they had left behind. For those who'd joined the temple when they were young and knew only how to read the scriptures and serve the Buddha, this was a long and excruciating process. Relearning how to herd and milk and gather yak pats was easy enough, but having to put aside the Buddhist prohibition against killing and take up hunting in order to keep themselves from starving was torturous.

On the day that a group of communists brandishing copies of the *Little Red Book* and wearing shabby fur-lined robes stormed into Cuoe Temple, Gongzha was sheltering in a crevice higher up the mountain, counting the wild yaks in the river valley. The yak herd had arrived two days earlier and Aba had told him to keep a close eye on them and see that they didn't run off. If he did as he was asked, Lunzhu promised he would take Gongzha with him to kill one of the yaks. The family had nearly run out of meat and would soon be going hungry.

Whenever Lunzhu took his old rifle with the forked stand out on a hunt, he always came back a day or two later with enough meat to last the family for several days. And even though Gongzha was not yet as tall as the gun, he'd been well taught by his father; he never wasted his bullets and could already take down antelopes and foxes.

Each time Aba came home from a hunt, he paid a visit to the temple, prostrated himself three times and presented the monks with some meat. Tibetan monks ate meat. Han Chinese Buddhists and Theravada Buddhists might have disapproved of this practice, but Tibetan Buddhism was rooted in the mysterious land of Tibet itself. On the cold, high plateau, yaks and sheep were essential for survival and anyone who did not eat meat would find it hard to scrape by. According to the theory of reincarnation, everything on earth had life, and that meant respecting not only animals that walked but also plants and other lifeforms. Everything had the potential to be the present incarnation of a person's brother, sister or parents from a past life. Entering a temple and putting on the crimson robes of a monk might change a person's status, but it did not take away his human needs. As Buddha's representative among men, a monk's first duty was to stay alive.

Hunting had to be done mindfully and with restraint. If an

entire herd was wiped out, there would be nothing but grass for people to eat. If humans were to continue living on the plateau, then animals had also to be allowed to continue living there. Cuoe Temple's Living Buddha Zhaduo would say this each time Lunzhu visited, and each time Lunzhu would bring his palms together in acknowledgement, nod, and exit the temple hall.

Gongzha had always wanted to go on a yak hunt with his father. Killing a wild yak was a serious challenge – they were massive, almost three times the size of domesticated yaks, and if you didn't kill them with a single shot, they would fight for their lives and quite likely cause you an injury. For the last two nights, Lunzhu had been called to political study sessions with the rest of the production team and hadn't been able to go hunting, which was why he'd told Gongzha to climb the mountain each day and check that the wild yaks were still there.

The herd in the valley were females. There were at least twenty of them, as well as four calves born at the beginning of the year. Male yaks were solitary creatures and only joined the herd for the mating season, during which time they burnt off all the fat they'd accumulated over the winter. Then they left the females again and began rebuilding their strength.

Gongzha suddenly heard shouts coming from the temple. Was it another group of communists looking to smash up the old way of doing things – the Four Olds, as they called them (old habits, old customs, old ideas and old culture)? Gongzha slipped excitedly out of the crevice and climbed round to a grassy viewpoint overlooking the temple. He wanted to see what was happening, but he was too young to join in.

The temple was halfway up the mountainside and from his vantage point Gongzha could see everything clearly. A group of monks were sitting in the dirt yard in front of the temple while a revolutionary held up a copy of the *Little Red Book* and lectured them through a megaphone. Gongzha recognised the young revolutionary: it was Luobudunzhu, from another production team. He'd gone to middle school in the same commune and had then joined the Red Guards. When he returned to the commune, he set up a Revolutionary Command Centre and was now its commander. He usually wore a soldier's belt around his sheepskin *chuba* and liked to strut around self-importantly.

When Luobudunzhu finished speaking, he ordered the monks to leave the mountainside and return to their homes. From now on, he said, the temple would be the Red Guards' headquarters. The Red Guards began yelling revolutionary slogans, hurling the bodhisattva statues to the ground and smashing them to pieces with hammers. The valley echoed with the clang of destruction and the despairing cries of the monks. In the blink of an eye, the revered Buddhas and bodhisattvas that had presided over the temple hall became nothing more than scrap metal.

The back door of the temple opened quietly and an old monk emerged carrying a yellow cloth bag. He looked as if he was in a hurry; he didn't take the path but scrambled on his hands and knees straight up the side of the mountain. Gongzha recognised him. He was the temple's Living Buddha Zhaduo, the most learned man of his generation. He often chatted with the hunters and was a very self-disciplined old monk.

A young man in a soldier's cap poked his head out the door. When he saw the old monk halfway up the side of the mountain, he started to yell, 'The cow-ghost snake-spirit is getting away. Hurry and bring him back!'

A gang of young revolutionaries brandishing the *Little Red Book* swarmed out of the temple and began to chase after him, shouting and yelling. The old monk kept glancing back nervously. Tucking the bag into his robes, he climbed faster towards the top.

Gongzha was worried for him; he feared Zhaduo would get caught and beaten up. The revolutionaries had subjected him to a lot of criticism at the production team's recent political meetings, tying a wooden board around his neck announcing in Tibetan that he was a cow-ghost snake-spirit. The old man was getting frailer, and after each such struggle session, as the revolutionaries called these meetings, he was bedridden for several days. Lunzhu often sneaked over with Gongzha to see him, bringing him food and comforting him.

Zhaduo's pursuers were closing in. The living Buddha was clearly exhausted and his leg was injured. His route up the mountain was blocked by a large boulder. He would soon be caught.

'Quick, quick!' Gongzha urged quietly. 'There's a way up to the right of that boulder.' He didn't dare speak loudly: if the Red Guards found out that he'd helped the cow-ghost snake-spirit, Aba and Ama would suffer for it.

In these troubled times, it was hard to distinguish between men and demons.

Zhaduo looked up and was startled to see Gongzha, but he took his advice and edged his way round the side of the boulder. With no time to lose, he stuffed the yellow cloth bag he'd been clutching into Gongzha's leather *chuba*, put his palms together and said, 'Please help the Buddha, child.' Then he turned and went back down. He cut a noble figure against the rocky mountainside.

The revolutionaries soon caught him. They pinned his arms behind his back and walked him back down the mountain, jostling him as they went. Zhaduo staggered, and just before he re-entered the temple, he turned his head and glanced up the mountain.

Gongzha touched the bag and suddenly felt that he'd been brave in the face of danger. He waited until the revolutionaries had disappeared inside the temple, then stood up and made his way back to the other side of the mountain. He slid down the slope, returned to his hideout and squeezed into the crevice. If he bent his knees to his chest, he could just about sit down.

He pulled the cloth bag out of his robe and opened it. Inside was the statue of a Buddha as tall as his arm and so black it gleamed. When he held it in his hand it felt cool and heavy. There were also some pages from a book. Gongzha glanced through them. On the top page was written in gold ink: *The Epic of King Gesar*. There was another piece of paper with a snow mountain drawn on it. In the centre was a triangle, and in the centre of the triangle was the image of a bear; on the bear's forehead was a tiny ¤ symbol.

Kaguo? Gongzha opened his eyes wide to look at the bear on the paper. How could it be Kaguo? What was the old living Buddha doing drawing Kaguo? And in a triangle? Gongzha looked at it upside down and right side up. He'd seen Kaguo enough times – in the distance when he was picking up yak pats, hunting foxes or herding. Sometimes Kaguo was hunting mice or catching rabbits, sometimes she was sunning herself or just lumbering about. They'd never actually had an encounter, but she felt as familiar as an old friend.

As he stared at the sketch on the rough paper, Gongzha felt as if a sheaf of grass had been stuffed in his brain. He thought and thought until he worried his brain would burst, but still he couldn't imagine why Living Buddha Zhaduo would draw Kaguo. He put the piece of paper and the other things away again. He couldn't take them home. The Red Guards came and searched the families' tents every couple of days for the Four Olds. If he took Zhaduo's things home and they were found, the family would be in big trouble. He would have to hide them while he worked out what to do with them. He looked around him, but there was nowhere in the rockface to hide things. So he got up, took out his meat knife and began digging in the crevice where he'd been sitting. After a while he'd excavated a hole just large enough for the cloth bag and the Buddha; he tucked them into it, covered them well and patted down the earth with his hands. Only then did he leave his hideout and descend the mountain, singing mountain songs.

That evening, Gongzha heard Bala and Ama saying that the temple's elderly living Buddha had been arrested and there would be a meeting to criticise him that night. He was accused of having hidden the Buddha statues handed down by generations of living Buddhas, including the statue of the Medicine Buddha, the most precious of Cuoe Temple's treasures. Nobody knew what it was made of, but it was said to be an ancient relic that had once belonged to King Gesar, and it was supposed to contain secret information about his legendary treasure. A very rare copy of *The Epic of King Gesar* written in gold ink had also been passed down. Luobudunzhu said that these artefacts were highly poisonous grasses that had to be rooted out and immediately handed over to the County Revolutionary Committee. But even though the Red Guards had turned the temple inside out, they hadn't been able to find them.

Everyone on the grassland had heard of the legend of King Gesar's treasure. It was said that there were two caches: one on Mount Chanaluo on Cuoe Grassland and the other by Tajiapu Snow Mountain in Shuanghu. Even if it was more than just a legend, even if there really was treasure up there, the herders knew that to take the story seriously would be to risk their lives. Chanaluo and Tajiapu were more like mountain ranges than individual peaks, comprising countless large and small snow mountains extending for thousands of kilometres. Up there among the peaks and ridges, at the mercy of the wind, frost, rain and snow, where the bears and wolves made their homes, how could anyone hope to find the treasure – or the corpses of those who died looking for it?

'What does the Medicine Buddha look like, Bala?' Gongzha was sitting in front of the stove and blowing the flames into bright tongues with the lambskin bellows.

'I've only seen it once, and that was five years ago. It was during a *cham* performance in the temple. The living Buddha was very excited and had it brought out so we could pay our respects to it. I think it was black, or perhaps a very deep blue-black, and very shiny.'

'Oh!' Gongzha's heart jumped and he opened his mouth to tell them what had happened on the mountain. But then he remembered Zhaduo's pleading eyes as he'd thrust the Buddha into his arms with the words, 'Please help the Buddha, child.' The living Buddha was usually so calm and composed, no matter who he was talking to. But today he'd been so flustered that he'd asked a mere boy for help. He must have been in a great deal of trouble, otherwise why would he have given such important objects to a child to look after?

For a living Buddha to have put such trust in him was a huge honour. The last thing Gongzha wanted was to betray that trust or let Zhaduo down. So he decided not to say anything.

The sun rose above the mountain peak like a great ball of fire, quietly surveying Cuoe Grassland. Far below, the herders advanced slowly with their yaks and sheep. Their long shadows stretched across the plain like an animated scroll painting in black ink. Occasionally a man quickened his pace or an animal lingered and the shadows intersected, creating a new image. The lake shimmered in the distance, its clear water sparkling like diamonds beneath the sun's rays. The snow mountain had always stood there, for a thousand years, even for ten thousand years; it seemed immutable, and yet each day it was different. There were always eagles overhead, swooping or circling, embellishing the landscape at just the right point. This ink painting had life – it had a quickness and grace.

It should have been an auspicious, tranquil scroll painting. It could have been heaven, if it weren't for the man in the red armband patrolling up and down outside people's homes and yelling through his megaphone: 'Struggle session tonight! No absences! No asking to be excused!'

The sun had not yet sunk behind the snow mountain's peak when the first of the herders began arriving at the empty yard in front of the production-team tent. Ciwang, the director of the Commune Revolutionary Committee, would be leading this struggle session himself. Although he was from Cuoe Grassland, Ciwang had never been a herder or a hunter. Instead, he'd drifted all over the grassland, turning up wherever there was a wedding or a funeral, eating and drinking his fill. Grassland elders used to single him out as an example to other lazy young men of how not to behave. But when the Cultural Revolution came, this bullyboy wastrel somehow managed, overnight, to become the Communist Party's local representative, to lead a gang of other violent layabouts in an orgy of destruction and looting, to rise up the hierarchy and in the blink of an eye.

When the herders arrived, they found Cuoe Temple's Living Buddha Zhaduo tied to a prayer-flag pole. His crimson robes were torn and covered in dust. Some of the herders were curious or even excited to see him like that, others were upset. Five-coloured prayer flags still fluttered from the pole, the six-syllable mantra of the bodhisattva Avalokitesvara dancing in the wind. It was a strange world. People cried out to destroy the Four Olds, to deny the existence of spirits and ghosts, but at festivals they still strung up banners petitioning for peace and prosperity.

At a table in front of the tent, three men sat on a bench: Ciwang in the middle, Luobudunzhu to his left and Team Leader Danzeng to his right. Ciwang took in the size of the gathering and saw that most people had arrived. He glanced at Danzeng. Danzeng stood up to quiet the crowd. He told them that the meeting was about to begin and that Director Ciwang would be instructing them.

Ciwang raised the *Little Red Book* high and led the people in the reading of a passage. Then he sat down, cleared his throat, glanced round the crowd and said, 'We called you here today, comrades, to clear out once and for all the highly poisonous grass that we have weeded, but not weeded thoroughly, that we have burnt, but not yet burnt to the ground. We all know that Chairman Mao has had us grasslanders in mind for a long time. He wanted us serfs to liberate ourselves and become our own masters. We have yaks, we have sheep, we have food and clothing. But there is someone here who cannot stand to see us serfs living comfortably. He cannot stand to see us happy. Who is that person?' Ciwang scanned the faces of the crowd as he shouted this last question.

Asked in that way, the crowd became agitated and countless pairs of hands pointed at the living Buddha tied to the prayer-flag pole, their strange cries echoing to the clouds.

'It's him! Beat him to death! Beat him to death!'

Ciwang nodded contentedly. A wisp of a smile floated around the corners of his mouth. 'Cuoe Temple is hiding the most poisonous grass on the plateau. Not only has he refused to bring it out so it can be destroyed, but he's hidden it, ready for the day when he can begin poisoning us with it again! You decide – can we let him do this?'

'No!' Another round of raised fists and savage shouts from the crowd.

Ciwang was delighted. He stood up and strolled over to the prayer-flag pole. He stooped a little and looked down at the drooping head of the former living Buddha of Cuoe Temple, now the capitalist roader Zhaduo, and laughed coldly. 'Speak! If you tell us where those things are hidden, perhaps the people will forgive you.'

Zhaduo lifted his head and glanced at him, then said lightly, 'The things you are looking for are not in the temple.'

'I'm asking you: where is that black Buddha?' Ciwang stared at him, a fierce smile pasted on his face.

Zhaduo met his gaze, his expression calm and peaceful. 'My temple has never had the black Buddha you speak of.'

This infuriated Ciwang. No one had dared to speak to him like that before. When people saw him, they bowed respectfully and smiled ingratiatingly – without exception. He despised Zhaduo, had despised him since he was young. How had Zhaduo become a highly respected living Buddha just by putting on some monk's clothes? Why should Ciwang have to bow his head and give Zhaduo the right of way whenever he saw him? Luckily, times had changed. Today the grassland was Ciwang's kingdom.

He raised his hand and slapped Zhaduo. 'Do you want to eat rocks?' he asked menacingly.

Zhaduo did not move. He didn't even blink. He just looked steadily at Ciwang. A trickle of blood began to creep down his forehead, but on that calm, still face it seemed like a torrent.

Ciwang turned to face the crowd. 'Even in the face of death he refuses to confess. What should we do, comrades?'

'Beat him to death! Beat him to death!'

Perhaps it was because Zhaduo was too calm; perhaps it was because of that trickle of blood; or perhaps it was because their darker natures had been stirred up by Ciwang's slap. The crowd began to get restless, to surge forwards, and then, flood-like, a chaotic barrage of kicks and cries crashed over the peaceable old man.

Gongzha clutched his father's robe. Lunzhu's hand clenched into a fist and his face twisted with pain. He and Zhaduo were the closest of friends – like father and son. To see his dear friend suffer such injustice was like a stab to the heart. It was as if each blow and kick was landing on his body too. Eventually, he could control himself no longer and forced his way into the fray of frenzied herders. But when Zhaduo saw him, his impassive face suddenly changed and he cried out loudly, 'Fuck off, you black demon! What do you think you're doing?'

Gongzha and Lunzhu were startled by his words. But the others surged forwards even more aggressively, piling into Zhaduo. In the chaos, someone thwacked Zhaduo's leg with a stick. Zhaduo screamed and his leg went limp. Purplish blood streamed out from beneath his crimson monk's robes, seeping into the sand and drenching the ground.

The scene in front of the black tent was grotesque: scarlet blood, dead grass, a monk's robes covered in sand, a calm face, fluttering prayer flags, crazed people. It was as if the door to hell had been opened by mistake.

*

Lunzhu sat slumped on the couch, his head drooping, sighing occasionally. His woman, Dawa, was sitting by the stove, mechanically adding yak pats to the fire. Their five children were huddled naked under a rough yak-wool blanket, looking at one another, not daring to make a sound.

'Gongzha, get up. Get dressed.' Lunzhu had finally made up his mind. His tone did not allow for questions.

Gongzha darted out from under the blanket, put on his sheepskin *chuba*, pulled on his boots, and stood by his father's side.

Lunzhu pulled a small yak-skin pouch from a basket by the door and took out a black medicine pellet that Zhaduo had given him some time ago. It was excellent for healing flesh wounds. There'd been two pellets: he'd used one when he was bitten by a wolf and there was one left.

Dawa looked anxiously at her man. 'Are you sure about this? If even his own sister won't look after him, why are you taking the risk?'

Lunzhu glanced at her, hesitated, and then stretched out his hand towards his son. 'Take this to Zhaduo.'

'Be careful! Don't let anyone find out.' Dawa saw that her man would not be dissuaded; she could only turn and fuss over her son.

Gongzha nodded, then turned and left.

It was very quiet outside. The dogs were all lying beside their tents, napping. When they sensed Gongzha walking by, they opened their eyes and looked at him briefly before lowering their heads and continuing to sleep.

Gongzha walked towards the field behind the tents, acting as if he was looking for a place to defecate. When he got to the small, lonely tent on the east side of the encampment, he glanced around to check there was no one nearby, then flung open the flap and hurried in.

Zhaduo was not asleep. He sat bolt upright. 'Who is it?'

'It's me!' Gongzha said quietly. He squatted by the couch and handed over the medicine. 'Aba wanted me to bring you this.'

Zhaduo took the pellet, put it in his mouth and chewed it up without a second glance. Gongzha quickly poured a bowl of cold water for him by the weak light of the moon. Zhaduo took a couple of sips.

'That Buddha—' Gongzha whispered, keen to tell Zhaduo that he'd hidden the statue.

'What Buddha? I don't know about any Buddhas. Go home now, go quickly,' the old man interrupted, waving him off.

Gongzha raised his head and looked at the old man on the couch. The old man looked back at him, his gaze both knowing and vacant, as if it contained everything and nothing. Gongzha kept his own gaze steady, but in his gaze there was both fear and confusion.

The old man and the young boy exchanged looks, then nodded simultaneously.

'I'll go and pick herbs for you tomorrow,' Gongzha said, and slipped out of the tent.

Zhaduo smiled peacefully and lay back down.

Gongzha glanced out at the empty wilderness then to the quiet encampment. He began to whistle, then returned to his tent as if he had just finished defecating.

In the days that followed, the fire of the Cultural Revolution continued to blaze. The adults were kept busy studying *Quotations from Chairman Mao Zedong*. Gongzha looked after the sheep and collected yak pats just as he always had.

Late one night, Lunzhu shook Gongzha awake. He'd slung on his rifle with the forked stand. Gongzha got up with silent understanding and put on his leather *chuba* and fox-fur hat. Dawa fastened Lunzhu's belt and warned him to be careful and to come back early if he couldn't get anything. Lunzhu nodded, pushed open the tent flap and went out, Gongzha following behind. They didn't dare ride; they took the sheepdog Duoga and walked quietly towards the river valley.

When a man went out hunting, it affected the rest of the production team, whether he was absent for just one day or whether he was away for ten days or more. The commune had issued a directive about this two days earlier: herders were no longer allowed to hunt for themselves. It disrupted the production quotas required to make the revolution a success. From now on, anyone who went hunting would be punished for being a selfish individualist and would lose their entire winter meat ration.

Directives were all very well, but they weren't always practical. It was too early for a harvest, and last year's meat had already been eaten. People just didn't have enough to fill their bellies. The adults liked to say that the children didn't care whether there was a revolution or not: when they were hungry, they cried.

Gongzha and his father walked along the river valley, the dog at their side. Save for the crunch of their footsteps, everything around them was silent.

3

Yaks were the principal livestock on the Changtang Plateau. Despite their bulk, they were docile and easygoing. But wild yaks had very different temperaments; they were unpredictable, aggressive and in the most remote reaches of the grassland often gored people.

August was mating season for wild yaks. The males were at their most aggressive then, sparring incessantly to establish dominance and win a mate. One by one, defeated bulls would be driven from the herd until the last bull standing became the new leader. Once exiled, the losers would turn their attentions to the domesticated female yaks. A domesticated bull was no match for a wild one and could be chased away in seconds, leaving the wild yak in sole command. The domesticated female yaks seemed to prefer the wild yaks and it was not uncommon for them to run off with one.

Father and son knelt on the mountaintop, looking at the yaks massing below them. Duoga lay by their side.

'How do we get them, Aba?' Gongzha's eyes were wide with excitement; he could not wait to hear the gunshot.

'What's the rush? Just be patient. If you wait until they lie down after they've eaten and find the right angle, you can kill a yak with a single shot. If you don't do it with a single shot, the yak might attack you in self-defence.'

The sky was a perfect blue, without a wisp of cloud. The sun warmed them, and the distant snow mountain gleamed silver. The mountains of northern Tibet were terrifyingly high, but when you stood in front of them, they didn't seem nearly as tall or remote as you might imagine. This was particularly true of the snow mountains of No Man's Land, which unfurled in layers, ridge after ridge. It was as if an immortal being had scattered precious stones across the empty grassland. Wild yaks, wild asses, antelopes and herders were also part of the landscape: they animated the plateau, they were its lifeblood.

Lunzhu nudged the drowsy Gongzha, who stirred and sat up. Rubbing his eyes, he looked down at the valley. It had a dreamlike beauty in the evening light. The golden rays of the setting sun lit up the dark cliff face, colouring it tangerine, and a little way off, the snow mountain burnt red and emitted golden rays of its own. In that light, the parched grassland looked idyllic. Black yaks lay on the ground and calves romped by their mothers' sides, occasionally butting heads with a playmate. It was a scene of shifting loveliness: quiet but full of life.

Gongzha twisted his head and saw that his father was loading his gun. 'Which one will we kill, Bala?' he asked.

'We can't kill the ones who have young. If the mother dies, the calf won't have anyone to protect it, which will make it hard for them to survive. We mustn't be greedy, son – we need to leave seeds so that new grass will grow.' This was one of Lunzhu's favourite sayings.

With that, Lunzhu lay on the ground, set up the forked stand for his gun, and slowly took aim at the yak herd below.

As the sound of a single gunshot pierced the air, a thin, weak-looking yak on the fringes of the herd fell to the ground and did not move again. In a flash, the rest of the herd lumbered to their feet and began to run, the calves in the middle and the strongest adults on the outside. They thundered off, turf kicked up behind them, the rumble of their hooves echoing across the valley.

Within moments, they'd vanished from sight.

'We got it, Bala! We got it! We won!' Gongzha jumped to his feet, punched the air, and raced down the mountain with a grin on his face and Duoga by his side.

Lunzhu watched him go with a smile. Unhurriedly, he

gathered up his gun and allowed himself to relax. He opened his box of snuff, poured out a little, inhaled deeply and sneezed happily. He wiped his mouth with his hand, picked up his son's leather *chuba* and headed down the mountain.

The ground was littered with steaming yak pats. The yak that had been shot lay dead, a tiny bullet hole in its neck. Lunzhu took his knife from his belt and began to skin it. With no horse or ass to assist them, they wouldn't be able to carry a yak of that size home in one piece; it would have to be chopped up and taken back in chunks.

At the herders' encampment on the eastern shore of Cuoe Lake, Luobudunzhu, wearing his soldier's belt as usual, took up his megaphone and announced that every man and woman was required to come to the Revolutionary Committee's tent that night to study the important directives of Chairman Mao.

Before the Liberation, the herders of the Changtang Plateau were mostly nomadic. They moved from pasture to pasture with their yaks and sheep, depending on the season, and had no fixed place of residence. After the Liberation, government officials arrived and divided the area into communes. The population of the grasslands was small and the distance between tents was often well over five kilometres, so to organise even a small meeting, the commune had to despatch riders ten days in advance, and even then they wouldn't necessarily find everyone. To make their work easier, the County Revolutionary Committee decided to group the herders into production teams and have them live in one fixed location and pool their food. This was convenient for the revolutionaries, but it made the herders' lives a lot more difficult. They had to walk for tens of kilometres to put their livestock out to pasture and sometimes could not get back home inside of a day.

When she heard Luobudunzhu summoning them to the meeting, Dawa began pacing back and forth inside her tent, unsure what to do. Her man had gone looking for wild yaks and was still not back. If he missed the study meeting, he'd have to go to a struggle session, but that would be no big deal compared with losing a meat ration for having ignored the directive against hunting. They had barely enough to eat as it was – if they lost an entire meat ration, how would they get through the next year?

She thought and thought, then put on her leather *chuba* and white lambskin hat, told her second son Gongzan to watch his brothers and sister, and walked over to the team tent.

As she stood outside the tent, she heard Team Leader Danzeng talking to Revolutionary Committee Director Ciwang and the people he'd brought with him. Ciwang rarely went back to his own home these days; he mostly just stayed out on Cuoe Grassland. He lived in the team tent, saying he was determined to root out every last one of Cuoe Grassland's poisonous grasses.

Dawa stamped her feet loudly and deliberately. From inside came Danzeng's deep voice. 'Who is it?'

'It's me, Team Leader!' Dawa opened the door flap and stood there smiling.

Although Dawa had given birth to five children, her waist had not thickened and her breasts and buttocks still managed to look shapely, even under her leather *chuba* and silver belt. Wherever she went, men stared at her. The men in the team tent were no different. When they saw her, they stopped talking and turned towards her. Ciwang was particularly attentive. He couldn't stop himself from going over to her, helping her off with her coat and holding it for her. 'Well, well, the celestial maiden of the moon that lights the grassland has arrived! Please come in and sit down.'

'Director, Team Leader, no thank you. I have come on behalf of the head of my household. He… he's sick. He has a fever and can't leave the tent,' she said, glancing at the men and laughing nervously.

'Sick? We're studying the latest directives from Chairman Mao tonight. The County Committee has told us that we must transmit them effectively and that everyone has to study them.' Ciwang stared lecherously at Dawa's face; he was practically salivating at the sight of her. Dawa, a woman as beautiful as the moon, had been the object of his frustrated desire when he was a young man. He'd gone to her tent several times but had always been driven out; once, her dog had chased him right across the grassland while she stood by her tent howling with laughter. He'd sworn to himself that he would have her. She was the real reason he spent so much time on the grassland now; it wasn't because his wife tried to make him stay home or because there were poisonous grasses that needed rooting out. No, it was because of the woman standing in front of him, the woman he'd never been able to have.

'Director, he… is really sick – he can't get up!' Dawa avoided Ciwang's eyes; she lowered her head to look at her toes and spoke in a small voice.

'He can't get up?' Ciwang looked at her doubtfully. 'I'll go and check.'

'Director…' Dawa quickly raised her head. 'Our tent is very dirty. How could we invite you in – you would soil your boots.'

'What difference does that make? If a great beauty like you can live there, why should I be afraid to come and have a look?'

'It's not that, Director, believe me. If you really want to come, I need to go on ahead and clean up.' Dawa turned towards Team Leader Danzeng and shot him a pleading look.

Danzeng stood up and said, 'How about I go instead? I often go to her family's tent – it's tatty and there are yak and sheep droppings everywhere, so it wouldn't be appropriate for you to go, Director. I'll go and check up on him. You sit here for a while: the butter tea is coming soon and the girl who's bringing it is one of our lake's wildflowers – we'll get her to sing for you!'

Hearing this, Ciwang stopped in his tracks. 'Alright. You go and check on him, but come back quickly – we'll wait until you return before we start drinking.'

'Good!' Danzeng left the tent with Dawa.

Once they'd checked that there was no one else around, Danzeng whispered, 'He's gone hunting again, hasn't he?'

Dawa glanced at him. 'We're almost out of food,' she said softly. 'We adults can manage, but the children are only small and they can't go without.'

Dawa and Danzeng had grown up together and their happy childhood memories lived on in their hearts. When the time had come for love, they'd hoped to be together for life. Danzeng's first go at dog-driving had been to Dawa's tent and he'd wanted to marry her. But his parents were against it; they said that because Dawa was an only child, Danzeng would have to care for her family's elders if he married her and wouldn't be able to get out of it. They made him marry another woman. Not long after, Dawa found Lunzhu and started her own family. Even though they now both lived beside the lake, they were careful to practise self-control and had not had an encounter since. Neither of them wanted to bring conflict into their otherwise peaceful lives. When there were no deep feelings, it was easy for people to sleep together, but because Danzeng and Dawa loved each other, there would be discord in their tents if they were to become involved again. Men and women with deep feelings could not play the adult games of the grassland.

'You have lots of children – the commune knows how difficult things are for you and we're thinking about giving you some help. Oh, the times we live in... Try to hold on. I've heard that the government is thinking of breaking up the collectives, putting a stop to group rationing, and returning the pastures, yaks and sheep to the herders. Things will be a little easier then.'

'Thank you, Danzeng. I know it's you that often leaves meat outside our door.'

'I'm so sorry, Dawa. Long ago I promised to marry you, but then I married another woman. You have only one man, your children are small, and your life has been hard – I wish I could help you. But you know what a fierce temper my mother yak has, and if she found out, she might come looking for you and make trouble, so...'

'I know, I know, Danzeng. I know what's in your heart. It's not your fault. When did our parents ever understand their children's hearts?'

'You mean you feel the way I do?' Danzeng's pulse quickened and he snatched up Dawa's hand.

Dawa quickly pulled it away, looked around to see if there was anyone nearby, and whispered, 'I'm scared someone will see. Our time has passed – don't take it to heart. I'm going back to my tent and you need to go back inside too – the director is waiting to have a drink with you!'

Danzeng watched meditatively as Dawa walked along the lakeshore, then he turned and strode back to the team tent.

The moon rose and travelled as far as the mountaintop, but still Dawa's man and eldest son had not returned. The four little ones were already asleep. She stood outside the tent until her hands and feet grew cold. When she turned, she suddenly sensed someone watching her, but although she looked carefully, she could see nothing but the crowd of tents. She shook her head and went inside. In the middle of the night she went out to urinate and saw the silhouette of a person flash by her tent. Strange – who else would be out so late? Again, she searched carefully, but apart from the cooing of the night wind, there was nothing.

Before dawn broke, Gongzha and his father came walking up the track from the river valley, carrying their meat. But just as they got to the encampment, a dozen torchbeams were shone in their faces, blinding them. The dogs began barking wildly.

Luobudunzhu emerged laughing from the darkness, wearing his red-star cap and with a sarcastic smile plastered across his face. 'Aren't you meant to be sick? The Sniper, so sick he couldn't leave his tent, so sick he couldn't study the Great Leader Chairman Mao's important directives – how come he's bringing meat home at this hour? Ha, and it's wild-yak meat too! He truly is the grassland's sharpshooter, never comes back empty-handed.' He leant forward and added nastily, 'But he won't be keeping it.'

A troop of Red Guards pushed forwards, grabbed the meat off Lunzhu's and Gongzha's shoulders, and jostled Lunzhu away under detention. Gongzha was badly frightened. He ran behind them yelling 'Aba!', but one of the revolutionaries thrashed him with his leather belt and he had no choice but to turn back and run home.

He burst into the tent crying 'Ama!' and told Dawa what had happened. Alarmed, Dawa got dressed, pulled on her boots and raced over to the Revolutionary Committee's tent without even buckling her belt.

The clearing in front of the tent was lit with a kerosene lamp and a press of people were circling around it. Lunzhu had been tied to a tent pole. There were traces of blood at the corner of his mouth; he had clearly just been beaten.

Dawa pushed her way through, sobbing. 'What do you think you're doing, beating him up? What crime has he committed?'

'You don't know what crime he's committed?' Luobudunzhu said. 'Hunting without permission, avoiding studying the important directives – if that's not counter-revolutionary behaviour, what is it?' he said coldly.

'We have nothing to eat. Do you want my family to starve?' Dawa stared at him, her eyes flashing cold like a mother leopard's. 'What harm does it do you if he goes hunting?'

'You get a meat ration, same as everyone else, do you not?' Commune Revolutionary Committee Director Ciwang walked over. 'Other families can manage, why can't yours?'

'Director, I—'

'They have a lot of children, Director,' Danzeng interjected in a soft but authoritative voice. Unable to stand by and watch, he'd come over to join them. 'Can't we just overlook it? He only went out because they had no choice.'

Ciwang glanced at Dawa. 'How many children does he have?'

'Five. The eldest has just started collecting yak pats; the smallest is still breastfeeding.'

'Are they all his?' Ciwang pointed at the pinioned Lunzhu. It wasn't that he didn't recognise Lunzhu – who around there didn't know the Sniper? – it was that the Sniper's time had passed. The country belonged to revolutionaries like himself now.

'Yes, Director. He moved in with his wife's family,' Danzeng said carefully but with a smile.

Ciwang walked over to the captive and said, 'You've got some fucking luck – having a woman all to yourself.' He leered at Dawa. 'How about this: I'll look into it and if things really are difficult for them, we'll consider letting him off lightly.'

'Yes, yes, Director. I'll get a report to you right away.' Danzeng nodded, cueing Dawa with his eyes.

Dawa hurried forward, bowed to Ciwang and clasped her hands together. 'Thank you, Director, you truly are a good man!'

'Enough. I haven't said I'll let him go – that depends on your behaviour.' Ciwang fixed Dawa with a meaningful stare. Then he turned to Danzeng and said, in words also loaded with subtext, 'You don't need to write a report. I'll look into it myself, to avoid any conflict of interest.'

Danzeng waved away the chattering crowd. 'You can all go back home now. There's nothing to see.'

The onlookers headed off, muttering to each other.

As Danzeng too made to leave, he glanced at Dawa and pursed his lips towards Ciwang. Dawa nodded her understanding.

When Ciwang saw that all the spectators had disappeared, he said to Luobudunzhu, 'You take your men and go home too. We'll speak again when this has been cleared up.'

'Yes, sir,' Luobudunzhu replied loudly. Gesturing at the men behind him, he barked, 'Let's go.'

Within minutes, Dawa and Ciwang were the only ones left in the clearing, apart from Lunzhu, still tied to the tent pole. Dawa pleaded with him, 'Can't you set my man free, Director? He hasn't eaten all day!'

'You come with me first.' Ciwang didn't even look at her, just turned and walked into his temporary tent.

Dawa glanced at Lunzhu. Seeing his body striped with blood, her eyes flashed fire. Her man, respected by so many, as proud as an eagle, why was he being treated with such contempt? She could not allow him to suffer like this again. Her home couldn't function without him. Women did not need to hide behind their men, basking in peace and happiness; they could stand shoulder to shoulder with their men. She hesitated briefly, then followed Ciwang into the tent. She knew perfectly well what would happen next.

Ciwang sat on a chair and gave a cruel laugh as he looked at Dawa. 'Do you really want to save your man?'

'Lift your hand and let him go, Director. Our family has been pushed to the brink, our five children are going hungry.'

'You say you've had five children, so how come your waist is so slender? You're not at all like the woman in my house. She's only had two children and her waist is as thick as a bear's.'

'Director—'

'Your man's really lucky – a woman all to himself! Every night he gets to hold you, a woman as beautiful as the moon. How cosy. It's not like that at my house: we are three brothers to one woman, and you can't always be sure that when it's your turn, the woman will be... available. What do you say – is my life not hard?' Ciwang gazed at her, his small eyes ravenous.

Dawa looked at her toes, tears dripping. Even though the women of the grassland didn't take sex that seriously, it had to be consensual. If it wasn't pleasurable, what was the point? Dawa's thoughts turned to her man, still tied to the pole. She forced herself to lift her head, put on a smile, loosen her belt and slowly take off her leather *chuba*.

Ciwang was in no hurry. He threw some dried yak pats into the stove and waited for the tent to warm up. This woman was Cuoe Grassland's moon, a figure from his dreams. Because of his status as Commune Revolutionary Committee Director, he didn't dare go dog-driving like the other herders, for fear of being knocked back. He'd been forced to wait, to wait until the opportunity presented itself.

He finished piling on the yak pats and turned round. Dawa was standing by the window, her snow-white chest half bare, her hand pulling at her collar. A shaft of moonlight was shining directly on her and it really was as if a celestial maiden had descended to the black tent.

He beckoned to her and Dawa walked over slowly. He grabbed her by the waist and tore off the robe she was clutching. Pressing her down onto the couch, he began biting savagely at her breasts. Dawa hissed in pain.

Ciwang had no intention of cherishing her. He had subjugated her, had used his power to get her, and having finally got what he wanted, he was going to make the most of it. He quickly stripped and then penetrated her brutally, his hands grasping clumsily at her breasts and buttocks, leaving purple bruises on her pale white skin.

Dawa wanted to cry, wanted to yell, but she didn't dare. Her body was the one thing that could save the lives of her husband and children. Whether or not they could get through this difficult time depended on whether or not her body could endure this trial.

When she eventually emerged from the tent, it was if she was stepping on cotton bracts. Clenching her teeth, she walked over to her man and began undoing his bonds. Gongzha ran over and together they quickly released Lunzhu.

When Lunzhu saw the bruises on his woman's neck, his eyes looked as if they would spurt blood. He turned towards the black tent, braced to burst in there, but his woman hung onto him as if for her life, gripping his hand, her face streaming with wounded tears. Lunzhu turned back, and, seeing Dawa at his feet and his beloved son sobbing by her side, he too let the tears fall, from eyes that did not weep easily.

4

Two days earlier, the commune had sent people round to inform everyone that the men of each tent were required to travel into town for study sessions on Mao Zedong Thought. The morning Lunzhu left, he swatted the naked Gongzha awake and told him to take care of his sister and three brothers and to watch over the production team's sheep. He said that he'd be back in a few days and would bring Gongzha a fruit sweet. At the promise of a sweet as his reward, Gongzha nodded at his father without even wondering whether he was old enough to take on such responsibilities.

Gongzha's mouth watered whenever he thought about fruit sweets. Two years ago, when a group of Han men had come to the grassland prospecting for oil, he and some of the other children had gone along to see what they were doing, and the men had given them each a sweet. Gongzha had been desperate to make the sweet last as long as possible. He would get the sweet out and lick it twice, then close his eyes and let the sweetness roll off his tongue, slip down his throat and spread through his body. Then he'd wrap the sweet up again and put it back in his *chuba*'s front pocket. The sweet had lasted a month. It was Gongzha's favourite childhood memory.

Lunzhu smiled and rubbed Gongzha's bare head. Then he put on his old sheepskin *chuba*, opened the thick door flap and went out. Gongzha raced after him in his bare feet, calling after his father's horse, 'Bala, don't forget to buy me a sweet!'

'Don't worry, son!' Lunzhu waved to his woman and children by the tent, whipped his horse and clattered off into the distance.

Gongzha went back to the tent and stuffed his feet into his boots. His father had made them for him two years ago and he'd long since grown out of them. His toes poked out the front and both big toes were black with dirt. The adults had no time to worry about their children's feet: during the day they were busy working, and at night they had to study Mao Zedong Thought. When winter came, they just packed their boots with wool; as long as the wind didn't get in, they would be alright.

Dawa made butter tea and gave each child a small piece of half-cooked meat. Gongzha finished the tea in a few gulps and tucked the meat into his *chuba*'s front pocket. He knew they would soon be out of food. Aba had had to spend a lot of time studying recently and wasn't sure when he'd be able to go hunting again. Gongzha took his slingshot from the basket by the door and with a word to his mother raced off to the commune's sheep pen.

Today it was the turn of their tent and another tent to tend the sheep. Shida, the boy from the other tent, joined Gongzha at the enclosure. Shida's tent had three men to look after him and his brother – his father and two uncles – but they'd also gone to the study session in town, and Shida's older brother had joined the army last year, so Shida was also looking after the sheep today, in place of the grown-ups.

He was a bit older than Gongzha and looked almost like a small adult, but the two of them were like brothers. They often gathered yak pats, tended sheep and searched for wolf cubs together. At the sheep pen, they smiled at each other and whistled for their sheepdogs, who were playing in the distance. The dogs came bounding up, tongues lolling. Gongzha's dog, Duoga, was brown; Shida's was black and was called Duopuqing.

The boys crouched down and petted the dogs. Then they opened the gate of the enclosure and the sheep flooded out, keen to roam free after being penned in all night. Duopuqing and Duoga were well trained. They kept the sheep together, taking one side of the flock each, racing to the front or back and rounding up any strays, following the lead ram along the side of the lake to the grazing area, which had lots of marsh grass.

Once the sheep began to graze, the boys had nothing else to do, so they decided to collect yak pats. The herders used the manure from their livestock for fuel. Not many shrubs survived the harsh conditions of the grasslands, and those that did grew very slowly and were far too puny to use for firewood. Instead, they used yak pats to keep them warm in winter and for boiling water in summer.

Shida pulled a lambskin pouch from his *chuba*, took out a piece of meat and handed it to Gongzha. Gongzha accepted it with a smile and stashed it in his *chuba*. Then he picked up his manure fork and the two boys took a slope each. Gongzha wanted to get up the mountain before the sun climbed too high and before he'd used up all the energy from his two bowls of butter tea. If he collected enough yak pats for tomorrow, maybe Ama would let him go to the tent school for half a day. Gongzha longed to be able to go to school, to sit with other children his age and learn about things he'd never heard of. But his family was too large and too poor, so they needed him to work. It was different for Shida, and Gongzha envied him that.

When his stomach began to growl, Gongzha straightened his back, tightened his belt, and called to Shida. Shida was already lying spread-eagled on the other slope; when he heard Gongzha, he waved. Gongzha smiled, put down his bag, sat on the grass, pulled out the piece of meat and began to nibble at it slowly. He knew from experience that you could trick yourself into feeling full if you nibbled your food rather than wolfed it down in one go.

As he sat there, he watched the sheep down below. The two dogs were clearly tired as well. They no longer kept close to the sheep but had found a place to curl up and nap. Cuoe Lake looked clear and dark, like a beautiful piece of ancient jade, reflecting dazzling beams of light. A yak-skin boat was coming across the water towards them, gentle ripples spreading out from its sides. It was the team boat, the one that ferried the students to school and back twice a day. It ran at fixed times and between fixed locations. As he watched it, Gongzha imagined being on board. Today was Saturday, so only the students in their final year had school.

He began to feel drowsy. The afternoon sun was making his forehead tingle. He spread his sheepskin *chuba* on the ground and lay down to take a nap; he would get back to work again later. Perhaps tomorrow he could go on that yak-skin boat himself. He had long forgotten the things he'd learnt the last time he went; if he didn't go again soon, he might not be able to keep up.

He had only just shut his eyes when he heard a girl yelling from the other side of the mountain. She sounded frightened.

'Help! Help! Is anyone there? Come and help me, quick!'

It was Cuomu's voice. Cuomu was Production-Team Leader Danzeng's daughter and she was different from the other grassland girls. Her face was white, not ruddy like theirs. Zhaduo, Cuoe Temple's former living Buddha, was her uncle. He used to teach Cuomu her letters at the temple and then she would teach Gongzha. That was why, even though Gongzha had only ever attended school a few times, he could write the thirty letters of the Tibetan alphabet. It was tragic how Zhaduo was derided now as a cow-ghost snake-spirit, forced to live on the edge of the encampment with a broken leg, all alone in the world. Gongzha often went with Cuomu to take him food and fuel when no one was paying attention, so the two of them had become close.

When Gongzha heard her shouts, he rolled over, leapt up, and without even stopping to put on his *chuba*, dashed round to the other side of the mountain. When he got there and looked down, he was terrified. Cuomu was trapped on a crag: a sheer precipice dropped away steeply below her, and her only route back up the mountainside was blocked by a hungry-looking snow leopard, not three metres from her, who was looking for a way down.

Snow leopards were smart. This one was well aware that if it moved too quickly, both it and the girl would fly off the precipice in a cascade of rocks and scree. So it was clawing its way carefully down the loose shingle. It was this sound that had alerted Cuomu and made her yell out in a panic. She had also come up the mountain to gather yak pats. Distracted, she'd got stranded on the crag, not expecting to meet a leopard.

Gongzha had no time to hatch a plan. He simply picked up whatever rocks he could find and hurled them at the snow leopard. The snow leopard whirled around, saw Gongzha, snarled and sprang at him. Gongzha drew his knife from his belt and raced back towards the other side of the mountain, yelling, 'Duoga! Duoga, come quickly, there's a leopard!'

How could a child outrun a famished snow leopard? Within seconds, the snow leopard pounced and sank its teeth deep into Gongzha's calf. A stab of heart-stopping pain made his head spin and he almost fell to the ground.

Gongzha had been at his father's side in the wilderness since he was small and there was no animal he had not encountered. He knew that when man and snow leopard met, one of them had to die. He twisted round and stabbed blindly with all his strength, sinking his blade into the snow leopard's back. With a yowl of pain, the snow leopard loosened its grip on his leg and prepared to strike again. Gongzha didn't have time to pull his knife out. He quickly rolled down the slope. But the snow leopard wasn't about to give up on a meal it was close to finishing. It shook itself vigorously and the knife popped out and dropped to the ground. Then it sprang after Gongzha, the loose stones beneath its paws clattering down the mountainside.

Gongzha's cries for help had raised Duoga and Duopuqing. Barking wildly, they raced over and just in time managed to plant themselves between Gongzha and the snow leopard. The leopard and the dogs stopped in their tracks, dust swirling around them, and glared at each other like tigers.

The fight erupted without warning. It was unclear whether the snow leopard or the dogs had attacked first, but within seconds there was a whirl of biting and flying dust. The animals on the grassland all had their own rules: they knew who they could attack and who to avoid. The snow leopard was starving, otherwise it would not have risked its life in a fight. If there had just been one dog, it would not have hesitated, but it could only defeat two dogs with effort. It assumed that if it killed one of them, the other would back off. That way it could conserve its energy and end the fight quickly. But the two dogs had realised they were no match for this leopard and had decided to play the long game: one fought for a time, while the other stood by and barked supportively; when it got tired, they switched places. The snow leopard was fighting for its life on an empty stomach and its energy reserves were quickly used up. It did not have the strength to continue.

In the distance, a pack of mastiffs was yelping and tearing towards them. Dogs were the most group-minded of the grassland animals: if a dog heard a commotion even from five kilometres away, it would always come and help. Now the leopard knew it would not get its delicious meal, so it retreated hastily, disappearing up the mountainside.

There was no way a pack of mastiffs, masters of the grassland, would let an exhausted snow leopard vanish from under their noses. The quick-witted sheepdogs glanced at each other. Duoga chased after the leopard while Duopuqing veered off in a different direction. Duoga caught the leopard and bit its hind leg and the leopard impatiently turned and began to fight again. Just then, Duopuqing reappeared higher up the slope, cutting off the snow leopard's exit. Below them, the pack of mastiffs had finally arrived and began encircling them to the left and right.

Gongzha seized the chance to go back round the slope and rescue the petrified Cuomu.

The battle on the mountainside was over very quickly. The snow leopard's body lay on the sand and rocks and the dogs stood baying at the sky, the clear, high sound reverberating across the grassland.

Gongzha patted his dog and praised its bravery. When he looked up, he noticed a bear with a white circle on its head watching them with interest from a distant mountaintop. 'Kaguo!' he shouted. This was the first time he'd said her name. After his close encounter with death, Gongzha's heart was full of joy and he wanted to share his happiness with someone. He'd been familiar with Kaguo since he was small – she was like an old friend, and he couldn't resist calling out her name.

'What are you yelling?' Cuomu tugged at his arm and tilted her small face towards his.

Gongzha smiled. '"Kaguo" – that's the bear's name!'

'A bear?' Cuomu asked fearfully. 'Where?'

'There, on that mountaintop!' Gongzha pointed into the distance.

Cuomu looked up in the direction he was pointing, but she didn't see anything.

When they returned to the encampment, the news of their encounter spread fast. Team Leader Danzeng embraced Gongzha and loudly praised him as the little hero of the grassland. He said he would go to the commune and ask that he be commended.

Danzeng carried Gongzha back to his tent. Dawa had already spread a sheepskin on the couch. She made her son sit on it, then with hot water and a cloth she cleaned the bite wound on his leg and rubbed butter on it. Afterwards, she set about boiling water to serve to the other herders. Grassland mothers learnt early to take their children's injuries in their stride. It was normal for a child to pick up several on their journey to adulthood; their scars were like milestones that had to be passed, each one signifying that they were growing up. How else could a child mature into a courageous herder of the grassland?

The leopard was suspended from a wooden beam and a fire was lit beneath it. Two young men began to skin it with small knives under the watchful eye of several elders, who stood nearby and offered advice. 'Careful! Be careful, don't damage the pelt.' Later, the pelt would be cured by rubbing it with butter and *tsampa*. After some discussion, it was agreed that the pelt would then be presented to the Commune Secretary, who would go to the county town and ask for a commendation for the grassland's little hero.

Nights on the grassland were very quiet. Apart from dog-driving, people had nothing else to entertain them. So the story of how a child had rescued a girl from the jaws of a snow leopard spread quickly and took on almost mythic proportions. Even people who lived five kilometres away heard about the young leopard-fighting hero Gongzha who lived beside Cuoe Lake. Wherever Gongzha went, he was asked to tell his story. No matter that the herders had heard it many times already, they couldn't get enough of it. Cuomu watched her hero from afar, her dark eyes shining. Gongzha had saved her life, and the little girl's heart was stirring.

The news of Gongzha's heroism soon reached the town, fifty kilometres away, where someone told Gongzha's father and urged him to hurry home. Late at night, five days after the snow-leopard attack, as the moon rose over the tops of the tents, Gongzha's father duly returned to the encampment. But he had not walked home. He'd been carried. And now he was laid out on the frozen, sandy ground.

Dragging his wounded leg, Gongzha limped out of the tent to find his mother clasping his father's corpse. Her hair was wild and she was shrieking. His sister and three brothers were hanging onto her leg, wailing helplessly.

The herders gathered round, murmuring.

'We got caught in a landslide – a huge boulder rolled down the mountain. Oh, it's too sad.'

'It was lucky we managed to run so fast, otherwise it would have been over for us too.'

'How will they live – and the children so small! No man will be willing to take on so many children.'

'That's true. Beautiful as she is, that's not going to help her now. It'll be hard to find another man.'

The moon that night was exceptionally cold and mournful, the wind exceptionally bitter.

Two women went over and lifted Dawa to her feet. She had to accept that her man was dead, they said. She should think about having the sky burial soon, so that his soul would not get restless.

Team Leader Danzeng had two young men stay and help but dismissed everyone else. Gongzha stood by the tent flap and listened to Danzeng and his mother talking quietly.

'I'll get someone to take him up to the sky-burial altar tomorrow, but that's all I can do. We won't be able to get anyone to chant mantras for him – no one would dare. The commune is determined to pursue its Four Olds policy, and the lamas are struggling to fit in. What do you think?'

'I'll do as you say. Him going like this, leaving five children and the smallest still not weaned... How will we live?' His mother started sobbing again.

'Don't cry. Gongzha is growing up fast – and he saved my daughter's life. Do you think I can just stand by and watch you all suffer? As long as there is food in my tent, I won't let you go hungry.'

That night, while his mother was coaxing his siblings to sleep despite her red, swollen eyes, Gongzha leant on a stick for support and went outside to sit with his father. Lunzhu's tanned, ruddy face looked as if he were asleep. There was a trickle of frozen blood at the corner of his mouth. Gongzha stretched out his finger and picked it away. His tears dripped onto the back of Lunzhu's cold, stiff hand.

The moon continued to shine clear and mournful. Gongzha felt his own bones turning to ice. He gripped his father's hand. It was clenched into a fist and Gongzha began to gently unfurl his fingers. To his surprise, lying in the palm of his father's hand was a fruit sweet. It was wrapped in clear plastic with a flower printed on it. Gongzha had seen a sweet like that before, placed by an elder in front of the bodhisattvas in the temple. The sight of it had made the children's mouths water. Cuomu had said that this kind of sweet cost one fen. One fen! The herders rarely had any actual money; when they needed something, they would trade something for it. If you added one fen to another, you could buy a box of matches.

Gongzha carefully picked up the sweet, peeled off the wrapper and licked it. He shut his eyes and let that sweet taste spread across his tongue and slowly slide down his throat. After a long while, he wrapped it up again and put it in his *chuba*. His tears fell in fat drops.

From now on he was the man of the tent. It was down to him to take care of Ama and his siblings.

Danzeng used his authority as Production-Team Leader to order people to do this and that. Under his instruction, just after dawn the following day two young men tied Lunzhu onto the funeral master's back. Carrying the butter lamp used to light the way for the souls of the dead, they began to walk towards the sky altar at the foot of the snow mountain.

Despite his injured leg, Gongzha ignored his mother's shouts and limped after them. The lamp moved slowly across the plain, its light receding into the distance. He followed as best he could, but when the light disappeared into a fold in the mountain, he headed for a nearby hill and clambered to the top on his hands and knees. From the summit, he watched as the lamp reappeared, ascending and then descending as it wound its way slowly into the mountains. Finally he saw the curl of incense smoke rising. They had reached the sky-burial altar.

The encampment's dogs, wild and domesticated, also began to race towards the sky altar, baying hungrily as they went. When a man didn't have enough food for himself or his tent, he couldn't be expected to feed his dogs, so the dogs fended for themselves. Once they'd all but exhausted the supply of mice and rabbits on the grassland, they began to look to the sky altar for meat, where they quietly set about eating its corpses. Traditionally, it was the vultures who fulfilled that role, picking the corpses clean and accompanying the dead on their last journey. But the dogs had driven the vultures away. There was a death every two or three days at this time of year, but even that wasn't enough to fully satisfy the dogs, though it was better than nothing.

As the incense smoke spiralled, Gongzha saw the vultures circling. The brave ones darted down but were quickly driven off by the dogs. He couldn't bear to watch. Aba had loved Duoga, his dog. Whenever he went hunting, he would always take his gun with the forked stand, and Duoga. And when they came back two or three days later with a wild ass or an antelope, he would always save his dog a big piece of meat, saying that Duoga had worked harder than he had. If Gongzha were to see Duoga in that pack of dogs around his father's corpse, the pain would be unspeakable.

He wiped away his tears and began to make his way back to the encampment. At the foot of the mountain he ran into Cuomu's Uncle Zhaduo. He was wearing regular clothes, white hair was growing out of his once-shaven head, and one leg was lame. He was carrying a basket, as if he was going to collect yak pats.

Gongzha yielded the path out of habit and waited for him to go by. This was what his father had taught him to do: when you saw a monk, it didn't matter what age he was, you were deferential. Monks were learned people, they practised Buddhism and deserved to be respected. It was just that recently, all of the grassland people's customs had changed. Monks had become cow-ghost snake-spirits, and temples were seen as part of the Four Olds. The elders who had faithfully worshipped the Buddha seemed overnight to have ingested some kind of inflammatory medicine. They became frighteningly violent, brandishing the *Little Red Book* in raised fists behind a crowd of adolescents, bellowing slogans Gongzha didn't understand as they rushed into the temple, driving the monks out of the prayer hall, then bringing out the bodhisattvas, smashing them and throwing them into the lake.

Zhaduo glanced at him and continued walking, his back hunched and his head hanging low. When they passed each other, the old man said softly, 'He's gone to Shambhala, to heaven.'

Gongzha was startled and wanted to ask him what he meant, but Zhaduo walked quickly by and clearly didn't want to speak to him. Gongzha carried on home with a heavy heart. When he passed Zhaduo's lonely tent, he noticed the old man had put a small incense burner by the door and lit a stick of incense. People only did that to commemorate a deceased family member. Gongzha's heart hurt; Zhaduo was honouring his father's dead spirit.

There was no chanting of mantras and no one held a ceremony to help Lunzhu's soul find peace. Ama also placed a small burner by the door of their tent and lit a stick of incense three times a day. Seven days later she gathered up the burner and Aba disappeared from their lives completely.

With the death of his father, Gongzha became the encampment's youngest head of a household. Whenever the production team was dividing up supplies or having a meeting, he went to represent his family, and his signature in shaky Tibetan script replaced his father's fingerprint.

The family had not had any meat in two days. Ama took the younger children to pick wild plants, which she stewed with yak bones that had been used so many times there was no fat left on them. The herders were used to eating meat, and when they ate anything else they got diarrhoea; the women began to look sickly, and the men lost their vigour and sat around listlessly in the sun like old people.

As Gongzha was coming past Cuomu's tent on his way back from collecting yak pats, he heard her mother yelling, 'Why is it only you that's taking an interest? No one else is bothered! Isn't it just so you can see that face the colour of egg-white and that waist as soft as butter? Why don't you just move over there? The tent is certainly big enough – are you not man enough for it?'

'She's a widow and I'm the team leader. What's wrong with asking after her? Your yak-mouth talks too much!'

'My yak-mouth talks too much? That wild yak's mouth doesn't talk at all! Why don't you go be the head of the wild yak's household?'

The tent flap flew open and Danzeng plunged out with a leg of mutton in his hands. When he saw Gongzha, he was startled and gave an embarrassed laugh. 'Your auntie is crazy. Let's go!'

'Uncle Danzeng, don't worry about us. Things aren't easy for your family either.' Such grown-up words sounded a little odd coming from someone so small.

'No matter how hard things are for us, they're nothing like as hard as they for you. Child, don't be angry at your auntie. That's just her way. Let's go.' Danzeng put his hand on Gongzha's shoulder and they walked along the lakeshore towards his tent.

At the tent, Dawa invited Danzeng to sit and passed him some clear tea; there hadn't been any butter for a long time.

'I talked to the local PLA unit – they'll be looking for soldiers this winter. You should get Gongzha to enlist; at least they've got food there.'

Dawa glanced at Gongzha doubtfully. 'He's still so young, will they accept him?'

'Why not? He's from a serf family, his father's dead, his family is in difficulties and needs help, and let's not forget, he's already saved someone's life. If the army doesn't want someone like him, who do they want?'

Dawa sighed. 'When he's gone, there won't even be anyone to collect yak pats.'

'I won't go and be a soldier, Ama. I'll go hunting and look after you all,' Gongzha said, putting the meat Danzeng had brought into a basket.

'Good for you, Gongzha – you've got deep feelings and you're loyal. You're our Cuoe Grassland hero. But you can enlist with an easy heart. I've already talked to the production team. They know how difficult things are for your family and they'll try and do something to help.'

Not long after, Danzeng went to the town and when he came back he told Gongzha that he'd signed him up. He just needed to wait for his notice to arrive.

Gongzha worked harder than ever. As well as gathering up each day's yak pats, he made time to shoot wild asses. Everyone knew his family's situation, so they turned a blind eye to his private hunting.

Springtime was the busiest part of the year on the grassland because of the lambing. The lambing always happened in a special pasture in another valley. Changtang's river valley lay between two mountains and from a distance it didn't look that big, but when you were there, it seemed to go on for ever, and the landscape changed around every bend. The herders had used the same lambing pasture for many years. There was lots of water there, it was warm and sheltered from the wind, and because it was fenced off during the summer, the animals hadn't trampled it, so the grass was soft and plentiful. This made it perfect for the ewes, who could feast on the grass and produce lots of milk for their lambs, which is what they needed before they got big enough to go grazing out on the grassland.

The team had issued the order to move the evening before. The herders were to drive the sheep directly to the lambing pasture. Individual families were responsible for moving their own tents to the new encampment, and they had to move within a day.

The cart hadn't been used since the previous summer and its wheels had rusted. Gongzha repaired it and then went into the tent to bring out the things his mother had packed. The older two of his younger brothers used all their energy to bring out the pots and baskets of belongings. His youngest brother was put in charge of his sister, who could not yet walk, and was to make sure she didn't fall off the couch.

After moving everything out, Gongzha and his mother took down the tent poles and began to roll up the tent. The yak-wool tent was good at keeping the wind out, but it was heavy and even though mother and son spent a long time trying, they couldn't quite roll the whole thing up. In the end they stuffed it onto the truck, along with the small wooden chest and the stove. To make sure their baskets of belongings stayed on the cart and the pots and bowls didn't fall out, they covered everything with a yak-wool blanket and tied it down with a yak-hair rope.

Since her man's death, life had become increasingly difficult for Dawa; she began to realise that a family without a man was like a tent without a main pole. A number of men had approached her – some with good intentions, some not – and had taken to hanging around the tent at night, unwilling to leave. But Dawa had her own plans.

The new site for the encampment was in a flat part of the mountain valley. When you looked up, you could see the peaceful blue of Cuoe Lake.

By the time Gongzha and his mother had finished putting up their tent there, cooking smoke was already rising from the other tents. Cuomu came to help them move in and arrange their things. After Gongzha had risked his life to save her from the leopard, Cuomu had begun to see him in a different light. As time passed, new and different feelings crept into the hearts of the two friends who'd spent their childhood chasing each other across the plains. Children matured early on the grassland and girls were considered adults at twelve. Cuomu and Gongzha were at the age for love. They both had feelings for one another, but neither had yet spoken of this.

After Cuomu left, Gongzha had something to eat and fell asleep. When he woke in the middle of the night to get a drink and did not see his mother, he didn't think anything of it; he assumed she had gone to urinate.

Dawa came back just before dawn; her hair was tousled and there was a twinkle in her eye. She called to her son to get up and told him he didn't need to collect yak pats that morning and that he should go to the other side of the lake for a half-day of school.

Gongzha's eyes widened. He must have heard wrong. 'Ama, if I don't collect yak pats today, what will we burn tomorrow?'

'We have yak pats. You go ahead. It'll be good for you to learn some words!' Dawa laughed and began to boil the tea water.

Gongzha raced over to where they stacked the yak pats outside the door and, sure enough, there was a pile already there.

'When did you go and get them?'

'Your Uncle Danzeng brought them. Alright, go quickly after you've eaten something – don't be late!' Dawa spooned some butter into the wooden bucket, added the boiled water, then poured out their tea.

After Gongzha had drunk two bowls of butter tea and eaten a little bit of dried meat, he dug his wrinkled textbook out of a bamboo basket.

Dawa watched her son walking off into the distance, then gathered up the four younger children, closed the tent flap and went off to the sheep enclosure. It was the women's job to deliver the lambs, and they remained at the lambing pasture. The men meanwhile concentrated on the other livestock, changing shifts every three days as they tended the separate herds of sheep, yaks and horses. The children who did not go to school stayed by their mothers' sides, cuddling the lambs. Gongzha liked to watch the little lambs as they sucked eagerly on his outstretched fingers; it made him shout with laughter. Lambing season was an exciting time. As one new life after another appeared, the grassland that had lain dormant through the winter was suddenly revitalised.

5

Gongzha sat in the classroom, propping his eyelids open, staring with incomprehension as his teacher's mouth opened and closed. He had no idea what the teacher was talking about. No matter how hard he tried, he could not make sense of the Mandarin pinyin. This was not Gongzha's fault; he was keen to study, but he wasn't able to come to school very often. The lecture was like a lullaby, and his eyelids drooped.

Cuomu nudged him and Gongzha immediately opened his eyes and sat up straight.

The tent school only had three grades; students who were in fourth grade or above went to the town school. Not everyone in the same grade was the same age; there were seven-year-olds in first grade and there were also ten-year-olds in first grade. Regardless, everyone shared the one tent. When the teacher was teaching the first graders, he made the other grades do homework or read. When he taught the other classes, he made the first graders do homework and read. One tent, one school and one teacher for all three grades: this was the unique feature of the tent school.

When school was finished for the day, Gongzha, Cuomu and Shida got in the yak-skin boat and sat in the stern.

'I'm not coming next time,' Gongzha said. 'I can't understand a thing.'

'You wouldn't have long to study anyway,' Shida said. 'My brother says you're on the list of candidates that will enlist this year.'

'Really?' Gongzha and Cuomu both turned towards him.

'Yes, really. My brother's friend is in the local PLA unit, and my brother heard him say so.'

Gongzha's eyes lit up, but a moment later they went dark again. 'If I go, what will my mother do?'

Shida patted his chest sympathetically. 'You don't need to worry. When I collect yak pats, I'll just collect more.'

'Yes, Gongzha, you should go,' Cuomu said. 'I'll help your mother with her chores, don't worry.'

'Thank you.' Gongzha looked at his two friends and smiled. Like every other boy in the encampment, it was his long-held dream to exchange his heavy *chuba* for a green soldier's uniform, to wear the cap with the five-pointed star, to leave the grassland... He would be the envy of all his friends!

After they got off the boat, the three of them walked across the plain.

'Gongzha, you promised you'd take us to see Kaguo. When will you take us?' Shida asked.

'How about tomorrow? It's not a school day, so we can all go to Chanaluo and gather yak pats. You can usually see Kaguo over there.'

'Alright!'

'Don't tell the grown-ups, otherwise we won't be able to go.'

Shida and Cuomu nodded.

The next morning, Gongzha spoke to his mother and then set off, taking two bags and the dog. Shida and Cuomu were waiting for him by the lake. They could see Chanaluo's snow-white peak from the shore, but reaching it on foot was no easy matter. The three friends talked and gathered yak pats and by midday their bags were full. They found a hollow out of the wind, stashed their bags in it, ate some of the dried meat they'd brought, then raced each other all the way to Chanaluo Snow Mountain.

'Once we get over that peak,' Gongzha said, gesturing just ahead of them, 'we need to be careful. Kaguo often hunts mice there.'

'There are people up there!' Shida said suddenly, pointing at the slope. 'It looks like Luobudunzhu and his crew. What are they doing here?'

'Strange.' Gongzha could see the figures too, skulking on the mountainside. 'Let's go up the other way – we can circle round and look.'

Sticking to the dips and using boulders for cover, the three of them made their way up stealthily. They could see that Luobudunzhu and three other men were hiding behind a pile of rocks and watching another part of the mountain. As Gongzha followed their gaze, another figure came into view at the foot of the snow mountain.

Cuomu pulled at Gongzha's leather *chuba*. 'It's Uncle!' she said quietly.

'Why is Luobudunzhu following him?' Shida muttered.

Gongzha motioned for them to keep quiet. He had an uncomfortable feeling in his heart. Luobudunzhu had lost his way recently. The Red Guards had been disbanded, and a directive had come down saying that the cow-ghost snake-spirits were to be rehabilitated. The troublemaker and self-styled lord of the grassland no longer commanded the herders' respect, and naturally he was disappointed about this. He was also bitter. He'd got used to strutting around and barking orders, so to suddenly have to listen to others was difficult. He also understood that there was no turning the clock back.

When a group of outsiders had turned up on the grassland and said they were looking for old artefacts, Luobudunzhu had accompanied them (he had nothing else to do) and learnt quite a bit. It turned out that these old, unremarkable items were called antiques and were very valuable. It was then that Luobudunzhu remembered how insistent Commune Revolutionary Committee Director Ciwang had been that he and his Red Guards find the ancient Buddhas of Cuoe Temple. So insistent that he'd ordered them to tear the temple apart.

Once Luobudunzhu recalled this, he immediately turned his

attention to the lame and apparently crazy former living Buddha of Cuoe Temple, Zhaduo. Even though they hadn't found anything valuable in the temple at the time, that didn't mean there was nothing valuable to be found. For a start, there was the black Medicine Buddha, which many elders had seen. It was said to be very old and it was also said that whoever found it would be able to open the great door to King Gesar's treasure. Luobudunzhu had kept Zhaduo under observation for three months, but neither persuasion nor threats had elicited even half a clue. In fact, the old man grew crazier by the day. In the end there was nothing else he could do and on Ciwang's orders he'd let Zhaduo go. But Luobudunzhu continued to have people secretly follow Zhaduo.

On this particular morning, the old man had left his tent with a ragged bag. It looked as if he was going to collect yak pats, but he was walking fast and didn't even glance at the yak pats on the pasture. Luobudunzhu suspected he was up to something, so he quietly gathered some men together and followed him all the way to the foot of the snow mountain. The old man did not realise there were people behind him; he just climbed doggedly upwards.

Gongzha did not know what Zhaduo was doing there, but his instincts told him he might be in danger. Ever since Luobudunzhu had caught him and his father coming home from hunting that time, Gongzha had hated the pointy-faced, beady-eyed man. No matter what Zhaduo had come there to do, Gongzha did not want anything to happen to him, and nor did he want Luobudunzhu to be successful.

He called Cuomu and Shida over and whispered a few sentences in their ears. Cuomu nodded, and then Gongzha and Shida crept back down the slope a bit, keeping a low profile. When Gongzha turned and saw the distance was about right, he waved to Cuomu. Cuomu started to shriek, 'Brother Gongzha, Brother Shida! Come up here quick! I saw a fox.'

Shida and Gongzha shouted back, much louder than necessary. 'Where? Where's the fox, Cuomu?'

'There!' Cuomu pointed up the mountain. She pretended to have just noticed Luobudunzhu and his men, and said in a surprised voice, 'Brother Luobu, what are you doing here?'

Luobudunzhu and his men could no longer hide. They could only stand, glance balefully at them, and say, 'We also came to hunt foxes!'

When Zhaduo, who was climbing the opposite slope, heard the noise, he came to a standstill, then suddenly turned and ran back down, crying, 'Ghosts! Ghosts!'

'Brother, what's that crazy man doing here?' Shida asked Luobudunzhu, his eyes on Gongzha.

'Who knows? People with disturbed minds will do anything!' Luobudunzhu said unhappily. He glared angrily at the three half-grown children. He knew there would be no catch today, so he took his men and went back down the mountain.

Gongzha and the others waited until Luobudunzhu was a long way off, then turned, slid down the mountain another way and raced to catch up with the bellowing old man.

'Let's go back, Uncle. What did you come here by yourself for?' Cuomu took his bag and led him down carefully by the hand.

The old man seemed not to have understood what Cuomu said. He just gurgled and muttered to himself.

'He's always like this,' Cuomu said. 'One minute he makes sense and the next minute he's confused.'

'You should talk to your mother and take your uncle to the county town to see a Han doctor,' Shida said. 'My brother says they can treat a lot of strange diseases.'

Gongzha gripped the old man by the back of his belt to keep him from stumbling down the slope.

Cuomu used her foot to clear some stones out of the old man's path so he could walk more steadily. 'My mother? Forget it. Uncle was accused of being a cow-ghost snake-spirit and Mother couldn't avoid being tarnished by association – why would she take him to get help?'

By the time the three children got Zhaduo back to the encampment, night had fallen. They parted ways in the field behind the tents. Cuomu's mother had forbidden Cuomu from spending time with Gongzha, so to avoid getting a scolding, she took a different route home. Shida also went back to his tent.

Gongzha helped Zhaduo back to his solitary tent and tipped out half the yak pats he'd collected by his door. Then he went inside, poured a glass of water and handed it to him. The Zhaduo he saw then was not mad or wild. He sat there calmly on the couch. Behind the dirty, messy hair that hung down over his face, Zhaduo's eyes were bright and clear.

'Kaguo has grown up!' the old man said suddenly.

Gongzha looked up in surprise. 'You've seen Kaguo?'

The old man nodded. 'She's grown into a large bear!'

'We wanted to go and see her today, but then we ran into you. What were you doing there, Bola?'

'I—' They heard footsteps outside and the old man kept what he was about to say to himself.

'I must go. Ama is waiting for me.' Gongzha lifted the tent flap and saw Luobudunzhu and his men sitting in the field nearby. They appeared to be playing with their dogs, but their eyes frequently flitted across to Zhaduo's tent.

Gongzha picked up the bag of yak pats and walked off, whistling, towards his own tent. Luobudunzhu could not touch him for occasionally meeting Zhaduo, firstly because Gongzha was young, and secondly because for the last eight generations his family had been serfs.

'Please help the Buddha, child.' The old man's pleading look often came into Gongzha's mind. For a child to be able to help the Buddha was an enormous honour. He made some time to go and check on the things he'd buried in the mountain crevice. They were still there. Should he give them back to the old living Buddha? He pictured the draughty tent and the unkempt old man and reburied the Buddha and the pages of the book.

Gongzha went out early every day and returned home late. Sometimes he came across the old living Buddha deep in the grassland. When they were sure there was no one else around, they would find a comfortable grassy nest to sit in, out of the wind, and Zhaduo would tell him the strange stories of King Gesar.

Zhaduo didn't just share his stories with Gongzha. He also taught Gongzha about traditional medicine, about the structure of the human body, and about which medicines should be used to treat which illnesses. When they were picking up yak pats on the grassland, the old man taught him to distinguish between different herbs and minerals, and he made Gongzha memorise how to combine them into medicine pellets. Whenever other people appeared, the old man would suddenly begin to babble. Gongzha realised that Zhaduo pretended to be incoherent as a way of protecting both of them.

Luobudunzhu sought out Gongzha many times and asked him what the old man talked about when they spent their days together. Gongzha would reply that Zhaduo was insane and that sometimes he said there were dragons in the sky and other times he said there were strange creatures in the lake which wanted to bite him.

Gongzha had just come back from herding the horses. He threw his whip onto the couch and was scooping up some cold water to drink, when several people surged into his tent, buzzing with news.

'Gongzha, your notice to report came; they want you to go to the local army headquarters tomorrow,' Shida said excitedly, holding up a piece of paper.

Gongzha leapt up and snatched it. He looked at it closely, then handed it to his mother. She couldn't read it either, but the large red stamp printed at the top made her laugh so hard she couldn't close her mouth. 'You keep it, Gongzha,' she said, giving it back to him.

Gongzha rolled it up and carefully tucked it into his *chuba*.

As the news spread round the encampment, the herders came by one after the other to congratulate Gongzha. Having a People's Liberation Army soldier in your tent was something to be proud of. At the very least, at a time when everyone was preoccupied with social status, it showed that Gongzha and his family did not have any political problems. From another perspective, the army paid a wage, and for a poor herding family that was no small thing.

To Gongzha's surprise, Dawa brought out the dried fruit they'd served to guests at last year's Spring Festival and offered it to the herders who dropped by. Lunzhu had bought the fruit in the county town a couple of years ago and Dawa usually only produced it when important guests visited, quickly returning it to the cupboard once they'd gone.

Gongzha was thrilled at the prospect of becoming a PLA soldier – no longer would he need to covet other people's army caps. But he was also worried at the thought of there being no one but his mother left to do all the chores. How would she keep going? Uncle Danzeng had said he'd help them, but he had his own family to take care of, and besides, his woman didn't like him getting involved.

That evening, Gongzha went out to fix the sheep enclosure. They didn't have many sheep, but once he'd left, his mother would be busier than ever and wouldn't have time to mend it herself. He would do as much as he could for her before he went.

'Gongzha, Gongzha...'

It was Cuomu.

Gongzha smiled and wiped the sweat from his forehead. 'Hello!'

She waved at him and he dried his hand on his *chuba* and walked over.

'I have something to say to you. Can we go for a walk over there?' Cuomu dipped her head. She was blushing.

'Can you wait a bit? I want to finish this – it won't take long.'

'Alright, I'll help you.' Cuomu shrugged off one *chuba* sleeve, tied it round her waist, and began helping Gongzha shift some rocks.

Before long, the two of them had repaired the rundown sheep pen. Gongzha went into his tent to get some water for Cuomu to wash her hands. Then they left the encampment together and walked down to the lake.

'You leave the day after tomorrow?'

'Yes. I report the day after tomorrow!'

'So... you won't be coming back?'

'Why could I not come back? I'm going to be a soldier – I'll be back in three years.'

'I mean, will you come back to the grassland?'

'Of course. The grassland is my home. Where else would I go?'

'They say that people who become soldiers and see the big wide world want to live in the city, not back on the grassland. Shida's brother is like that. When he leaves the army this year, he's going to stay in the county town.'

'I won't. I like our grassland and I like hunting. Do you remember, you made a hat from the first fox I killed? My father used to tell me I was a good hunter with strong instincts. My aim still isn't that good, but once I'm in the army, I'll improve for sure, and then I'll kill you a red fox.'

'Really? You'll really come back?' Cuomu grabbed Gongzha's arm excitedly; her eyes were sparkling and her face was flushed.

'Mmm!' Gongzha nodded energetically.

The two sat on the shingle beach beside the lake as the water lapped lightly against the darkening shore.

'Brother, why don't I sing you a song?'

'Good! I like hearing you sing.'

Cuomu looked out at the gently rippling surface of the lake and began to sing softly.

'The stars in the sky
Are like Brother's eyes
Watching Sister's silhouette.
The butter lamps ablaze all night
Cannot see your eyes, Brother,
As they fall inside the tent
To light up Sister's heart.'

When she finished singing, she stayed staring at the lake. Two glistening tears hung from her long lashes.

'Cuomu...' When Gongzha saw how sad Cuomu looked, his heart flexed. The two of them had been together since childhood, as close as siblings, but today something seemed different. Cuomu's song and her tears, the lake, the moonlight – all of this created a strange feeling between them. He quietly put out his hand, brushing his fingertips against the shingle, and slid it towards Cuomu.

Cuomu seemed to sense something. She put her right hand down on the black pebbles and bashfully turned her face away.

When Gongzha took Cuomu's hand, a hotness raced through him as if he'd been burnt, but he held on tight. He didn't dare turn and look at her but kept his eyes fixed on the lake ahead. His heart was pounding.

Cuomu didn't speak either, just trembled slightly.

Light clouds veiled the moon and lent the grassland an air of mystery. Insects called non-stop. Pleasant sounds, clear sounds, all kinds of sounds mixed together and with the lapping of the water against the shore created a beautiful symphony.

The lake glimmered in the moonlight and its tiny ripples had a gentle beauty. Far out on the water, a thin layer of mist was rising; under the moonbeams, it seemed like a young woman's feelings – sometimes visible and sometimes not.

'Brother, this is for you.' On their way back to the encampment, Cuomu suddenly drew out something from her *chuba* and thrust it into his hands.

'What is it?' Gongzha took it and examined it: it was a red belt.
'I knitted it!'

He cast her a doubtful look. 'Where did you get the yarn?'

'I unravelled the arm of my sweater.'

'But your mother went to a lot of effort to get that for you from the county town. Won't she tell you off?'

'She doesn't know. Don't think about it so much. Do you like it or not?'

Gongzha nodded. He put the belt in his *chuba* and escorted Cuomu back to her tent.

When he reached the fork in the track on his way home, he hesitated, wondering whether to go via the solitary tent at the back and say goodbye to Zhaduo.

A weak light illuminated the inside of the tent. Gongzha sat down in front of the couch and said softly to Zhaduo, who was wrapped in his old sheepskin *chuba*, 'I'm leaving to join the army soon.'

'That's a good thing.'

'How's your leg?'

'It's quite a bit better. Thank you for the herbs you brought.'

'I only brought what you asked for. I gave some to an old man with a dog bite and they really helped him. He's better now and he's out collecting yak pats again.'

'These treatments have come down to us from our ancestors. You must remember the ones I've taught you – they may come in useful. Tibetan medicine is a rich discipline: it can heal people's minds as well as their bodies.' He sighed. 'It's a shame you aren't interested. I'm worried that when I die, our traditional medicine will vanish from the grassland.'

'It won't. You can teach someone else.'

'Someone else? Who else would dare come anywhere near someone like me?'

Gongzha remained silent.

'Five and a half thousand metres up Chanaluo Snow Mountain grow the best snow lotuses in our region. Only seven of them grow each year. You must pick them when the Rigel star rises, so that their healing effects are at their strongest. When Rigel appears, the shadow of the large black boulder will point due south; that long shadow will be the Buddha pointing the way for those who are lost,' Zhaduo muttered.

Gongzha listened and pretended to understand.

'Remember what I've said. That long shadow now, that's the Buddha pointing the way for those who are lost.'

'I will remember.'

'You should go now. When you get to your army unit, be sure to work hard and learn Mandarin. And remember, all people in this world are equal: no one is taller than you and no one is shorter.'

'Mhm.' Gongzha nodded. As he rose, he dusted the grass off himself. 'I must go. Please stay well. If you need anything, you can ask Cuomu. She's not like her mother.'

He left the tent. The light went out and he heard no sound from inside.

The morning of his departure, Gongzha set off just after dawn. The area in front of his tent was crowded with people. Some had a *khata* in their hands, others had tucked their ceremonial scarf into their *chuba*, deliberately leaving a corner showing. Their faces were all smiles. Even though Gongzha was not their child, they were from the same encampment and everyone was glad for him.

Gongzha stepped out of the tent with a flushed face, wearing a green uniform that was too large for him and a large red flower on his chest. The crowd began to bubble with good wishes; white *khatas* flapped in the wind and were hung around his neck, the traditional way to mark a special occasion. Gongzha smiled broadly, tied the many *khatas* into a knot and embraced the herders one by one. After he'd mounted his horse, he turned to look back and saw Cuomu in the crowd, her eyes full of tears, looking as if she couldn't bear to say goodbye. Gongzha nodded at her as if to say, 'You can be at peace. I won't forget what we said the other night.' He swept his eyes over the crowd and saw Zhaduo appear briefly at the back. He smiled happily, whipped his horse, and tore off.

And so Gongzha left the grassland. On his household register that year, he said he was sixteen, but he hadn't even turned thirteen.

6

The army unit was stationed in Gyangze, which couldn't have been more different from Gongzha's homeland: a series of large fields stretched into the distance, people sang, they yoked yaks together in pairs, they dressed fashionably to work in the fields, they ate *tsampa* and vegetables, and their robes were made of finely woven wool. When they addressed each other, they used courtesy terms, and when parents called to their children, they always added a 'dear' to their name. Coming from the grassland, Gongzha found all this very strange.

His biggest problem was the language. He could barely understand anything the locals said, let alone the Mandarin spoken in the unit. There was only one other Tibetan soldier in his platoon and he was from Chamdo. Their dialects were so different, it was like they were speaking different languages.

The company commander was from Shandong, a large man with a square head and a voice so loud that when he was angry it sounded like he'd opened fire. The day Gongzha arrived, the commander called the squad leader and Gongzha into his office and said, eyes bulging, 'Gongzha is from a nomad area. He's young. He can't speak Mandarin. Arrange for two older soldiers to look after him!'

The squad leader saluted, and dragged Gongzha, who hadn't understood a thing, away.

Gongzha liked guns, and when he saw the rifle he'd been issued, he was as happy as if he'd found a piece of treasure. On his first day at the range, it took him only a few rounds before he was hitting the centre of the target every time, stunning the company commander, who was training the new recruits.

'Fuck, Gongzha, how come your marksmanship's so good?'

Gongzha understood that the commander was yelling excitedly at him, but he had no idea what he was saying. The only word he could pick out was 'cigarette' – although that was because the Mandarin word for 'fuck' and the Tibetan word for 'cigarette' sounded almost identical. He thought the commander wanted a cigarette, so he scampered off to the corner shop and bought a five-fen pack of Economy cigarettes. When he came back, he gave them to the commander and, beaming, said, 'Here are the cigarettes!'

The commander didn't know whether to laugh or cry, but he swore cheerfully as he took the cigarettes. 'Fuck, Gongzha, if you don't hurry up and learn Mandarin, I'm going to end up kicking your ass.'

Again, Gongzha had no idea what he was saying. He heard only the word 'cigarette' and assumed that the commander wanted a different brand, so he scampered off again, bought a pack of Da Qian Men cigarettes, and, chuckling, handed them over. 'Cigarettes, Commander!'

The commander took the cigarettes and rolled his eyes in exasperation. It would be inappropriate to keep them, and he would normally have thrown them away, but he didn't want to hurt this minority soldier's self-respect. He ground his teeth impatiently, pulled a five-mao note from his pocket, stuffed it into Gongzha's hand, turned round and walked away.

Looking at the five mao in his hand, it took Gongzha a long time to react. He'd only spent one mao and five fen on the cigarettes – why had the company commander given him so much money? Clearly he was meant to buy more cigarettes for him in the future.

Because his marksmanship was so good, Gongzha became the unit's model new recruit. The regimental commander and the company commander both liked taking him on their hunts.

By the time he'd been there a year, he could just about make himself understood in Mandarin. Of course he still occasionally made a fool of himself, but compared to the fools the new Han recruits made of themselves with the Tibetan locals, he did fairly well.

Six years passed. The sun and the moon rose and set over the plateau, and the children grew, changing a little with every day. Basking in the grassland sun, Cuomu slowly matured into a young woman. Her beauty and her naturally lovely voice were Cuoe Grassland's most vibrant scenery, and she began to draw the eyes of young men from tents near and far.

Cuomu was the only child in her tent. To her father, mother and two uncles, she was as precious as their own eyes. So when she announced that she was now old enough to live by herself, her two uncles immediately set about making her a charming little white tent to stand beside the family tent. The day it went up, several young men circled around it. Cuomu knew exactly what they wanted. She peeked out through the tent flap at the glances being cast in her direction and giggled. The young men assumed that she would now be free to do as she liked after dark, but when they saw the fierce dog her uncle had led over and was now chaining up beside the tent, their eyes darkened.

As night fell, the dogs stationed outside the tents of the encampment's unmarried women would bark without let-up at every visitor. Only if their mistress came out and called them off would they desist. Her graceful figure would appear in the doorway, and a shy smile would play across her face. That meant that the man outside her tent had captured her heart.

That night, Cuomu amused herself by watching the shadows flitting past. She laughed loudly, shut the tent door, opened the roof flap and sat on her brand-new rug. Her younger uncle had exchanged a fox-skin for it and it was the palest blue, like the lake water in springtime. Beyond the roof flap, stars glimmered against the black night. She began to sing the old herders' song with great feeling.

> 'The stars in the sky
> Are like Brother's eyes
> Watching Sister's silhouette.
> The butter lamps ablaze all night
> Cannot see your eyes, Brother,
> As they fall inside the tent
> To light up Sister's heart.'

'Our snow lotus has grown up,' Cuomu's mother Baila said as she heard Cuomu's song. She was pouring milk into a wooden bucket and taking a rest between pours. 'Her buds will open and bear fruit. It's just we don't know which young man will be able to climb to the mountain peak and pluck our tent's flower!'

'Luobudunzhu has already circled the tent quite a few times!' Cuomu's elder uncle, Niduo, said, looking up from the shoes he was repairing.

'Luobudunzhu? Would Cuomu accept him?' Danzeng put down his tea and glanced out at the white tent. 'A girl's first night always goes to the man she likes. I don't see Luobudunzhu getting into our Cuomu's tent.'

'Then who? Shida? They do get on very well,' Cuomu's younger uncle, Duoji, said.

'I don't think it'll be Shida. If they were going to get together, they would have done so already – no need to wait until today!' Baila said, laughing and keeping her eyes trained on the goings-on around the white tent.

'Do you think she's waiting for Gongzha?' Danzeng said. 'She's been unsettled ever since he left.'

'You'd like that, wouldn't you?' Baila said unhappily. 'If your old lover's son marries your daughter, it would be quite reasonable for you to move in, wouldn't it?'

'Cut the sarcasm, can't you? That family's having a hard time.

74

What's wrong with me checking up on them regularly – has it meant you've had any less to eat or drink?' Danzeng set his cup down heavily and left the tent in a huff.

He walked over to his daughter's tent and kicked the dog, which was staring at him. Dragging its chain, the dog whimpered and went off to lie down.

'Aba.' Cuomu saw her father and stopped singing.

'This is not at all bad – you've made it very neat.' Danzeng sat down and gazed at his precious daughter's moonlike face. 'Have a little chat with your *aba*.'

Cuomu got up and moved over to sit beside him. She lay with her head in his lap, her long, skinny plaits fanned out around her. 'Aba, would you say I've grown up?'

'I would. My snow lotus has definitely grown up,' Danzeng said, stroking his daughter's cheek.

'I want to ask you a favour, Aba.' Cuomu traced her finger aimlessly across her father's *chuba*.

'Tell me, my snow lotus. What would you like to ask your *aba*?' Danzeng smiled indulgently. All four adults treated Cuomu like a pet and did everything they could not to overburden her with chores. When she was young, a wandering monk had told them that she was a maid from King Gesar's palace and that she would remain in their tent for only twenty years. She was eighteen now.

'Can I choose my own man?' Cuomu said, biting her lower lip, her face reddening, her voice as soft as a mosquito.

'What did you say? Speak up – Aba can't hear clearly.'

'I said… will you and Ama let me choose my own man?'

'Of course we will. Isn't that why you've got your own tent, so you can choose for yourself? Don't worry, we definitely won't interfere.' Danzeng was laughing loudly now that he'd understood.

'That's not what I meant.' Cuomu's finger wandered across her father's *chuba* again. 'What I mean, Aba, is can I choose the man I marry?'

'You want to get married?' Danzeng's eyes widened in surprise.

'I'm talking about later on. Will you and Ama let me choose for myself?'

'You want to find your own man?'

'Mmm... Will you let me do that, Aba?'

'I certainly have no objections, but your *ama*... I doubt she'll agree to it.'

'I'm begging you, Aba, let me decide for myself. I want to spend my days with a man I like.' Cuomu jiggled his knees and pouted at him.

'Alright, alright. Aba agrees. But you'll have to persuade Ama yourself.' Danzeng laughed resignedly. He'd never been able to refuse his stubborn daughter.

On this vast wilderness, where wind, sand, rain and snow battered the land and its inhabitants throughout the year, the only way humans could continue generation after generation was by relying on one another for help. It was the tight bonds of marriage that guaranteed this help would be given. The people of the grassland knew from experience that strong relationships made life more stable and more prosperous. Their sons and daughters could do what they liked with their bodies, but they had to do what their parents said when it came to marriage. This tradition had been handed down from ancient times; it was an established custom and everyone stuck to it. If a family were to have a child decide for herself, they would be seen as having turned their back on tradition and experience and would become the laughing stock of the grassland.

The reason Cuomu had dared to suggest to her father that she be allowed to find her own man was that she knew he was bitter about not having been able to decide his own marriage. Who on the grassland did not know about him and Gongzha's mother, Dawa? Her father's feelings for Dawa were complicated – when did a man looking for a simple fling seek out the same woman for decades?

That night, the herders watched the goings-on around the small white tent with interest. Everyone wanted to know who would be the first to pluck Cuoe Grassland's snow lotus. Cuomu's dog repeatedly leapt up and barked fiercely, inciting the neighbouring dogs to bark with him, but no one heard Cuomu call out to him. If she had, everyone would know who she'd chosen and that would have been the end of it. But Cuomu never made a sound, quietly letting the dog howl. Finally, she called her youngest uncle over, saying she was afraid and wanted him to keep her company.

Many tents accommodated entire families, but that didn't stop the young men from making their nocturnal visits. At night, when everyone was in their own corner of the tent, they would still come and try their luck, and the adults weren't bothered by this at all. But Cuomu was on her own and when she suddenly called her uncle over, that sent a different message. It told the young men she wasn't interested in any of them. They turned away mournfully and for the rest of the night the grassland was silent.

Three days later, Cuomu and her good friend Yangji were sitting by the lake. A herd of sheep were grazing behind them. Yangji picked up a flat rock and skimmed it. She watched it skip three times, then turned to Cuomu and told her the gossip.

'You know what, Cuomu, they're betting on which man you'll pick.'

Yangji was Ciwang's youngest daughter. No one knew why, but Ciwang had suddenly been removed from office and had recently returned to the grassland. For a former Commune Revolutionary Committee Director to return home and become a herder again was a significant fall from grace. Some people said he'd been chasing a Han cadre – Han cadres weren't like the women of the grassland and didn't let men go dog-driving. They also said that because he'd never properly dealt with the living Buddha or found the Medicine Buddha, the higher-ups were unhappy and had fired him.

Cuomu and Yangji were the same age. They'd grown up together.

Cuomu shrugged off one sleeve of her leather *chuba* and tucked it into her belt. She gazed at the ripples on the lake and laughed. 'They're crazy.'

'So who will you pick to be your wild stallion?'

'Don't worry, I won't pick your man – I know you like Shida.' Laughing, Cuomu pulled Yangji's plaits. 'Didn't he visit you last night?'

'Screw you.' Yangji blushed and splashed water at Cuomu's hair and face.

'You're still embarrassed about that? Even so, Yangji, you need to be careful. Your father looks down on Shida and wants you to marry someone from the town.'

'Why are you still going on about it? If you mention it again, I'll kill you!' Yangji pushed Cuomu, who laughed as she fell back against the rocks, spreading out her arms and letting the sun warm her face and body.

Yangji caught a ladybird on the shingle and called to Cuomu. 'Get up! Get up! Let's see where our men are.'

Cuomu came over and crouched behind Yangji, and they both stared at her cupped hands. Young girls often played this game: whichever direction the ladybird flew off in would be the direction in which they'd find the man they would marry.

Yangji slowly opened first one hand and then the other. The ladybird crawled up her palm and flew off to the left.

'Your man is that way.' Cuomu giggled, slapping Yangji on the shoulder.

'And your man is that way!' Yangji turned round and pinched her.

The two girls laughed as they tussled on the stony shore.

After they'd had enough, Yangji propped herself up on one hand and, looking sideways at Cuomu, asked, 'Be honest, who do you really like? Is it Luobudunzhu?'

'Him?' Cuomu laughed disparagingly. She lay back on the

ground and with her eyes half closed watched a white cloud creep across the sky. 'He's not worthy of entering this celestial maiden's tent.'

'Then who is worthy of this celestial maiden?' Yangji laid her face next to Cuomu's and looked into her eyes, full of curiosity.

'None of your business!' Cuomu gave Yangji's head a little shove. 'It's not Shida, anyway.'

'You still miss him, don't you?'

'Who?'

'You know who. It's been years, and he's only come back to see you twice. Are you going to wait for him forever?'

'Who's waiting for him? It's just there's no one I like on the grassland.' Laughing, Cuomu pillowed her head on her hand as her heart conjured the image of Gongzha in his uniform.

'You need to stop thinking about him. Your mother will never agree to it, anyway, and if you keep waiting for him, Miss Snow Lotus, you'll wither. You should find a man while you're still young and pretty.' Yangji lay down, following Cuomu's example.

'Spoken like an old matchmaker.' Cuomu smiled and nudged her friend's waist.

Yangji rolled away with a laugh.

Three horses clattered up. Luobudunzhu and his two companions dismounted and came towards them.

'I was wondering who was laughing so prettily! It was our snow lotus! Cuomu, do you want to see what I've brought you?'

Cuomu turned over and sat up. 'Luobu, what are you doing coming here instead of going home?'

'I was going home, but the laugh of the celestial maiden led me here.' Smiling, Luobudunzhu drew a red cotton headscarf out of his *chuba*. 'What do you think? Do you like it? I actually sent someone to the county town to buy it!'

'Thank you, but I can't take it. You should keep it for the woman you like!' Cuomu laughed, sprang up, dusted herself down and set off towards the distant herd of sheep.

'You are the woman I like,' Luobudunzhu said eagerly, grabbing her by the arm. 'Cuomu, I'm serious, I want to marry you.'

Cuomu whooped with laughter when she heard that, as if it was the funniest joke in the world. 'Luobu, you want to make me your woman? I'm afraid my parents would disapprove!'

'They wouldn't – your parents like me.' As he looked into her flower-like face, he couldn't resist dipping his head to kiss her, but Cuomu blocked him.

'My mother likes you, but I don't like you.' She peeled his hand off her arm and ran towards the herd, her laughter drifting back on the wind.

Luobudunzhu's expression changed as he stared after her. Most people saw him as a young man with prospects, and all the other girls greeted him with a smile. Only Cuomu thought him unworthy.

Yangji shot him a sympathetic look, then raced off after Cuomu.

The grassland was as empty as it was vast. As the girls' bodies matured, so did the workings of their hearts. For girls with something on their mind, there was plenty of room to roam by themselves, alone with their thoughts and their turbulent hearts, free to yearn and to dream.

Cuomu often sat alone in the remotest parts of the grassland, absorbed by the rolling mountains. Her longing for Gongzha would creep up on her without warning. Yes, Gongzha, her childhood sweetheart, her companion in herding and singing, her friend who in the space of just a few years with the army had become an eagle.

The first time he came back to visit his family, the two of them had sat together by the lake. As they gazed at the water under the light of the moon that first night, they pledged to marry each other.

The green grassland turned brown; the brown turned to green again. As the seasons changed, any unrest on the grassland slowly settled; peace returned and people's hearts grew calm again.

Cuomu knew her mother's feelings. It was not Gongzha she disliked; it was Gongzha's mother, Dawa. Everyone on the grassland knew about Aba and Dawa's relationship. Even though they were both old and the passion was no longer there, Aba still frequented Dawa's tent. This made her mother furious; she said Dawa was a disruptive jenny who'd seduced her father. Once, her mother had even gone cursing to Dawa's door and fought with her. Danzeng stayed home for two days after that, but on the third day he crept back to see her again.

The next time Gongzha came home to visit, Cuomu kept out of her mother's sight and quietly went with Gongzha to an unused sheep pen. The two of them tumbled together on the dried sheep droppings.

'Brother, I missed you so much. When you're not here, I miss you every day, and I keep wondering when you'll come back for good.'

'I miss you too. I miss you when I'm eating and when we're doing drill. Cuomu, Cuomu, you are my celestial maiden, you are my one and only celestial maiden!' Gongzha gazed at the woman in his arms, the person he cherished most in the world.

'Yes, I am your one and only celestial maiden. I am your Cuomu.' Cuomu caressed his tanned and ruddy cheeks, her tears glistening. From the moment she'd understood what love was, she'd given her heart to him; she had never considered taking another man, and her tent was open only to him.

'My celestial maiden, we just need to wait a bit longer. My senior officer says I should wait until I've got a work assignment before I leave the unit. So let's wait till then. Trust me – I promise I'll come back and marry you. I promise I'll make you the woman of my tent.'

'Alright. My man, do not forget the grassland, and do not forget that your woman is waiting for you.'

This was their vow, made in a tumbledown sheepfold full

of dried droppings. As they held each other, the faint smell of sheep dung wafting up their nostrils, light clouds racing across the blue sky overhead, and the clear, jade-blue waters of the lake in front of them, they promised to spend the rest of their lives together.

And so they waited, month after month and year after year.

He'd said that this winter he would come home for good. To Cuomu, this was a promise, and motivation enough to continue quietly waiting. She wanted to be his woman, to be with him and only him for the rest of her life. Such strength of feeling was unusual on the grassland. Her friends got tents of their own and began raising children, and meanwhile Cuomu waited, day after day and year after year.

Baila was always dropping hints to her daughter, saying that Luobudunzhu was a good man, that he was kind to the elderly, courteous to others, and wise, but Cuomu never responded. 'You need to get married,' Ama repeated at every opportunity. 'You need to find a man to spend your life with.' Today, Cuomu had escaped her mother's nagging and was sitting on the grass, hugging her knees and staring at the distant mountains. Her longing surged through her like the floodwaters of Cuoe Lake, covering everything in its path.

Recently, Ama had taken to going out early and coming back late; when she returned, she would whisper secretively to Aba and the uncles, and as soon as Cuomu walked in, they'd fall silent. Cuomu knew what they were discussing, so one afternoon when they were all home she said, 'Ama, there's no need for you to find me a man. Stop interfering in my life.'

When Baila heard this, she jumped up, shouting that Cuomu had been spoilt by her father and would not even listen to her elders.

Cuomu had stood up too, and stabbed her knife into the yak meat. Tilting her head towards Danzeng, who seemed to be buried in his cup of tea, she shouted, 'Aba, if you and Ama find a man for me behind my back, I'll leave the grassland and become a nanny in the city!' In the last few years, several girls who were unhappy at home had gone to the city to become nannies, cooking and taking care of other people's children. When they came back they wore showy clothes and no longer seemed like grasslanders.

'Just you try it!' Baila slammed down her tea and stared at her. 'If you dare go, I'll break your legs!'

'If you find me a man behind my back, you just see if I dare!' Cuomu snorted. She slammed down her fist and strode out of the tent.

As she clasped her shins and gazed at the mountains, Cuomu's tears fell like rain. Behind her, the black tents stood in rows; in the distance, the yaks and sheep wandered slowly. Gongzha, I miss you so much – do you still miss me?

Just then Shida walked over, sat down beside her, and said quietly, 'Are you thinking about him again?'

'He said that next time he comes home, he won't leave again. Do you think he'll really stay, Shida?'

'If he said he'll stay, he'll definitely stay. When do we grassland men not keep our word?' Shida plucked a blade of grass and put it in his mouth.

'That's true – he's still one of us!' Cuomu laughed and was a little ashamed to have doubted her lover.

'Is your mother still against it?'

'I've thought about it, Shida, and when he comes back this time, whether Ama agrees to it or not, I'm going to marry him.' She had a determined expression on her face.

After a brief silence, Shida said lightly, 'Would you never consider anyone else?'

'Shida, I'm sorry. I know you have feelings for me, and I know you've tried twice to come to my tent, but my heart only has room for him and no one else.' Cuomu spoke with her head lowered. 'Yangji's a good girl – go and have a serious talk with your father and marry her.'

'They've already made a marriage arrangement for her, didn't you know? With someone from across the lake.' Shida gave a dry laugh.

'Isn't that because you gave up?' Cuomu turned to look at him. 'Yangji's been waiting for you all these years, but your father has never sent anyone to her family to discuss marriage.'

Shida avoided her gaze. 'Cuomu, I—'

'Shida, you and Gongzha are good friends. I've never hidden my feelings from you. I will never marry anyone but Gongzha. Yangji likes you – if you go to her family, you'll still be in time.'

Shida shook his head obstinately. 'If you can wait for Gongzha, I can wait for you!'

'That's asking for trouble!' Cuomu laughed bitterly and turned back to the mountains.

While Shida and Cuomu were talking, Luobudunzhu was at Cuomu's family tent. He gave Baila a thick shawl, and Baila cheerfully busied herself making tea for her guest.

'Cuomu just went out, Luobu, dear. Sit and I'll pour you some tea.'

'I'll help you, Ama.' Luobudunzhu wasn't sure when he'd started calling Baila 'Ama' instead of 'Auntie', but Baila had tacitly agreed to this change.

'How are things with you and our Cuomu, Luobu? Have you made any progress?'

'Ama, Cuomu... she... doesn't seem to like me.'

'How could that be? You're so capable and handsome. Luobu, you're a man – you need to be more proactive.'

'I've already gone to her several times, but it's no good. The dog at her door is fierce and I can't get into her tent.'

'That's easily dealt with. I'll get her uncle to take the dog away tonight.'

'Thank you! Thank you, Ama.' Luobudunzhu was so delighted that he gave the table a vigorous kick and the tea water went flying.

That night, Cuomu brought the sheep back, took the two lamb chops her mother had prepared specially for her, threw one to the dog at her door and chewed on the other herself. She lit the stove, poured in a shovel of sheep droppings, closed the door against the wind and put the kettle on to boil; the tent soon warmed up. Humming herders' songs, she took off her thick *chuba* and changed into a long silk dress. The hearts of all the young men watching ached at the sight of her lovely silhouette, clearly visible on the outside walls of her tent.

Hearing movement outside, Cuomu stopped washing her face, lifted her head and asked, 'Who's there?'

'It's me.' It was her youngest uncle's voice. 'I'm taking the dog. We're afraid the wolves will come tonight, and the sheep-pen needs him.'

Cuomu agreed and thought nothing of it. These past couple of days there'd been a rumour flying around that the chain that tethered the Wolf Spirit to the top of Mount Chanaluo had stretched, and that meant wolves would be coming to terrorise the grassland again. Every family had sent people to the sheep pens to keep watch through the night. The yak-pens weren't such a worry; yaks were large and the young men who watched over them were the strongest in the encampment, so the wolves wouldn't bother them. But sheep were docile by nature and wolves understood them better than anyone. Faced with danger, sheep would immediately try to escape, and that made them an easy target. As long as the wolves didn't run into any humans, there would be rich pickings.

The wolves of northern Tibet tended to act alone, unwilling to share their food unless they were desperate, or to put themselves in unnecessary danger. When a pack of wolves went out, they risked getting picked off by a gun before they'd even got near their prey. Guns were unpredictable and could move in any direction; even the fiercest wolf was no match for a hunter.

There were many people in Cuomu's family, so night-watch duty had not yet fallen to Cuomu herself. And being the only child with four adults doing everything they could to keep her safe and well, it was unlikely she'd be asked to go. How could they make her spend the night at the sheep pen in the company of a group of foul-smelling men?

Baila thought well of Luobudunzhu, and Cuomu's father and uncles had nothing against him. Among all the young men of the grassland, Luobudunzhu stood out, and his family circumstances were good. There were four brothers; he was the eldest and he was clever and hard-working. He'd recently fallen in with some Khampas who'd come to the grassland on business, looking for antiques. Rumour had it that he'd made quite a bit of money. A smart man could make life comfortable for a woman, protecting her from the worst of the relentless wind and sand. Even though Danzeng secretly approved of Gongzha, he knew that his brothers and his wife were angry about his relationship with Dawa, so when they paid repeated visits to Luobudunzhu, he didn't dare say anything.

Shida didn't know why, but that night he couldn't sleep. The news that Yangji was going to get married made him uncomfortable. He was not unaware of Yangji's feelings for him, but he'd always liked Cuomu. Even though he often went dog-driving to Yangji's tent, that was just how the young men and women of the grassland spent their lonely evenings. There were no promises, no spiritual bonding, just two bodies coming together. No one expected it to be a long-term thing.

That was the way Shida thought, and the way he acted. Even as he gave his body to one woman, in his heart he was thinking of another. But Yangji felt quite differently. She loved Shida and she was hurt by his behaviour. She'd waited so long for him to come and seek her in marriage, and when he didn't, her heart froze like the waters of Cuoe Lake in winter, and she was angry.

That night, as she'd watched Shida and Cuomu sitting talking together on the plain, so close they seemed like lovers, her tears had fallen uncontrollably. She had intended to wait for Shida to come back, but in the end she welcomed another man to her tent for the first time. For no other reason than to forget.

Shida stood outside Yangji's tent in the moonlight. When he heard the laughter inside, he retreated silently. He felt strangely unmoved. Letting his body do the talking had been easy enough, but his heart was a lot more choosy.

All of a sudden, screams and curses ripped through the quiet night. They came from Cuomu's white tent.

Cuomu had been in a deep sleep when suddenly she felt someone pressing down on her and pulling at her clothes. She yelled out and reached for the dagger by her pillow, but before she got the chance to use it, her arm was grabbed.

'Cuomu, it's me!'

'Luobudunzhu, you bastard, get out!'

'Cuomu, my snow lotus, be my woman. I think of you every night – I think of you so much, I can't sleep.' Luobudunzhu lay down on top of her and began smothering her face with kisses.

'You bastard, fuck off!' Cuomu pushed him hard and shouted for her uncles, mother, and father in the next tent, but no one responded.

'Don't shout – your mother agreed to my coming. If she hadn't made your uncle take your dog away, how could I have got in?' Luobudunzhu lifted up her underwear. As she lay there trembling, her full breasts gleaming in the moonlight, her body seemed to glow. He was mesmerised.

'I don't want to! I don't want to!' Cuomu shrieked, kicking and scratching and leaving a bloody trail across Luobudunzhu's face.

'Hey, hey, don't yell. Tonight I will make you my woman, and tomorrow I'll get my family to come and discuss marriage. Come on, my snow lotus!' Luobudunzhu tried to tug down her pants.

'No!' Cuomu screamed piteously. No matter how hard she tried, she couldn't break free of this man, so fired up with lust. 'Luobudunzhu, Gongzha will kill you when he comes back – if you dare touch his woman, he won't let you get away with it.'

'What right does he have to compete with me? What has he got that I haven't?'

It would have been better if Cuomu hadn't brought up Gongzha. At the mention of his name, a burst of ruthless anger surged through Luobudunzhu. He thought of the night they'd had a struggle session for the old living Buddha and how Gongzha's angry eyes had remained fixed on him throughout, as if it had been his own father they'd tied up. He was a little afraid of those eyes, because their expression was like that of a bloodthirsty leopard, and he was its prey.

Just when he was on the point of getting his way, the tent flap moved and a figure came in, followed by a rush of freezing wind.

'Cuomu...'

'Shida, help me!' Cuomu shouted in desperation.

'This is none of your business,' Luobudunzhu snarled at Shida from where he was lying on top of Cuomu. 'Get the fuck out.'

Shida immediately withdrew. According to the rules of the grassland, when a man was visiting a woman's tent, regardless of whether she had agreed to it or not, no one else could interfere.

'No, Shida, help me!' Cuomu repeated. 'I beg you, help me!'

Shida spun round and went back into the tent. He yanked Luobudunzhu upright and punched him in the face. Luobudunzhu stumbled to one side, clutching his cheek.

Cuomu leapt up, pulled down her clothes and grabbed her knife, ready to rush over.

Shida held her back.

'Let go of me! I'll kill him, the bastard – how dare he touch me!' Cuomu struggled and waved the knife in the air, her eyes burning with hatred.

Shida pulled at her arm. 'Forget it, Cuomu. Just be a little more careful next time.'

Luobudunzhu scrambled up, a streak of blood at the corner of his mouth. He glared viciously at the two people by the bed, especially Shida. If Shida hadn't burst in, Cuomu would have been his tonight. The more Luobudunzhu thought about it, the angrier he got. Eventually, without any thought for the consequences, he grabbed the gurgling pot of boiling water from the stove and swung it at Shida. Shida dodged, but the pot hit his leg. The boiling water soaked through his trousers and the stabbing pain made him stagger.

'Shida!' Cuomu cried as she held him upright. Turning to Luobudunzhu, she laughed coldly. 'What a bastard you are, Luobudunzhu – you fail to seduce me, so you resort to violence instead? If you think you're going to be my man, you're dreaming. I'll never accept you.'

'Fine. You won't be my woman, you want to be Gongzha's woman, you want to be that nothing's woman... Fine, fine...' Luobudunzhu bellowed, his eyes red. He pulled his knife from his belt and hurtled over. Shida pushed Cuomu out of the way and the knife plunged into his chest. Warm blood spurted out.

Danzeng, Baila and Yangji came running into the tent at Cuomu's screams. When they saw the blood on Shida's chest, they froze. Danzeng was the first to react and quickly helped Cuomu support Shida out of the tent. Luobudunzhu fled immediately.

When Shida's parents saw Danzeng helping their bloody son into their tent, they were so frightened, they didn't know what to do. Danzeng called to the women to help Shida onto the bed. Then he told everyone what had happened.

Shida's uncle stood up with a roar, drew his knife and was about to rush out, but Danzeng held him back. 'Help the boy first. Deal with the rest later.'

'Uncle, Father, forget it. Don't go after him!' Shida also tried to stop his raging uncle.

Yangji helped Shida's mother take off Shida's robe and use clean strips of cloth to bind the wound, but the blood continued to gush out. Shida was obviously and rapidly losing colour, and his vision began to go cloudy.

'What can we do?' Yangji started crying.

There was no doctor in the encampment. Before, the herders used to consult the living Buddha of Cuoe Temple when they were sick. But now the living Buddha had been forced to resume a secular life, had been beaten into a cow-ghost snake-spirit, and had become the lame Zhaduo. With that kind of history, who would dare ask for his help? Especially given that, back during his struggle session, Shida's parents had been the first to rush at him.

'It's after midnight – we can't go to the town,' Danzeng said.

'Find Uncle. Doesn't Uncle know some medicine?' Cuomu said, looking at her father expectantly.

Shida's father also looked at Danzeng. He was the team leader. If he nodded, that would make whatever followed a little better.

'We can't overthink it. Cuomu, go and get your uncle and explain everything to him,' Danzeng said, looking first at Shida and then back at his daughter. 'Shida's mother, light two more lamps and make the tent brighter.'

Cuomu ran out. A short while later she returned, bringing lame Zhaduo with her.

Zhaduo did not greet anyone; he went straight to the bed and glanced at Shida, then pulled a medicine pellet from his *chuba* and stuffed it into Shida's mouth. Yangji served Shida a little hot water.

After watching him swallow, Zhaduo began to undo the strips of cloth. 'Bring a bowl of water!'

Shida's mother quickly did as he'd asked.

Zhaduo used a cloth to carefully clean away the blood. Then he pulled a bottle of medicine from his *chuba* and shook some powder onto the wound. Once the bleeding had stopped, he found some clean cloths and bound up the wound again. By the time he'd finished, it was almost dawn. Zhaduo straightened up and said, 'He's lost too much blood. Once it's light, find some Party medicine for him to take.'

'Party medicine' was what north Tibetan herders called Western medicine. In the past, the grassland hadn't had Western medicine, but after the Eighteenth Army Corps had come to Tibet and the Han doctors had walked out onto the Changtang

Plateau to treat the herders, it began to spread. Because the Communist Party brought it, the herders called it Party medicine.

Danzeng left for the town in the morning. He returned shortly before nightfall, bringing with him a bespectacled Han army doctor with a medical bag on his back. The two of them went straight to Shida's tent.

When the people in the encampment heard that a young Han doctor had come, they gathered outside Shida's family tent, gossiping about the new arrival. Because Cuoe was deep in the grassland, it seldom saw outsiders, let alone a Han doctor. 'I heard my man say his last name is Zhuo – he's called Zhuo Mai,' Baila whispered to her neighbours, deliberately mysterious. 'He's in the Border Defence Regiment. My man ran into him in the town. When he told his leaders about Shida's injury, they told him to come and take care of it.'

The herders began swarming up to the tent door, craning their necks and trying to catch a glimpse of Shida with all the white cloths wrapped around his chest. His father was standing by the bed, holding up a bottle with a tube coming out of it, and the tube was stuck into Shida's wrist. Shida's colour was much better than it had been that morning and people were clicking their tongues in amazement. Those at the back couldn't see, so they kept jumping up and supporting themselves on the shoulders of the people in front of them, which won them a stream of curses.

Dr Zhuo stood up and smiled at the people around the door. 'Come in, dear friends,' he said. 'Let me give you all a check-up.' His fluent Tibetan shocked the herders.

They shuffled in sheepishly, pushing one another along.

Danzeng took control. 'Come on in. Line up one by one and don't crowd,' he said.

Young and old alike were curious to see what was happening, and the queue was long. One at a time, they stood in front of Dr Zhuo, their heads bowed. When the doctor lifted his stethoscope to listen to their chests, some of them couldn't help doubling over with laughter. Danzeng put on a sober expression and shouted, 'Be a little more serious. If you carry on laughing, you won't be examined.' The laughers straightened up and deliberately kept their faces taut so he couldn't tell whether they found it funny or not. Those who got a pellet or two of medicine left proudly under envious gazes.

On the grassland, conflicts were traditionally resolved either by taking revenge in blood, or by accepting money instead. On the third day, under the supervision of a clan elder, the two families came together and a yak was give in compensation for Shida's injury.

7

Zhuo Mai was now the grassland's most popular guest. People went to see him for ailments as minor as a headache or a warm forehead. They even took their livestock to him if a yak or a sheep wasn't producing offspring. When it was discovered that Zhuo Mai was single, unmarried women from near and far began coming to the lake for any reason or none. It was well known that Han men were capable, didn't hit their wives, and would help with the housework. On top of that, Zhuo Mai was a doctor and a cultured man, and he spoke Tibetan. All this made him quite different from the rough, heroic men of the grassland, and so it would have been strange if the women hadn't tried to snatch him up.

Zhuo Mai greeted everyone with a smile. As for the cow-ghost snake-spirit Zhaduo, whose tent was set apart from the rest, the doctor visited him often and stayed for hours; no one knew what they talked about. Because of this, the herders no longer avoided Zhaduo; they even nodded when they ran into him.

One day at around noon, when Cuomu hadn't seen her uncle come out to collect yak pats all morning, she went to his tent. When she saw that he was sleeping, she called softly to him, and then tried again. Zhaduo woke up and struggled to sit up but did not have the strength.

'What's the matter? Are you sick? Uncle!' Cuomu hurried over to help him up. When she felt how hot his hand was, she was frightened.

'I'm going to go, Cuomu.' Zhaduo leant back against the

cushion, gasping for breath, his face flushed. 'It looks like I won't be able to wait for Gongzha. You tell him, tell him... he must... he must find... find Kaguo, and make the Buddha's... Buddha's light... shine once... once more... on Cuoe... Cuoe Grass... Grassland!'

Cuomu had no idea what her uncle's words meant, but she nodded anyway. 'Don't talk any more – I'm going to get Ama and Aba.'

She hurried out of the tent and raced home to call her parents, then she found Shida and urged him to go to the army base and get Dr Zhuo.

The evening clouds were already stained red by the time Zhuo Mai arrived. Shida helped him carry his medical bag and the two of them went straight to Zhaduo's tent. Cuomu was sitting by the bed. When she saw them come in, she quickly stood up and got out of the way.

Dr Zhuo nodded to everyone, then took out his stethoscope and put it inside Zhaduo's robe. He listened for a while, then put it away, his face solemn.

'How is he?' Baila asked in a small voice, stepping forward with a face full of worry.

'His body was already weak. And now that it has to fight off a cold as well, I'm afraid...' Dr Zhuo turned away. He couldn't bear to say the words. This benevolent old man was one of the few learned people he'd met on the grassland and the knowledge of Tibetan medicine that Zhaduo had shared with him had introduced him to a new world.

Just then, Zhaduo opened his eyes, their expression clear. He signalled for Cuomu to help him sit up and Baila quickly got a pillow for him to lean on. 'You all go out for a bit,' he gasped. 'There are some things I'd like to say to Dr Zhuo and Cuomu.' Despite his wheezing, his words were clear.

Pulling his woman with him, Danzeng went out with Shida.

Zhaduo watched them go, then turned to look at Zhuo Mai, still gasping. 'Remember, you must pick the snow lotuses of Chanaluo Snow Mountain only when Rigel rises. If you go earlier or later, it won't have the right medicinal effect. And when you pick them, you must always leave one for the Mountain Spirit.'

'Alright.' Zhuo Mai nodded. 'Rest assured, I will remember.'

'You must wait for Gongzha to come back to get the notes on the Four Medical Tantras. Don't try and do it by yourself – it's too dangerous. There's one last antidote I haven't completed and I've heard that the herb can be found on Tajiapu Snow Mountain in the No Man's Land area of Shuanghu. You can ask Gongzha to take you.'

'Alright.' Zhuo Mai squeezed his hand, nodding thoughtfully.

'Don't... don't let it be forgotten.' Perhaps because he had spoken too much, the old man began gasping again.

'You can rest easy. I will of course follow your instructions, and your knowledge of Tibetan medicine will be passed down on the grassland.'

Zhaduo looked into his eyes and gave a relieved smile. He instinctively trusted Dr Zhuo. Though they were of different ethnicities, faiths and generations, the two men understood each other; the geography was irrelevant.

After resting a moment, Zhaduo raised his head again and saw that Cuomo was crying as she sat to one side. 'Cuomu, my good child, don't be upset. Everyone has to leave sometime; whether they leave early or late is of no consequence. I'm going on ahead and I'll be waiting for you in Shambhala. When Gongzha comes back, you must tell him from me that he has to find Kaguo; then he'll know where the Buddha is. He must invite the Buddha back and make the Buddha's light shine on the grassland again.'

'Alright, Uncle. You can go in peace.' Cuomu nodded, even though she was heartbroken. Her face was wet with tears.

'You've chosen well – Gongzha is a good boy,' Zhaduo said. He tried to raise his hand and caress her, but he lacked the strength. 'Go and call your parents.'

Cuomu wiped away her tears with the back of her hand. Lifting the tent flap, she called out to her parents, who were standing a little way off.

Danzeng and Baila hurried in and stood by the bed. Zhaduo lifted his head and laughed warmly. It was as if he was back in his dim temple hall, a single ray of light shining through the window, incense drifting, sutras being chanted, the compassionate eyes of the Buddha behind him, and believers gazing up reverently in front of him. He was going home, finally going home. The place that the Buddha longed for, that was his real home, the resting place for his soul.

'Baila,' he called softly, just as he used to when he and his beloved sister were young and he'd nudge her awake. They had loved each other so much then. His little sister had never wanted to leave her brother's side, and he had always watched out for her. Later, when he'd been identified as the reincarnation of a living Buddha and had become an exalted disciple of the Buddha, respected by all, she'd had to make an appointment just to see him. There were no more warm, loving looks – in the temple hall there was only reverence. When you were a disciple of the Buddha, you could decide nothing yourself. He didn't blame his sister; everything in this life was the fruit of seeds planted in a past life. 'I am going. You must take care. Don't be too wilful; listen to your man; look after the household.'

'Oh, Brother...' Baila was suddenly overcome with sadness. All the love she'd once had for her brother flooded back into her heart. Their parents had died when she was young and it was her brother who'd brought her up and found a man to support her tent. How was it that when the communists arrived, she'd drawn a clear line between herself and her own brother? She should not have allowed her heart to be clouded, should not have denied her own family and stopped caring about him. 'Please forgive me. I was wrong, Brother. Don't abandon me! Aba and Ama didn't want me – do you not want me either?'

'Baila...' Zhaduo stroked his sister's cheek, tears streaking his face. He was no longer the living Buddha; he was just a simple herder, unable to forget his family before he went, unwilling to leave them behind and go. 'Sister, you must look after your health. There are some things you need to be more relaxed about – try not to lose your temper so often. Trust your man; he is an eagle of our grassland and no matter how high eagles fly, they will always return to the eyrie at sunset.'

'Brother, Brother...' Baila buried her face in the bed and sobbed so hard she could barely catch her breath.

As he stroked his sister's greying hair, Zhaduo's tears also fell one after the other. After a while, he raised his head and, looking at Danzeng, called out, 'Dear Danzeng...'

Danzeng bent down and forced a whisper of a smile to his mouth. 'Yes, Brother?'

'My sister is wilful. I did not teach her well when she was younger – you must forgive me.'

'Baila is very capable, she looks after the household very well. Brother, go in peace.'

Zhaduo nodded. A compassionate smile spread across his face. He did not speak again. His gaze passed beyond the tent flap to the sky beyond. It was as if he'd returned to that blustery, snowy night many moons ago when he was a young man. Back then, he'd been wandering in the wilds of No Man's Land, in Shuanghu, with no idea where he was going. Green eyes had glittered in the distance, but he hadn't been afraid. He'd picked his way through the unfamiliar territory calmly and cautiously. He remembered thinking that if he were to fall, he might never return to the grassland. But he wasn't worried; if the Buddha had arranged things that way, there must have been a reason for it. In which case, he was ready to let the new life begin, and when he reincarnated, he hoped he would have more time to study and more opportunity to help people in distress. These thoughts had occupied him as he wandered, until his body had no more strength. Two crimson-robed figures had appeared on the snowy ground before him. The shade of red had given him hope for his new life. And then he'd woken to find himself floating in a warm lake, naked like a newborn infant. As he bathed in the white mist, the concerned eyes of those crimson figures, half hidden, half visible, had made him feel safe and full of joy. He'd thought he was in Shambhala.

Was he going back there now? Would he return to the warm lake of No Man's Land, to sit by the side of the lamas and listen to their teachings? Would he be able to practise reverently with no concern for worldly matters and live his days in peace? As these thoughts came to Zhaduo, he smiled contentedly and his soul slowly left the grassland.

In keeping with the traditions of Tibetan Buddhism, as the reincarnation of a living Buddha, Zhaduo should have been given a stupa burial or been cremated. But on the grassland the coals of the Cultural Revolution still glowed here and there, so the herders could only take him to the sky-burial altar and let the vultures dispose of his flesh.

Danzeng's tent stopped all forms of entertainment. They did not wash their faces, comb their hair, sing or dance. The encampment cancelled all its festivals, because one of their elders had passed on. All the anger that had been present before his death vanished with the dead man, dissipating like smoke.

It wasn't until the winter of the following year that Gongzha heard that the man he cherished was dead. The night of his return, he went to Cuoe Temple, and as he stood outside the tightly sealed wooden door, two lines of tears rolled slowly down his face.

Gongzha was not easily moved. He'd started burying his feelings deep in his heart when his father died and he'd had to take on the role of head of the household. Life was tough for grassland men and they couldn't afford to be too emotional. Where Lunzhu had been Gongzha's instructor in how to live day to day, Zhaduo had been his instructor in how to be an adult. His father taught him to hunt, taught him the essential skills for surviving on the grassland. Zhaduo taught him how to be a person, how to respect and value all living beings. The departure of the old man plunged Gongzha's heart into darkness; he felt like a man walking along a night-time road with a lamp that had suddenly been extinguished.

The light of the moon was desolate. The ground was bare, save for Gongzha's long, unmoving shadow.

On Gongzha's second day of leave, Cuomu took advantage of her mother having gone to the pasture and sneaked off to meet him in a mountain valley deep in the grassland. When she saw her man standing waiting at the mouth of the valley, her heart began to pound. She gave a savage crack of the whip and her horse flew towards him.

When she reached him, she rolled straight off the horse and into her man's arms.

'Cuomu, my snow lotus!' Gongzha murmured quietly. He hugged Cuomu's feverish body, gazed at her slightly trembling lips and could not resist kissing them.

Cuomu hung onto his neck, greedily devouring him with her lips, wanting to be part of him, wanting to be one with him.

The golden plain stretched to the edge of the sky, so far you could not see its end. The two snow mountains on either side glistened with a silvery light and their silver peaks seemed to pierce the curved dome of the heavens. The day was extraordinarily blue, like an enormous piece of jade without a single blemish, and the clouds were as white as the lambskin hat on a girl's head, tumbling across the blue curtain in irregular curls.

The two young people rolled together on the thick, soft grass as the sun's rays shone warmly down. Their desire for each other was urgent and all-consuming, as if they'd been separated by many worlds and had at last found each other again.

Gongzha held his beloved woman. He slowly pulled down her fur-lined robe and admired the curves of her gleaming body as, little by little, they were revealed in the sunlight. He caressed her, covering every centimetre of her with kisses.

'My woman!' He laid his body over hers, tasting her lips, biting her earlobes and nipples. Watching the woman he loved sigh happily beneath his caresses, his heart soared and his happiness knew no bounds. He gripped her waist more tightly, brought the two of them together and slowly began to take her. He wanted to show her how much longing had accumulated, he wanted to slowly enter her heart, he wanted to become a part of her and gradually dissolve into her.

'Gongzha, I missed you so much, did you know that? I missed you every day and every night...' Cuomu circled her arm around his neck and gazed tenderly into his eyes.

'I missed you too, my woman!' Looking at her blushing cheeks, Gongzha felt as if his chest would burst. He could not control his body any longer; he only wanted her more deeply.

In the same way, the snow mountains and the plains have been together day and night for thousands of years. In the same way, the beach and the lake have lived out their days together and will never part.

Later, as Cuomu lay in his embrace, her calves poking out, her wheat-coloured skin gleaming like butter in the sunlight, she remembered what Zhaduo had told her. 'Uncle said I had to make you go and find Kaguo. He said she will take you to the Buddha, and then Buddha's light can shine on the grassland once more.'

'Strange!' Gongzha looked towards the snow mountain's peak, his brow furrowed. 'How are Kaguo and your uncle connected?'

'I don't know. He just said I was to tell you that. Have you heard of Mount Tajiapu in No Man's Land?'

'I know it – it's by Shuanghu. I've been hunting there before. What about it?'

'When Uncle was young he often went to Mount Tajiapu to pick herbs. He said Tajiapu and our Chanaluo are a pair of lovers.'

'A pair of lovers? Like us?' Gongzha kissed her, his eyes smiling.

Cuomu raised her head and gazed at him, full of feeling. Gongzha dipped his head again, pressing her pink lips to his, and they were lost once more in their passion.

After some time, Gongzha finally released her. 'You were saying that Tajiapu and our Chanaluo are a pair of lovers?' he murmured, his forehead resting on hers.

'Uncle said so. He said that in the time of King Gesar, Tajiapu was a handsome young man and Chanaluo was a beautiful young woman. They both lived in No Man's Land. Chanaluo's father didn't want her to marry Tajiapu and quietly betrothed her to a sorcerer and arranged that they be married the next day. When Chanaluo found out, she ran away in the night and eloped with Tajiapu to Shuanghu Grassland. The sorcerer caught up with them and turned Tajiapu into a mountain and dragged poor Chanaluo back. When they got to Cuoe Grassland, Chanaluo said that she wanted to rest for a bit. Then, when the sorcerer wasn't looking, she drank some poison she'd prepared and turned herself into a mountain – Chanaluo Mountain. Uncle said Tajiapu and Chanaluo once had hearts that beat, but that they didn't have hearts any more, he didn't know why, only cavities where the hearts should have been.'

'Cavities?'

'Yes, that's what Uncle said. He also said that Kaguo was once King Gesar's favourite steed, and she helped King Gesar beat the demons. The Buddha gave Kaguo the heart cavities of Tajiapu and Chanaluo to live in.'

'Kaguo lives in the heart cavities of Tajiapu and Chanaluo?'

'Yes.' Cuomu patted Gongzha's thoughtful face. 'It's a good story, isn't it?'

'Yes, yes...' Gongzha said absently. Looking at Chanaluo's cloud-draped peak under the blue sky, he muttered to himself, 'Heart cavity?'

'What is it?' Cuomu sat up and put her red silk dress back on, and then her fur-lined robe. Leaning on him, she rearranged her long and now rather dishevelled plaits.

'Nothing. When did Uncle tell you this story?' Gongzha also stood up and put on his clothes.

'A couple of days before he died. He told me I had to tell you.' Cuomu tilted her head and looked at him. 'He said you liked hearing King Gesar's stories.'

Seeing her smiling face, Gongzha went over and held her waist from behind, resting his chin on her head. 'Uncle really was a strange man. But since he wanted me to find Kaguo, I'll go and find her. It's just that it's such a huge area – who knows where Kaguo is?'

'Let's talk about it once you've left the army. Are you coming back to the grassland or not?'

'Of course I'm coming back. Isn't my snow lotus here? What is it – are you desperate to give me a son?' Gongzha could not resist kissing her again and laughing softly.

'Fuck you. If you want a son, you have to come back first!'

'Well, you never know...' Gongzha circled around her, inspecting her willowy waist. 'Maybe you'll have one after today!'

'You...!' Cuomu turned away, looked down and blushed.

'Lots of the grassland girls your age are already mothers. That's my fault. Will you wait a little longer for me? My senior officer says there'll be jobs in our area for those of us who leave next year. Don't worry, I promise I'll come back and marry you.'

'Mmm,' Cuomu said, with a lowered head and the voice of a mosquito.

Gongzha drew her into his arms again.

The snow mountain's shadow fell across the plain and the sunbeams cast a golden road through the valley. As the lovers sat whispering to each other, the whole world seemed to stop turning.

8

For several days it seemed as if Cuoe Grassland had gone mad. In the mornings, a beautiful sun shone overhead and clouds drifted across the blue sky. In the afternoons, before the sun had passed the mountain peak, the wind howled and blew the sun back, black clouds piled one on top of the other, and the grassland was shrouded in a cloud of sand. The wind demons dragged a swirling vortex in a wild dance across the plateau. Women used thick scarves to cover their eyes and noses, but still their mouths felt as if they were full of sand. When the herders returned home, all you could see were two eyes moving, the rest of their face was smothered in dust. Everyone was cursing it – 'The weather is crazy!' they said – and the old people talked of a mad demon wandering the grassland trying to make it lose its true nature.

There was not a drop of water in the air. It was if the heavens wanted to suck the moisture from every living thing, from the people and the land. The Tibetan antelopes suffered especially badly; when the sand blew into their large eyes, they became infected, and the antelope went blind and starved to death. More and more antelopes were staggering around aimlessly, bleating piteously. The wild asses hid in mountain crannies, nibbling at the yellowed grass stalks. When the yaks and sheep that had been out at pasture all day returned to the pen, their bellies were empty. The elders' faces grew increasingly solemn. They feared that the windstorm would be followed by another disaster.

That winter, when the first wolf howl came, the herders had just returned to their tents and were preparing to eat and sleep. The howl pierced the sky and startled everyone. Taking up their knives, meat and bowls and with their children in their arms, the men and women came out of their tents one after the other, scanning the skyline for signs of where the howl had come from.

They were used to fighting the elements and they were used to fighting other animals. As their ancestors had lived, so would they. When the elders heard the wolf howl, they shook their heads, sighed and went back inside. The women stared in alarm at a spot on the mountain and turned to each other, their faces white. The children clutched at their parents' robes and gazed in fear at the scary grassland.

The experienced herders knew that the first wolf howl would be followed by three howls, then four, then a wave of them. When that wave of howls came, trouble would follow. Sure enough, in the middle of the night, there was more howling, and it was getting closer. Danzeng called the head of each family to the team headquarters for a meeting about how to defeat the wolves. A wolf attack would be catastrophic for the encampment, but there was also a quiet anticipation among the herders. Their blood was up and as the sandstorm raged around them, they prepared themselves excitedly.

As he stared up at Mount Chanaluo, Gongzha remembered Zhaduo's story about the chain on the top of the mountain that tethered the Wolf Spirit. When the chain stretched, the wolves descended to the plains to wreak havoc; when the chain became taut again, calm was restored. Had the chain stretched? Some of the herders said it had, which made people alarmed.

The grassland was the herders' barn, and the livestock was the grain they stored there. If anything happened to that stash of food, the following year would be hard. This was especially true for the newborn children: if their mothers had no milk, how could they survive the harsh winter?

For the wolves, competing with humans for food was an enormous risk. As long as their usual prey, the smaller wild animals of the grassland, were not forced into their holes by snowstorms or sandstorms, the wolves had no need or inclination to bother the livestock. But sometimes it was a question of survival. Experience had taught them that in those circumstances they were better acting in packs; they would sacrifice some members of the pack so the rest of them could carry on. Humans were not the only ones who got desperate.

Gongzha began to clean his old hunting gun. It had been passed down to him from his grandfather. Even though such guns were rarely used on the plateau now, he was reluctant to give it up. Looking at it was like looking at his father or seeing his elders galloping across the grassland amid the wind and clouds. He feared losing the traditions that his elders had passed down, so when he went hunting he took this old gun to remind himself that the grassland was not his alone, that all lives had to share the gifts of nature.

He sat on the grass, adjusting the balance of the forked stand. This kind of gun had to be unique to Tibet; it was utterly unlike the guns they used in the army. The fork was made out of two antelope antlers and supported the barrel of the gun. When he was out in the wilderness, no matter what the terrain was like, he could balance the gun on the fork and his aim would be steady and accurate.

Gongzha lay on the ground and slowly turned the muzzle of the gun. He set his sights on a distant Tibetan antelope. He was only taking aim; he didn't plan to shoot it. Hunting such an easy target didn't interest him. He preferred going after bears, yaks, snow leopards and even wolves – fierce animals that gave him a sense of accomplishment.

He continued adjusting his gun. Beneath the blue sky and white clouds, he watched as Cuomu and Zhuo Mai came towards him, Zhuo Mai wearing his white doctor's coat. The silver snow mountain was behind them and in the distance there were two black tents, one of them with smoke rising from it. With his sophisticated bearing and her beauty, Zhuo Mai and Cuomu looked like the perfect couple. It made Gongzha's eyes hurt.

'Gongzha!' When Cuomu saw him, she sped over, her multiple tiny plaits flying out behind her.

'You're not wearing your hair net, Cuomu!' Gongzha stood up. As he watched her running over to him with the sun behind her, he made himself smile.

'Well, I don't like it. This is much better!' Cuomu smiled and spun round, her turquoise-studded plaits swirling around her. She giggled and posed in the sunlight. 'Am I not beautiful, Gongzha?'

'You are. Of course my woman is beautiful!' Gongzha glanced at Zhuo Mai and deliberately emphasised 'my woman'.

Cuomu twirled happily into his arms and kissed his face.

Gongzha noticed that Zhuo Mai had stood to one side and was looking at them with interest. He felt a bit embarrassed, scratched his head and asked Zhuo Mai with a smile, 'I heard her uncle took you to birth some more lambs?'

'He did – I've become Cuoe Grassland's full-time doctor!'

'Full-time vet!' Cuomu looked at Zhuo Mai and laughed loudly.

'No, that's only part-time!' Zhuo Mai gave a dry laugh.

'The herders say you once saved a child's life, Zhuo,' Gongzha said, his arms around Cuomu's waist. He was afraid of mispronouncing the doctor's first name, so he used only his last name.

'Yes. There was an avalanche and his parents and brother died. So I took him in and brought him up, and now I'm getting ready to send him to school in the interior.'

'You are our grassland's lucky charm. You've brought us health and happiness – we all like you.' Cuomu spoke from the heart as she leant against Gongzha.

'And I like the grassland! When I retire, I'll get myself a tent and grow old here.' As Zhuo Mai looked at Cuomu's lovely face, the image of another long-haired young woman urging her horse forward flashed through his heart. The two of them really were very similar, especially when they showed their teeth and laughed, so pure and light. He wondered how she was. It was three years since he'd left Chamdo; she must surely have become a mother by now. Did she still miss the Han doctor who used to pick mushrooms and collect yak pats with her? The memories of the two of them walking hand in hand through the dusk on that narrow path would stay with him forever; they could never be erased.

Gongzha watched Zhuo Mai's face as he stared at Cuomu; at times his gaze was unfocused and at others appreciative. It made Gongzha uncomfortable. Had this Han man who spent all day hanging around the grassland taken a fancy to Cuomu? Did they spend a lot of time together when he wasn't around? Had they developed feelings for each other? Had he visited Cuomu's tent?

'Do you want to stay on the grassland?' Gongzha asked meaningfully.

'Yes, I do.' Zhuo Mai smiled. He thought of Chamdo's high mountains and deep valleys, and the fields halfway up the mountainside. She used to drive her flock of sheep towards him with an open, happy smile. Those had been his most blessed and contented days.

'Do you want to marry a herder?'

'Mmm.' Zhuo Mai nodded. He'd wanted to marry her so much, to stay together, to live at the foot of the snow mountain and never leave her.

'Good, good!' Cuomu said loudly with a smile. 'We have so many young women here on Cuoe Grassland, and since you arrived, they've all been coming to see you. Zhuo, you could have your pick of any of them.'

Seeing Cuomu's smile, Zhuo became downcast again. 'Too alike,' he muttered to himself. 'They're really too alike.'

'What?' Gongzha and Cuomu asked in unison. Neither of them had understood what he said. 'What's too alike?'

Zhuo Mai did not have time to reply. From a distance they heard Cuomu's mother Baila calling.

'Cuomu, Dr Zhuo – the meat's ready, come back!' When she saw Gongzha, her expression changed and she snorted in disgust.

Cuomu made a face at Gongzha and walked off with Zhuo Mai towards her family's tent.

Gongzha frowned again as he stared after them.

The howl of a lone wolf pierced the air and the grassland lost its colour in the dusk light. Gongzha scowled and looked up at the mountains. They'd waited anxiously for several days, but the wolves had not come. There was only that occasional howl.

People were getting tired of waiting. But long experience made Gongzha fear that tonight would not be peaceful.

He caressed his gun as if he was caressing his lover. His heart shivered with anticipation. During all his years in the army, he'd mostly gone hunting only when his seniors had asked him to accompany them. He'd fired the occasional shot but hadn't enjoyed it. He was longing for the day when he could return to the grassland fulltime, take up his old forked gun, mount his horse with his beloved woman behind him, and, like his father before him, gallop across the mountains and plains, savouring the life of a Cuoe herder.

A good hunter could not rely on experience alone; instinct was equally important. As his brothers were cutting up their meat that evening, Gongzha warned them that the wolves might come that night. He told them they should take it in turns to sleep, keep their boots on and get Ama to set the dog loose. Everyone nodded in agreement. Even though Gongzha was hardly ever at home, he was still the centre of their world, still the calm older brother who'd cared for them when they were younger.

The sandstorm continued to rage.

The exhausted herders watched anxiously from their tents, as if the grassland might not be there anymore once the night was over. The men were always the calmest. They comforted their women and children, restored peace to their tents, then made sure their guns and knives were within easy reach. They needed to reassure themselves they were ready, whether or not anything happened.

The wolf howls began to come one after another, sparking terror in people's hearts. But after midnight the howling suddenly stopped. The night-watch breathed a sigh of relief.

Gongzha took his gun and went to the sheep pens with his three brothers. They found a hollow to shelter in about fifty metres from the enclosures. The wind continued to scream as madly as ever and the sand still swirled. The four brothers did not speak. They pulled their fox-fur hats low and concentrated on watching the far edges of the grassland.

Gongzha's nostrils flared imperceptibly, as if he wanted to smell the stench of the wolves. He flattened himself even closer to the ground and signalled for his brothers to go to the pens and alert the night-watchmen. They headed off, their backs bowed. Gongzha adjusted his position again, and under the faintly stirring brim of his fox-fur hat fixed his eyes on the darkness in front of him.

The tension increased as everyone prepared for battle, but still the wolves did not appear.

Gongzha was in no hurry. He knew they were coming. He could even picture what they were doing right then. They wouldn't be running, for fear of alerting the night-watch. They would be drawing close stealthily, padding along carefully as if they feared snapping so much as a blade of glass. The howls of the previous ten nights or so had been a distraction, meant to lull the herders into thinking they wouldn't actually attack. When he was younger, Gongzha and his father had fought many wolves together and he knew their habits as well as he knew his own. They were the smartest animals on the grassland and they knew how to keep their losses to a minimum.

Slowly, a few black dots became visible through the sandstorm. They were a long way off, but he could still see them creeping forward. Someone less observant might have mistaken them for little mounds of earth, but Gongzha did not – the shape of this land had been in his bones since he was small.

More and more dots materialised and grew into a dense pack.

Gongzha still didn't move. He watched silently.

The pack gradually split into three groups and fanned out slowly towards the three sheep pens.

Gongzha knew he couldn't stay hidden any longer. He would have liked to, because the closer the wolves came, the more of them he could kill and the more chance he'd have to show off his hunting skills. But the three sheep pens contained the herders' food for a whole year. The army had taught him that acting like a hero must not come at the expense of the collective good. So he lifted his gun, took aim at the front-most wolf in the centre group and gently pulled the trigger. The sound of the shot was heavy and short, and the wolf fell almost immediately.

The other wolves came to a standstill and glanced around in fear. But the pack didn't break formation. Gongzha couldn't help respecting them for that, but he didn't stop. Within moments, his gun had sounded again, and another wolf fell.

The pack began to lose cohesion. A few wolves even pulled back their necks and loped off. Then a long howl went up from somewhere. The scattered wolves quickly rearranged themselves and continued their advance towards the enclosures.

They weren't cautious any longer. Now they bounded towards the pens, legs fully extended, truly wild as they raced freely across the plain that should have been theirs. Even the moonlit night was wolf-like. It was as if the entire landscape was there for the wolf pack. The manic wind continued to hurl sand and ruthlessly attack the plants. It shrieked as if it wanted to grab the earth by the throat and strangle it. In this hopeless night, the human inhabitants and everything they possessed seemed to be the weakest of the weak, suitable fodder for the wolves in their desperate attempt to regain control of the grassland. By the light of the desolate moon, the wolf pack seemed magnificent: they would fight to the death, undaunted and fearless.

Gongzha couldn't stay lying down any longer. He stood up, raised his gun and shouted heroically, 'Come on then!'

Bullets flew like drops of freezing rain trying to douse the consuming fires of the wolf pack. Gunshots resounded from all around. The raging wolf pack had fanned the flames of anger in the men. Bullets and hearts burnt fiercely in the screaming wind.

From inside tents near and far, women and the elderly banged loudly on pans, bowls and anything else that would make a noise, yelling their declaration of war against the approaching wolf pack at the tops of their voices.

The harrowing noise of battle echoed through the night. Gunshots, dogs barking, the clanging of metal, children's cries, adults cursing, the bleating of sheep... It was both terrifying and defiant, pitched against the competing howls of the wolves and the blood-curdling shrieks of the wind. Man versus beast, the wind versus the plants – it was an elemental struggle for dominance, for the right to survive.

The gunshots got closer together and the clashing of the pots grew sharper. The herdsmen's defence had brought the attack to a temporary halt.

The wolves lay on the ground together, their inscrutable eyes occasionally shifting from side to side.

The wind blew on, and the sand continued to swirl.

Nights like this were really not suitable for hunting. The sand made the hunters' hands tremble and lose their accuracy. But could this even be called hunting? Hunting was one man against one beast; it was calm, unhurried. Here there was a pack of wolves, a pack of wild wolves, a pack of starving, wild wolves! The herders were defending themselves against an invasion.

A short howl and the wolves began to move again. This time they avoided Gongzha, who was directly in front of them, and separated into groups. Their actions seemed unplanned, but they were advancing in coordinated units.

Gongzha fired two shots and took down two wolves, then swiftly ran over to the largest sheep pen. But the wolves were surprisingly quick. Gongzha had only just climbed onto the wall of the pen when the sounds of bleating sheep and the alarmed shouts of herders began coming from the other two pens. No matter how powerful a gun was, it could take only one life with one shot. It seemed the wolves were ready to sacrifice the majority of their pack in order that a few of them could live. 'Sacrificing the self, supporting the collective' – this was not a phrase invented by the human race. In the face of danger, wolves were the most collectivist of animals. The wild wind and the freezing cold had driven them to a point from which there was no retreat. Set against the surging, desperate wolf pack, human strength seemed frail indeed.

Wolf after wolf was killed, dog after dog was hurt, sheep after sheep had its neck snapped. The wind blew without let-up, and the gloomy moonlight was torn to shreds by wolf claws. Wound after wound was ripped open, life after life was lost. Sheep's blood, wolves' blood, dogs' blood, human blood – the gritty air was thick with the stench of it. The strange, dry taste of sand mingled with salty blood made the herders vomit.

The wolves were extremely well organised. There were wolves that concentrated on attacking: as long as they could stop a dog or a human, they cared nothing for their own safety. There were wolves that concentrated on biting sheep, killing them in a single snap of their jaws. And there wolves that were responsible for moving the sheep, dragged them off one by one, forcibly pushing them out of the pen. The sheep bleated pitifully and jostled each other as they tried to crowd together, making it easier for the wolves to pick them off.

The sandstorm strengthened. The fires the herders had lit to help drive off the wolves smoked and didn't catch and didn't appear at all threatening to the wolves. Shida took a bowl of burning yak pats and threw the smouldering droppings into the fray. Gongzha turned his gun on the wolves streaming into the pen. But one man and one gun were no match for an entire pack.

A gunshot sounded from another side of the pen. The shooter was good – killing one wolf with one shot – a worthy partner for Gongzha. As the two began to coordinate their fire, they temporarily stopped the wolves' attack on the large pen. But the other pens were in a bad way: the sheep's pained bleating was continuous.

In situations like this, failure to act only made things more dangerous. The herders without guns used their fists or their knives to open a close-range battle with the wolves. They paid no heed to their wounds and had no idea if the blood on their bodies was the wolves' or their own. Cuomu was with the rest of the women, beating pans as big as her face, shouting encouragement to the men. With each second that passed, things got more desperate.

Occasionally, one or two short sharp howls rose from the ranks of the advancing pack, upon which the wolves either quickly re-formed, increased the ferocity of their attack or replaced the wounded or tired animals with fresh fighters. Gongzha climbed onto the wall of the pen to look for that lead wolf. He knew the others would scatter once it was dead.

The other sheep pens were in a state of emergency, so the centre pen started to send people to help them. Cuomu ran behind her younger uncle towards the lower pen. When the wolves realised the humans' plan, the short sharp howl sounded again and some of the wolves raced over to attack.

Because he'd been using one eye and keeping the other shut for a long time, the left side of Gongzha's face was tired. After beating another wave of wolves into retreat, he lifted his head to give his face a rest. As he did so, he noticed a white circle among the wolves. *Kaguo?* He opened his eyes wide and in the yellowish moonlight could just about discern that four straight lines radiated out from the white circle, creating the familiar ⌧. He watched Kaguo dart into the wolf pack, snatch a sheep from a wolf's jaws and run away, her grey figure disappearing in a matter of moments.

There was another short, urgent howl and the wolves surged forward. Thinking no more about the marking on Kaguo's forehead, Gongzha looked around and discovered that the sound was coming from an insignificant-looking wolf that had been keeping its head low. This was an experienced wolf: it had hidden itself deep in the pack, neither too near the front nor too near the back; it kept its head down and its hind legs set back, but its ears were raised. In this position it could attack or retreat with ease and without attracting attention.

Gongzha moved the muzzle of his gun. Just as he was about to pull the trigger, the wolf raised its head and flashed him a cold glance. Perhaps because it sensed its own death, it had a look of despair on its face. As Gongzha stared at it, his heart softened a little. How many years of bloody battle had it endured? His sudden burst of sympathy made him unwilling to shoot. But he had no choice; in this, he was no different from the hungry wolves. The gun sounded and the chilly light in those two eyes went dark. Two teardrops the size of beans welled in Gongzha's own eyes.

Just at that moment, Cuomu's screams rent the air. Gongzha raised his head and saw that she had a wolf to either side of her and they were closing in. Other wolves had surrounded them and were eagerly joining the fray.

Gongzha was so frightened he felt his heart would burst. He shouted to Cuomu and aimed his gun at the wolf in the back. At the same time, a gunshot from elsewhere took down the wolf in the front.

'Cuomu, don't worry! Gongzha, cover us!' Zhuo Mai's loud shout came from the other side.

Zhuo Mai jumped down from where he'd been standing and used the butt of his gun to open a bloody path. Gongzha used his bullets to stave off another wolf and covered Zhuo Mai as he ran over and dragged Cuomu away.

Without the directions from the lead wolf, the rest of the pack dispersed to east and west. They didn't re-form or organise another attack as they had earlier and before long they'd scattered like chaff. The herders followed behind, chasing them and yelling, driving them far away.

Finally it was quiet.

Gongzha was at last able to jump down off the wall. He wanted to wrap Cuomu in his arms but discovered she'd long since been hauled away by her mother. Zhuo Mai was leaning on an old gun, staring into the distance; who knew what he was thinking.

The corpses of wolves and sheep lay all around in the gloomy moonlight. Sheep that had not yet died continued to bleat. All that for a full belly. To survive on the grassland, sometimes it was necessary to pay a price ten times higher than elsewhere. When hungry people pointed their guns at other animals, they were no different to wolves.

The following day, as they cleaned up the battleground, they counted the cost. The large pen had lost twenty sheep and the two small pens had suffered even worse: one lost eighty-two sheep and the other seventy-six. There were more than thirty dead wolves. The herders sighed, skinned the wolves and gave the meat to the dogs. They did not eat it themselves, both because the taste of wolf-meat was too strong, and because after years of warring with the wolves and seeing them go to battle for their stomachs, they had some sympathy for them in their bones.

The sun rose and extended its golden rays across the grassland, the yaks and sheep bounded out of their pens and scattered, the herders cracked their whips and sang, and the horses began to prance once more. It was as if the previous night's tragedy hadn't even happened.

After the wolves had gone, life on the grassland settled down once more. The loss of the sheep made things a little harder in the early spring. The men started looking towards the other grassland animals: wild asses, antelopes and even bears. Now, no matter the usual rules, if they encountered one and could take it down, they would bring it back.

Still, difficult times had no impact on weddings and funerals, and Ciwang's family began preparing to marry off their daughter, Yangji. It was rare to see a smile on Yangji's face and that afternoon there were the sounds of a fight coming from her family tent. People bent their heads and turned their ears to the rumours: it was said that Yangji had cut her hair and was going to be a nun.

A crowd gathered in front of their tent. Ciwang was standing outside yelling at his daughter, Ciwang's woman sat inside weeping, and Yangji sat on the bed, her hair haphazardly chopped. The crowd whispered among themselves: some of them were there out of nosiness, others loved a scene. Ciwang, once one of the most feared people on the grassland, had lost his power in the blink of an eye, and the herders' respect for him had gone with it. To them, a powerless Ciwang who could neither hunt nor herd was less lovable than even a government official.

Hearing the herders' chatter and especially seeing Dawa's disdainful face in the crowd made Ciwang even angrier. That woman, who'd given herself to him in exchange for her man's life, that woman, whom he'd possessed – she too had come to see the joke. He shot her a hateful glance. Unexpectedly, she met it with a smile. It was intolerable: the smile, the way her mouth lifted at the corners, the contemptuous expression that was like a dull blade scraping at his heart. Ciwang snatched up the tongs used to gather yak pats, charged into the tent and thwacked his daughter around the head.

Blood streamed from the top of Yangji's forehead and Ciwang's woman darted over to her, wailing. The crowd outside began to stir. Two men pushed through, went into the tent and dragged Ciwang outside. Dawa looked at him, standing there with his head hanging, gave a cold laugh and strode off.

This whole thing had come about because Yangji was pregnant, and the child was Shida's.

Becoming pregnant before marriage was nothing to lose face over on the plateau. Visiting tents was the most popular form of nocturnal entertainment. Of course, such entertainment had a consequence, which was that the woman could fall pregnant.

Since everyone saw these nocturnal activities as a kind of game, they also had to respect its rules; if there were consequences, everyone had to bear them. The woman who had the child would bring it up herself, and the man would give some yaks and sheep in compensation. These were the rules. Their ancestors had done it this way and the current generation followed suit.

Ciwang asked Shida's parents to come and discuss the question of compensation for the baby in Yangji's womb. He also asked the clan elder and Team Leader Danzeng to attend. The family agreed to give two yaks and twenty sheep. And so, in less than fifteen minutes, the fate of Yangji's baby had been decided, and it hadn't even been born yet. Was that strange? On the grassland, it wasn't the least bit strange.

The grasslanders had their own moral code. The most important thing was that life was to be respected. No matter whose line a life came from, it was a grasslander, a member of the next generation of herders, and of course it should have sheep and yaks like its peers. It didn't matter whether the child knew its father or not; it was enough to have a mother. A mother's back was the child's cradle. Look at the animals on the grassland: which of them had been raised by their fathers?

Yangji's marriage was postponed; they had to at least wait until after the child was born. If she wanted to, Yangji could take the child with her to the marriage; her man would not abandon it. Or she could leave the child with her parents to raise. As long as the souls of the grassland had meat to eat and water to drink, they would grow as soon as they felt the wind; in just a few years, they would be running all over the place tending the yaks.

However, Yangji did not want to get married, which had made her father angry and sparked this round of conflict between them.

As Yangji's stomach grew, so Shida became increasingly troubled. He was conflicted. His heart longed for Cuomu, but his body was irresistibly drawn to Yangji. Even though he'd half expected to find himself in this situation one day, when it came to it, he still didn't know what to do. When the game became reality, when a bit of fun turned into love, it was difficult for either party to extract themselves. Now, whenever he caught sight of Yangji, he either went out of his way to avoid her or quietly ran off. He hated seeing the resentful look on her face. That look could break a person's heart.

'What's wrong with me?' Yangji had cornered him round the side of a tent, blocking his escape route. 'What don't you want me?' she asked in a faint voice.

'It's not... It's... You're already betrothed!' Shida looked at the tips of his boots. His voice was so low, it fell straight to the ground.

'If you want to, I can ask Aba to break the betrothal any time.'

'No, no, no. Yangji, don't... Ah... If you break the betrothal, your parents will be incredibly angry.'

'So you're afraid of my parents being angry? Shida, I still don't know what you're thinking. You want to make Cuomu your woman, but she is the snow lotus of the snow-mountain peak; how can Shambhala's celestial maiden go to your tent?' Yangji glared at him and her tone was sharp. She had loved this man as soon as she understood the meaning of the word, and she had spent forever waiting for him to speak up, waiting for him to send someone to discuss a betrothal, waiting, waiting, right up until now, when the child in her belly was getting bigger by the day. And he still tried to escape at every opportunity. Might he actually be one of the grassland's stones? Could she really not warm his heart with her body?

Her words cut to the most tender part of Shida's heart. His face changed. Raising his head to look at Yangji, he said, 'My family has already given your family yaks and sheep. What else do you want? Who I want to marry is my own affair – what does it have to do with you?' When he was finished, he swung his arms and left.

Yangji was so angry, tears sprang from her eyes. She took out her slingshot, bent down to pick up some stones, and shot them right into Shida's back.

Feeling the stone strike his back, Shida turned and stormed over, breathing heavily. 'What are you doing, Yangji? Don't assume I wouldn't dare hit you just because you're pregnant!'

'Go on, hit me. I don't want to live anyway.' Yangji cocked her head and stared at him, a resolute expression on her face.

'You...' Shida stared back at her tear-streaked face, but after a while he turned and hurried away.

Watching him disappear around the side of the tent, Yangji went limp and sank down on the sandy ground. Her tears fell uncontrollably. From time to time she wiped her eyes with her hand and after a while her face was smudged as if she were a character in an opera. She was heartbroken. No matter what she did, he was unmovable. Could they really not be together? Was she really not good enough? Up until she became pregnant, he'd always acted the same as when he came visiting. His behaviour then and his behaviour now were as different as water and sand.

Even sheep developed an affection for their masters after their masters had taken care of them for a long time. She had used her body to care for him for many years, so why was he not even the slightest bit moved? The more she thought about it, the more it hurt; in the end she opened her mouth and wailed.

Shida hadn't got far, he was only at the back of the tent, and Yangji's cries rang in his ears. Listening to her sobs, he crouched down and held his head, wishing he could find a tent to hide in. He thought about Yangji's affection for him through the years, how it had slowly gathered force, as pure as the white clouds in the sky and as beautiful as the wildflowers on the grassland. Had he only seen her as someone to visit? Then why did he feel so upset when he heard her cry? Should he marry her? She was carrying a child, his first child; if he married her, the child would call him Aba.

So Shida stood up with a cry and strode back. He would tell Yangji that he wanted to marry her, that he wanted her to be his woman, that he wanted the child to call him Aba. But Yangji was gone.

The next day, when Yangji's mother woke up and discovered her daughter's bed was empty, she thought Yangji must have gone to draw water, so she lit the stove and poured the rest of the water into a pot. When the water had boiled but Yangji still hadn't come back, she began to suspect that something wasn't right. She went outside and searched around but couldn't find her. She hurried back to the tent, turned out the clothes chest, and discovered that all of Yangji's clothes were gone. She shook her man awake and told him that Yangji had disappeared. Ciwang looked at her strangely, thinking she was joking.

'She's really nowhere to be found and her clothes are all gone. You should get up and see if the horse is still here,' his woman urged, her tears falling.

Ciwang turned over and climbed out of bed. Draping his *chuba* around himself, he went out to take a look, then came back and sat on the bed. 'The horse is gone.'

When his woman heard this, she went limp and had to sit down on the pile of dried yak pats.

So Yangji vanished from the grassland. Her family kept searching but found no news of her. A pregnant woman wandering through the night across a plateau hungry with wolves and leopards – where could she have gone? On the fifth day, some people in No Man's Land found Yangji's headscarf; it was covered in blood. That night, Ciwang's woman cried until dawn. That night, Shida rode his horse back and forth across the grassland in a frenzy.

9

The weather slowly warmed up. Having suffered through the harsh winter, people and livestock alike began to stretch their limbs and show sparks of life. It was spring, time to cut away the sheep's thick woolly winter coats and free them from their burden. They emerged freshly lightened from the fold and fattened up quickly on the nourishing new grass.

It was a mild day and the men and women of the encampment would have been getting on with their chores had it not been for Dawa's pitiful screams coming from the sheep pen. Her head and face were covered in blood and she looked as if she was about to keel over. Baila stood frozen by her side and the sheep that had caused all the trouble had run off and disappeared.

Baila had been holding a ram as she stood alongside Dawa, who was stooped over, tending to one of the sheep. As Dawa had raised her head, Baila's leg had suddenly given way for some reason and the ram had sprung away from her. It caught Dawa with the sharp point of its horn, stabbing her forehead and making her yell out in pain as blood poured from her wound.

Ciwang happened to be standing by the two of them at the time and quickly went to Dawa's aid, keeping her upright. He shouted at Baila, who was too shocked to move, 'Baila, you're really too much. Your man visits her tent, that's all – do you have to try and kill her?'

'No... It wasn't...' Baila looked at Dawa's bloodied face and was too frightened to talk sense. 'I didn't... The ram itself...'

'I saw you throw down the ram with my own eyes and yet you won't admit it,' Ciwang said. He picked up Dawa and pushed his way through the crowd. They ran into Danzeng at the gate and Ciwang fixed him with a fierce stare. 'Your woman is really too horrible, treating a woman with no head of the household like this. How can you let this carry on?'

Seeing Dawa covered in blood, Danzeng was dumbfounded. When his woman ran over, crying, he raised his hand and slapped her. Baila cried even louder and scurried off to her tent.

Cuomu didn't know what had happened, but she quietly tugged Shida's arm and urged him to get someone to go to the army base and ask Dr Zhuo to come as soon as possible. Then she hurried after her mother.

When Dawa's three sons saw their mother covered in blood, they drew their daggers and rushed over to Danzeng's tent. Everyone followed them. Danzeng's youngest brother, Duoji, had also taken up his dagger and was guarding the door to their tent. He watched the three raging youths approach with a cold light in his eyes.

A few people tried to plead with them and pull them away, but it was no good. The three young men were like young bulls, afraid of nothing that earth or heaven could throw at them. They raced up to the tent door and set upon Duoji. Danzeng's second brother, Niduo, pushed through the crowd and entered the fray. The five men wrestled with each other. When Danzeng pulled one of them away, another plunged in. Meanwhile, Baila continued sobbing inside the tent.

No one knew who had stabbed whom, but there was blood on the ground. One of the young men fell to the floor, then another followed him. Then they got up again and started over.

Shida arrived, supporting the tottering figure of Wangjiu, the clan elder he'd brought back with him from another part of the grassland. The crowd automatically made way for the old man.

'Stop it, all of you!' Wangjiu's body was ailing; he shivered constantly when the wind blew and it was getting worse. He did not want to see the clan at war with itself and hoped that the sight of his frail old body might shake them into calling a halt to the bloodshed.

As society had changed, so the role of the clan elder had all but disappeared. Even though Wangjiu was still highly regarded on the grassland, he was rarely called upon to get involved in clan affairs. In fact, there were no affairs that required his input. Team Leader Danzeng was the government's representative and had authority over the herders in political matters. As for people's private matters, the head of the household took care of those.

Wangjiu had spent decades roaming the grassland, and though the wind and sun had weathered his body, he still had a wise head. He'd been a mighty man in his youth, afraid of nothing, but in old age he was peaceable, restrained and self-aware, and he knew exactly when and when not to intervene. This was not such a common quality – how often did people rate themselves too highly or too little because they'd forgotten who they were? As a result, Wangjiu commanded great respect from clan members whenever they saw him.

Hearing the clan elder's angry instruction, the six men separated. All of them except Danzeng were wounded. They stared menacingly at one another.

'Go home, the rest of you!' Wangjiu straightened up and glared at the assembled onlookers. His voice was not loud, but it had strength and authority. The onlookers smiled with embarrassment and returned to their tents.

'So tell me, does someone have to die before you call this off?' Wangjiu gave a dry cough. He sat down on a chair that Cuomu had brought over and stared down the six men in front of him.

Under the glare of those cloudy eyes, the men who'd just been baying for blood lowered their heads and looked at their boots in silence.

'Drawing your daggers to resolve an argument between two jealous women – you really are quite something! What fine grassland men you are – killing people is so much easier than killing yaks.' Wangjiu's face flushed with anger.

'Gela, don't be angry! It's because I didn't teach them well. I'll reprimand them shortly.'

'Danzeng, I'm not talking about you. You're a production-team leader, but if you can't manage the affairs of your own tent, how can you manage the team?'

'Yes, yes, Gela has spoken correctly. I have not managed them well.' Danzeng bowed in response.

Cuomu poured a cup of water and offered it to Wangjiu with both hands. 'Bola, please drink.'

The old man accepted the cup, took a sip and said, 'Call your mother out.'

Cuomu went back into the tent and pulled the weeping Baila in front of the old man.

'You have quite a few men in your family, don't you? If you kill one, there will still be two left, right?'

'I...' Baila was racked with sobs and her hair was dishevelled; she did not dare raise her head.

'The only woman in your family, and you spend all of your time watching someone else's tent – do you have no self-respect? Has Dawa taken any space in your tent or any of your belongings? Does your man not come back? Has he left you and become her support instead? How could you be so vicious – using a ram's horn to stab her!'

'I didn't... I don't know how, but the ram sprang out of my hands.' Baila raised her head, cast a nervous glance at the elder, then looked down again.

'The ram sprang out of your hands by itself? Baila, how can you say that? Everyone on the grassland knows that your wild jenny personality will never change and that when your man visits another woman's tent you flare up. Why not tie him to your waist so he can't leave at night!'

'Gela... I...' Baila could only cry piteously.

'Enough. Go and see her and take her some butter. Unless you really want to see a war between your men and her sons?' Wangjiu gave her a sharp look. He was angry and upset, which brought on another coughing fit. He covered his mouth with his hand and Cuomu quickly massaged his back with her fingers.

'You three, come over!' He beckoned to Gongzha's three brothers.

The three young men were covered in blood. They walked quietly over to the old man, bowed and stood up straight.

Wangjiu looked them up and down. 'So you're all grown-up and you want to avenge your mother? Your father died young, and Gongzha is away in the army. If it hadn't been for your Uncle Danzeng, wouldn't you have been food for the wolves long ago? Now that you've grown up, you take your knives to your Uncle Danzeng's tent for something like this? Your hearts have been eaten by wolves!'

The boys looked at one another. Eventually the second eldest, Gongzan, walked over to Danzeng, bowed and said, 'I'm sorry, Uncle Danzeng!' Without waiting for Danzeng to reply, he turned and kicked his brothers – 'Let's go' – and the three of them raced off across the grassland.

It was not helpful to measure grassland distances in kilometres; much better to count the number of hours you'd need to ride it. If someone said how many hours it took by horse, everyone knew how far it was; if someone used kilometres, everyone rolled their eyes. Zhuo Mai's border unit was based at least four hours' ride from Cuoe Grassland; getting there and back took a whole day.

'How is she, Dr Zhuo? Will it leave a scar?' Ciwang asked warmly when Zhuo Mai arrived two days later.

'A cut this big? Of course it will leave a scar!' Zhuo Mai replied without turning his head.

Ciwang gasped and took a step back. 'Will... will it look ugly?'

'Well, it won't look like it did before.' Zhuo Mai took out a syringe and said to Dawa, 'I'm going to give you some anaesthetic. The cut is deep and I'll need to put in some stiches for it to heal.'

Dawa nodded and smiled drily. 'Thank you, Dr Zhuo. If it's going to be ugly, then let it be ugly. This face has never brought me any luck; things will be simpler if it's ruined.'

'What are you saying? Such a beautiful face, how can it be ruined just like that?' Ciwang tapped his foot. 'I need to find Danzeng.'

'What can you achieve by finding him? Don't you think his woman has caused enough damage? Go home, Ciwang. My sons are here; they can take care of me. Thank you for helping me yesterday.'

'Well... alright.' Ciwang made his way slowly to the door, then glanced back at Dawa. 'If there are any problems, send Gongzan to find me.'

Dawa waved at him and closed her eyes.

Ciwang left and returned to his own tent, humming a song. When he stepped through the door, he called to his woman to serve tea and whistled cheerfully.

'Managed to flatter your way into her heart, did you?' Ciwang's woman banged the wooden tea bowl down in front of him. 'There's just one thing I don't understand: how come the ram managed to escape Baila's grip so easily?'

Ciwang chuckled darkly and did not reply.

'Baila has a sharp tongue and she's always hated Dawa for taking her man, but she wouldn't go so far as to hurt her. It's very strange.'

'That's Buddha's punishment to her.' Ciwang laughed coldly.

'Why would Buddha want to punish Dawa? That woman only had one man on this grassland. Wouldn't Buddha get a little tired if he concerned himself with private family matters like that? I don't think it's Buddha's punishment – I think it's yours. Because she likes Danzeng and she doesn't like you.'

'What foolish talk is this?' Ciwang pounded the table and stood up, slapping her so hard that her body spun. 'You've gone crazy.'

His woman gave a hollow laugh. 'I saw Baila being pushed by someone – the ram only got away because she couldn't stay upright. I'm not crazy – you're the one who's crazy!' She dabbed the trickle of blood at the corner of her mouth and stared at her man with reddened eyes.

Ever since their daughter Yangji had run away, she had blamed everything on her husband. As a mother, she couldn't stop thinking of her child out in the empty wilderness. Where had she got to? Had she run into a wolf or a bear? Her man wasn't worried; her man's eyes were fixed on another woman; her man's heart was fixed on driving away the other men around that woman and bringing her into his embrace. That made her angry; it made her hate her man even more. So when, from another corner of the sheep pen, she'd seen her man give the ram that Baila was holding a surreptitious shove, she'd felt crushed. That hateful act turned her heart as cold as a chunk of ice frozen for a thousand years.

'You'll be punished for this!' She sank to the ground, her hair dishevelled. Her wrinkles had got a lot deeper in recent days. She looked across at her man, who was humming a tune, fumbling open a bottle of *baijiu* and pouring it into his mouth. There was nothing she could do but suffer.

After her wound healed, Dawa took a bandage she'd got from Dr Zhuo, cut it into it circles, squares and triangles the size of her fingernails and carefully pasted them onto her cheek. This was apparently very popular in the city, so Danzeng had told her after coming back from the county town one time. Dawa had sought out Dr Zhuo and asked for a bandage, saying her leg hurt, but she'd never used it. She took it out now because she didn't want to give that woman of Danzeng's the satisfaction of thinking that just because she was no longer beautiful, she had also lost the power to attract. She wanted her to understand that even if her face was ruined, Danzeng would still want her.

When the sun had warmed the grassland, Dawa left her tent wearing the silk dress that Danzeng had bought her, deliberately letting its soft collar show outside her sheepskin *chuba*. She had washed her hair and used butter to smooth it down until it gleamed; then she'd asked Ciwang's woman to help her braid it into tiny plaits. She fixed pieces of turquoise around her head and gathered her plaits into a net inlaid with yellow jade. With great ceremony, she led her horse to Danzeng's tent, then called, 'Danzeng, dear Danzeng, come out!'

Baila came out. When she saw the lively, healthy Dawa, her face changed colour and she disappeared back into the tent.

Danzeng walked over, smiling. 'Has your wound healed? You're leading your horse – where are you going?'

'I want to go to the town to send Gongzha a letter. But I heard that bears have been making trouble along the road through No Man's Land, so can you come with me?' Dawa smiled, her face as fresh as a spring breeze.

'Alright. Wait a minute.' Danzeng went into his tent and came out with his rifle on his back. He unhitched his horse from beside the tent.

The two walked down the road side by side and after a short distance leapt up onto their horses at the same time. Dawa knew Baila would be watching. She wanted her to watch, she wanted her to know that the man at her side would come away with her anytime she asked. Baila should not think she could tie down her man's heart just because she had a tent. Men's hearts were like shooting stars: the flowers on the ground could not determine where they would fall on a given night. Catching this falling star was not something that could be achieved through treachery.

There was another pair of eyes following them – Ciwang's.

Ciwang's woman was also standing beside her tent, watching the two horses disappear into the depths of the grassland. She laughed coolly. 'Someone really wasted his efforts,' she said.

Ciwang swung his foot back and kicked her in the side.

'Go on, kick me!' his woman said, scrambling to her feet. 'Kick me to death and you still won't get your prize – she doesn't like you at all.'

Some days later, Dawa began to sense that something wasn't right. When she went out in the middle of the night to urinate, it was as if someone was watching her, but when she turned round there was no one there. What was going on? One night, when it happened again, her heart began to pound. Was she thinking too much or was there really someone watching her?

The next day, everyone else in the encampment went to the pasture. But Danzeng said that she hadn't yet recovered her strength after her injury and he gave her special dispensation to stay close to home and look after some sick lambs.

Dawa gave the lambs some tea water to drink, closed the pen and tied the dog up at the gate before returning to her tent. She pulled out a shovel and began to clean her own tent's sheep pen while humming a herding song. Suddenly everything went dark. A black cloth had been thrown over her head. Then came a forceful blow to the back of her scalp, and that was the last thing she knew.

That night when everyone came home from the pasture, they found Dawa wandering aimlessly around the encampment, hair tousled and stark naked.

Gongzan was shocked. He quickly pulled off his leather *chuba*, wrapped his mother in it and took her home. Dawa's two legs hung bare, kicking uncontrollably. She shouted wildly, 'Danzeng, come on, come and visit my tent! No need for you to drive the dog away; I've tied it up! Hee hee hee... You've knocked out my dog – I don't want you. You dead ghost, you've already gone, you won't take care of me anymore, how will I look after so many children?'

How could a healthy person lose her sanity so quickly?

When Gongzha got the news, it was already ten days after the onset of Dawa's madness. He ran to the company commander's office with the telegram in his hand; he didn't even knock, just pushed the door open and burst in.

'Gongzha, you fucker, you've been in the army eight years and you still haven't learnt to knock?' The old company commander was now the regimental commander. He'd been looking at a map with the new company commander. When he saw that it was Gongzha making such a noisy entry, he swore at him affectionately.

Gongzha chuckled. 'I'm sorry, sir. I forgot again!' He went back to the door, snapped his heels together and roared, 'Reporting!' His shout frightened the orderly serving tea so much his hand shook and the teacup smashed to smithereens on the floor.

'Gongzha, you fucker, if you don't yell "Reporting!", you scare people to death, and when you do yell "Reporting!", you scare them even more.'

'Ha ha, sir...' Gongzha strode over, scratching his head with an embarrassed laugh.

'Give it to me, give it to me. Is it that you want to go fucking hunting again?' Because Gongzha was both a skilled marksman and a local, the regimental and divisional leaders always liked taking him when they went hunting, and it was usual for him to accompany them for several days.

'No, sir, it's not for the regimental commander to go hunting...'

'Of course I'm not going hunting. Gongzha, you fucker, what level of Mandarin have you actually reached?' The regimental commander took the piece of paper from his hand. 'Oh, your mother's unwell? You want to ask for leave to go back home?'

'Yes, sir. I didn't have a father, only a mother. Now that she's poorly, I'm sick worried.'

'It's "worried sick", not "sick worried",' the regimental commander chided with a laugh. He passed the company commander a leave slip. 'Where did you come from, if you didn't have a father? You can't even speak!'

The company commander signed the leave slip and passed it to Gongzha. 'Off with you.'

Gongzha laughed embarrassedly, took the slip, snapped his

heels together and saluted, then ran out of the office, repeating, 'Worried sick, worried sick, worried sick.'

The regimental commander and the orderly doubled-over laughing.

Gongzha repeated 'worried sick' all the way back to the barracks.

'Old Squad Leader, how did it go? Did they approve your leave?' Gongzha had been the squad leader for five years, so the new recruits all called him Old Squad Leader. He should have retired from the army long ago, but the regimental commander liked him and had persuaded him to stay on until a suitable job became available. This year a directive to that effect had finally arrived. Gongzha could soon hope to return home for good.

'Approved, approved – two months!' Gongzha smiled contentedly and with this smile forgot 'worried sick' again. He quickly asked the other men, 'What was I saying when I came in?'

'"Worried sick." You were saying "worried sick" over and over. Old Squad Leader, what are you were worried sick about?'

'Right, right, right, it's "worried sick". I'm worried sick about my mother's illness.' Gongzha laughed, smacked his head and began to get his things together.

When his fellow soldiers heard that Gongzha was going home to see his family, they all brought him specialities from their hometowns and stuffed them one after the other into his backpack. The regimental commander's orderly also came and gave Gongzha a bag of fruit sweets, saying they were from the regimental commander for his mother.

'The regimental commander really likes you, Gongzha.'

'I'm honest, alright? Not like you lot, visiting women's tents all over the place, trouble the regimental commander giving,' Gongzha replied in his distinctive Mandarin. He continued organising his things.

'Weren't you the one who took us? When trouble came, you ran faster than a fox.'

'I was just your translator. I tried to get you to study hard, but you didn't want to, and even now you can't speak Tibetan. That's not like me at all, I studied Mandarin so diligently, I'm...'

'Sick worried!' a couple of soldiers said in unison, laughing together.

'Right, I'm off. My brothers, when I come back, I'll bring you some of our grassland's wind-dried meat – it's much better than the greasy stuff we get here.' Gongzha lifted his bag onto his back and walked out; ten or more soldiers crowded around to see him to the gate.

The sunbeams sparkled, the sky was completely clear and waves rippled on Cuoe Lake. The warm breeze was making both people and animals lethargic. The yaks in the distance and the antelopes closer to hand were all extremely still, eating or resting, enjoying the gentle caress of the beautiful day.

Gongzha hurried home in a cloud of dust. After hearing what had happened, he suspected that Baila had something to do with it. His hand flew to his dagger and he raced even faster across the plain.

As he reached his family tent, Gongzan came out to greet him. 'Brother, Ama's acting up again.'

Gongzha strode into the tent to find a tousle-haired Dawa trying to get up off the couch and his little sister tugging at her clothes and crying. 'What's this, Ama?' He walked over and pressed down on Dawa's shoulder, holding her steady, then sat down beside her. 'Ama, do you know who I am?'

Dawa looked at him, laughing crazily. 'Ha ha, which tent did you go to that you're only coming back now after such a long time?'

After she was calm again, Gongzha set off to collect some herbs for her. He took out the old gun and weighed it in his hand. He hadn't used it in a long time and it felt unfamiliar to the touch. He slung the gun across his back, put on his leather *chuba*, hung the leather bag of gunpowder off his belt, and led his horse out from behind the tent.

On his way out of the encampment, just as he was about to mount his horse, he saw Baila coming towards him. When he thought of the scar on his mother's forehead, his face fell.

Baila rolled her eyes when she saw Gongzha, snorted at the ground, and cursed. '*Bairuo!*'

'*Bairuo*' meant 'your father is a corpse' and was the most vicious insult on the grassland. His father's untimely death had left a deep wound in Gongzha's heart and even if he'd been of a calm disposition, he probably wouldn't have let such a hurtful insult pass. But Gongzha was not known for his even temper. He pulled his foot out of the stirrup, turned and glared at Baila, his face trembling with rage.

'*Bairuo!*' Baila cursed again as she passed him.

Gongzha immediately raised his hand and slapped her, hitting her so hard that she spun round several times before she fell to the ground. 'You stay away from me from, you hear? Otherwise I won't be responsible for my actions,' he said coldly. Mounting his horse, he cracked his whip and disappeared across the grassland in search of his mother's herbs.

A crowd gathered when they heard Baila's cries. They asked her what had happened.

'The son of that wild jenny Dawa hit me! How dare he!' Baila smacked the ground, stirring up a cloud of dust. 'Danzeng, is that the sort of woman you spend your time with – a woman who raises her sons to hit your own woman? You're really something. The punishment for your tent visits has come, and it's come to your own woman!'

'Ama, how could Gongzan have hit you?' Cuomu pushed through the crowd and helped her mother up. 'Isn't he in his tent looking after his mother?'

'What Gongzan? It's that yak Gongzha. I'm telling you now: if you carry on seeing him after today, don't blame me if I don't recognise you as my daughter.' Baila wiped away her tears, leaving streaks of dirt across her face.

Cuomu's eyes lit up. 'Gongzha's back?'

'I've told you, I forbid you from seeing him again.' Baila clasped her back with her hands. 'Ow! My back… That dead yak, *bairuo*…'

'Ama, don't curse!' Cuomu supported her mother back to the tent; when they were almost there, they ran into her two uncles, who were on their way back from herding.

'What's wrong with your mother?' her elder uncle, Niduo, asked.

Cuomu was about to speak when her mother butted in. 'It's that woman of your brother's – yet again. She told her son to hit me. I can't even straighten my back, and as for my face, well, see for yourselves.' Baila turned the swollen, reddened right side of her face towards them, her tears falling thick and fast. 'Oh, my three men have all become grass-eaters. Their woman gets beaten up by a wild yak and all they can do is look!'

Her words had the desired effect. A grassland man could take being called stupid, he could even take being called useless, but to say he was no better than the grass-eating livestock was an insult that struck deep. A man without the bloodlust fundamental to survival on the grassland was no man at all. If a man lost that, he lost the respect of his woman, and if even his own woman didn't look up to him, he had no standing on the grassland.

'Let's go.' Niduo jerked his chin at his younger brother, Duoji, who was standing next to him. Ignoring Cuomu's shouted protests, they headed off, taking with them a stave from beside the tent.

The two enraged brothers plunged into Gongzha's family tent. Gongzan and his siblings were tending to Dawa. Sensing something was wrong, they automatically reached for the knives at their waists. Niduo and Duoji didn't even look at Gongzan; they just took their staves and lashed out in every direction.

The pressure cooker and bowls clattered noisily to the ground, and clothes were thrown across the floor. Gongzan and his two brothers defended themselves with whatever household items came to hand. Their little sister Lamu was badly frightened, she only knew to protect her mother Dawa and hid sobbing in the corner.

By the time Danzeng and Cuomu had hurried over, Niduo had been stabbed in the back. He lay on the ground trying to hold his wound, blood staining his fur-lined *chuba*. Gongzan had been hit on the head with the stave and blood was trickling down his forehead.

'Don't fight, don't fight...' Cuomu quickly tried to help her uncle up, but his body was so weak he couldn't stand. When she saw how pale his face was, she was badly frightened. 'Aba, Uncle is done for!' she yelled.

Her shout made everyone else freeze. They all stared at Niduo.

'Why don't you come and help me?' Cuomu called to her Uncle Duoji.

Danzeng and Duoji carried their brother Niduo out of the tent and took him home on their backs. As soon as they'd laid him on the couch, Zhuo Mai raced in, pulling his son with him and carrying his medical bag. He felt for Niduo's pulse, pulled up his eyelids and then sighed, shaking his head.

'He's dead.'

Cuomu sat on the floor, her face deathly pale, wanting to cry but unable to shed any tears. Danzeng could barely stand; he staggered and put out a hand to steady himself on the chest. His youngest brother looked on in a daze. Baila's eyes rolled and she fainted.

Zhuo Mai caught her and signalled for a glass of water.

When Baila woke and saw Niduo's bloodied corpse at the side of the tent, she let out a great cry.

'Brother Danzeng, things have already gone too far,' Zhuo Mai said, giving Danzeng a sympathetic look. 'Being upset is not helping – you need to resolve this quickly.'

Duoji's eyes flashed fire. He fixed Danzeng with a stare and spoke in a low, steely voice. 'Second Brother cannot die like this. Oldest Brother, it's for you to say: what should we do?'

What could Danzeng say? Could he say they would not seek revenge? No, he didn't dare say that. No matter what he felt in his heart, he had to deal with this. His brother was dead, his corpse laid out right there in front of him. He was the head of the household, the backbone of the family. It was his responsibility to ensure that the people of his tent were not wronged. Danzeng was a man of standing. His brother had been killed and this was a blood feud that could endure for generations – how could he not take revenge? How could it stop here? And yet, what sort of revenge should he take? Should he kill one of her sons? A life for a life. Blood for blood. Thinking of her now, so delusional that she didn't even know him, how could he bring another bloody disaster on her tent?

'Brother, I know you like that woman, but now her son has killed our brother. No matter how much you like her, is a woman really more important than a brother?' Duoji looked at him, his face tense.

Looking down at Niduo's mute, motionless, bloody body, Danzeng's heart was like an eagle about to pounce. Blood rushed to his head. 'Alright, let's avenge Second Brother.' Danzeng looked at his youngest brother, grimaced, and forced the words out from between gritted teeth. He lifted his feet and prepared to go out.

'No, Aba, Uncle, don't kill again! Uncle Niduo has already gone. No matter how much more blood is spilt, it won't bring him back.' Cuomu held onto her father's leg, her tears falling like rain.

'Will your Uncle Niduo die for nothing? A debt of blood must be repaid in blood.' Baila's eyes were bloodshot and she was hungry for revenge. 'That woman... Your father was so good to her, and for what? He helped her bring up her son, and now see what's happened – bitten by the leopard you raised,' she said viciously. 'Let go of your father, Cuomu. Don't make the people of the grassland look down on him.'

When Danzeng heard his woman say that, he knew he had to go. He turned to leave.

'Wait, wait. Will you just let me say one thing?' Zhuo Mai glanced round at everyone in the tent. His voice was not loud, but it was full of authority. 'When I've finished, you can go and kill people or burn down tents, whatever you want.'

Danzeng looked at his brother and his woman and sat down without saying a word.

'Times have changed, and things are different here on the plateau now. Outsiders used to dismiss this land as a place of evil ghosts. They said that once you came up here, you could never leave. So no one wanted to come. And you yourselves never left, never mixed with the outside world. You settled everything among yourselves. If a man killed another man, the following day someone would come and kill him, and on it would go. If you wanted to put an end to the generations of blood feuds, you discussed how much would be paid in compensation, but the price for the lives lost was never equal.

'Now it's different. The Liberation has come. You're not anyone's serfs anymore, and you no longer have to run around for other people. Everyone is equal before the law: if you kill someone, you die, and if you owe a debt, you pay. There's no difference in the value of a life now.

'We can't keep holding on to the old ways, paying blood debts with blood. I suggest that you go quickly to the town to report this matter and let the government handle it. Brother Danzeng, you're the team leader and you're well known on the grassland. If you set an example by changing the way justice is done on the grassland, future generations will thank you.'

'Dr Zhuo is right.' Wangjiu, the old clan elder, stooped in under the tent flap, supported by Shida and another young man. 'That is the history of our grassland. If you kill a member of my family, I will kill one of yours. Year after year there is blood and sacrifice, and it goes on for generation after generation.'

Danzeng got up to let Wangjiu sit.

'People say that we people of northern Tibet are *abuhuo*, that we're hot-headed and unreasonable, that we're dirty and unruly. We murder one another, turn our knives on each other. Why can't we control ourselves? Why can't we let the government help us deal with problems when they arise? Blood-letting doesn't solve anything.'

'Elder Wangjiu, I...' Danzeng looked up at the old man, then clasped his head in his hands and knelt on the ground in front of him. His eyes slowly filled with tears.

'Danzeng, your grandfather died in a revenge killing and your father died in a revenge killing. Now your brother is gone. Will Cuomu have to die before all this stops?' Wangjiu spoke with feeling and patted Danzeng's shoulder.

His words made Danzeng and Duoji hold their heads and howl. Danzeng agreed to go to the town and report the case the next day.

While all that was going on, Gongzha was halfway up Mount Chanaluo, carefully searching the rocky crevices for herbs. Loose stones occasionally rolled past him. The upper slopes, above five thousand metres, had snow year round and the summit got a fresh covering every day. The smallest disturbance could trigger an avalanche and bring down half the mountain, so Gongzha moved slowly and kept his breathing as light as possible for fear the vibrations might bring the snow crashing down on top of him.

Mount Chanaluo's eastern face overlooked the lake. There were ravines on both the north and south sides, and to the west lay the endless sweep of Cuoe Grassland. The mountain was a haven for yaks, wolves and bears, and according to the legend of the Wolf Spirit it was forbidden by the Buddha to go there. The herders didn't dare, and only the older, braver hunters ventured up there with their guns, in groups of two or three, but they always hurried away.

Gongzha's father had often hunted up there, taking Gongzha with him. Zhaduo had also gone there to gather herbs and he'd told Gongzha the mountain's story. He said that beyond the first layer of the mountain range was a snow valley and that this was the bears' haven. When you were almost at the ledge just below the summit, there was a large black boulder, and on the boulder lay the magical chain sent from heaven that King Gesar had used to tether the Wolf Spirit. The main gate to Shambhala was right next to the chain.

Shambhala was the heaven that occupied many a herder's heart. Was it really on this earth? Gongzha shook his head. He'd heard these kinds of stories since he was young. The children of the grassland could easily tell several days' worth of stories about Shambhala. But no one could say what Shambhala looked like; they just put whatever they imagined was most beautiful into their stories. As he looked at the cloud-veiled mountain peak, he thought of the story that Cuomu had told him. How Chanaluo had once had a heart that beat, but that now, no one knew why, the heart was gone and all that remained was a cavity. Was that ledge Chanaluo's heart cavity?

He stared hard at the mountain peak. He wanted to explore up there, investigate that mysterious ledge, the heaven-sent magical chain and the legend of the Wolf Spirit. But not tonight. Gongzha tilted his head and looked at the sky: the moon had already reached the mountaintop and Ama would be waiting for him. He checked the herbs in his pack and, stepping onto the packed snow, carefully slid down the mountain.

Just after he rounded a large rock, he suddenly saw Kaguo standing on a nearby boulder. Her thick fur stirred lightly in the breeze, and in the moonlight her small eyes shone bright and clear. She watched him quietly.

Gongzha froze, then instinctively reached for his gun. But slowly he lowered his hand. Under the light of the moon, man and bear looked at each other across the snow mountain. The mountain was utterly silent save for the in- and out-breaths of the man and the bear.

Then Kaguo jumped down from the boulder and bounded back up the mountain. In a little while she'd completely disappeared.

Gongzha stood staring after her for some time. He thought about how Zhaduo had instructed him to find her, how she would supposedly lead him to the Buddha and let the Buddha's light shine on the grassland once more. This was what Zhaduo had requested and it had become Gongzha's burden. Kaguo was a bear, what could she do? What did the Buddha have to do with a bear? Gongzha didn't understand. He thought of the black Buddha he'd buried when he was a child and the book that looked like a religious text but wasn't. Maybe he should find them and move them to another place. With these thoughts in mind, he continued his slide down the mountain, found his horse, mounted, and with a crack of the whip raced back to the grassland.

He got back to the tent before dawn to find his home in a shambles. The pressure cooker, washbowls and blankets were strewn all over the place and their one small wooden chest had been smashed to pieces. His three brothers were clearing up and his mother was asleep. When his sister saw him, she buried herself in his arms and sobbed.

'What happened?'

Gongzan explained.

Gongzha's face darkened. He put the medicinal herbs he'd collected beside the window and began to help his brothers clean up.

When morning came, Gongzha made his youngest brother, the brother who'd stabbed Niduo, go to the town and turn himself in.

Because the guilty party had proactively reported themselves, the situation was now a lot less inflammatory. The government had stepped in and, whatever the outcome, that would at least guarantee there'd be no ongoing blood feud. As for settling Niduo's funeral arrangements, the clan elder called Gongzha and Danzeng to Zhuo Mai's tent to discuss them.

Wangjiu coughed, drank a little water, raised his head, and said, 'What's done is done. You are your respective tents' head of household. I called you here today to discuss the funeral of the dead man.'

'It is we who were in the wrong,' Gongzha said. 'How much money do you want? We are willing to pay.' He saw that the hair on the side of Danzeng's head had begun to go white and his heart sank. The Danzeng he remembered was a strong, authoritative man. How could he have lost that overnight? His back was stooped, his leather robe hung loose around his waist, and his hair was dirty and unkempt.

Ever since Gongzha had come to understand such things, he'd been witness to Danzeng's comings and goings in their tent. In the lean years, it had always been Danzeng who went hungry so that they could eat; he'd looked after Gongzha and his siblings like a father. Then when Gongzha had grown and could look after his own tent, Danzeng had put him forward for the army. In Gongzha's heart, Danzeng was like his own father. He'd always hoped that one day he would return to the grassland, marry Cuomu and take good care of Danzeng in his old age. But now this had happened.

'Let's say three hundred. Things aren't easy for his family.' Danzeng glanced at Gongzha then quickly lowered his head. It was hard to look into the eyes of this young man whom he had once loved and cherished as his own child, whom he had taken hunting and herding. How could he have grown up so fast and become his enemy? Was fate so impossible to anticipate, so impossible to fathom?

'Alright.' Gongzha took out a large wad of ten-yuan bills and tossed it to Wangjiu. It was two months' salary and even after the two hundred he'd given his youngest brother, there was still more than a thousand left.

'There's no need for that much,' Danzeng said. 'His mother needs money for the doctor.' He grabbed a wodge of notes, put it in his *chuba* and returned the rest to the clan elder, who passed it to Gongzha.

'I don't need it,' Gongzha said in a muffled voice, and pushed the money back.

The elder sighed and motioned for Zhuo Mai to put the money in Danzeng's *chuba*. 'You should take it,' he told Danzeng. 'Accept the gesture.'

Danzeng lowered his head and his eyes blurred with tears.

Gongzha glanced at Danzeng; he wanted to apologise, but his pride wouldn't let him. He rose, bowed to the clan elder, turned and went out of the tent.

Cuomu was standing outside in the sunlight. She looked at Gongzha askance, and his feet froze to the ground.

Danzeng also came out. Seeing his daughter, he said in a low voice, 'Let's go.'

Cuomu walked mechanically behind her father, looking back every three steps.

Zhuo Mai came over to Gongzha's side. 'You must give her time, and give her family time.'

With such hostility between the two tents, would it ever be possible for the pair of them to be together?

The wind began to blow, increasing in strength, turning every which way and howling. It was always like that on the grassland: the wind and rain came and went at whim.

Five days later, people from the county town came to take Gongzha's youngest brother away. Everyone in the encampment turned up to watch. After all, this was the first blood feud the government had stepped in to resolve, a new way of seeing justice done on Cuoe Grassland.

The affair stopped Gongzha and Cuomu's love in its tracks. How could love flourish amid the pain of a family member's death? Their love was no longer protected and carefully tended, no longer unconditional but smothered under hurt and dust.

The once singing, smiling Cuomu changed overnight, like the summer grass. She became silent and withdrawn; she no longer joined in with the other young people's activities. No matter how large the dance circle or how exuberant the singing, she wouldn't even look at it. She just searched for something else to do: cleaning the lamb pen, carrying water, washing clothes... If there really was nothing to do, she would sit by herself out on the plain, staring vacantly at the distant snow mountain.

She got thinner by the day. The young men sighed when they saw her, shocked that such a free-spirited beauty could become skinnier than a two-month-old lamb in such a brief space of time. In the dead of night, the white tent that they'd all once been so interested in now often emitted the sound of stifled sobbing.

Gongzha was also withdrawn, but like the mountains on the grassland, he stood tall and immutable. Seeing Cuomu get thinner and weaker, seeing her deep silence and deeper pain, made his heart so sore it grew numb. Every day, he followed Cuomu with his eyes. Watching her wander lonely on the grassland, his heart was like dried grass bending in a fierce wind; it twisted with such pain he could barely stand it.

Deep down, he blamed himself. If he'd controlled himself that day, if he hadn't raised his hand against her mother, everything would be different. Her uncle would still be alive, his brother would not be cowering in jail, and the two of them would still be slipping away to a corner of the grassland and whispering their warm, bewitching words.

His mother's mental state had become much more stable, at least, thanks to the herbs. Most of the time she sat quietly in the tent, neither speaking nor moving. But Gongzha could not suppress his longing for Cuomu. When he could bear it no longer, he would go out into the vast wilderness and yell hysterically, or he would take his old gun and go hunting, killing wolves, or foxes or nothing at all, simply riding on and on until he was exhausted.

10

Blood flowed, tears flowed, life went on.

Gongzha took advantage of the moonlight and climbed the mountain behind Cuoe Temple. The path was overgrown with prickly shrubs, but he made his way steadily to the top, carrying a length of wire with him. He looked down at the grassland. It was deep in sleep; only that small white tent still kept its lamps lit. She always went to sleep very late, and sometimes not at all: some nights, her lamps burnt on till morning. Whenever Gongzha saw that, it was as if the butter lamps were scorching his heart.

Was she planning to go without sleep again tonight? Did she not know how much he worried about her, how he ached for her?

Gongzha forced himself to look away. Taking a deep breath, he walked round to a dip on the other side of the mountain. The boulder still stood tall. He looked at the crevice: he had often hidden there as a child, sheltering from the wind and rain, but he was too large now and could no longer squeeze inside it. He bent the length of wire into a hook, reached into the crevice, and began to carefully prod around.

When he felt the hook catch on something, his heart leapt. The Buddha had blessed and protected the items, and they were still there. He suppressed his excitement, steadied his hand, and edged it carefully upwards, centimetre by centimetre. When he finally drew the object out, he saw clearly by the light of the moon that it was the book. He snatched it up and flipped through the pages; apart from some sand on the outside, it was still in good condition. He put it carefully in his *chuba*, then took up his wire and began searching again. He could feel something but could not draw it out. He removed the wire hook, adjusted it and reached in again. That made it much easier and he quickly hooked out the Buddha. He used his wool sleeve to dust off the sand. In the moonlight, the black Buddha gleamed as brightly as it always had.

Gongzha sat down with his back against the boulder and examined it. The Buddha was heavy, but he couldn't tell what it was made of. He remembered how, long ago, Luobudunzhu had been so desperate to find it that he'd subjected Living Buddha Zhaduo to struggle sessions and had even broken his leg. Was it very valuable – so valuable it merited destroying a temple?

Gongzha examined the Buddha from every angle and turned it upside down. He felt something like a raised line on its back and when he held it up to the light he saw that what should have been a smooth surface actually had the image of a small ¤ engraved in it. What did it mean? Gongzha looked at it curiously. Was it a name for the Buddha? He'd never come across it before. But then he raised his head and an image flashed through his mind: an old man in tattered monk's robes sat by the side of the lake, staring absently at Chanaluo Snow Mountain across the water. The old man drew a ¤ in the sand with his finger. But when he saw that someone was coming, he wiped the sand smooth and began laughing wildly.

Why was this image on the Buddha? What did it mean? Gongzha squinted thoughtfully at it for some time, but he still didn't have a clue. He decided not to think about it. He put the Buddha in his fur-lined robe, brushed the sand off himself and returned to the mountaintop. When he looked down and saw the dark temple below, he suddenly got the idea to go and explore it.

He clambered down, slipping on scree and scratching his way through shrubs. The wooden door in the courtyard wall was still there. When he pushed it gently, it creaked and two terrified wildcats streaked off into the distance.

He went into the courtyard. The large complex was now completely empty. The Red Guards had made their headquarters there, then it had served as a storage place for the commune's meat, and after that it had been abandoned, left to the mice, rabbits and wildcats.

Gongzha turned on his torch and made his way through the empty rooms. A few of the murals were still intact, their colours just as vivid as before. When he got to the main hall at the front, he saw that the once highly revered bodhisattvas had disappeared. They must have been casualties of the Cultural Revolution, either hurled into the lake by a frenzied crowd or smashed up and recycled for some other purpose. Only their platform remained; several mice scurried across it. Four great pillars still stood in sturdy support, though of course their imposing gold and silver casings were long gone. The temple's serene, esoteric atmosphere had been obliterated in that extraordinary, turbulent period. A thick layer of dust now covered a floor once so clean you could see your reflection in it, and the sweet smell of incense had been succeeded by a sharp, noxious odour. Lacking spiritual purpose or any believers, the temple had reverted to being the house it had been before, and a decrepit house at that; it had nothing like the warm, safe feel of a black tent.

Gongzha took out the Medicine Buddha and set it on the platform. He stepped back two paces to look at it. The Buddha as tall as a child's arm gleamed brightly in the faint moonlight. He contemplated it for a while, then picked it up and put it back in his *chuba*, turned away and went out.

The path ran down the side of the mountain to the plain, through grass so withered it wasn't even heel height. When he got to the encampment, his feet automatically took him in the direction of that small white tent. He stopped about ten metres away, from where the huge guard dog fixed him with a suspicious eye and a threatening growl.

The stars were already vanishing from the sky and the moon had crossed the mountain peak – why had Cuomu still not blown out her lamp? Was she going without sleep again? Even the healthiest body couldn't endure so many sleepless nights.

Gongzha was full of longing: he wanted to kick the huge dog aside; he wanted to throw open the tent flap and go in; he wanted to pull her into his embrace and fall sleep beside her. But in the end he merely sighed, circled the tent and walked away to the west.

Just as he was heading off into the lonely distance, the small tent behind him slowly opened a crack. Cuomu's pallid face and tear-swollen eyes stared out and followed him bitterly as he went.

In his heart, Gongzha continuously apologised to Cuomu. I'm so sorry, Cuomu... We can't go on like this... I miss you so much, and I want to marry you... That's all I want – to marry you.

His solitary figure roamed the plain for a long time.

The regiment established a small school and brought in a teacher, temporarily solving the problem of how the border guards' children would be educated. Once Zhuo Mai had settled his son Yihang into the school, he took some time to return to the grassland. He was planning to leave the army and return home the following year and he wanted to find the notes on the Four Medical Tantras and fulfil the old man's wishes.

He sought out Gongzha, but Gongzha wasn't interested. Without even waiting for Zhuo Mai to explain why he'd come, Gongzha just picked up his gun and led his horse away. Impatient to get on with things, Zhuo Mai went to find Shida and ask him to go with him to find Kaguo.

'Find Kaguo? You want to find Kaguo? You want to rush off up Chanaluo Snow Mountain?' As they sat together on the plain, Zhuo Mai cradling his guitar, Shida's eyes widened so much he looked like a yak. It was as if Zhuo Mai had just told him a joke.

'I do. Why's that so strange?' Zhuo Mai was tuning his guitar and he turned his head to look at Shida while he listened to the twang of the strings. He always brought his guitar when he came to the grassland. His guitar and his medical bag were the two things he was never without.

'This is avalanche season – did you not know that? There was one just a few days ago, and it buried two hunters from the other side of the lake.'

'If we're careful, we'll be fine. Besides, if there's just been an avalanche, the next few days should be safe.'

'Brother Zhuo, it would be better if you didn't go. Honestly. Besides, you don't have to go to Chanaluo to pick herbs, other places have them too. You don't want to mess around with that Kaguo, she's hurt many hunters.'

'Thank you, I'll go by myself.' Zhuo Mai picked up the guitar and plucked a few chords. He sang while gazing at the distant snow mountain, and his bittersweet song spiralled above it.

'Today I must go to a faraway land
When we parted you said, "Please don't forget me."
Our promise hangs high in the sky
Those white clouds, those stars, that moon
Bear witness to our promise that in the next life we will
    meet again
And never forget each other.

'Beautiful shepherdess, I love you
No matter how the world changes, you are forever in my
    heart.
Beautiful shepherdess, your laughter echoes under the blue
    sky
And deep in my heart.

'Oh, give me a tent
I want to take your hand and live together free of pain.

Oh, give me some land
I want to dance with you there, slowly and forever.

'Shepherdess, sweet shepherdess
When will you return and make our love run smooth?
My greatest hope is not to be separated
Has our love in this life already scattered?
Could it be that loving you brings only despair?
Every day without you is a tragedy.'

As the silk strings sounded, Zhuo Mai was submerged in pain. Beloved shepherdess, are you well? We've been apart so many years, do you still smile like you used to? Do you remember the young Han doctor who picked mushrooms with you and sang with you?

Shida was also staring into the distance. Yangji's hate-filled eyes flashed before him. Yangji had left with venom in her heart. She had left so quickly, so definitively, he'd had no chance for regret.

Across the plain, Cuomu stood in front of her tent wrapped in a wool-lined robe, her two hands gripping the pole of her butter churn, tears streaming down her face. Zhuo Mai's mournful song made her think of Gongzha. Their love had disappeared with her Uncle Niduo's spirit. She would never smile or be happy again.

Gongzha also listened to the mournful song. Nothing could suppress the regret and pain in his heart. He whipped his horse and thundered across the grassland.

'Shepherdess, sweet shepherdess
When will you return and make our love run smooth?
My greatest hope is not to be separated
Has our love in this life already scattered
Could it be that loving you brings only despair?
Every day without you is a tragedy.'

As the sound of the strings faded, the sad beauty of the words intensified.

On the empty plain, the herders stared up at the white clouds and dreamt. The yaks, sheep and wild asses came to a standstill. The grassland was suffused with unspeakable grief.

Zhuo Mai prepared to take on Chanaluo himself. During his years in Tibet, he'd crossed countless snow mountains and forded countless streams; he did not believe that Chanaluo would defeat him that easily.

He rolled up his uniform tightly and wrapped it in a blanket. He put on a borrowed sheepskin *chuba*, took two dried legs of lamb and set off with his horse in tow.

Cuomu came up to him, leading her horse and accompanied by the dog that watched her tent. 'I'm coming with you.'

'What?' Zhuo Mai thought he'd heard incorrectly.

'I said, I'm coming with you.' Cuomu looked at him and spoke firmly and clearly.

'Do you know where I'm going?'

'Chanaluo...' she said quietly.

'And you still want to come?'

'If you can go, why can't I? Besides, I'm a local, born and bred – I know snow mountains better than you.'

'In which case you should be well aware of what the hunters say – that Mount Chanaluo is where the bears and wolves live. It'll be hard enough for me as it is, but if I've got to look after you – a girl – as well, it'll be twice as dangerous.'

Cuomu looked him up and down, taking in his slight frame, and pursed her lips. 'You think it's *you* that'll be looking after *me*? I don't think so!' She mounted her horse and nudged Zhou Mai with her whip. 'I know what you're thinking: you're afraid I'll be mauled by a bear or eaten by a wolf – or that you will... Don't worry – if you get mauled or eaten, I'll be fine. Let's go! Two people are always stronger than one.'

And with that, she whipped her horse and tore off, the dog bounding behind.

Zhuo Mai shook his head in exasperation and sighed, then mounted his own horse and chased after her.

When the two of them reached the foot of Mount Chanaluo, they unbuckled their saddles and threw them aside, leaving the horses free to graze on the plain. Cuomu instructed the dog to look after the horses, then she and Zhuo Mai took the bags they'd packed with meat and began to climb.

'Be careful!' Cuomu frequently looked back to see Zhuo Mai crawling up the mountainside on all fours – it was funny. The grasslanders often crossed snow mountains and they would never resort to doing so on all fours, as clumsily as a bear. 'Don't step on the ice, it's slippery.' Just as she said that, Zhuo Mai landed flat on his face.

As she'd explained, Cuomu was a local and had lived in the wilderness for many years, she was much more experienced than Zhuo Mai. He watched admiringly as she moved easily and energetically through the snow. It was a mistake to assume that just because grassland girls were cheerful, all they could do was pour tea, do the milking and look after their men. When trouble came, they never hid behind their men but stood shoulder-to-shoulder with them, keeping a cool head.

His thoughts flew back to eastern Tibet. He was just eighteen and his army unit was stationed in the mountains there. As an army doctor, he often went down the mountain to tend to people in the surrounding area. That was how he met her, a young woman as beautiful as the moon who loved to laugh loudly at anything and nothing. She loved to sing and always sang for him. They went for walks together, and she played with her slingshot. She giggled incessantly. Zhuo Mai liked to see her laugh; he had only to see her laugh and anything that was troubling him would fly away. He often stayed at her house and when he went on his rounds in the town, she would carry his medical bag for him. They would return home in the evenings by the light of the moon.

He clearly remembered her expression the first time he held her hand. She who feared nothing that earth or heaven could throw at her was suddenly overcome with shyness: two rosy clouds rushed to her cheeks, her gaze dropped to the ground and her thick eyelashes fluttered.

How could those days have changed so quickly? How could she have become another man's bride in a single night?

The night she was married, he was walking along a path high up the mountain and he heard her heartrending cries from all the way down at the foot of the slopes. He longed to steal her away, to carry her off to the interior of the country, to flee the place that could never make her happy and protect her for the rest of his days. If he hadn't been wearing a green soldier's uniform, if the army hadn't had rules of iron, he might have actually done it.

From that day since, her tears had lain on his heart and never dried.

Cuomu and Zhou Mai crossed a ridge and a valley deep with snow appeared before them. There was not a speck of dirt on the pristine snow; it was if the ground had been covered with a layer of soft white sugar. It was so quiet in this snow-white world that apart from their breathing, they could hear no other form of life.

Such valleys were a common sight in Tibet – they nestled within every one of those mountains ranges. And yet they were also Tibet's least common sight, because they lay beyond the Changtang Plateau. These mountains were the support beams of the roof the world. But the support beams were not that stable. No one knew when the beams would tremble, shaking the piled-up snow and causing it to tumble down with a roar and redraw the landscape of the place.

'Is that Chanaluo?' Zhuo Mai said with awe, looking at the peak.

'Yes, Chanaluo. I see it every day, but this is the first time I've got this close. It's truly beautiful, isn't it?'

'Like a celestial maiden.'

'She was a celestial maiden once. Uncle said that in her previous life Chanaluo was the faithful handmaiden to King Gesar's daughter and looked after some of the princess's treasure. When she reincarnated, she lost her way and became a herder.'

'She was in charge of the treasure? No wonder the mountain's so beautiful. It's like an enormous diamond, flashing light in all directions.' Zhuo Mai withdrew his gaze and glanced at Cuomu, his eyes half closed as if he was thinking of something else.

The lined robe Cuomu was wearing was black, and curly white lambswool showed around the edge of the collar. The *chuba* was fastened with an intricately wrought silver belt. Dozens of long plaits held by silver bindings hung to her waist and swung when she walked. In the middle of her shiny forehead, above her sad eyes, lay a red carnelian shaped like a droplet of water. It had been a present from her uncle the living Buddha to her mother on her marriage; when Cuomu turned thirteen, her mother gave it to her to celebrate her becoming an adult. In that silvery-white world and with her air of sadness, it was if Cuomu herself was the mountain's celestial maiden.

'Zhuo, what's that?' Cuomu stepped forward and pointed at the snow in front of them.

'What?' Zhuo Mai came over and looked in the direction she was pointing. A wiggly line of small holes stretched across the snow and disappeared into the distance.

Cuomu went closer and examined them. 'Bear tracks,' she said, raising her head.

'There are bears here?' Zhuo Mai was a little surprised and instinctively reached for his hunting gun. 'We've run into bears?'

'Not yet. These tracks must be several days old. Look, some of them have begun to blur. Zhuo, you were the one who wanted to come! Are you afraid now?' Cuomu stood up, brushed off the snow on her hands and laughed as she looked at him.

Zhuo Mai also laughed. 'Afraid? I'm not afraid of bears. I'm more afraid of what Gongzha would do to me if something happened to you! He'd kill me!' He deliberately straightened his back. After all, he was a border defence soldier protecting his country – how could he show fear in front of a woman?

'Zhuo, how's your aim?'

'I'm a PLA soldier, Cuomu!' Zhuo Mai retorted.

'A PLA soldier maybe, but a doctor first, no? You're good with a knife, but what about with a gun – not quite so good?'

'I wouldn't say that. Back when the wolves came, I shot a good number. Don't worry, bears are bigger than wolves – I can definitely hit one.' Even as he said it, Zhuo Mai was not at all confident that he could kill a bear.

'Could you definitely kill a big one?' Cuomu looked at him and started to regret having been so hasty. Was rushing into this bears' den with a scalpel-wielding doctor anything other than a death mission? 'You know, Zhuo, I think we should just go back.'

'No, no, no. Didn't you say these tracks are from several days ago? We might not run into them. Let's go a bit further, and then if it's really too much, we'll go back – alright?' Zhuo Mai waggled his head and looked at Cuomu reassuringly, keen for her to stay positive.

'Weren't you the one who didn't want me to come? Now you know that I have my strong points.' Cuomu laughed, pleased with herself. 'Let's go, Vet Zhuo.'

'It's Dr Zhuo.' Laughing, he shouldered his gun and on they went.

They followed the bear tracks through the snow. Eagles hovered, sometimes swooping down from the peak, sometimes flying slowly by, as if gliding. After they'd walked for a short time, they found there were two more lines of tracks on the ground and they were very muddled.

'How can there be three bears?' Zhuo Mai said, looking at the messy tracks.

'It looks like two bears came down from up there. You can see those tracks are a little smaller. Maybe they're this one's cubs. We should go a different way – a bear with cubs is ferocious, we need to avoid running into it.'

'Alright.' The two of them left the bear prints and took a different route up the mountain.

In that silver-white world, it was impossible to know what lay under all that snow, where to step or where to avoid. They had to trust their instincts. Cuomu led the way. She sometimes turned to laugh, encouraging Zhuo Mai or pulling him along. The two rarely spoke, and when they did, they talked very quietly. They understood in their hearts that in that pure, unsullied world, the slightest sound could cause a disastrous avalanche.

Before night fell, they dug out a snow hole beneath a large boulder, using layers of snow to build walls on three sides. They ate a little dried meat and snow and wrapped their sheepskin *chubas* tightly around themselves. Leaning against the boulder, they did not find it cold.

'Will we be able to get to the peak tomorrow?' Zhuo Mai asked quietly.

'Yes!' Cuomu said.

'Will we be able to find the medical book tomorrow?'

'Yes!'

'Will we really?' Zhuo Mai stuck his head out of his sheepskin *chuba* and looked at Cuomu doubtfully.

'I don't know. Is that book really so important to you, Zhuo?'

'Of course. I'm interested in anything that will help my profession. Your uncle spent his whole life studying the Four Medical Tantras, and from what he said, he kept detailed records of every treatment he gave as well as the patients' responses. With those notes, it will be as if I've gained your uncle's decades of experience. Do you see?'

Cuomu nodded. 'I understand. Before I was born, Uncle was the best doctor around. It's a pity he was made into a cow-ghost snake-spirit.'

'No matter what other people thought of him, he will always be the best teacher I ever had,' Zhuo Mai said earnestly, looking out at the still-light day.

'I know why Uncle liked you so much, Zhuo. You and he are so much alike – you're both honourable, and whatever you do, you do it well.'

'And the same also goes for Gongzha. Your uncle must have held him in great esteem, otherwise he wouldn't have left him with such an important task.'

'Important task – what do you mean?'

'The rebuilding of Cuoe Temple. Your uncle hoped that one day Gongzha will rebuild the temple!'

'Rebuild Cuoe Temple? Zhuo, you are joking?' Cuomu tilted her head and shot him an incredulous look.

'The grassland won't always be like this, Cuomu. It's like the waters of Cuoe Lake: when it rains, the water's choppy, and when it's fine, the water's clear. When I came out here this time, I heard the regimental commander say that this revolution won't last long – the central government has already started rethinking it. Perhaps not long from now, people's lives will go back to being peaceful.'

'Go back to being peaceful? Do you mean herding for a lord again?'

'No, it won't ever be like that again. It'll never go back to how it was before the Liberation, when the government called this region the Black Land, made out that there were ghosts all over the place and wouldn't let the herders come here to pasture. When there was no electricity and local herders had nothing to eat or drink and wore clothes that were ragged like a beggar's. Isn't life better now? It's just that the Revolution stirred people up into going around and making trouble. I've heard – and it is only a rumour at the moment – that the government might divide up the livestock for people to herd themselves, and maybe build you roads and electricity stations.'

'Divide it up for us to herd ourselves? And build roads and

electricity stations?' Cuomu looked at him with disbelief. 'If that happens, won't our lives be the same as the people in town?'

'It's just what I've heard – I don't know if it's true or not,' Zhuo Mai said, laughing. He drew his head back inside his sheepskin *chuba*.

Cuomu glanced outside, then drew her head into her *chuba* too. The two did not speak again.

In the middle of the night, a bear roared and frightened Cuomu and Zhou Mai awake at the same moment. Zhuo Mai felt for his gun and crawled softly to the front of their snow hole. Looking down into the snowy valley below, under the clear bright light of the moon, he saw seven bears. They were stretching their necks and turning around on the spot. He had no idea what they were doing.

Cuomu squeezed in beside him and craned her neck to look outside.

'What are they doing?' Zhuo Mai asked lightly.

Cuomu stared down at them. 'Look at that shape in the snow – it's a circle with lines radiating from each corner, isn't it?' Her eyes sparkled with excitement and her voice shook a little.

Zhuo Mai glanced at her, wondering why she was so excited. It was a troop of bears; if the bears were to discover them, would they have any hope of surviving? 'Er, yes, it is. Strange, what are bears doing here in the middle of the night?'

'Don't talk, look carefully!' Cuomu said and continued to stare, unblinking, at the bears.

Sometimes, two bears lumbered forward together; at other times, they walked separately, taking different sides. But they always kept to the lines of the image in the snow; they never missed a step. It was if their task was to tamp the lines of the image deeper and tighter. Eventually, a large bear gave a low roar. The six other bears retreated to its side and stood in a line, lifting their necks and howling towards the peak in a loud, clear chorus.

Cuomu signalled Zhuo Mai to look at the leading bear on the right.

Zhuo Mai saw that its forehead had a white circular marking with lines off it in four directions. 'Is it Kaguo?'

'It seems so.' Cuomu nodded, then shook her head. 'But I wouldn't want to say for sure.'

The bears finished howling before the dawn sun broke through the clouds. They formed a line and raced off to the valley on the right, disappearing into the vast mountain in a flash.

The sun slowly sent out its first rays, and the valley fell silent.

Zhuo Mai and Cuomu scrambled out of their snow hole and stood on the slope. Looking down from above, they had a clear view of the wide valley. The snow around the lines was soft and undisturbed; apart from the tracks the bears had made when they'd arrived and left, there was only the strange motif the animals had trodden out. The image of the ¤ was like an enormous seal stamped onto the pure white snow.

'It's the same pattern as the marking on that bear's forehead. Was it really Kaguo?'

'I don't know. I've never seen Kaguo up close. I've heard Gongzha say she has a white circle on her forehead, but I've never seen her clearly.'

'They seemed to be worshipping something. Strange!'

At that moment, the sun burst through the clouds and a wash of golden light fell over the valley. The vast snowy land turned orange and the unusual ¤ emitted an eerie glow.

Behind the encampment there was a low hill covered in thorny scrub. Dressed in an old sheepskin *chuba* and a leather hat, Gongzha sat cross-legged on its brow, his mind lost in the rolling clouds on the horizon, his dog sitting by his side.

'Gongzha! Gongzha!' Shida came scrambling into view. 'Cuomu... Cuomu and Brother Zhuo went to Chanaluo Snow

Mountain yesterday and they haven't come back. Danzeng and the others are worried sick and want to go and find her.'

'Why did they go to Chanaluo?' Gongzha stared at its distant peak, only partially visible, and his tanned face darkened.

'Brother Zhuo wanted to go and pick herbs. He said that if he could find Kaguo, he'd be able to locate the herbs he needed – whatever that means. He asked me to go with him, but I didn't dare. How could I know Cuomu would go with him?' Shida added nervously as he glanced at Gongzha.

'He's crazy. Going to Chanaluo at this time of year, with so many avalanches – he's playing with his life.' Gongzha got to his feet and began striding irritably back down the hill. Shida hurried along behind him.

Gongzha returned to his tent and told his brother Gongzan that he needed to go somewhere and might be away for two or three days. He instructed Gongzan to take care of their mother and to continue steeping herbs for her to drink. Then, taking his old gun, he led his horse out of the encampment. He stopped at Danzeng's tent on the way and called him outside.

'Uncle, I'm going to find her.'

Danzeng looked at him and nodded slightly. 'Will you be alright?'

'Mmm,' Gongzha affirmed, and mounted his horse.

'Wait.' Danzeng turned, went into his tent and came back out with his own leather *chuba*, which he laid on the back of Gongzha's horse's. 'It's cold on the mountain. You and Cuomu come back soon.'

'Alright.' Gongzha looked at Danzeng's worried face; he wanted to say something comforting but stopped himself.

As Danzeng watched Gongzha ride off, his eyes were full of trust. Was it possible to hold a grudge in the face of such tremendous kindness?

Gongzha couldn't return his gaze; he feared his tears would fall. He whipped his horse and rode off into the distance in a whirl of dust.

Danzeng stood on the plain for a long time, staring after him.

When the sun came out, earth and sky slowly warmed.

Chanaluo's early mornings were lively. The little animals began to emerge from their holes, and on the ground were all kinds of prints: bear, fox, rabbit and eagle. Those that could fly and those that could not began to dart out of their safe hide-aways, starting the new day in their own way.

Zhuo Mai and Cuomu ate a little dried meat and washed their faces with snow. Cuomu melted some butter in her palm and gave half to Zhuo Mai, then they rubbed it on their cheeks. The glare of the sun's rays as it reflected off the snow was very strong and it was easy for skin to burn. Butter was an excellent protection against that and the herders always took some with them when they went out.

'Let's go!' Cuomu took off her leather *chuba*, revealing the red silk dress she was wearing underneath. She tied the two sleeves around her waist and took the lead up the mountain.

The slope got steeper and the deep snow meant they couldn't always go straight up but sometimes had to make wide detours. They only had one goal, though: to climb to the ledge just below the summit. They wanted to see if there really was a chain left there by unknown people from an unknown time. As for the Four Medical Tantras, if they searched that vast snowy wilderness randomly and without purpose, they would never find them. True, Zhaduo had said they were in a cave, but he hadn't specified whether the cave was large or small, or where on the mountain the cave was.

They were finally climbing Chanaluo's highest peak. On the other side was the vast deep blue of Cuoe Lake. Rippling under the blue sky and white clouds, the sacred lake was so beautiful, it didn't seem real. Tired, the two sat on the snow.

'It's gorgeous, isn't it? Our grassland, our Cuoe Lake!' Cuomu said, almost to herself, as she stared at it.

'Beautiful!' Zhuo Mai said, gazing at Cuomu sitting there in the snow. She'd taken off her hair net so that her long thin plaits fell like a fishing net around her shoulders. Her cheeks were lightly dusted with red from the high altitude, and her eyes were round and bright, glittering with colour like the stars in the grassland's night sky.

'Zhuo...' Cuomu turned her head with a gentle laugh. He often stared at her like that. No wonder Shida joked that he liked her. If she hadn't known that Zhuo had someone else in his heart, a look like that could have been misinterpreted. 'Should I... go and find him?'

'Yes, I think you should. I've seen Gongzha staring at your tent many times – sometimes he stands there for a whole night.'

Cuomu took a deep breath and laughed. 'Alright. If we make it down the mountain safely, I'll go and find him.'

'Why wouldn't we make it safely down the mountain?' Zhuo Mai asked in surprise. 'We'll climb up to that ledge and have a look around, and if we can't find the cave, we'll just forget about it. I'll come another time.'

'Zhuo, it's obvious you have no idea how moody a snow mountain can be,' Cuomu said, standing up and shaking the snow off her robe. 'This is avalanche season, and if we do get caught in one, we won't have a hope – it'll be enough to bury ten people, not just the two of us. And even though this mountain looks silvery-white and empty, do you know how many wolves, how many bears are behind that ice watching us? Did you not see all those bears this morning?'

'Then why did you come with me?'

'My life without Gongzha is no life – I may as well be dead. Besides, you're my best friend and our grassland's most honoured guest. How could I watch you risk so much and not care?' A bitter smile twitched at the corners of her mouth. She rarely smiled properly these days, this once open and high-spirited grassland girl.

The weather on the mountain followed no discernible pattern. It could be bright and sunny and as warm as spring and then in the blink of an eye crow-black clouds could mass into a pile, causing snowflakes to fall. Cuomu put on her leather *chuba* and buckled her belt. 'Let's go. We've come this far, we should go up to the top and have a look.'

The snow was knee-deep. They trod cautiously, one slow, careful step at a time, never knowing how deep they were going to sink. Eventually they reached the ledge.

The ledge was as large as a football field and neatly angled; it looked as if someone had built it that way. The snow up there was deep but no longer up to their knees.

'Where's the chain?' Zhuo Mai pushed at the snow with his feet and used the fork of his gun to try and clear it away, throwing it up in clouds as he searched.

'There's no hurry. Let's look slowly,' Cuomu said, using her boots to kick up the snow. 'I've heard the chain is on a large boulder – they say it's as if it's actually coming out of the boulder.'

'It looks like there's a boulder over there.' Zhuo Mai pointed at the side facing the lake and dragged the gun over; the fork of the gun traced two wriggly lines through the snow.

Cuomu walked over with him.

There really was a large black boulder, standing about a metre proud of the ledge. Zhuo Mai climbed up, and suddenly his eyes widened. 'Come here, Cuomu! Quick!'

Cuomu clambered up.

A jet-black chain lay motionless in the snow.

Zhuo Mai brushed most of the snow off the boulder and stood beside the chain; when he saw that four lines of stones radiated from the round boulder in four directions, he was dumbstruck.

'Look at this boulder, Cuomu, and think about that symbol the bears stamped out this morning. This is the same, isn't it?'

'You're right, it's very similar. No, it's exactly the same! How odd.'

'This chain really does look like it grew out of the boulder.' Zhuo Mai squatted on the ground and used his knife to pick at it. 'Strange. What's it made of? It's not iron and it's not copper, but it's still so heavy.'

'It's not iron?' Cuomu crouched down and pulled at the chain with both hands, but it didn't budge.

'It's not iron. Iron wouldn't be this heavy. Also, it hasn't rusted at all, and it's quite shiny, and the snow hasn't settled on it. It's all very odd.'

'My uncle said that this is what King Gesar used to tether the Wolf Spirit. He was afraid the wolves would bring disaster to the grassland, so he brought the wolves' ancestor here to control them.'

'That's just a myth, Cuomu.' Zhuo Mai looked at the black chain. It seemed to be naturally connected to the boulder. The links were so tightly forged that even a blade of grass wouldn't fit between them. He racked his brains but couldn't work out what such an obviously manmade thing was doing on the summit of this snow mountain. When was it installed and who put it there? What purpose could a chain in a boulder on the top of a snow mountain possibly serve?

'People say that it's been here ever since our clan came to Cuoe Grassland. But no one knows how it got here,' Cuomu said and stood up. From the look of the sky, the clouds weren't going to disperse and the snow was actually getting heavier. 'Don't worry about it. Let's go back down sooner rather than later; if the snow gets any thicker, we might not be able to get back.'

'Alright,' Zhuo Mai said. 'Let's go down this way, it's not as steep.'

The two slid down from the side of the boulder. They hadn't gone more than five steps when they heard a series of cracking noises coming from the peak.

'Avalanche! Stand still and hold on to me,' Zhuo Mai said, instinctively grabbing Cuomu. He'd been through an avalanche in Ngari and he knew to spread his arms and feet wide and to bend his back a bit to create as much space as possible. As long as there was air to breathe, the two of them should be able to climb out of the snow.

There was a roar from the peak and the snow thundered down like a mountain crashing into the sea.

The whole earth-shattering process was over in less than two minutes.

Zhuo Mai wriggled his right shoulder and packed the snow around it, creating a hole to work in. Then he scooped and packed the snow along his arm, and dug through to Cuomu.

'Don't worry, we can definitely get out,' he said, and pulled out his bag of dried yak meat. He felt for his meat knife, cut off two pieces and put one in Cuomu's hand. 'Eat something. We'll dig our way back up along the boulder.'

They didn't say anything else, and their snowy chamber echoed with the sound of them nibbling and breathing. Eating was a good tranquilliser – it restored their strength and quieted their hearts. When they'd finished, their bodies felt stronger and their minds clearer.

Zhuo Mai began using his knife to dig towards where he thought the boulder had been. The avalanche snow was soft, which made digging through it fairly easy work. If he could locate the boulder, there was hope for them, because the boulder was only a metre high.

'I've got a lighter, Zhuo. What if—'

'No, no, no, Cuomu. The flame will use up the oxygen and if there's no oxygen, we'll die faster. We'll just dig like this, going in one direction.' But Cuomu's mention of the lighter reminded him that he'd brought the little torch he used for surgical procedures. He hurriedly fished it out and turned it on.

He clenched the torch between his teeth and scooped at the snow, throwing it behind him. The two of them advanced like this bit by bit. They'd been digging for a while when suddenly Cuomu cried out in surprise, 'Zhuo, there doesn't seem to be any snow on my side. I think it's empty!'

'Empty?' Zhuo Mai stuck his hand out along Cuomu's arm. There really was nothing in front of them. He quickly took the torch from between his teeth and looked through the hole. To his surprise, he saw there were walls of broken rock to either side and empty darkness ahead.

They swiftly pushed away the snow around them. Cuomu carried the meat bag and Zhuo Mai did not forget his gun. They stared stupidly at one another, neither sure what to do. After a little while, Zhuo Mai turned the torch up and shone it ahead of them, but there was nothing for the light to bounce off, only darkness. He looked at Cuomu. 'What should we do?'

Cuomu shook her head. 'I don't know. I've never heard of a cave up here.'

Gongzha had already followed the pair's footprints as far as the snow hole they'd slept in the night before. When he saw the tiny space, Gongzha's heart tightened. As he faced the snow mountain, his heart beat fast and loud. He knew he could not lose Cuomu or allow anyone else to share her affections.

He couldn't bear to look at it any longer, so he turned away. As his gaze swept the valley, his eyes suddenly alighted on that strange and exaggerated ¤ symbol. It was as if he'd been struck with something heavy, and he began to feel very anxious.

The smooth ¤ on the black Buddha's back, the ¤ that Zhaduo had unconsciously drawn on the sand and the ¤ he'd seen on Kaguo's forehead during the wolf attack all rushed into his mind. Why would the same symbol also appear in this snowy valley, so far from any sort of human life? Gongzha couldn't suppress his surprise and excitement. He slithered quickly down the slope, rolling and scrambling as he went, and was covered in snow by the time he landed in front of the image. The ¤ was very regular; the four lines extending out were of exactly equal length and width, as if they'd been drawn using a ruler.

Gongzha walked around examining the image, sometimes stooping down to scrutinise its edges. They were ragged and revealed muddled footprints, as if some kind of animal had stamped it out with its feet. He raised his head and scanned both sides of the valley; eventually he found a line of tracks on the right side.

He didn't need to look carefully to know what animal had left them. Any grassland hunter who couldn't recognise a bear track was a fool.

He followed the tracks with nervous excitement. He even forgot why he'd come up the mountain – he just followed the tracks instinctively as any seasoned hunter would. It would have been impossible for Cuomu and Zhuo Mai not to have seen that the bears had drawn that strange symbol in the snow. The valley bore no trace of a struggle and that at least told him they were safe. He gave a sigh of relief and climbed carefully, still following the tracks.

At a cliff on the north side, the tracks suddenly disappeared. 'Strange!' Gongzha looked over the clifftop; it was high, and its face was covered in glimmering, unmarked snow. 'How could they just disappear?' he muttered as he sat on the ground. He looked at the crisscrossing bear tracks in front of him. Up until this point, the tracks had been neat and orderly; here they became disordered. It reminded him of standing in front of a tent and walking around in circles while waiting for someone to come to the door. A door...? Gongzha's curiosity mounted.

He scrambled up and searched carefully all around him. He found two clear prints going up the left side of the slope and disappearing by a thicket of red bushes. The ground around the prints looked as if something had rolled over it. Gongzha bent down to look more closely and picked up two silver-brown hairs. 'Strange, why would they roll on the snow? What are they trying to hide? Could there be cubs inside?' He knew that when cubs couldn't leave a den, the mother bear would find a way to mask the entrance for fear of another animal finding and hurting them; she'd take a circuitous route back for the same reason.

Gongzha went a few steps closer. Squatting in front of the red bushes, he pushed aside the thick branches and discovered that there was indeed a cave behind them. The mouth was just large enough to allow a grown bear to enter. These bears were really very clever: they hid the mouth of the cave under bushes and deliberately crossed their tracks so that when the wind and snow came it would be well hidden. He looked back at the tamped-down snow and laughed. Who said bears were stupid? Every time they left or returned to their den, they made the last two bears cover their tracks. While one bear stood at the bottom, another rolled down from the top. When the last bear returned to the cave, it cleared away the tracks of the bear before it. Once Gongzha had figured this out, he had even more respect for them.

He turned round, climbed to the mouth of the cave and sniffed. The faint foul odour that greeted him proved that bears had been there, but the fact that it was faint told him that the cave was very deep and that the musky smell was just a trace left by one of the bears on their way in or out. Gongzha was not there on a bear hunt and had no interest in the cubs; he was there to find Cuomu and her safety was much more important. Now that he knew where the mouth of the cave was, he could come back any time.

Just as he was turning to leave, he saw that above the entrance there was a tiny ☿, etched so faintly that you could only see it if you were looking closely or your eyes were used to the dark. As soon as he saw it, his stomach began to churn; he wrenched out his torch and crawled in without a second thought.

The cave was deep and tunnel-like and he had to wriggle his way in. After two or three metres, it began to slope downwards. There was no room to turn round, so he had no option but to carry on. He gripped the torch between his teeth and began to crawl on all fours. By the weak light of the torch, he saw that niches had been cut into the tunnel walls. He didn't think too much about it, just used them as handholds as he continued edging his way down it. When he finally reached the bottom, he found that the tunnel started to climb again, and there were more niches on either side. Gongzha was a brave man and he continued on without worrying about the consequences.

He finally reached the highest point and emerged into a small stone chamber. The floor was level and there were rocks on either side, like seats. On the walls were paintings of bears, in all kinds of poses. Some were playing, some were breastfeeding, some were catching small animals.

'Kaguo...' Gongzha was looking at the bear in the centre; there were two bear cubs by her side, one with a black circle on its forehead, the other with a white circle.

Could this be the cave of the Buddhist ascetics? Gongzha slowly shifted his feet as this idea began to take hold. His father used to say that there were ascetics living on Mount Chanaluo, but he'd never seen them. Gongzha searched the chamber with his torch. When he found that a passage had been opened on the right and that on the roof of the passage had been painted the Kalachakra mantra, he became even more convinced that this was the Buddhist ascetics' cave. Kalachakra was an advanced tantra. But if it was an ascetics' cave, why would the bears come in? Unless the ascetics had died and the bears had made it into their den? What did the painting of the bears on the wall mean? And that mysterious ☒ symbol? There had to be a thread connecting all the different places he'd seen it – in the valley, on the black Buddha's back, drawn by Living Buddha Zhaduo in the sand, on Kaguo's head, on the entrance to the cave – even if he had no idea what it was.

Without thinking, Gongzha followed the passage. He was a curious person and now that he'd discovered this place, he wasn't going to leave until he'd understood it. The passage was easily wide enough for one person but would have been a squeeze for two people walking side by side. The walls had clearly been worked by human hands and every few steps there was a small niche containing a butter lamp. Gongzha pulled out his lighter, flicked it a few times, and lit one of the lamps. The passage quickly became much brighter.

He continued along the rock-hewn corridor, lighting more lamps as he went and following the passageway as it twisted round a number of bends. Eventually he came to another chamber, about twice the size of the last one, very regularly shaped, and also with paintings on its walls. The mural on the right showed people transporting wood on the mountain; in the one in front of him they were building walls; and the one on the left showed a group of monks in red reading scriptures in front of a dazzling temple.

That temple... that temple, particularly the exterior of the large hall in the centre with the prayer flags, red edges and yellow walls, why did it seem so familiar? Gongzha walked a little closer and looked carefully at the painting. The image of Cuoe Temple's main hall flashed before his eyes; it was just that there were many more buildings surrounding the Cuoe Temple in the picture than there were in the temple as he knew it – they almost covered the mountain.

Gongzha frowned; if Cuoe Temple had looked like that when it was constructed, why were none of the other buildings there now? Had they been destroyed or never even built?

What connection did this cave have with Cuoe Temple? Why were there pictures of Cuoe Temple's construction on the walls? That black Buddha, said to be Cuoe Temple's greatest treasure, why did its back have a ⌖ like the one on Kaguo's head?

A string of questions popped into Gongzha's mind. Each one was enough to cloud his brain and mist his eyes, and he couldn't answer any of them. As he contemplated this, he suddenly heard screams – Cuomu's screams. They were coming from another direction. Without a moment's hesitation, Gongzha turned and rushed into the tunnel that opened out from across the other side of the chamber.

'Cuomu, are we inside Mount Chanaluo?' Zhuo Mai rubbed the stone wall, unwilling to believe his eyes.

They had no idea where they were. It was like a maze down there, with one tunnel leading to another tunnel and then another and so on. They didn't know which was the route out or where the end of the tunnel system was.

'We must be. Strange, I've never heard of Chanaluo having a cave like this,' Cuomu said, using a lighter to light the butter lamps on the wall.

Zhuo Mai glanced around – they'd been in the cave for hours.

Every tunnel ended in a small stone chamber, each of which had four painted walls and a lamp. In one chamber, they even found some *tsampa* in covered stone bowls, but it had stuck together in clumps and had clearly not been moved in a long time.

The people of the northern Tibetan wilderness weren't in the habit of eating *tsampa*; their staple food was meat. The presence of *tsampa* in the cave didn't chime with what Cuomu had first thought, that this was a cave for local Buddhist ascetics. In Tibet, there were lots of hermit ascetics. They sought out somewhere remote, far from other people – deep in the mountains, in the old forests, where other men would never come – and stayed there for many years, communicating only with the Buddha. The caves they sheltered in were always small and basic, and as soon as the ascetic left, the cave fell into decay. But this cave was clearly not the work of a single ascetic – it had multiple chambers connected by passageways. The whole network was very well preserved, especially the murals: the colours were vibrant, as if they'd been painted yesterday. The space was far too big for a solitary Buddhist ascetic, it was large enough to house scores of people, more than a hundred perhaps.

Zhuo Mai peeled off the sleeves of his leather *chuba* and tied them round his waist. Suddenly he cried out as if he'd just thought of something. 'The mountain cave, the mountain cave...'

'Zhuo, you've gone crazy!'

'No, Cuomu, I... I remembered, the mountain cave, the mountain cave.'

'I know this is a mountain cave – what's come over you, Zhuo!'

'I'm saying... I'm saying... Didn't your uncle say that the Four Medical Tantras and his medical notes were hidden in the mountain cave?' Zhuo Mai was clearly enormously excited since he stuttered as he spoke.

Cuomu clapped her hand over her mouth.

From the time they'd entered the cave, their curiosity had made them forget their reason for coming to the mountain in the first place.

'Let's look for it! Come on – quick!' Zhuo Mai put his gun on the ground and began searching the chamber.

The stone chambers only had so many places to put things and it didn't take long to complete their search. They scoured chamber after chamber but didn't think to leave any markers to help them find their way out. When they found themselves back at a chamber they'd searched before, they realised the seriousness of the situation. They were lost.

'It seems we've come back to where we started,' Zhuo Mai said dejectedly when he saw the murals.

'Let's check how much meat we have left and work out how long it will last us,' Cuomu said, setting the pack down on the stone seat. 'We still have a little less than half what we started with. We haven't touched yours, so there's enough for two or three days. The main thing is water. We've been in here for hours, but we haven't found water anywhere.'

'There has to be an exit, otherwise the air wouldn't be this fresh. We'll search slowly and methodically.' Zhuo Mai picked up a stone. 'We have to mark our route so that we don't pursue a passage we've already been down. In all mazes, as long as you keep going in one direction, you can always find the exit. Let's start by going left.'

Cuomu agreed and slung on her pack again.

They entered the left-hand passage, lighting the lamps as they went. After about ten minutes, they came to a very large chamber, like a great hall, inside which were some shadowy silhouettes that looked like seated monks. Cuomu, who was in front, leant against the wall and motioned for Zhuo Mai to join her.

'What should we do?' Zhuo Mai craned forward to look. The great hall had no lamps, and though the lamps along the passage gave off a faint light, they could only see part of the hall. It was silent and had a mysterious air about it.

'It looks like they're studying, but they're not making a sound. Let's go over and look,' Cuomu said, slowly moving forward.

When they got to the entrance to the hall, their shadows stretched across it, blocking out some of the light and making the place seem even dimmer. All of the people were sitting cross-legged facing the inside of the room. They looked very much like monks reading the scriptures, but their clothes were those of common herders.

Zhuo Mai coughed lightly, bowed and said, 'I'm sorry, brothers, we were caught in an avalanche and ended up in here by accident. Please forgive us.'

There was a deathly silence. Apart from their own breath, there was no other sound in the hall. Zhuo Mai and Cuomu looked at each other in surprise.

'I'm sorry, brothers...' Zhuo Mai raised his voice and repeated his words, bowing once more. His voice echoed around the hall.

But still no one replied. The silhouettes didn't move but maintained their dignified posture as if in meditation.

Cuomu strode forward to one of the silhouettes. She put out her hand and tugged at the man's clothes. 'Brother!'

Her finger poked through the clothing as the fabric immediately disintegrated and streamed to the ground in a flurry of dust. She stared in disbelief at the spot she'd touched, which was now a hole. The rest of the clothing seemed to have remained undamaged. She grabbed another exploratory handful, and once again the clothes turned to dust at her touch. She lightly tapped the figure's head and, finding it was a white skull, was so frightened she cried out.

Zhuo Mai hurried forward and scanned the hall with his torch. Everything – the beams, the floor, and even the mysterious people – was covered in dust. He craned his neck to look at the seated people. 'Oh my goodness! Cuomu... they're all dead!'

Cuomu trembled and her teeth chattered. 'All of them... all of them... are... are dead...?'

'Yes, all—'

Zhuo Mai hadn't even finished his sentence before Cuomu ran out screaming and rushed straight into someone's arms. She became even more frightened, kicking, wriggling and screaming, 'Demon! Demon!'

'Cuomu, Cuomu, it's me, Gongzha!' Gongzha held the sobbing Cuomu close and stroked her face.

'Gong... Gongzha?' Cuomu's face was deathly pale; she was still in shock.

'Yes, I'm Gongzha – I'm not a ghost.' Looking into her eyes and seeing her distracted expression, he couldn't help tenderly drawing her into his embrace and lightly patting her back. 'There, there... I'm here now. Don't be afraid. You have me. I'm here now. I came to find you.'

'Gong... Gongzha, Gongzha...' Recovering herself, Cuomu hugged him round the waist and wept.

'You must really have a death wish, coming here,' Gongzha said, rather melodramatically.

'If I don't have you, I really don't care whether I live or die,' Cuomu said softly and sadly, staring into his eyes.

Gongzha held her close. 'I'm sorry, I really am – it was all my fault.' He knew Cuomu was still his. He wanted to tell her that without her he too was a walking corpse. His heart was bursting and he flushed to the roots of his hair.

Zhuo Mai came into the passageway and was very excited to see Gongzha. 'How did you find this place, Gongzha?'

'When you didn't return yesterday, I came up the mountain to look for you. I tracked some bears in the valley and they led me here. I was lucky to run into you,' Gongzha said, holding Cuomu and looking at Zhuo Mai.

'Did you see that image in the valley? The ones the bears trampled?' Cuomu had finally calmed down and now raised her head embarrassedly from Gongzha's embrace.

'I did. Was it really done by bears?'

'They trampled it with their feet – we saw them do it,' Zhuo Mai said. 'The lead bear had a white circle on its forehead exactly like the image. We thought it was Kaguo, but we weren't certain.'

'I came into this cave because there's an image at the entrance that's exactly the same as the one on Kaguo's head,' Gongzha told them. 'And there's a painting of Cuoe Temple being built on the wall of one of the other chambers. There are also lots of paintings about bears, and in one of them the image on the bear's forehead is very clear.'

'Kaguo... what does she have to do with all of this?' Zhuo Mai furrowed his brow.

'We can't work that out right now.' Gongzha shook his head, instinctively clasping Cuomu's hand, and then asked, 'How did you get in here?' His gesture dissipated the tension between them, and both their hearts were filled with affection once more.

Zhuo Mai explained what had happened.

Gongzha looked at them with surprise. 'Did you see the chain?'

'We did! We came from that direction.'

'In which case you must have come in under the boulder.'

'Maybe. We were digging through the snow towards the boulder; originally we were hoping to dig as far as the boulder and then up.'

Gongzha thought for a while. Then he asked Cuomu, 'What did you see just now that scared you so badly?'

'That... that hall... has... has ghosts!' she said, stuttering and trembling at the memory of what she'd just seen.

'It has ghosts? Woman, are you sure you haven't lost your mind?' Gongzha looked at her with amusement.

'There really are ghosts! Those people appear to be just sitting there quietly, but if you touch them, they turn to dust and... and they're all skeletons!' Cuomu said, unconsciously inching closer to Gongzha. She'd been cool and collected on the hike up, because she was used to the grassland and the mountains. And anyway, even if she didn't have her man by her side, she could still hold up the sky. Women could occasionally allow themselves to be weak and to cry, but only in front of the man they loved. She had never seen or heard of anything like what she'd just encountered and of course she'd been afraid, but she hadn't wanted to let Zhuo Mai see that. Now all was well: her man was with her, and he could take care of everything; she didn't need to be strong anymore, she could show her vulnerable side.

'Let's go and look,' Gongzha said. Taking Cuomu's hand, he walked forward.

Once inside the hall, they shone their two torches all around it. Gongzha saw that there were large butter lamps along the walls, so he went over with a lighter and used oiled paper to light them. The hall quickly became much brighter, but the shadows seemed that much more mysterious.

11

The hall was vast. There were four stone pillars in the centre and six lines of cushions with six people seated in each line. Each person sat in the same position: legs crossed, both hands resting on their knees, their head bowed. Some had shrugged off just one sleeve of their sheepskin *chuba*, others had tied both sleeves around their waist. At the front, one man sat on a high stone chair facing the others, his palms pressed together. There were only a few skulls in the hall; most of the faces were still intact, their eyes closed in a placid expression.

'Could it be that all these people died at the same time?' Gongzha swept his eyes over the vast hall; the way the different shadows were thrown together was a bit eerie.

'Gongzha, it looks like there's writing here!' Zhuo Mai shouted from the other side.

Gongzha walked over. Cuomu held on to him, never more than a few centimetres behind.

On the wall were red Tibetan letters, written in a neat script. Gongzha shone the weak light of his torch on the wall and read quietly:

'In the Year of the Earth Ox, the Jialong people invaded Nacangdeba. The clan elder ordered that all the old people and all the women and children be sent to the place the Buddha had prepared. We, the soldiers of Nacangdeba, remained behind to defend the grassland. We swore to heaven that we would guard it with our lives. The Jialong are at the foot of the mountain and have blocked every route out. They want us to surrender and become serfs. The cave has no meat or *tsampa*. Cuoe Grassland is the heaven left to us by our ancestors and we lost it. The grassland is no more; it has been stolen from us. We have no way to fulfil our promise, so we have retreated from the grassland to honour the vow of our ancestors: "As long as the grassland is here, our soldiers will be here. If the grassland dies, we will die. We are the fearless soldiers of Nacangdeba and we will follow our ancestors' footsteps to Shambhala."'

'Nacangdeba? What does that mean?' Zhuo Mai asked.

'I've heard our area used to be called Nacangdeba and afterwards it was renamed Shenzha, because the terrain was like a pair of bellows,' Gongzha explained, looking at the script on the wall. 'After the Liberation, the government combined our area with Shigatse's Yayaodi, Bazha, Zhunbutaerma and Jialong into the county we have today.

'The Jialong were many and aggressive and they made their living by going on raids. There was a gang of them active in No Man's Land. They used to say they were just hunting there, but they were actually looting other areas. After each raid they'd rush back to No Man's Land and hide their plunder. Then, once the news had died down, they'd take it back to their homes bit by bit. Of course, that's just hearsay.'

'"As long as the grassland is here, our soldiers will be here. If the grassland dies, we will die."' Cuomu read the words quietly. 'The grassland hasn't died – we still have new grass every year, and the yaks and sheep still wander everywhere, but these soldiers can't see it.'

'According to this, the Nacangdeba were invaded by the Jialong and the women and children were sent away,' Zhou Mai said. 'So where did the people who now live around Cuoe Lake come from? Are you the descendants of the Jialong?'

'Cuomu's uncle once told me a story,' Gongzha replied. 'He said that the herders of Cuoe Grassland used to live in the

Shuanghu area of No Man's Land; at that time, Cuoe Grassland was occupied by a demon. Every day, the demon would eat children's hearts with fish meat and he turned the beautiful grassland into a wasteland of sand and stone. After a while, King Gesar could stand it no longer, so he came to Cuoe Grassland and fought the demon. They did battle for three days until finally King Gesar cut off the demon's head. The grass grew again and the sun returned, and it was then that the herders started to migrate over.'

'That's just a myth,' Zhuo Mai said. 'If the Jialong were in Cuoe, they must have had a reason to leave, right? Did they just give up or were they chased off? Could it be that the Jialong took over the grassland, developed it, and made it what it is now?'

'I remember hearing Aba say that my grandfather's grandfather was originally from the foot of Mount Tajiapu in No Man's Land,' Cuomu said, 'and that the clan moved here when they discovered the water and the grass were good.'

'My father's old home was in Shuanghu, near Siling Lake. This is really quite strange: I remember Shida's family is from Wenbu, and they even had a visit from some Wenbu relatives once. Didn't they, Cuomu?'

'Yes, they did, and there was a girl with them of about my age, called Danwangmu. She said they lived beside the sacred Dangreyong Lake. Their direction for circumambulation isn't the same as ours; we go clockwise and they go anti-clockwise,' Cuomu said.

'Anti-clockwise? So they follow Bon practices rather than Tibetan Buddhism?' Zhuo Mai asked, looking at Cuomu.

'Probably, seeing as only Bon go anti-clockwise.' Gongzha looked at the writing on the wall again. The letters were vivid, as if they'd been written yesterday. 'It says only the soldiers remained and that the old people, the women and the children went to the place Buddha had prepared for them. Which means the Nacangdeba weren't completely wiped out by the Jialong.'

'So the people living around Cuoe Lake are the descendants

of the Nacangdeba who moved back?' Zhuo Mai asked. He shook his head. 'In which case, where did all the Jialong on the grassland go?'

'I don't know. We can have a think about it and ask the clan elder once we get back to the encampment. From what it says here, when the Jialong attacked, the defenders were outnumbered and eventually retreated here. Let's search carefully and see if there's any more writing,' Gongzha said, sweeping his torch over the wall.

Zhuo Mai took his torch and walked off. He was particularly interested in the corpses; he wanted to figure out exactly how they died and how come the bodies had neither decayed nor fallen over in all the years since.

'Gongzha, Cuomu...' He gripped his torch and stared at the ground. He called again loudly and as the other two came over, he pointed and said, 'Look!'

A few faint letters were visible in the torchlight:

The smoke is rising and the door to Shambhala has been opened. I must go. Duojilamu, my woman, you must raise our child. When he's grown, he must avenge his father and drive the Jialong off our grassland.

'There are more here,' Zhuo Mai said as he checked the ground in front of each corpse. 'Gongzha, there's writing in front of each person – are these their last words?'

'It looks like it. They must have written them just before they died. It seems that they died from inhaling some sort of poisonous smoke, and they were all suicides,' Gongzha said. He walked up to another of the corpses, looked at the words and read: '"The Jialong are demons from No Man's Land; they eat everything. The Buddha will punish them."'

Gongzha frowned. 'They came from No Man's Land – that makes sense. That group is still around – they hunt Tibetan antelopes and sell their wool.'

'The poachers of today are their descendants?'

'Not all of them. But some are, or that's what I've heard. They mostly stay in No Man's Land now, because they don't dare come out raiding anymore. So now they've changed to hunting antelopes. It would be difficult to find them.'

'But the No Man's Land of back then and the No Man's Land of today that you're talking about must have been very different places,' Zhuo Mai said. 'The population back then was very small and there were many places deep in Changtang where there was no human life at all. The herders were free to move where they wanted and the tents were scattered over a vast area. It was normal not to see anyone for tens of kilometres or even a hundred kilometres.' His thoughts turned in another direction and he began muttering to himself. 'What kind of smoke could kill people so peacefully? If the dosage was properly controlled, could it be used as an anaesthetic?' He was always interested in the medical angle of things.

'Thieves always hide in the places where Buddha's light does not shine.' Cuomu leant against Gongzha, her eyes brimming with tears. 'So many people, all dead in a moment. Why did the Jialong block all the routes off the mountain? To not even give them a single way out – that's crueller than the wolves.'

Gongzha squeezed her hand even more tightly. 'When people turn cruel, they can be ten times worse than any animal on the grassland. Come on, let's see what else Zhuo's found. He really is as curious as a lamb.'

Zhuo Mai was standing stunned in front of the stone chair that towered over the rest. On its back was the symbol of a white ☿ with stark, protruding lines. The person on the chair was sitting cross-legged; the lines on his face were clear and his expression was as serene as if he were alive.

Gongzha was no longer surprised to see the symbol. From the moment he'd entered the mysterious cave complex, he knew it had something to do with the marking on Kaguo's forehead, though he still didn't know what. Were the people who made the cave the remnants of the Nacangdeba? He assumed the person on the chair was the Nacangdeba's clan leader, but why would the strange ⌻ be cut into the back of it? Could it be that the Nacangdeba had used this image to worship Kaguo's ancestors?

Gongzha still hadn't collected his thoughts when Zhuo Mai gave a sudden yell, even louder than before; the sound echoed around the chamber and the light from his torch wavered back and forth as if he'd been frightened by something. 'Gongzha, you two must come and look at this!'

The wall had been polished smooth and gleamed black in the torchlight. On it had been carved a large ⌻ in such high relief that the symbol stood proud of the rock, and at its centre was an even more prominent relief of an imposing black Buddha. It looked as if it was about to jump out of the wall.

Gongzha looked at the Buddha in the centre of the circle and the image of the Buddha Zhaduo had given him to protect years ago flashed through his mind.

'"Teacher of Medicine, Buddha of Lapis Lazuli Light, please protect this impoverished land and these tortured souls. Keep them from leaving again, from fighting again. Make all the lives share this sky and this grassland together. *Tayata Om Bekandze Maha Bekandze Radza Samudgate Soha.*"' Zhuo Mai read the words beneath as if he were reading a scripture.

'The part at the end is the Medicine Buddha's mantra. I often heard Uncle repeat it,' Cuomu said.

As Gongzha gazed peacefully into the Buddha's eyes and the Buddha's eyes gazed peacefully back, it was if heaven and earth, past and present, became one. 'Please help the Buddha, child!' Living Buddha Zhaduo's urgent tones sounded again in his ears.

'When Cuomu's uncle was teaching me Tibetan medicine, he always started with the story of the Medicine Buddha,' Zhuo Mai said, almost to himself. 'He said that the Medicine Buddha ruled the pure land of Eastern Lapis Lazuli. He made twelve great vows, including to wipe out all sickness, to bring happiness, to free people from evil, to bring sustenance to the hungry and thirsty, and to give beautiful clothes to the naked. Zhaduo also said that with the help of the Medicine Buddha his own dream was to wipe out sickness among the herders so they could live without illness, avoid disaster and enjoy peace and happiness.'

'I think this image must be the symbol of the Nacangdeba clan, and it must have something to do with Kaguo's family.' Gongzha touched the relief carving of the Buddha. 'It's the same material as the wall, so it wasn't added later but was made at the same time as this chamber. So that means—'

'They were the ones who made this cave system?' Cuomu joined in excitedly. 'And they worshipped the Medicine Buddha!'

'Right. Cuoe Temple was built in the Nacangdeba period. I saw a painting of the temple's construction in another chamber. But I still don't know what this symbol has to do with the Medicine Buddha,' Gongzha said.

Cuomu was suddenly reminded of her uncle and the reason she and Zhou Mai had come up the mountain. 'You know, Gongzha, just before Uncle died, he said that you should go with Zhuo to find the Four Medical Tantras and Uncle's medical notes. He said it was too dangerous for Zhuo to go by himself.'

Seeing that Zhuo Mai was now out of earshot, Gongzha asked, 'That's why you came – to find the notes to the Four Medical Tantras?'

'Yes.'

'Why didn't you get me to come with you? The two of you just deciding to head off to Chanaluo is a pretty brave thing to do.'

'Weren't you... weren't... weren't you ignoring me?' Cuomu said quietly, lowering her head and blushing.

'Who said I was ignoring you? Every night I...' Gongzha wanted to tell her that every night he'd gone to her tent to wait for her, but he was too embarrassed. 'When Shida told me you two had gone up Mount Chanaluo to pick medicinal herbs but hadn't come back, my heart almost jumped out of my body.

Woman, if you want to scare people, that isn't the way to do it.'
Gongzha gripped her hand hard.

Cuomu stole a glance at him and when she saw how tense and stern he looked, her heart suddenly felt very sweet. Just then, Zhuo Mai shouted out as if he'd seen a ghost.

'Zhuo, if you yell like that again, you'll scare us all to death!' Gongzha shook his head and sighed. Holding Cuomu's hand, he walked over.

'Look!' Zhuo Mai pointed to the traces of a line of blurry white script and stammered, 'How... how...?'

'It's not Tibetan and it's not Mandarin. Strange,' Gongzha said, looking at the untidy script.

'It's English,' Zhuo Mai said. 'How come there's English here?'

'English?' Cuomu and Gongzha said together in surprise.

'Foreigners use it. It's no good explaining it to you; it's not my language or yours.'

'Can you read it?'

'I studied it.'

'Then you'd better translate it quickly!' Cuomu fixed him with a look that made Zhuo Mai's mind wander back in time. His face took on an inappropriate expression.

Looking at Zhuo Mai staring at Cuomu, Gongzha frowned. He glanced at the woman beside him. His heart was bitter, but he couldn't show it.

'Zhuo, have you lost your mind?' Cuomu prodded Zhuo Mai with her toe.

'Oh, I'm sorry.' Zhuo Mai came out of his daydream. 'What's written here is: "Every step I take here increases our knowledge of the world; every name I give is a new kind of territorial occupation. Until January 1907, we knew as little about this part of the planet as we do about the dark side of the moon. Sven Hedin, Sweden."'

'Sven Hedin? Where have I heard that name before?' Gongzha muttered to himself.

'What would have brought this Swede here?' Zhuo Mai looked at the blurred letters and his brain moved as slowly as if it were covered in glue. This cave complex was full of surprises, each more startling than the last. He'd long believed that magic existed on the Tibetan plateau. The snow mountains and lakes had so much imagination invested in them and exuded such an air of divinity, how could there not be something magical about them? But if you chased down the root of a legend, you could always pull out a thread of historical fact relating to some dynasty, some era, some unarresting corner. This Swede had stepped into this place decades before them: how did he get there and why did he come? And how did he get out? Was there no history to check, no one to ask?

'In 1907... that long ago?' Cuomu said in surprise as she stared uncomprehendingly at the letters like tadpoles.

'Gongzha, where did you hear this name?' Zhuo Mai asked.

'I think it was the old clan leader. When his father was young, he acted as a guide to a foreigner and took the man to No Man's Land to find rocks. I think that foreigner's name was Sven Hedin.' Gongzha looked at the wall and said thoughtfully, 'Outsiders rarely come to the grassland, especially big-nosed, blue-eyed ones, so I remember pretty clearly.'

'When we get back, let's ask the clan leader,' Zhuo Mai and Cuomu said in one voice.

Gongzha nodded, and the three of them turned to look at the silent hall. None of them knew what to think. The walls of crushed stone had been smoothed over with a paste of ground grass and *tsampa* that emitted a faint black gleam in the smudged orange glow of the butter lamps. The flames barely wavered and the shadows of the pillars and the cross-legged figures overlapped and intersected like otherworldly demons. All the dead men sat placidly, showing no signs of fear or panic. Their clothes were unruffled and they were as quiet and calm as if they were living.

Gongzha put his arm around Cuomu's shoulders and pulled

her into him. Zhuo Mai stood by the stone chair in the centre, resting his chin on the end of his upturned gun. The three stood quietly and fell into a deep silence.

Finding nothing else in the hall, they continued into the tunnel. Zhuo Mai led the way and, as before, each time they turned a corner, he drew a line with a stone. Two tunnels appeared in front of them: one went up and to the left; the other went down and to the right. They stopped to discuss which route to take.

'Let's try going up first. Didn't you come down when you came in? There might be another exit,' Gongzha said.

Zhuo Mai and Cuomu nodded and they continued along the left-hand passageway, lighting the lamps as they went. The tunnel wended its way upwards and was a bit different from the other passages. Its walls had clearly been carefully worked and were very smooth. The butter lamps were also different: no longer simple copper bowls but instead beautifully engraved with auspicious figures.

Eventually the tunnel ended at a scarlet iron door, the first door they'd come across in the cave complex. The three of them stood looking at it in silence. There was no lock. On the lintel was painted in bright colours the Kalachakra mantra, and over the door was an extraordinarily white ♅, which seemed both benign and mysterious.

Gongzha pushed the door and it creaked open. Dust fell from the top, obscuring their vision.

They didn't rush in but waited a while, letting the foul air escape before getting out their torches and going in. They lit the two ornate lamps by the door, and once they could see the inside of the chamber clearly, they entered, their mouths open, unable to speak.

In the centre of the chamber stood a tall rectangular stone platform supporting a wooden box. The box was obviously made of sandalwood because the whole room was filled with a light sandalwood scent. Lined up in front of the box was a series of small gold Buddhas.

Gongzha looked up at the little Buddhas. There were at least twenty of them and he recognised them immediately. He'd seen them countless times as a child, when he'd gone with his father to Cuoe Temple to pay his respects to Living Buddha Zhaduo. The Red Guards hadn't been able to find these ancient statues when they'd stormed into the temple, which was why they'd interrogated the monks so intensively. It seemed Zhaduo had moved them here long before.

Zhuo Mai passed his gun to Cuomu. When he looked up at the sandalwood box, his heart raced and his blood surged. The box was exactly like the one Zhaduo had described. 'The heart's blood of my life as a travelling doctor is in that sandalwood box,' Living Buddha Zhaduo had told him. 'I put it in a very safe place. If it is your destiny to find it, please treasure it. Do not forget to act with the benevolence and compassion befitting of a doctor.'

Zhaduo was the elder Zhuo Mai respected the most and he would never forget him. The old living Buddha had stuffed everything he'd learnt into Zhuo Mai's head, saying that he didn't want what he'd spent so long studying to be lost; he hoped that Zhuo Mai would one day bring Tibetan medicine back to the grassland.

Zhuo Mai was a surgeon and had had no knowledge of Tibetan medicine, but the old man's sincerity had moved him. He became an enthusiastic student and carefully observed and absorbed the methods the old man taught him. He'd studied diligently under Zhaduo while he was alive, but since the old man's death he'd redoubled his efforts. He felt unworthy in comparison: Zhaduo had always been true to his values and would always help others, regardless of the circumstances. Zhou Mai was determined to fulfil his final wishes. He would go to No Man's Land and find the last herb Zhaduo hadn't managed to classify.

There were three steps up to the stone platform, but Zhuo Mai didn't race up them. Rather, he respectfully prostrated himself on the ground three times in the Tibetan way. Then he straightened up, and with the dust from the floor still on his forehead, he mounted the stairs one at a time, his gaze fixed on the box.

'Gongzha, there are words on the platform, and they're addressed to you!'

Gongzha flew up the stairs. When he saw the words, his eyes reddened. He was very familiar with Living Buddha Zhaduo's script, and the words were indeed addressed to him.

Gongzha, my good child, when the time is right, please return these Buddhas to Cuoe Temple and let Buddha's light shine on the grassland once more.

'He really was a clever old man. Who would have thought he would hide the Buddhas in a mountaintop cave? But how did he know you would find this place?' Zhuo Mai muttered.

'Because Kaguo lives in this cave. I would only need to find Kaguo to find this place. That was why he repeatedly told me to look for Kaguo.' Gongzha jumped down and motioned for Zhuo Mai to pass him the Buddhas.

Zhuo Mai handed them to him one by one. When only the sandalwood box was left on the platform, his heart began to race again. He reached out his hand but suddenly drew it back. This was the heart's blood of the old man, his life's work. Touching it was like touching the old man's soul.

Eventually he picked up the box with both hands, slowly descended the steps and sat down cross-legged on the ground. He brushed the dust off it. The box was made of red sandalwood and was ornately decorated; on the top was carved an auspicious jewelled parasol.

After wrapping the little Buddhas in Cuomu's headscarf and placing them in her backpack, Gongzha squatted next to Zhuo Mai and asked quietly, 'Is that what you were looking for?'

'It must be.'

'How does it open?' Gongzha took it and turned it this way and that, checking the top and bottom and the left and right sides, but there was no lock or any other sort of fastening.

'There's a secret lock under here – a sunken disc,' Zhuo Mai said. He slid a small panel off one end of the box, beneath which lay an ornate golden disc in the shape of a 岱.

Gongzha stared intently at the tiny 岱. 'How did you know?'

'Cuomu's uncle told me about it. He said that when I found the box, I had to be sure not to hit it or force it open, otherwise everything inside would be ruined.' Zhuo Mai lifted the box and shook it gently. There was a faint splashing sound. 'Maybe there's some kind of corrosive liquid in there and if you force the box open, it'll spill out and destroy the contents.'

He pulled out his small meat knife and used its point to rotate the disc. He turned it clockwise three times, then anti-clockwise three times, then clockwise once and finally anti-clockwise twice. The box snapped open.

There was a roll of paper inside, which Zhuo Mai gently lifted out. As he looked through it, his eyes welled with tears. 'This is wonderful,' he muttered. 'So many descriptions of illnesses and the medicinal herbs needed to treat them. Cuomu, your uncle really was a living Buddha.'

Cuomu didn't reply. There was nothing else in the chamber except the stone platform, so she was fully absorbed in investigating the rifle that Zhuo Mai had handed her. Women rarely had access to guns on the grassland because the men monopolised them. She set up the forked stand, balanced the gun on it, sat down with her finger on the trigger and practised turning the muzzle. As she pointed it towards the door, a shadowy figure suddenly stuck its head through. Cuomu was so startled, her finger twitched and the gun went off.

The figure in the doorway fell to the floor with a thud. Cuomu dropped the gun in fright and began to scream.

From the outside came the sound of something running away. Then there was quiet.

Without a thought for the frightened Cuomu, Gongzha dashed out through the door.

Zhuo Mai swiftly rolled up the medical notes, put them in the box, closed the box with a snap and stuffed it into his leather *chuba*. Then he got up and also raced outside.

A bear cub lay at the door, blood streaming from a hole in the centre of its forehead. They could hear other bears growling in the distance. At first there was only one, then two, three, four... Eventually there were too many to count; all they knew was that they seemed to be surrounded by angry bears in all directions.

Gongzha and Zhuo Mai set up their gun stands, lay on the floor and trained their muzzles on the far reaches of the dark tunnel. Cuomu stood pale and trembling behind them.

The growling continued for some time, and then it gradually went quiet.

After a while, Gongzha and Zhuo Mai glanced at one another and sat up.

Zhuo Mai looked at the bear cub next to him. 'It's dead.' Looking at Cuomu, he joked, 'Woman, you're not a bad shot. You killed a bear on your first attempt.'

'But I hit it completely by accident – I didn't even mean to fire the gun,' Cuomu said, a panicked expression in her eyes. She was still in shock.

Zhuo Mai looked at Gongzha. 'How can there be bears in here?'

'I got in here by following a pack of bears. Look!' Gongzha lifted up the bear cub's head and pointed to a white circle on its forehead. 'It's the same marking, isn't it?'

'I don't understand this at all – what do the bears have to do with these caves?'

'I don't know. There's no question that this bear cub is Kaguo's and that Kaguo and the other bears have something to do with the construction of this place. It's just that we haven't figured out what yet. Did you hear anything just now?'

'It sounded like something running?'

'Bears. We need to be careful and do our utmost to avoid running into them.'

'I've been in Tibet all these years,' Zhuo Mai muttered, 'but apart from a mother with her cubs, I've never seen three bears together. It's very strange.'

'It's the first time I've seen this many bears together as well,' Gongzha said. 'But it's not so strange that they're here. This cave system is an ideal hibernation hideaway – it's out of the wind and it faces west – and grassland bears always hibernate for a long time. We don't see them for three or four months. And this is the time of year they have cubs. We need to be careful: even though bears are often gentle, they can be ferocious if they come into sudden contact with people, and we've already killed one of their cubs. Bears' sight and hearing might be poor, but their sense of smell is good.' Gongzha tugged Cuomu's arm. 'Come on, let's go and look at the other chambers. Now that we're here, we may as well do some exploring.'

The three of them left that chamber and Zhuo Mai closed the door carefully behind them. Even though there was no lock, it had been closed when they arrived, so they felt they ought to close it again when they left. Having come upon the cave complex unexpectedly, they now felt a little like intruders, as if they'd burst into someone's house without permission.

Gongzha continued to the far end of the tunnel. There was a door there too, also without a lock. It seemed that there were surprises waiting for them in every part of the cave complex and they had no way of guessing what might greet them on the other side.

The sight that met them was equally shocking. This time the door didn't take them into an enclosed chamber but instead opened onto blue sky, white clouds and the rippling vastness of Cuoe Lake beyond. Ten steps away from them was the edge of a cliff, below which they could hear the sound of water relentlessly pounding against rock. Ice clung to the rocks around them, but on a nearby ridge seven snow lotuses bloomed and a light, clean scent drifted over on the wind.

To the left, a path wound down the mountain.

Both Gongzha and Zhuo Mai could almost see Zhaduo standing there solemnly in the void, in his tattered robes, looking at them compassionately. They both recalled his words: 'Five and a half thousand metres up Chanaluo Snow Mountain grow the best snow lotuses in our area. Only seven of them grow each year. You must pick them when the Rigel star rises, so that their healing effects are at their strongest. When Rigel appears, the shadow of the large black boulder will point due south; that long shadow will be the Buddha pointing the way for those who are lost.'

The two men looked at each other and smiled. 'We won't leave until Rigel rises.'

Gongzha opened the door a little wider so they'd be able to see if there was any movement outside. Then they took out the dried meat and the three of them sat on the ground and started to refill their empty bellies.

The distant snow mountains looked a bit like a troop of soldiers ranged in order of height, and below them the clear dark blue lake rippled with wavelets. Cuoe Lake was not one of northern Tibet's most famous lakes, but it was still an impressive sight. Anyone standing there facing the vast, misty body of water couldn't fail to be awed by the mysteries of its creator: the pairing of the snow mountain with the lake's unique and complementary beauty made a truly harmonious picture.

'The interior of the cave complex is so perfectly preserved,' Zhuo Mai mumbled indistinctly through a mouthful of dried meat, 'it seems no one else can have been there apart from the bears.'

Gongzha glanced up at the blue sky and said thoughtfully, 'We've still got some time before nightfall, so why don't you take a good look at the notes Living Buddha Zhaduo left. I suspect he has other things to tell us in addition to the medical stuff.'

Cuomu cut the meat into pieces and laid them on a handkerchief on the ground. All the men had to do was put it in their mouths.

Zhuo Mai pulled the box out of his *chuba* and set it on his thigh. He used the point of his knife to twist the disc as before and again the wooden box sprang open. The box was divided into sections and the first thing Zhuo Mai did was to carefully lift out a bag from between the sections. 'If we hadn't opened the box properly, the bag would have been damaged and the liquid inside it would have spilt out and destroyed all the notes.'

'He can't have gone to all that trouble just for the Four Medical Tantras and his notes,' Gongzha said. 'They're of no use to people who don't understand medicine. And even if someone did take them, it wouldn't have mattered much to the grassland.'

'That's where you're wrong,' Zhuo Mai said. 'It would be bad if these notes fell into the wrong hands. They contain the details of many lost medical practices, including prescriptions for making people unconscious and recipes for poisons.' He paused for a moment. 'I never understood why Zhaduo was so keen for me to memorise the names of all your mysterious Tibetan plants or why he wanted me to learn to read Tibetan plant books. I thought my Tibetan was good enough, perfectly sufficient to read normal books and the newspaper. But now that I see his notes, I can see that he decided very early on that he would give these to me one day.'

'I think you were the only suitable choice. You studied medicine and you're interested in these things.'

Zhuo Mai picked up the last page and read: '"To the person who acquires these books: your destiny must be connected to my Cuoe Temple. When the grassland has become quiet again, please return these medical notes to Cuoe Temple. No matter how you got in, please do not look back. There is a route out running from the left side of the stone chamber by the lake; turn right at the second intersection and you'll be able to get out if you keep going up. After you exit the cave, turn the upright stone to close the stone door. Once you've left, please forget everything you saw here and don't tell anyone else about it."'

'There's nothing else?' Gongzha raised his head to look at Zhuo.

'There's one more sentence. "When Rigel appears, the shadow of the large black boulder will point due south; that long shadow will be the Buddha pointing the way for those who are lost."'

'What does that mean?' Gongzha took it and looked at the last line.

Zhuo Mai shook his head.

'We'll find out once we've left, won't we, if we go and look at the boulder when Rigel rises?' Cuomu said.

Zhuo Mai and Gongzha looked at one another. 'You mean the large black boulder he mentions is that boulder up there?'

'Of course. Where else is there a big black boulder?' Cuomu said lightly as she cut up some more meat.

Zhuo Mai and Gongzha laughed at the obviousness of her comment.

Cuomu handed them each a piece of meat. 'I'm surprised the cave wasn't discovered by the Jialong.'

'There are too many riddles here – we can talk about it once we're out,' Gongzha said. He put the meat in his mouth but kept his eyes on the door. He fully expected the mother bear to appear at any time and take revenge for the killing of her cub. Until now, though, apart from that chorus of growling, the cave complex had been eerily quiet, which was very odd. Every grass-lander knew that a mother bear would defend her cubs to the last. In most circumstances, bears did their best to avoid people and rarely attacked them. But if cubs were involved, a mother bear would ignore any threat to her own safety and do battle, even if it cost her her life.

By the look of its teeth, the bear cub Cuomu had killed was not even two months old. Its curiosity had been its downfall. The mother bear must have been nearby and had presumably only run off at the sound of the gun, for fear of more bullets.

The longer the quiet continued, the more unsettled Gongzha became. Many years of hunting experience told him that some animals were smarter than humans and had very clear ideas as to when an attack would be most successful.

The sun finally sank behind the snow, leaving just enough light to make the sky glow.

Rigel eventually appeared in the blue curtain overhead, sparkling and splendid.

Suddenly there was the smell of dust in the air and mixed in with it was a faint whiff of something more unpleasant. Gongzha opened the door wide and snatched up his gun, shouting, 'Zhuo, the bears are coming! Remember, you have to shoot to kill. Otherwise there'll be trouble if they attack again.' As he spoke, he set up the forked gun stand, lay on the ground and gripped the trigger. 'Cuomu, crouch down by the side wall and don't move!'

Zhuo Mai had been studying the notes. He closed the box, stuffed it in his *chuba*, dragged his gun over and set it up, all the while keeping watch on the door with narrowed eyes.

Before long they could hear the thud of running paws, followed by a long, cold, piercing howl. Several bears appeared in the passageway across from them. Gongzha took down one with a single swift shot. Zhuo Mai toppled another at the same time. The other bears froze, then quickly turned and lumbered off. Everything fell silent again.

There was no time to take a closer look. Gongzha stood up, shouting, 'Cuomu, shut the door.'

She pushed the rusted iron door shut with a clang. 'There's no lock,' she yelled. 'What shall we do?'

Zhuo Mai and Gongzha carried over a rock from the edge of the cliff to close it.

Through the door came the sound of more bears arriving, and then their pounding and snarling rolled like thunder around the stone chamber.

'Zhuo, go and pick the snow lotuses – we need to go!' Gongzha called, holding the door.

Zhuo Mai ran up to the little ridge and used his knife to dig away the stones around the roots of the snow lotuses. Heeding old Zhaduo's instructions, he only dug up six and left the last one for the Mountain Spirit.

'Go!' The three of them raced off: Cuomu in front, Zhaduo in the middle, and Gongzha last.

The snarling bears finally pushed open the iron door and bounded after them. Because the way was very narrow, they could only run in single file. Gongzha fired the occasional shot, but all that did was frighten the bears temporarily and hold them at bay for a little while longer.

As they were rounding a bend, one of the bears got close enough to sink its teeth into Gongzha's leg, ripping open his flesh. Gongzha didn't think about the pain, just instinctively took out his knife and stabbed down. The bear opened its jaws, and Zhuo Mai took advantage of Gongzha's turned body to fire a shot, at the same time ordering Cuomu to support Gongzha at the front. He would take the rear.

At last there was a thread of light ahead. Gongzha and Cuomu raced to the cave mouth. 'Zhuo, left or right?'

'Right!' Zhuo Mai fired another shot into the darkness.

Gongzha had already turned the smallish upright stone as Zhaduo had instructed, and stones of all sizes now began to fall from above the cave exit.

'Run!' Gongzha yelled. Pushing Cuomu, he ran out and Zhuo Mai followed.

Just after all three had exited the cave, they heard a thundering noise from inside. The whole cave mouth, including the snow-covered rocks above it, collapsed. When they glanced back, it looked no different from the rest of the mountain face.

After their near-fatal encounter with the bears, the three of them were very shaky, but they could all clearly see where they were: right at the upper part of the ledge, not twenty metres from the peak. Half of the ledge had already collapsed, and although the mystical large black boulder still stood steady, a lot of snow had fallen on it. The dark chain was buried beneath the piled snow but still emitted a faint light. The Rigel star was now right over the peak and it shone so clear and bright that the large black boulder cast a long shadow pointing due south, towards the lake.

Gongzha walked over, squatted down, took up the chain and stared at it. 'Zhuo, do you know how this was done?'

'I don't. All I know is that it's neither copper nor iron,' Zhuo Mai said. He slung his gun across his back and surveyed all around them. The layers and folds of the snow mountain were just as they had been before, and in the starlight the lake down below had lost none of its mystery. It was only the ledge that had changed its appearance. But if they hadn't seen what had happened, they would have put that down to the normal shifts that happened high up on any mountaintop. No one would have guessed that under this ledge lay a mysterious series of caves or that the ledge hid so many enigmas.

'Come here! Quick!' Gongzha was looking down at the lake and waved them over urgently.

The other two climbed swiftly to the top of the large black boulder and squatted down beside him.

'Look at the surface of the lake,' said Gongzha, his eyes not leaving it.

Cuomu and Zhuo Mai followed his gaze and they too stared in silent, slack-jawed amazement.

On the rippling surface of the lake appeared an extraordinary sight.

There was a valley encircled by three mountains, with a steaming lake at its centre. Several naked elders were floating on the lake, their legs and arms paddling idly. On the lakeshore were horses, sheep and yaks. A few stone huts were scattered across the mountainside and from their roofs hung strings of prayer flags. Monks bustled along the mountain tracks, carrying things.

'It's a mirage!' Zhuo Mai said.

'"When Rigel appears, the shadow of the large black boulder will point due south; that long shadow will be the Buddha pointing the way for those who are lost,"' Gongzha reiterated.

'Shambhala!' Cuomu's eyes widened as she gazed eagerly at the mystical apparition on the lake.

Before long, the apparition disappeared and Cuoe Lake was covered once more in dark blue ripples, as mysterious as ever.

The three of them continued sitting and staring at it.

The moon was straight ahead of them, the contours of its blazing surface unclear.

When their three figures appeared halfway down the mountain, the group who'd been waiting at the bottom for a day and a night burst into tears. Shida put his fingers in his mouth and let out a piercing whistle, and they all hugged each other and pounded one another on the back. The hearts that had worried for so long could finally rest.

Danzeng's youngest brother, Duoji, and two other young men ran up the mountain and took the things from the adventurers' backs. Duoji squatted down and put Gongzha, who was so injured he could barely walk, on his back.

When they returned to the encampment, Cuomu had her younger uncle take Gongzha straight to her own tent. Just like a young wife, she nursed her injured man with great tenderness. She no longer cared about her mother's rolling eyes or the sidelong glances of the other grasslanders. She had chosen her man and she would not be parted from him again.

After this adventure, Gongzha and Cuomu's relationship was back on track. Danzeng was delighted: he liked Gongzha and didn't want to see the two youngsters repeat his own mistakes. Baila still bore a grudge, but there was nothing she could do. After all, Gongzha had taken an injury for her daughter – what more was there to say?

Gongzha, Cuomu and Zhuo Mai agreed not to tell anyone else about the cave. Subconsciously, none of them wanted the fallen heroes to be disturbed again.

Because of Gongzha's injury, Zhuo Mai extended his leave by

ten days and remained on the grassland. When he had nothing else to do, he stayed in the tent the team had prepared for him, its door flap shut tight, and studied the medical book and notes that Living Buddha Zhaduo had left for him. Occasionally he went out to pick large bunches of herbs and then made broths or medicine balls. He tried them himself, and if they didn't make him nauseous he gave them to his patients. He cured many ailments that had not been cured before, and herders came from tens of kilometres around to be treated by him. Slowly the herders began spreading stories, saying that the Han doctor Zhuo must have met King Gesar's doctor on Chanaluo and had the mystical art of Tibetan medicine transmitted to him for he'd turned into an expert overnight and was now the most famous miracle healer on the grassland.

Zhuo Mai did not explain; he just kept his head down and ministered to his patients or studied the herbs he'd gathered.

When Gongzha's injury had marginally improved, he went with Zhuo Mai and Cuomu to find the clan elder and began talking in a roundabout way about the old stories they'd heard.

The old clan elder Wangjiu sat on the couch, leaning against a pillow. 'At first, our grassland was occupied by the Jialong, and they practised the Bon religion. The Nacangdeba came from elsewhere and they practised Buddhism. To escape the heavy taxes levied by the old government, they led their people to Cuoe Grassland and drove off the Jialong. The grassland was already barren at that time.' He began coughing and broke off for a while, then resumed. 'It is said that Cuoe Temple was built after the Nacangdeba came, so afterwards the people recognised a Nacangdeba clan elder as the first living Buddha. It is also said that the Nacangdeba were good at training bears, but no one ever saw proof.'

'Put that way, we're also from elsewhere.'

'Of course. We were originally from the Mount Tajiapu Shuanghu area. One year a great snowfall made the mountain inaccessible and many yaks and sheep starved to death. The clan elder led the migration here, but it was difficult and many people died on the way. My father was only two at the time. Some people say that the Nacangdeba were the original ancestors of Tajiapu; others say that we have nothing to do with the Nacangdeba and are actually the descendants of the Jialong.

'Bola, does Cuoe Temple really have one of King Gesar's Medicine Buddhas?'

Wangjiu seemed shocked by Gongzha's question. 'Are you looking for it too?'

'I'm just curious. There's a saying on the grassland that if the Medicine Buddha appears, the people's hearts will find peace.'

'What does the peace of the people's hearts have to do with the Medicine Buddha? They need to find it for themselves.' Wangjiu stared past Gongzha at the vast grassland outside. In the distance, yaks grazed, their heads lowered, while the herders sat to the side rolling balls of yarn.

'You don't believe in that saying?'

'Gongzha, you're a good hunter and a good hunter always relies only on his own judgement. I've seen that Medicine Buddha. There's a strange symbol on its back and I don't know what it means. Zhaduo always looked after it himself. I once heard my *aba* say that the statue came from the sacred lake in No Man's Land. He said that the sacred lake welcomed all living beings as equals, and whether they were animals or humans, if they went into the lake, they all floated on its surface.'

'The statue came from the sacred lake in No Man's Land?' Gongzha repeated.

'I don't know the details. I've just heard the elders say that.'

'Before we moved here, did anyone herd on Cuoe Grassland?'

'Yes, but very few. There were many wolves. When we first came here, the hunters spent three months clearing this area round the lake. This vast grazing land that we have was all ripped from the wolves' mouths.'

'What about the monks at Cuoe Temple? Did they all come later?'

'Not at all. It's said that when we arrived there were two monks in the temple but no living Buddha. Our people rebuilt the temple and asked the great lama to come and conduct the ceremony to search for the living Buddha's spirit in a child. In the end they identified Zhaduo. Zhaduo suffered a lot for the peace of the grassland!'

'Suffered a lot? What do you mean?'

'There was a plague on the grassland and many people died. Zhaduo went off to pick herbs in No Man's Land and disappeared for more than three months.'

'The living Buddha disappeared for three months?'

'Yes. He said he wanted to go to No Man's Land to pick a herb that could heal the plague sickness. He took three disciples with him. There was a blizzard and he and the disciples got separated. The clan sent out several search parties, but they couldn't find them. We all thought the living Buddha had gone to Shambhala. We didn't expect that three months later he would come back on his own, in high spirits and bringing with him many medicine balls for healing the plague.'

'He didn't talk about how he'd spent those three months?'

'He did not. It was enough that he'd come back. The plague was raging and in some tents had killed every single member of the family. The living Buddha was working flat out to save people – when would there have been time to talk about where he'd been? I remember we set up lots of large pots in the courtyard of the temple to brew medicine that would keep the survivors safe.'

'So no one knows what happened to him during those three months?'

'That's right. No one asked, and he never told. Why are you asking about all this?' Wangjiu turned his head and motioned for Cuomu to pass him the medicine tablets from the small table. They were from Zhuo Mai's supply of Western medicine. When Zhaduo died, there was no one left on the grassland who knew Tibetan medicine. It was lucky that the Han doctor Zhuo

Mai was there, otherwise the herders would have had to go all the way to the town for medical treatment.

'I'm just curious.' Gongzha stood up and passed the old man a glass of water.

Wangjiu took his medicine and put the glass back on the small table. 'When Zhaduo came back he had the Four Medical Tantras with him. He read that book whenever he had time and often went to pick herbs. He tested them on the yaks and sheep first, to see what effect the medicines had.'

Zhuo Mai had been sitting on a bench and keeping quiet. Now he lifted his head and said quietly, 'Clan Elder, I've heard that when your father was young he was a guide for a foreigner. Is that true?'

'Yes, that's right. My *aba* mentioned it often. He ran into the foreigner while he was herding; the man was on his own, he had a big nose and blue eyes and he didn't look anything like us. It seemed he'd come from over by Chanaluo and was lost. His clothes were in tatters and he was as thin as a ghost. When he saw my father, he hugged him and began to cry. No one understood what he said, but he kept pointing to himself and gabbling something, which Aba thought might have been his name. He had to draw lots of pictures on the ground before my father could understand: it seemed that he'd come across some kind of cave and had then run into some bears. All the people he'd gone with disappeared and only he escaped. At the time, there were lots of avalanches on Chanaluo. My *aba* took some people with him and searched for two days but couldn't find anyone. They also went to No Man's Land but found nothing there either. The foreigner wasn't able to say where the cave was, so they couldn't do anything except take him off the grassland.'

Zhuo Mai glanced at Gongzha; Gongzha nodded. Cuomu helped the old man lie down and covered him with a blanket.

'We're leaving, Bola. Have a good rest,' Gongzha said.

'Wait, I've just thought of something.' The old man suddenly opened his eyes and looked at the three thoughtfully. 'Once when I went to the temple, Living Buddha Zhaduo was looking at King Gesar's book. He said that the book was written in gold ink and had been given to him by Buddhist ascetics living beside a sacred lake in No Man's Land.'

Gongzha thanked the old man and the three of them left the tent together.

Thanks to Zhuo Mai's thoughtful care, Dawa no longer ran wild and naked, but her spirit was still troubled. Gongzha's leave was almost up and he started to prepare his things ready for his return to the army base. The night he left, he went to Cuomu's tent.

'I will wait for you. You can go in peace.' Cuomu lay in Gongzha's embrace. They were covered with a soft lambskin blanket with only their naked shoulders showing. The yak pats burnt in the iron stove, the flames leaping occasionally, and the small tent was as warm as spring.

'My senior officer says I can leave the army next year. When I come back, we'll set up a tent together.'

'Yes!' Cuomu nodded and wrapped her hair around Gongzha's neck. 'I will take care of your *ama*. You don't need to worry about her. Remember to write to me.'

'Woman, I will miss you.'

'I will miss my eagle.'

12

On the ninth of September 1976 the clouds were thick over Cuoe Grassland. The herders had gathered outside the production-team tent and were staring at the little radio on the table. A young man wearing a cotton Tibetan robe climbed onto the table to adjust the frequency, and out from the radio came muffled Mandarin. The herders could not understand Mandarin, but they still listened intently because Luobudunzhu had come back from the commune saying that the central government had some incredibly important information to convey and that everyone had to listen at the appointed time.

Danzeng had invited Pubu, the teacher from the tent school across the lake, to translate. He was the only one in the team who spoke Mandarin. Pubu had graduated from middle school and stayed at the tent school to teach the children their letters. Right now he was gripping the radio and listening carefully; his face was looking more and more serious.

'Our Manjushri has really left us!' When the radio began to emit nothing but static, he turned around. His eyes were full of hot tears. Seeing the expectant expressions on the faces of the waiting crowd, he sobbingly translated the message into the dialect of northern Tibet.

'Manjushri' was the herders' respectful name for Mao Zedong.

The sounds of mourning erupted suddenly from every part of the crowd. Manjushri was gone and it seemed like the grassland's sky was about to fall in. As they gazed at the image of Chairman Mao on the front of the tent, people's eyes filled with tears. They bowed, took a *khata* into their hands, carefully hung it over the frame of Mao's portrait, and bowed again with each step. In the hearts of the grasslanders, Chairman Mao was the bodhisattva who had saved them from a sea of suffering.

They honoured the great man in their traditional way: one year of not washing their faces, combing their hair or wearing make-up; one year without dancing; one year of sorrowful remembrance and cold loneliness. There was now one more spirit to honour in their shrines, one more sad day lodged in their hearts.

That year, Gongzha retired from the army. The minute he'd reported to his work unit, he set his horse for home, galloping off straightaway, not even stopping to eat lunch. The lure of Cuomu's passionate eyes made his heart almost leap out of his chest. The grassland was both his heaven and his home and his spirits soared as he urged his horse onwards, faster and faster into the wind. He would be with the woman he loved and they would never part; they would have two or three children and he would return to the grassland for holidays, taking up his rifle with the forked stand and going hunting. He would definitely shoot a red fox this winter and make her a hat. When he pictured Cuomu's moon cheeks set off against the red fox-fur, he couldn't help chuckling to himself.

He opened his sheepskin *chuba* and began to sing at the top of his voice. The loud lyrics of the herders' song and the horse's thundering gallop shattered the grassland silence, scattering the mice and rabbits and even sending the foxes and antelopes dashing through the short grass, their bodies flattened, vanishing in an instant.

> 'The stars in the sky
> Are like Brother's eyes
> Watching Sister's silhouette.
> The butter lamps ablaze all night
> Cannot see your eyes, Brother,
> As they fall inside the tent
> To light up Sister's heart.'

The track stretched across the plain to the horizon and beyond, seemingly without end. Occasionally the sound of pounding hooves scattered a flock of skylarks; they flew up into the air with a pop, waited until the horse passed, then settled again.

The sunshine was wonderful. It warmed and softened everyone in its embrace, so that the vast grassland was like a mattress, cushioning and wrapping everything in the afternoon light and tumbling it gently to the ground. Between the blue sky and the dark blue water, what warmth there was. It was the perfect weather for lovers, and Gongzha urged his horse on, welcoming the wind and laughing wildly. He was a man deeply in love. In no time at all he would be with the woman he loved and his whole body was alive with anticipation.

His horse tore across the plain, its athletic body rising and dipping. As it rounded a bend in the track and leapt over a stream into the next river valley, the sound of Cuomu's frightened screams suddenly echoed around them, accompanied by the faint snarl of a bear.

'Gongzha...!'

It was a truly heartrending cry.

Gongzha whipped his horse savagely, desperate to grow a pair of wings.

The strengthening smell of blood gripped his heart like an iron claw.

Then he saw his woman's turquoise-studded plaits flailing wildly; her despairing eyes.

As Kaguo extended her claws again, Gongzha's meat knife flew out of his hand without him even thinking about it and buried itself in her foreleg. Kaguo turned with a growl and ran off with her cub. Gongzha leapt off his horse, gathered Cuomu's bloodied body into his arms and howled like a wild animal.

In the blink of an eye, the warm, spring-like grassland turned into hell on earth. The sun disappeared behind a mass of black clouds and the wind hurled the sand ahead of it, screeching as it blew. The wild asses and antelopes looked at the sky in confusion and rushed towards the mountain valley with the wind at their heels. The earth was chaotic and the sky was dark.

All afternoon long, Gongzha staggered around the grassland with Cuomu's cold body in his arms, zigzagging aimlessly, directionless. His brown horse followed behind. Vultures circled overhead, occasionally swooping down then soaring back up again.

According to the traditions of the grassland, Cuomu's body should have been taken by the funeral master and swaddled in white cloth like a baby in a womb to symbolise that she was to leave the world as she had entered it. But Gongzha wouldn't let the funeral master do anything. He himself drew water from Cuoe Lake, washed his beloved's hair and body clean, rebraided her plaits and then tenderly wrapped her in soft white cloth. Through all of this he remained extremely quiet, as if nothing had happened. No one else's tears or words of comfort had the slightest effect on his demeanour. He just kept watch over Cuomu's body, neither eating nor speaking.

A burial was a significant event for a family. Guests came in a continuous stream, so the family had to prepare food, receive condolences, and get all sorts of things ready. But they were not allowed to cry. A relative's tears would unsettle the spirit of the departed and make it worry about its family in the material world, which risked delaying its journey and preventing its reincarnation. This life of Cuomu's had ended; her life to come had not yet started. They had to let her step onto the road towards that next life and whatever place of belonging that might be.

So her relatives could not cry, could not mourn. Letting the departed's spirit leave happily was the last thing they could do for it in this life.

Gongzha did not cry. During the brief periods when he wasn't keeping watch at Cuomu's side, he sat quietly on his own out on the grassland, staring ahead as the evening sun stained the sky red. Everyone who saw the lonely silhouette sighed and left their words of comfort unsaid. He was young and had waited so long for love, had seen it almost come to fruition, and then in a moment had watched everything good disappear. Like an antelope that had lost its mate in the spring, his every hair and pore dripped with despair.

The morning that Cuomu died, the commune had been mobilising the herders. The government wanted everyone to join together to help repay the national debt to the Soviet Union. A borax mine had been discovered in No Man's Land and the production team decided that every able-bodied young person should go and work there, not even returning home in the evenings. The elderly and those who were weak or ill would stay behind to look after the animals.

Zhuo Mai got leave and hurried back to the grassland; he wanted to see Cuomu off on her last journey.

The sun had not yet risen and there was a biting chill in the air. Gongzha carried Cuomu on his back. She was so light, it was as if a feather had settled on him and was slowly drilling into his flesh. That soft feather wiped the dust from his heart. The physical weight of the dead may have been slight, but yearning for them was the heaviest of burdens. When you missed someone, they were never absent from your thoughts, and your body never stopped aching for them. Year in, year out, you couldn't touch them, couldn't see them; longing for them became a habit, became part of you, something you could neither forget nor forego.

Zhuo Mai walked in front, carrying a smoking clay jar.

Neither of them spoke.

Dawn was breaking now, but the sky had not yet become fully bright. A light fog, white as milk, lay in a band across the gloomy grassland, soft like a *khata*, like a young woman's hair, graceful and dreamlike. The yaks and sheep had not yet woken, and even the skylarks seemed to be asleep. Everything on the grassland was quiet this morning, in honour of that kind, beautiful girl, seeing her off on her journey.

Three men walked across the measureless grassland: the funeral master, Zhuo Mai with the jar, and Gongzha carrying Cuomu.

When they arrived at their destination, Gongzha laid Cuomu gently on the large black boulder, opened the white cloths that swaddled her, and watched as the first rays bathed her in light, her four limbs spread like a baby's, pure and beautiful. He and Zhuo Mai stood quietly and though tears welled in their eyes, they did not let them fall. The funeral master lit the incense and its light blue smoke floated straight up. When a light wind blew, the whole valley was filled with its scent.

Zhuo Mai took out some prayer flags, and he and Gongzha hung them on the stones around the mountainside. When this was done, the two of them turned and hurried away without looking back. It was not that Gongzha did not want to watch; he did not dare to watch. When he reached the bottom of the mountain and heard the shrieks of the circling vultures, he could stand the pain in his heart no longer. He sat down heavily on the ground, defeated. Covering his face with his hands, he wept the tears he had tried to suppress, sobbing into the wind.

Zhuo Mai stood behind him, watching the slowly rising sun, and his eyes were wet.

The day after Cuomu's sky burial, Gongzha returned to his work unit. He did not smile again.

Zhuo Mai also returned to his unit and began to make a serious study of the medical book and notes that Living Buddha Zhaduo had left him. He chose two young people from Cuoe Grassland to be his pupils and taught them about Tibetan medicine as well as Western treatments.

The second year, when the snow began to fall, Zhuo Mai passed the medical book and notes to Gongzha and asked him to one day restore them to Cuoe Temple. Then Zhuo Mai returned to metropolitan China, to the great city of Shanghai, taking with him Zhuo Yihang, the son he had pulled out of an avalanche.

Without Cuomu, Gongzha was lonely, cold and cheerless, like the waters of Cuoe Lake. The lake looked beautiful on the surface, with its clear blue ripples. But when you put your hand in to feel it, the cold cut to the bone and froze your heart.

His body was haggard. He wandered from one wilderness area to another, from one drink to another; he wanted to drink himself into oblivion and never wake up. Day after day, year after year, he watched as other people married, had children, lived happy lives. His friends advised him to forget the past and start again, to find another woman to cherish, a new family to take care of. But Gongzha always responded with a bitter laugh: how could he cherish another woman and take proper care of a family when he could find himself swamped by a sudden burst of loneliness at any time and in any place. Along with the loneliness came an unquenchable longing that tore at him without remission. Its only salve would be having Cuomu returned to him.

Even so, he was still the head of the household for one tent.

When he came back to the encampment on annual leave, he appointed people to find wives for his three brothers, then held the weddings very quickly. He brought his mother, Dawa, to the county town and organised his sister, Lamu, to take care of her.

The day after Dawa left the grassland, Ciwang also disappeared. No one knew where he'd gone, and apart from his family, no one cared. When he'd been at the peak of his powers, he'd brought hatred to the grassland. With the grassland now peaceful again, Ciwang longed for the return of those glory days, but his was a solitary voice. His lot was cold and lonely, and he'd lost his status in the encampment to Luobudunzhu, who disliked him and often bullied him or beat him up. When Ciwang disappeared, the grasslanders just assumed that he'd lost some sort of bet with Luobudunzhu and was hiding at the tent of an old friend, biding his time until things settled down.

As for Zhuo Mai, he often called Gongzha from the city, and the two of them talked of the grassland, of Cuomu, and of days long past. Gongzha thought that Zhuo Mai's loneliness was because of Cuomu; he didn't know that his heart belonged to a different woman. Meanwhile, the sun continued to rise and set over the grassland and all its people, regardless of their hurts.

13

The lake water went from clear to blue and from blue back to clear again as the years slid by. There was some good news; it had spread through the country and had finally reached the grassland: China was bringing back the college entrance exam.

Everyone was excited: young and old, those who had gone to school and those who had not. To the herders, going to college had always been beyond their wildest dreams, but that dream was now a real possibility. Thirteen years earlier, when herders had not even had the freedom of their own homes, just learning a few words of Mandarin had been unthinkable, much less going to college. Then, in the early sixties, tent schools had been established on the grassland and children had begun to realise that they could do more than just herd yaks and sheep and collect yak pats. The Cultural Revolution had begun not long after.

Despite their limited education, the grasslanders anticipated the college entrance exam with enthusiasm. In the weeks leading up to it, Shida shut himself away in his tent and pored over his tattered schoolbooks, writing notes and memorising facts day and night. When he came across something he didn't understand, he went to find Teacher Pubu at the tent school on the other side of the lake.

'Do you think I have a chance of passing?'

Shida and Pubu emerged from the tent side by side as the sun sank behind the mountains. They followed the narrow path along the lakeshore to where the solitary yak-skin boat lay.

'Everyone's coming to this from more or less the same situation. And because we're a minority group, we're apparently eligible for extra points. As long as you put the work in, you'll pass.' Pubu glanced at Shida, who had a full beard and was already a father of two.

Shida nodded vigorously and got into the yak-skin boat. Pubu untied the rope for him and watched him row off into the distance.

Having a relative at college was a significant high-status achievement for the entire family, equivalent to having a highly educated *geshe* monk in the family, so when Shida got his results, Cuoe Grassland was exultant. He was the first person from the grassland to go to college and everyone came together in spontaneous celebration, singing and dancing through the night.

The day he left, Shida wore a large red flower and a portrait of Chairman Mao the size of his palm. His neck was hung with tens of *khata*. As he waved his goodbyes to the people who were seeing him off, he looked back at the grassland. The wife his father had chosen for him held onto their two children in the middle of the crowd and stared blankly at her toes. Shida's gaze didn't rest on her but travelled over the grasslanders' heads to the black gravel shore of azure-coloured Cuoe Lake where he and Yangji had played together when they were young. The two of them could have been a couple, a couple everyone spoke fondly of, but because he'd been weak and foolish, their story had become the great, indelible pain of his heart.

Then let the painful grassland stay only in his heart.

'You really don't want to ever come back?' That night, Shida stayed at Gongzha's house in the county town.

'I feel like it was me that drove Yangji to her death. Everything on the grassland reminds me of the times we spent together, and there's no escaping it, day in, day out, to the point where I feel like I'm going mad,' Shida said bitterly. 'I'm not planning on coming back. After I graduate, I'm going to move to a city and work there. I don't care where I go, as long as it makes me forget this place.' He clasped his hands behind his head and stared up at the fabric-covered ceiling.

Gongzha lay on the couch opposite, not knowing what to say. He thought of Cuomu, and the times they spent together, and his heart began to hurt.

'Don't forget to look up Zhuo Mai when you get to Shanghai. He's the director of the surgery department at a big hospital there. Yihang's grown up now and the two of them might come to the grassland for their summer holidays next year.'

'Time's gone so fast... When I think back to how we all used to sing and dance and hunt together on the grassland, it seems like a dream.'

'It does.' Gongzha inhaled deeply, then switched off the light. The room glowed gently in the moonlight. 'Yangji is gone, Cuomu is gone, Zhuo Mai is single but has a son. You're married, the father of two children, and about to go to college. As for me, I have a job but no Cuomu.'

As the two men talked, the night slowly fell quiet. The moonlight shone through the small window and made the terrazzo floor gleam.

Like every head of the household on the grassland, Gongzha took his family responsibilities seriously. He concerned himself with everything, no matter how important or how minor, from what sort of woman his brother should marry to what kind of clothing their tent should make that year. But always at the back of his mind was the knowledge that one day he must head off in search of Kaguo and avenge his woman's death. He could not forget Cuomu's bright black eyes and on countless nights would wake to her mournful cry: 'Find Kaguo, take revenge.' On one such night, frightened awake yet again, he stared up at the dark sky and resolved that he could put it off no longer; he had to find Kaguo and honour the fallen spirit of his lover with the bear's life.

The rain and wind of the grassland had long shaped the immature youngster into a hardy man. By now Gongzha had a full beard and hair that fell to his shoulders. His tanned face was as rough as sand and as he walked the dusty streets of the county town, his eyes glittered with a fierce light. He submitted his resignation and strode freely out of the door of his work unit. He had waited for many years and now the time had come. Cuomu's smiling face seemed to be getting more insistent, and his yearning for her only deepened.

He took his mother to Lhasa to consult a specialist there, arranged by an old friend of Zhuo Mai's who was the head of an army hospital. The specialist's conclusion was that Dawa was suffering from a psychotic disorder that may have been triggered by a significant trauma. He prescribed perphenazine. Gongzha and Dawa returned to the county town.

With his mother's condition now taken care of, Gongzha went back to his old home on the grassland. He still had one more significant task to undertake: to fulfil Zhaduo's wishes and make the Buddha's light shine once more on the grassland.

The day he got back to the grassland, the herders were meeting to discuss the allocation of pastureland. Other areas of the country had already begun using the land-contract system and that particular wind was now blowing across the grassland. Once the pastureland was divided up, the herders would no longer follow a nomadic existence, leading their animals to where the water and grass were. Whether fixing the herders' feet to one spot would be a good or bad thing, no one knew. There was no way of telling whether it would have a positive or negative outcome. But people were instinctively excited about yet another new idea for the grassland. They would have their own pasture and their own yaks and sheep and there'd be no more having to set off for work at the sound of a whistle or returning home at a specific time.

They had already discussed how many yaks and sheep a family of a certain size should get, and this then determined the size of their pasture. There was also the question of horses. Horses had big bellies. One horse ate more grass than five sheep, but when they divided up the pasture, a horse was only allocated as much land as a sheep, while a yak was given an area the equivalent of three sheep. Because this enormous consumer of grass could supply the herders with neither meat nor wool, herders no longer wanted to keep horses. And now that public roads were being built on the grassland, horses weren't critical for getting around either. Many horses now ran wild on the grassland.

Building roads on the grassland was straightforward. The land was mostly flat – apart from the mountain slopes that needed to be levelled and the marshy areas around the lakeshore – and a road was effectively in place as soon as a car drove across it.

Gongzha's second-youngest brother came back from the meeting about dividing up the pastureland. When he saw Gongzha, he waved. 'Brother, we've been given five *gang* and four valleys, over by the side of Chanaluo; the pasture there is pretty good.' A *gang* was a unit of area that all the herders in Changtang understood, though no one could say how many hectares it was and no one had ever tried to measure it.

Gongzha nodded.

Gongzan, the family's second son, was stacking yak pats. He turned and said with a grin, 'According to Luobudunzhu, the public road will reach us in ten days at most. When that happens, let's get a motorbike. It'll be faster for us to go see you and Ama in the county town.'

'Alright.' Gongzha was staring at the distant mountains and replied without turning his head.

'A lot of the household heads at the meeting today were talking about buying one. This is good – we won't have to ride horses to herd anymore.' Third Brother chuckled. 'Brother, if we get a motorbike, shouldn't we sell the horses?'

'You should hold on to two of the good ones – we still want to take part in the summer races,' Gongzan reminded him with a laugh.

'Keep mine. The others you can decide on as you see fit.' Gongzha turned and went into the tent. 'I'll go back to the county town in a couple of days and buy you your motorbike.'

His brothers' laughter circled the tent.

The herders' way of life, barely altered for a thousand years, began to change. With the pastures now divided between them, the herders worked harder than ever and their lives became fuller. Some of them even built small houses on their land near the public road and the elders and the children stayed there while the men went to the pasture. Gongzan's woman already had two children and their house was getting noisy.

Gongzha did not just buy a motorbike, he also bought a walking tractor. He and his brothers were busy – the three of them divided the workload and laboured hard every day. That Gongzha was still single troubled his brothers. They felt that their elder brother should either join them and become the real head of the household or find a woman in the city to take care of and start a home there. But Gongzha's mood remained sombre, and he rarely spoke.

It was unthinkable on the grassland that a man would stay single his whole life because of a woman who'd died long ago. Life on the Changtang Plateau was tough enough without giving yourself the extra challenge of remaining true to a long-dead love. The snow fell when it wanted and the rain blew when it wanted; the heavens might be unhappy at any time and disaster could come at any point. Even the thinnest layer of snow did not melt easily and when it blanketed the pasture, the yaks and sheep had no grass to eat and could only starve to death. In those harsh, inhospitable highlands, death was a fact of life.

No one understood Gongzha. Of course, Gongzha did not need anyone to understand him. He was only true to his own heart.

No one was sure on which day Cuoe Temple (still missing its bodhisattvas) began to have offerings again: at first some apples and fruit sweets quietly appeared, then a thread of light blue incense, then the five-coloured prayer flags. Nor could anyone say on which day an old monk called Basang appeared on the grassland, carrying a cushion and with a sheepskin *chuba* draped over his shoulders. No one knew where he came from. He went straight up the mountain, pushed open the temple door that had remained shut for so many years, and moved into one of the small rooms in the complex. The next day, he took up a broom and swept the temple clean inside and out.

Cuoe Temple slowly began to feel lived-in again.

The question was, where were the Buddha and bodhisattva statues hidden?

One day, Gongzha was sitting daydreaming in his brothers' tent halfway up the mountain when Gongzan came in.

'Elder Brother, Guxiula Basang is looking for you.'

Gongzha lifted his head and was about to stand when Basang, the old monk newly arrived at Cuoe Temple, came in bowing and coughing; his robe was dirty and his hair was dishevelled. He clasped his hands together in greeting. 'Dear Gongzha, I have something to ask of you.'

'Guxiula, please take a seat.' Gongzha stood up and invited the old man to sit on the main cushion.

Gongzan's woman poured butter tea and handed the old man and Gongzha their bowls with both hands, then turned away and went about her business.

'My name is Basang,' the monk said quietly. 'I was once a disciple of Cuoe Temple's living Buddha. Very soon after the Cultural Revolution came, the living Buddha told me to leave the grassland. Recently I heard that things here had calmed down again.' He looked at Gongzha then took a sip of tea.

'That time was hard; all the monks had to leave.' Gongzha sighed and refilled the old man's cup. 'Why have you come to see me?'

'I've heard that the government has started rebuilding damaged temples and I'd like to submit an application for the refurbishment of Cuoe Temple and the recasting of some new bodhisattvas. You, dear Gongzha, worked for the government and are familiar with the process, so I wanted to ask you to help me.'

After the Cultural Revolution was over, the government set about rectifying the mistakes of that period. Zhaduo had been restored to the status of living Buddha, and the grassland, which had been in turmoil for ten years, had settled down again. Many places were filing reports asking for their damaged temples to be repaired.

'Of course I'll help you,' Gongzha replied quickly. Hadn't it been Zhaduo's dying wish that the Buddha's light be restored to the grassland? Helping return Cuoe Temple to its former glory would honour his request, and the Medicine Buddha and those ancient little bodhisattvas he was hiding would have somewhere to go.

The application was swiftly approved. The government gave 150,000 yuan to fix the temple. During the Cultural Revolution, the temple compound had been taken over by the Red Guards and used as their headquarters, and afterwards it had served as a storage depot for the collective's food. This had actually helped protect the temple, and its original buildings and murals were still intact. The only things that were missing were the sacred Buddha statues and little gold bodhisattvas, which were national treasures, and an ancient tanka or religious scroll painting.

Using the budget of 150,000 yuan and under Gongzha's direction, the temple invited artisans from Chamdo to make replacement sculptures of the Buddhas and bodhisattvas. Gradually, the scattered monks returned to the temple. Some were known and others were not, but no one objected to this. When a man entered a temple and put on his robes, he was a disciple of Buddha and no one questioned his status.

Everyone in the area came to the unveiling of the Buddha, bringing tea bricks, butter and dried meat. The new great hall had two levels. On the upper level new rugs had been neatly laid out; on the lower level was a terrazzo floor. The believers sat on the floor and listened to the deep, resonant chanting of the scriptures. Butter lamps flared once more and the long-absent light of the Buddha filled the hall. Basang, who was in the first monk's seat, glanced at Gongzha's back and a smile appeared at the corner of his mouth.

The next day, when the monk on duty rose early to sweep the temple, he discovered that the door to the great hall was open. He was afraid that a thief had broken in, but on checking he discovered that nothing was missing. In fact, in front of the Jampa Buddha there now stood several small bodhisattvas from the collection of Vajrapanis that Living Buddha Zhaduo had personally taken care of. News spread rapidly that the Buddhas and bodhisattvas of Cuoe Temple had acted and made the lost bodhisattvas return to the temple.

That night, Gongzha sat in a field beside Cuoe Lake. Its deep blue water gleamed faintly and the vast grassland beyond was so silent it seemed to be from a different age. In the distance, Chanaluo Snow Mountain loomed, as striking as ever, stealing the radiance of the grassland by night just as it did by day.

Gongzha used a blade of grass to etch a ♅ on the ground. The symbol was always circling in his mind, tormenting him, but mostly he didn't dare dwell on its meaning because of the heart-breaking pain it conjured. Unlike most grassland men, who could make their home anywhere there was grass, as long as their tent had their woman in it, Gongzha could not find peace. His heart had stopped that afternoon all those years ago, when the sand and wind had ravaged the plain; had stopped in the darkness of that day.

He stood at the foot of the mountain and lifted his face to look at Chanaluo. It was so high, so bright, so formidable. Thin clouds drifted around the peak as they might around a flagpole.

Climbing the mountain was easy, and he reached the first ridge without even breaking a sweat. He stood motionless on the ridge, his old sheepskin *chuba* tied around his waist, his narrow eyes shining with a cold, hard light, his beard full, and his long, tousled hair streaming out behind him in the snowy wind.

On the frozen snow in the sunlit valley that enormous ¤ symbol had given off a strange glow. Why had the bears wanted to make that symbol? What did it mean? Gongzha closed his eyes; he had no answers.

He knew that Kaguo was still on the mountain. The light, acrid scent on the wind told him so; he was a good hunter and his nose never deceived him. He didn't head up the snow valley but instead climbed straight up the mountainside. He wanted to go to that ledge. He hadn't managed to get a close look last time because he'd been injured.

The mysterious large black boulder was still there, but the stones around it looked different because of avalanches. Gongzha walked round the boulder twice, but apart from confirming that it was not a natural feature of the landscape, he gleaned no other information.

He sat cross-legged on the boulder and lifted a section of the black chain. It was heavy and so cold to the touch that when he held it he felt as if he was being pricked by countless tiny needles. Its links were tightly forged, and its end looked as if it was growing out of the rock – no matter how hard he yanked it, it didn't budge. How had it got there? Why had it been set in there? The legend about the tethering of the Wolf Spirit had circulated generation after generation, and every generation's version was the same. But in the end, a myth was a myth, and it was not the same as a logical explanation. Gongzha didn't believe in myths, even though he enjoyed hearing them. He didn't believe that sacred beings came down to earth and he didn't believe that a spirit would save you if you didn't work hard. Everything originated somewhere, and everything had a purpose. But where had it originated, and what was its purpose?

Gongzha stood up, tightened his leather *chuba* around him and walked from one side of the large black boulder to the other, then back again. Then he began circling it, speeding up as he went, taking longer and longer strides. Finally he sat down and let his dizziness slowly settle until he could see the landscape in front of him clearly again. The snow mountain loomed tall, and far below, Cuoe Lake stretched into the distance, blanketed with mist as usual.

Gongzha got to his feet again and began to walk around the boulder once more. The vertigo returned.

Just then, the furious roar of a bear resounded; it came from some distance away. Gongzha would never forget that roar. It was Kaguo, and she only roared like that when she was angry. Cuomu had gone to Shambhala hearing that sound. Because of that sound, Gongzha had turned into a walking corpse, all happiness extinguished.

To find Kaguo and kill her, that was Gongzha's goal.

Even before the sound of Kaguo's roars had faded into the deepest recesses of the mountain, Gongzha was already racing across the slopes towards it.

He pursued her for three hours through snow that was knee-deep. Finally, after crossing a nameless snow mountain, he reached a spot crisscrossed with tracks. A quick glance told him there'd been one large bear, one small bear, and six wolves.

Wolves? Gongzha twitched one corner of his mouth and assessed the scene coldly. If he had guessed correctly, the wolves and bears were just around the bend, not three hundred metres away.

Kaguo, you took my woman's life, and I will take yours! That was the vow Gongzha had made, spoken out loud for his woman to hear, with the vast grassland and the endless blue sky as his witnesses.

He slowed his steps and zigzagged upwards. The packed snow crunched underfoot. He wanted to find a good vantage point; looking down from above would give him more control. The bears and wolves were ahead of him and were perhaps engaged in a fierce battle. Let them fight – better that they depleted their energy reserves and wounded each other.

Kaguo! Gongzha's heart repeated the name, and with the name came that heart-rending pain.

When several black shadows came into view, Gongzha was filled with a crazed joy. He crouched down, found a mound of snow to hide behind and quietly looked on.

Six wolves and two bears.

Wolves were usually active down below on the grassland – why would they have come up the snow mountain? He saw with interest that Kaguo was protecting one bear cub by her side and that she was encircled by six grey-brown grassland wolves baring their teeth and glaring. Her body had bloody gashes, and two of the wolves were also injured.

As the confrontation continued, the six wolves slowly separated into two groups, three in front and three behind, preparing to attack from both sides. There was a wisp of a smile at the corner of Gongzha's mouth. Wolves were the grassland's cleverest animals, and their ability to work together against their enemies was unmatched. Kaguo was done for. When Gongzha realised this, he raised his gun. He didn't want Kaguo to die in a wolf's jaws, he wanted her to die by his own gun. That was the only way he could pacify Cuomu's soul.

The three wolves in front were only feinting. The three at the back were intent on getting the cub. None seemed worried about the consequences. It was clearly the first time the cub had been in this kind of situation; it huddled close to Kaguo for protection, squealing with fear.

Two wolves got between the cub and Kaguo and waited, teeth bared.

As she faced the other three hungry attackers, Kaguo had to try and stop herself from getting hurt while protecting her cub at the same time; she clearly did not have the strength. She howled bitterly, sweeping her paws to left and right, her steps getting heavier. Even though her claws still had strength in them, they only sent the piled snow flying.

In a second, the cub would be gripped between the wolves' paws.

The gun fired.

But what fell was not Kaguo but the wolf that had set its paws on the bear cub's head.

Why? Gongzha was to regret having made that choice for a very long time. Why had his muzzle moved? He had clearly been aiming at Kaguo, but the bullet had hit the wolf. He bore no grudge against the wolves; whether he hit one today or hit another one tomorrow made no difference. But Kaguo... Kaguo was the object of his revenge; he had sworn to take her life. Letting her go meant that the coming chase would last a long time.

At the sound of the gunshot, Kaguo and the wolves froze, then quickly disappeared into the snow valley.

A snow-filled wind rose and howled.

Gongzha gripped his gun and sat down, a solitary figure in the barren wilderness. As he gazed absently at the overlapping tracks in front of him, his long hair whipped around his head. He was like an ancient statue, with the history of the grassland people carved on his face.

Eventually, he got up, put his gun over his shoulder, and walked cautiously out of the snowfield, singing the old herder's verse in a rasping voice as he went:

> 'The stars in the sky
> Are like Brother's eyes
> Watching Sister's silhouette.
> The butter lamps ablaze all night
> Cannot see your eyes, Brother,
> As they fall inside the tent
> To light up Sister's heart.'

He found the bush he was looking for; the cave walls were covered in wild grass. He sniffed, but there was no scent on the air; clearly the cave had been abandoned long ago. Without the bears' scent, Gongzha had nothing to go on. Why had they moved? Then he laughed. They were bears, wild animals, could they really have souls like humans? Did they need a reason to move? Here today, gone tomorrow: they moved as the urge took them and their need for food demanded.

He picked up a few dried branches, tossed them at the cave mouth and then kicked the snow to cover them. The bears had gone; let the cave rest forever in history. He slung his gun over his shoulder, began singing loudly again, and disappeared into the vast snowfield.

He returned to the encampment the next day. Early the following day, before the sun had broken through the clouds, he took his gun, threw a leg of yak meat that had been wind-dried and then rubbed soft with butter onto the back of his horse, and left.

The hardy young man set out on the road to revenge, carrying his boundless longing for his lover and his burning hatred for Kaguo. The autumn wind pierced his bones and blew his hair high, but he still wore his sheepskin *chuba* over only one shoulder; his other shoulder was bare, and his muscles bulged under his skin. He rode off slowly towards the distant snow mountain. The more alone he was, the more he could feel Cuomu beside him, singing softly, or following him with a blush, or looking at him, or talking to him. In this way, Cuomu travelled with him.

Behind him, Danzeng stood hunched over by his tent, a mournful expression in his eyes as he watched Gongzha go.

Part Two

14

Feng was the last one off the plane. As the cool air caressed her face, she felt a powerful sense of wellbeing. She took a deep breath, threw open her arms and shouted, 'Tibet, here I come!' causing everyone in front of her to turn round and stare.

She darted down the plane steps with a huge grin on her face, a deep red cashmere scarf patterned with black flowers floating behind her, and her brown curls dancing in the wind. An electric bus was waiting to ferry them to the terminal. Feng glanced at it but did not get on; she decided to walk over.

Lhasa Gonggar Airport was nothing like as big as she'd imagined and the grey terminal building was right there in front of her. Everything looked so vivid: the sky was bluer than she'd ever seen it and the clouds whiter. Her whole body tingled with excitement.

'The sun's strong, but the air is cool. It's stunning – like paradise.' That was the first thing she said to her boyfriend Yang Fan, who lived in America, once she'd found a public phone. 'I haven't felt any signs of altitude sickness; I don't feel dizzy and my head doesn't hurt.' Then she asked, almost automatically, as if out of habit, 'So, are you missing me?'

From the phone came the equally predictable reply, 'I miss you. Have a good time, and stay safe!'

Then Feng made another phone call, this time to her good friend Zhuo Yihang. 'I've already found your paradise,' she told him, 'and just as you said, it's gorgeous. Thank you for introducing me to it.'

'Be careful,' Zhuo Yihang replied, 'don't let a Tibetan man carry you off, otherwise Yang Fan will come back and eat me.'

Feng, Zhuo Yihang and Yang Fan had grown up together, gone to the same college, and were the best of friends. Feng and Yang Fan were a couple and Zhuo Yihang was their third wheel. Yang Fan often said that while other people dated in pairs, they dated as a threesome. After graduating, Zhuo Yihang didn't find a job with a company but started his own business, rode the economic wave and became an extremely wealthy eligible bachelor. Yang Fan went to America to study international business and got a master's and then a PhD. Feng joined an international company and became one of the most envied and highly regarded professional women in Shanghai.

The travel agency that was looking after her tour group had sent a handsome young Tibetan man to meet them. After he counted everyone, he took several *khata* out of his *chuba* and flung them skywards as if he was acting in a play; they fluttered up and down in his hand. Then he hung one around each person's neck, greeting them loudly with '*Tashi delek.*'

The atmosphere suddenly became very animated. Enraptured, Feng caressed her smooth, thin *khata* and her heart softened. She was only here because she'd helped her company win a multi-million-yuan contract and had been allowed to take a whole month of holiday. Zhuo Yihang had kept on at her, encouraging her to go, and so, finally, twenty-five-year-old Feng had set out, a little nervously, on her journey.

The people in her tour group were all from Shanghai, all about the same age and all very polite. They peppered their conversation with English, not to show off but simply because that's how they always spoke.

It was the early nineties and Tibet's tourist industry had not yet taken off. China was preparing to introduce reforms and open up and reinvigorate its economy. There was much discussion and uncertainty about the very notion of 'reform'. As they stood on the edge of this vast new sea wondering if they should take a dip, only a small number of locals and foreigners embraced China's new markets. Feng and some others were lucky and brave enough to get on the earliest wave: they had high-paying jobs, houses and cars, and lived lives that made their peers envious.

Each day had been carefully timetabled by the travel agency. They visited the Potala Palace, Jokhang Temple, Sera Monastery and Tashilhunpo Monastery. They travelled to Namtso Lake and to Linzhi to see virgin forests. Were there any problems? There were not. Theirs was a well-travelled route.

Their ten days slipped by. Most of the tour group left, returning to their normal lives after another week's relaxation. Feng still had ten days of holiday left. Alone in Lhasa, she wasn't sure what to do. Where next? Should she join another tour group and spend her time following another tour leader's little flag, mindlessly filling the hours taking the pictures you were supposed to take on trips like this? Feng was reluctant to do that. She gave Zhuo Yihang a call.

'Go to northern Tibet. I have an uncle who works in Shenzha. Go and find him – he speaks Mandarin – and make him take you to Cuoe Grassland to see the nomad herders. I lived there when I was young; it's stunning and I guarantee you won't be disappointed.'

'And where is Shenzha? Zhuo Yihang, don't forget I'm all by myself!' Feng was sitting propped against a wall facing the window, holding the phone to her chest.

'There are a lot of travellers in Lhasa. Go to Barkhor Street, have a look round, and leave a message in one of the teahouses; anyone interested in travelling with you will find you,' Zhuo Yihang said. He paused to issue instructions about one of his projects; he was clearly very busy.

'Alright, I'll give it a go,' Feng said and hung up. She turned to look out of the window at the radiant sun and began to daydream. She thought about phoning Yang Fan but decided not to in the end. The two of them were friends more than anything else. They'd been bored back in college, and when they saw that all their classmates were coupling up, Yang Fan had said, 'Let's date,' and she'd nodded in agreement. They'd been lovers ever since. Then they graduated, and Yang Fan left for America. Now they had to rely on the phone line and their own resolve to keep the relationship going.

Beside Potala Palace Square there was a small shop between two small lakes. Next to it were a garden and a teahouse. The pavements looked as if they would never be clean: there was rubbish everywhere and the air reeked of stale urine. Some dirty children swarmed up behind Feng, stuck out their grimy hands and yelled, 'Auntie, give us a mao! Auntie, give us a mao!' Feng pulled out all her change and handed it to them, but more and more children came over and grabbed at her clothes. She was so frightened that she froze; then she pushed through the children and ran off as if she was escaping something. She began to regret coming to Lhasa.

There were far fewer people on Yutuo Road and she gradually calmed down as she made her way along it. The sun was still warm, so she put up her small, delicate umbrella, hiding as much of herself under it as she could and stealing glances to left and right. Although the sun was fierce, she discovered that only a few women carried umbrellas on the street; at most they wore a hat that shaded only part of their cheeks, beaming as they hurried by.

What kind of city was this? Even though she was on a busy street and next to the sacred Potala Palace, she could smell all kinds of unpleasant odours. And yet it was a happy place: everywhere she looked she could see peaceful elders ambling along and spinning little prayer wheels in their hands, taking puppies or lambs for a walk, or giving an amicable smile to friends or strangers.

Feng's curiosity was piqued. On Barkhor Street, she studied the faces approaching her and smiled back at anyone who smiled at her. She got into the habit of smiling; even if someone didn't smile at her, as long as they noticed her, she smiled at them. It was very enjoyable: she had never felt so relaxed and cheerful.

If she'd been in Shanghai and had smiled like that at passers-by, she'd probably have been considered mentally ill and made people avoid her. As Feng was thinking this, she turned a corner and found herself in front of Jokhang Temple. She heard the sounds of people prostrating themselves and stood transfixed in front of its red door, watching them make their obeisance, repeatedly getting down flat on the ground and then standing up again. Their fervour stirred up all sorts of emotions in her. To Feng, who was used to worshipping material things, the Buddha was not necessary; she realised her dreams through hard work, not through reciting scriptures or prostrating herself.

As she stood there absentmindedly, all sorts of sympathetic thoughts went through her mind.

'Have you just arrived in Lhasa?' a voice next to her said suddenly.

Feng turned her head and stared. Beside her stood a battered bicycle being pushed by a man with a beaming face and shoulder-length hair who was carrying a bow and arrows and wearing armour. Had she gone back to the past? How come she was looking at a warrior from ancient times?

'I'm Agang. I've been in Lhasa a long time. Are you new here?' Agang asked, still smiling. He seemed unfazed by her surprised expression.

'Agang?'

'Right. What's your name, pretty lady?'

Feng finally collected herself. 'Feng. I've been here quite a few days,' she said with a smile.

'Where are you going next?'

'My friend suggested I go to Cuoe Grassland in northern Tibet, so I'm going to look for some people to come with me.'

'What a coincidence! We're planning to go to Shenzha – let's share a car.'

'Really? How many are you?'

'Seven. With you, we'll just fill two Beijing Jeeps. How about it? We can split the cost.'

'No problem. When do we leave?'

'Tomorrow morning!' Agang said. 'Do you have a sleeping bag?'

'A sleeping bag? No.'

'I'll take you to buy one. You can't go to northern Tibet without a sleeping bag; it's very cold there!' Agang turned his front wheel and, just like an old friend, took Feng to Beijing Middle Road, where he went into several outdoor-gear shops, haggled with the owners, and bought her a sleeping bag, a windcheater and a pair of hiking shoes.

Agang's warmth was disconcerting. Feng was used to keeping people at a distance and had always thought that overly friendly people had some kind of hidden agenda. Otherwise, why would they be so unguardedly generous to a stranger?

After buying the supplies, Agang took Feng back to her hotel, waved and said he would pick her up the following morning at seven. Then he hopped onto his battered bicycle and rode off noisily: the bell was broken, but his whole body was clanging. Feng watched the two luxurious golden pheasant feathers he'd stuck in the back of his armour disappear into the setting sun, and it was quite some time before she got her thoughts together again.

Laughing and shaking her head, she took her various bags into the hotel. She wanted to repack her luggage. She was travelling with an oversized medical bag that contained all sorts of vitamins and calcium tablets as well as standard medicines for colds. She piled up her sunblock, moisturisers, and moisturising masks. Making herself beautiful so that people would look at her was the kind of work that women like Feng had to undertake every day.

That night Zhuo Yihang called and gave her his Uncle Gongzha's phone number. He hadn't managed to get through to him, so he told her to go directly to his workplace in Shenzha and look for him there. 'It is the most pristine environment. You can't imagine how blue the sky is or how clear the lake, and I guarantee the people won't disappoint you either. Go! Don't worry. Just don't forget to come back.'

'You can't seriously think I'll want to spend the rest of my life there! I'm not interested in going back to basics and living a primitive life.' Feng laughed, picked up an apple and bit into it.

'Well, it's hard to say. Every time I go, I don't want to leave.'

'But in the end you always do go back to Shanghai, don't you? Forget about northern Tibet, you couldn't even make me stay in Lhasa. It's so unsophisticated – dogs roaming the streets, dust flying up whenever a car goes by. It's unbelievable!' Feng laughed and hung up. Humming 'Story of a Small Town', she began stuffing her bag full of chocolate.

15

Northern Tibet's No Man's Land was also known as Kekexili in Qinghai Province. It was barren, lonely country, and the land was so poor, it barely merited the term. It could not support crops or trees, and the only plants that grew were short, wild grasses and low shrubs, sparse and frail. Most of the land had not even a centimetre's growth of grass on it. In No Man's Land, mountains of six or seven thousand metres seemed like small hills. No matter the time of year, the peaks were permanently snowbound, flashing their silver light as they had for a thousand years, adding a sparkle of white to the otherwise green summers and brown winters. The bright blue sky and white snow complemented each other perfectly.

It was a paradise for wild animals. When people elsewhere on the plateau went crazy and started killing animals just for fun, the wild yaks, asses and sheep that had nowhere to hide fled there, to No Man's Land, where there were hardly any humans. Vegetation was also scarce: there was less food and the environment was harsher, but at least the animals' lives were not in danger, so they could find happiness.

Happiness was not something that just animals needed; people needed it too. On the vast plain, a brown horse walked slowly, as if it was taking a stroll. Its rider wore an old sheepskin *chuba* tied around his waist. A thick beard covered almost half of his face, his eyebrows were the colour of coal, his skin was rough, and his long hair was filthy and wild. He carried an old hunting gun on his back. He appeared to be asleep, but he was not asleep.

It was Gongzha. Twice on Mount Chanaluo he had tried to kill Kaguo, and twice he had failed. Even so, Kaguo was spooked and had fled to No Man's Land. Gongzha had followed. Cuomu had been dead for many years, but Gongzha's memories of her had only intensified with time. The more he thought about her, the clearer his memories became: in his heart, she was forever young and beautiful. Now he didn't even need to think about her; she was always by his side or in front of his eyes.

The day slowly fell towards night. As the evening sun began painting the sky red, the grassland and the snow mountains turned gold. In one small patch of that golden grassland stood a few tumbledown mud walls. An old woman carrying a wooden bucket on her back hobbled out from between them. She started when she saw Gongzha. 'Guest, are you lost?'

Gongzha sprang off his horse and led it over by the reins. He bowed and put his palms together in greeting. 'Dear Ama, I am a hunter. I've been chasing a bear here.'

'Oh, we haven't seen an outsider for many years. Respected guest, please come with me and rest your feet. I'll stew you some mutton ribs. An eagle only has the strength to fly when it is full,' the old woman said, and she led him to a black tent nearby.

Gongzha followed the old woman, tethered his horse to a post, entered the tent and sat down by the stove. She served him butter tea, then threw several yak pats into the stove and used the sheep-gut bellows to blow the fire until the flames leapt high. Her kindly, wrinkled face glowed in the firelight and Gongzha's thoughts turned to his own mother and to his brothers' children. His wanderer's heart was suddenly filled with bitterness. Women and children were a man's future, the hope in his tent. But his own future and his own hopes had disappeared at the sound of Kaguo's wild howls on that gloomy afternoon long ago.

With these thoughts preying on him, Gongzha's heart began to hurt again. He picked up his butter tea and gulped it down, hoping to suppress the pain.

The old woman stood up and refilled his cup. 'Where are you from, child?'

'Cuoe Grassland, Ama.'

'Cuoe Grassland?' The old woman lifted her head and stared through the window in the roof of the tent at the white clouds drifting overhead. 'Now that is a lovely place!'

'Has Ama been there?'

'No, but I've heard of it. A place like heaven!' The old woman withdrew her gaze. She used a fork to lift the meat out of the water and into a bowl, placed it in front of Gongzha, and passed him a small knife. 'Eat, my respected guest. I have nothing fancy to offer you; I can only give you this mutton to fill your stomach and give you the energy to journey across the grassland and over the mountains in search of your bear.'

Gongzha hadn't eaten stewed mutton in a long time. Like any hunter out in the wilderness, he ate what he could hit. He didn't stand on ceremony – to do so would have been disrespectful to his hostess. He took the meat in one hand and his knife in the other, and in a flash devoured a large part of everything in his bowl. The old woman grinned appreciatively, poured him some more tea, and passed him the salt and some hot pepper. When they heard someone approaching from outside the tent, the old woman lifted the door flap, smiled and went out.

When he finally got the point where he couldn't fit anything else in his stomach, Gongzha stuck the knife into the rest of the meat, stood up and went out of the tent. The old woman had been joined by a young woman and they were driving sheep towards the sheep pen. He went over to them, borrowed the old woman's slingshot and launched a few stones. They whirred through the air and landed squarely on the old ram that was trying to stray from the flock, forcing him back into line.

The young woman smiled at him. Working together, the two of them herded the sheep into the pen and shut the gate.

'I'm Yongxi. Who are you?' The young woman tilted her head to one side, flashing two large dimples as she smiled.

'Gongzha.' He strode over to take the bag of yak pats out of the old woman's hand, swung it onto his back and returned to the tent.

The old woman smiled, her eyes narrowing, and said to her granddaughter Yongxi, 'That child can really work!'

Yongxi giggled, swung her thin plaits behind her, and trotted over to catch up with Gongzha.

'Where are you from?'

'Shenzha County.'

'Our area here is called Ejiu, that snow mountain is called Tajiapu and we are all its children.'

'Tajiapu?' Gongzha squinted at the distant snow mountain.

'You know it?' As Yongxi looked at him, the evening sunlight slanted across her face and her delicate eyelashes were so defined, you could count them.

'I've heard of it,' Gongzha said and he looked away.

Yongxi kept up with him and chattered on. 'Tajiapu must be quite famous then, if even you've heard of it, but it has only a few children. There aren't even a hundred of us herders here. Granny says there used to be many people on Tajiapu Grassland, but they left.'

'They left? Why?'

'It's said that Tajiapu was invaded by demons, so it was always hailing. No grass grew, so the yaks and sheep starved to death, and the herders had no choice but to look for better pasture elsewhere. Granny said that some of them moved to Cuoe Lake.'

Gongzha turned to look at her. 'To Cuoe Lake? Are you Nacangdeba?'

'Yes, we're Nacangdeba. How did you know?'

'I'm from Cuoe Lake.'

'We're family?' Yongxi jumped in front of him and grinned at him in delight, her eyes wide. She called to her grandmother in the tent, 'Mo, he's from Cuoe Lake and he's Nacangdeba!'

The old woman glanced at Gongzha with a smile but said nothing.

The Nacangdeba on the grassland all had one ancestor. No matter where they wandered, they were all one family.

Gongzha stacked the yak pats by the stove. Then he went out again, found some stones and began to repair the yak enclosure. He got hot and took off his leather *chuba*, tying the sleeves around his waist; his weathered, coppery skin gave off a faint golden light in the evening sun. Yongxi stood by his side and helped by passing him stones. She didn't know why, but every time she looked at the full-bearded man from Cuoe Grassland, a strange new feeling arose in her heart.

That night, Gongzha slept in the little black tent in the wilderness. The stove gave off a rosy glow and made the tent quite toasty. In its innermost part, the old woman made a bed for Gongzha out of three cushions and a new rug. The auspicious blue images on the rug had taken her a year to create; she'd planned to give the rug to her granddaughter when she was grown up and started a tent of her own. Tonight she brought it out to welcome their relative from a faraway place. Only treasured guests received such treatment and Gongzha was moved, though he said nothing. He was not one to express himself, keeping both his gratitude and his anger buried deep.

When the stars had risen and the moon hung over the mountain peaks, the grassland became so still, it was as if it had entered a different dimension. The three of them sat on their rugs in the faint light cast by the stars and the old woman told Gongzha stories of the past.

'We were also once from Cuoe Grassland. My grandmother was called Duojilamu and her first tent was by the side of Cuoe Lake. When my mother was small, demons suddenly invaded the grassland. They went everywhere, stealing yaks, sheep and girls, and burning any tents they found. Our ancestors couldn't defeat them, so the men ordered the women to escape during the night, taking the elderly and the children with them. That was how my mother left her home; her mother brought her here to No Man's Land in Shuanghu. Her brothers froze to death on the road, and her father did not return. I heard that none of the men of the clan escaped; some said they were eaten by the demons.'

The old woman sat facing the fire, occasionally throwing yak pats onto the flames. The fire was perfectly hot enough, but she needed to do something to distract herself from her grief. Shaking the dust off the old stories had exposed the pain hidden beneath.

'The year I was five, there was a great blizzard here. The snow was up to our knees and it didn't melt for two months. The livestock all froze to death. Many people did too. The clan leaders had no choice but to tell the herders to go and find a new pasture. Most people left, but my parents only had me, so our life wasn't that hard, and they were used to it here, so we stayed.'

'Duojilamu? Cuoe Grassland?' Gongzha sat on the rug, his sheepskin *chuba* wrapped around him, staring at the serene old woman in the firelight. Her face was a mass of wrinkles, her hair was white and wild, and her spirit was peaceful, as if she'd seen everything in life there was to see. She was like the shaft of a bow, like the craggy mountain ranges that loomed over the grassland, ravaged but steadfast. Only mothers of the grassland had that kind of face; only mothers of the grassland had that kind of mountain-like spine.

As she spoke, Gongzha thought back to that strange cave, and he muttered to himself, 'Duojilamu?' The name was familiar – he'd seen it somewhere:

The smoke is rising and the door to Shambhala has been opened. I must go. Duojilamu, my woman, you must raise our child. When he's grown, he must avenge his father and drive the Jialong off our grassland.

That mysterious stone chamber, those peaceful corpses, that man who'd written his last words in the dust on the ground... Gongzha told the old woman about everything he'd seen in the cave on Chanaluo. As he talked about the men's final words, he heard Yongxi weeping quietly beside him.

Without looking at either Yongxi or Gongzha, the old woman rose to add some water to the pot on the stove. 'People come and people go. No matter how beautiful the grassland is, it will never belong to just one person.' She returned to her seat and squeezed the bellows twice to fan the flames again. 'It's like this fire – it will die down today, but tomorrow it will brighten again. The grassland too: its flowers wither, but next year they will bloom again.'

The night slowly grew silent, and all that remained of the fire were some faintly glowing embers.

In the middle of the night, Gongzha suddenly woke up. He heard footsteps outside the tent. From his many years in the wilderness, he'd cultivated a keen pair of ears: he could tell just by listening whether it was a human or an animal drawing close.

The person approached the tent slowly, then raised the door flap. A gust of cold wind rushed in. Squinting into the moonlight, even with his eyes half closed, Gongzha could tell it was a young man. He didn't move; he barely even drew breath.

The young man walked over to where Yongxi was sleeping, called her name softly and began to pull at her quilt.

Gongzha still didn't move. The grassland had its traditions. When a young man came visiting at night, pursuing the young woman in his heart, no one had the right to interfere.

Yongxi seemed unwilling; she clutched at her quilt, struggled, and began to cry, calling out, 'Mo! Mo...!'

The old woman didn't stir. Perhaps she was sleeping, or perhaps she was waiting for something.

Gongzha didn't stir either. He was simply respecting the customs of the grassland.

In that tiny space, Yongxi's struggles seemed all the more helpless, her muffled cries all the more piteous. But her tears didn't seem to have any effect on the young man. He began to pull vigorously at her arms and tear at her quilt.

Yongxi's cries got louder and she began to swear at him.

Now Gongzha got up. He crossed the tent in two steps, grabbed the young man's arm, twisted it behind his back and pushed him out of the tent without a word.

The last thing the young man had expected was an encounter with a man who didn't understand the rules. He whipped out his knife and rushed at Gongzha, who was standing by the tent door. Gongzha didn't move. He waited until the young man drew close, then grabbed his wrist, yanked him to the side and threw him to the ground, where he lay splayed like an old sheep.

He scrambled up and glowered at Gongzha, who stood there as strong and silent as an iron tower. The young man knew he was no match for him, so he turned away, cursing, clambered onto his horse and sped off.

Gongzha watched him disappear swearing into the distance. Then he went back inside the tent, walked over to his rug and crawled back into his *chuba*; within minutes he was breathing evenly.

Yongxi sat clutching her quilt around her, staring in confusion at Gongzha's sleeping form. Moonlight streamed through the little skylight and illuminated her face: her eyes were misty and her cheeks were still wet with tears. The old woman's snores were as peaceful as before.

Once this now tranquil night was over, could everything really remain unchanged?

When dawn broke the next day, Gongzha didn't leave straightaway. He helped the old woman tether the sheep together in pairs while Yongxi brought over the milking bucket. As she did the milking, the old woman said with feigned carelessness, 'Our household has no man and we need to move pastures soon. As it's just me and Yongxi, one old woman and one young woman, we'll have to ask a man to help us.'

'How long until you move?' Gongzha said lightly. He tied

the horns of the last two sheep together, straightened up, and looked over the two rows of sheep.

'Ten days. We'll move to another side of Tajiapu.'

'I'll help you move and then leave,' Gongzha said. He strode over to pour the full buckets of milk into the butter churn.

Yongxi and her grandmother stared after him as he worked busily in the morning sunshine and burst into smiles.

Gongzha said little, but his hands and feet never rested, and he kept himself occupied both inside the tent and out. He hated the thought of the compassionate old woman pushing a heavy cart over the snow mountain, and anyway, it didn't matter to him how many days he stayed. His purpose in life was to catch Kaguo; whether he did so sooner or later, the outcome would be the same. He knew Kaguo had come to this part of the country, and if he didn't chase her, she wouldn't go far. He would let her survive for a few more days.

Ejiu was a true wilderness and life there was fragile. The ground was covered in pebbles the size of fingernails. If heaven was gracious and sent more rain and less hail, wind and snow, then the people and the animals could live comfortably through the year. If heaven was not gracious, it took only one season of sandstorms for the grassland to become a place of starvation. The grass that managed to endure such hardships completed its cycle swiftly – it sprouted, made rapid growth, flowered, and dropped its seeds all within a relatively short period. If the herders moved their livestock to the pastures just when the grass was at its best, there was hope for the season ahead. It was the most labour-intensive task of their year.

Before they moved the cart to the new pasture on the other side of the snow mountain, Gongzha first wanted to relocate most of the livestock there. He asked Yongxi to be his guide. On Cuoe Grassland, moving pasture was something all the families did together. The busy sounds of moving would fill the air and nothing and nobody would even contemplate attacking them, neither wolves nor other people. But in the infinite wilderness of

Tajiapu, they were on their own: people had become an endangered species.

Gongzha had tied his *chuba* around his waist, and his long, wild hair blew in the wind. He walked with his tanned face to the sun, and his rough skin could have been used as sandpaper. Yongxi was by his side. She'd dressed carefully in a red robe with gilded edges that set off her figure perfectly; her freshly washed wavy hair had not yet dried and it rippled behind her in the wind. As she walked, she knitted something with yak wool.

The two occasionally exchanged a few sentences; usually it was Yongxi asking a question and Gongzha replying. A black dog travelled with them, racing back and forth and circling around them. As they crossed the snow mountain and meandered along the pathless slope, Gongzha and the dog worked together to push the yaks into one long line.

The reflection of the sun's rays off the snowy ground was extremely strong and Gongzha had to keep raising his hands to shield his eyes. Yongxi called to him, opened the yak-wool circlet she'd been knitting and placed it over his eyes. He smiled at her gratefully. It was a simple but effective device. When worn over the eyes, the knitted shade protected the wearer from the glare but still kept their line of vision clear. In the highlands, where sunglasses were not yet commonplace, the herders had developed their own way of preventing snow-blindness.

'Brother, you said that Chanaluo has an iron chain on top of it. Our Tajiapu does too!' Yongxi said, searching for something to talk about.

Gongzha lifted his head to look at the cloud-encircled peak. 'On the summit?'

'Yes. I've been up there to see it – it looks as if it's growing out of the rock.'

Gongzha's heart stirred, but he said nothing. He thought about the chain, that strange symbol, the vanished Nacangdeba, the enigmatic statue of the Medicine Buddha... Try as he might, he still didn't understand what it all meant.

'The elders say that the chain was used to tether a Wolf Spirit meant to keep watch over the part of Princess Gesar's treasure that was hidden on Tajiapu.'

'A Wolf Spirit?' How could there be another chained Wolf Spirit? Gongzha thought to himself. Chanaluo's chain was to bind a Wolf Spirit, Tajiapu's chain was also to bind a Wolf Spirit, although one was meant to guard the grassland and the other to guard treasure. Chanaluo and Tajiapu stood over five hundred kilometres apart and seemed unconnected, but there was apparently a mysterious, hidden thread that linked them.

By the time they'd crossed the snow mountain, the sky was already darkening. They found a place out of the wind, tethered the ropes to the ground, lined up the yaks and tied them together, and left the dog to watch them. Then they selected a yak each and lay down beside its soft, warm belly.

Under the night sky, Yongxi's black eyes gleamed like two stars. When Gongzha sensed her gaze resting on him as he lay in his nest by the yak's side, he was well aware of its meaning. But his heart had already followed Cuomu to a distant place. It would be hard for him to fall for another woman.

'Brother Gongzha,' Yongxi complained lightly, 'I'm so cold!'

Gongzha threw his *chuba* over to her.

'What will you do?' Yongxi lifted up the *chuba* and covered herself with it, looking at him with an air of quiet complaint. How could he understand so little about attraction? If it had been one of the shadow hunters in his place, they would have come over to her long ago.

'I'm used to it!' Gongzha said, and closed his eyes. It was not that he had no desire for a woman, it was that when he was alone at night, he usually thought of Cuomu's warm body. He could not allow another woman to take her place.

As soon as dawn broke, Yongxi got up and made a fire with some yak pats to boil tea. They ate some meat, then freed the yaks and continued on.

When they were almost at the pasture, Gongzha discovered

that two wild yaks were following them. That didn't surprise or worry him. Yaks were not like wolves: as grass-eating animals, they didn't hurt people unless they were angry. It was their mating season, and unlike the domesticated yaks, the wild bulls had to fight for the right to mate. Those that lost out would quite often set their sights on the domesticated yak herd, and because they were three times larger than the domesticated bulls, they were usually successful. The mating life of a yak was a real example of survival of the fittest. The main thing to watch out for was that the domesticated females didn't run off with the wild bulls. Gongzha instructed the dog to watch the yaks carefully and to keep the females from leaving the herd.

There was no one else at the new pasture; the black tent stood all alone between heaven and earth. Gongzha did not sleep that night but took his gun and rode around the area. When he failed to find any traces of wolves or bears, he was relieved. Even so, he was reluctant to leave Yongxi all alone in the wilderness, far from any signs of human life, while he returned for her grandmother. On Cuoe Grassland, a young woman of Yongxi's age would never have been out on her own on such a lonely pasture. She would have stayed with the family tent under the protection of her father and brothers. But Yongxi was used to that way of life, used to dealing with the wind and rain of the wilderness. She and her grandmother had struggled on by themselves since her childhood, and she knew how to keep herself safe.

When the sun had risen in the sky, it was time for Gongzha to leave. He didn't want Yongxi's grandmother to bring the heavy wagon over the snow mountain by herself.

Yongxi stood by the tent and handed the gun to Gongzha. 'You should take the gun – what if you meet some wolves? I'll be fine. I've got the dog for company, haven't I?'

'I'm a man!' Gongzha said, and leapt onto his horse.

As he whipped it to urge it forward, Yongxi said loudly, 'Brother...'

Gongzha turned and shot her a questioning look.

'You... you'll come back, won't you?' she asked gloomily, tears welling in her eyes. She truly feared he might not return.

'Don't worry.' Gongzha whipped the horse's rump fiercely and rode off into the reddened morning clouds, leaving a column of dust in his wake.

Yongxi watched his silhouette disappear into the light on the horizon. Then she turned around and began to tidy up, humming a herder's song.

A pack of wild asses trotted over. When they saw Yongxi busying herself around her tent, they were startled but not afraid. They'd got used to seeing that tent there over the years. The two wild yak bulls slowly drew close.

They had finally finished moving to the new pasture. Because Gongzha was there, the two wild yak bulls had left again. But now a trail of dust was floating towards them, kicked up from some distance away. Yongxi suddenly came running back to the tent from the foot of the mountain, waving her hands and yelling to Gongzha, 'Brother, you must leave quickly! Qiangba is coming with a posse!'

Yongxi was clearly scared out of her wits, but Gongzha had no idea why.

She ran over and began pushing Gongzha towards his horse. 'It's the man who came to the tent that night, he's brought a posse to take revenge on you for throwing him out. They have guns – they're poachers and they wouldn't think twice about killing someone. Go quickly, Brother! Quick! Once you get over the snow mountain you'll be on a grassland so vast that not even an eagle can spot a sparrow there.'

Gongzha stood his ground. He turned, patted Yongxi on the shoulder, then went into the tent and brought out his old gun. He placed the forked stand on the ground and kept one hand on the butt. His *chuba* was tied around his waist as always, its greying sheep's wool drifting in the wind. He stood in front of the tent with his legs planted wide and watched with narrowed eyes as the riders raced towards them from the mountains. It was as if he was observing a herd of wild asses running freely and considering whether or not to fire a shot to scare them.

The posse was heading straight for them. When they saw Gongzha and Yongxi, they tried to bunch their horses together, to look as threatening as possible. But the horses wouldn't obey; they scattered left and right and cast the formation into disarray.

The young man that Gongzha had thrown out of the tent that night was one of the posse. He leapt off his horse and glared angrily at Gongzha. Then he turned to the centre of the posse and addressed a stern-faced man wearing a red fox-fur hat and black leather clothes and sitting astride a black horse. 'It's him, boss, he's the one that chucked me out. An outsider who has the audacity to break our rules – he shows us too little respect.'

'Qiangba, this has nothing to do with him.' Yongxi moved to stand in front of Gongzha. 'He's only passing through – he's a guest of our grassland,' she said angrily.

Qiangba glanced at Gongzha. 'He must abide by grassland rules, Yongxi,' he said nastily. 'He has interfered in our affairs and now he must take the consequences.'

Gongzha pushed past Yongxi and gave Qiangba a cool stare. 'The grassland has another rule: if you want to win a woman, her heart is more important than her body.'

'What grassland man doesn't go visiting? You're an outsider, what right do you have to concern yourself with what I do?' Qiangba patted his gun.

'Since I have concerned myself, I'm not going to back down now,' Gongzha said lightly.

He looked at the man on the black horse: the image of an eagle about to take flight was displayed on the horse's bridle, a clear sign of its owner's status. The rider was Jijia, the leader of the shadow hunters. It was said he would kill a man without blinking and that it was he who was responsible for slaughtering the Tibetan antelopes in the area. It was also said that he had a good heart and that when disaster struck he would help the poor without leaving his name. One rumour followed another. Very few people on the grassland had seen him – they only knew that whenever his eagle appeared, blood and trouble followed.

'You don't like Qiangba?' Jijia asked, shooting Yongxi a playful look from under the brim of his fox-fur hat. The sound of his voice was dry and scratchy, like sand being ground over paper.

Yongxi raised her eyes and couldn't help shivering as she looked at the arrogant man. She lowered her head but her words were clear. 'I don't like him.'

Jijia looked at his men and said, 'Leave this woman out of it!'

'Boss...' Qiangba lifted his head to protest, but when he saw the serious expression on his boss's face, he dropped his gaze. Even though men were free to visit tents, the desire for an encounter had to be mutual. If it became known that a man had forced a woman, that would not go down well. Of course, out there in the wilderness, even if there was such a rumour, how many people would hear it? That was why Qiangba did what he liked.

Jijia turned back to Gongzha and said unhurriedly, 'However, you have broken our grassland's rules. This affair must be resolved.'

'How shall we resolve it?' Gongzha said, looking markedly unconcerned.

His cool attitude irritated Jijia. No one out there in the wilderness disrespected him: he was always treated with fear and reverence. That was the rule. So what gave this man, this grassland wanderer, the right to look at him with such levity? 'How about this?' he said. 'We will do as we always do on the grassland: you will shoot it out on horseback, from a distance of a hundred paces, and let fate take its course.'

'Boss...' Qiangba called back, clearly annoyed.

'Alright!' Gongzha said in a low voice. At his whistle, the old brown horse that had accompanied him all those years trotted over. Gongzha mounted and without a second glance at the posse rode out into the sandy wastes.

Qiangba glanced at Yongxi with irritation. He had no option but to climb onto the back of his horse and follow suit.

Yongxi looked at the horses, standing waiting in the distance, and hurried over to Jijia. 'Why are you making them gamble their lives? Why are you so cruel? Is slaughtering antelopes not enough? Do you have to slaughter people too?'

When the men around Jijia heard Yongxi's words, they straightened up and stared at her with wide eyes. In all their years roaming the wilderness with Jijia, they'd never come across anyone who'd dared raise her voice to their boss like that. For a moment they were so shocked, they forgot they were supposed to shout her down.

'Who is it that you don't want to die?' Jijia didn't seem to mind this herder girl shouting at him at all. He was calm, as if she'd just asked him something quite unimportant.

Seeing how cool Jijia was, Yongxi spat out her reply. 'Neither of them should die. It's you that should die.' She regretted her words as soon as she'd said them. What was she doing provoking this notorious demon, the most evil man in the wilderness? If she pushed too far, it wouldn't take a genius to imagine the consequences.

'I should die?' Jijia leapt off his horse and strode angrily over to Yongxi, his whip raised ready to strike.

The other horsemen were taken aback. 'Boss, she's a woman!'

'You...' Jijia's face was livid with rage. Looking at Yongxi's impassive expression, all he wanted to do was to thrash her. He had never hit a woman, but this woman had made him incandescent with anger. In the end, the whip did not fall. Instead, he inwardly cursed this impossible woman; he wanted to pick her up and hurl her into the void.

Jijia's eyes burnt fiercely, but Yongxi showed no fear. Only heaven knew how afraid she really was and how she longed for a crevice to rush into and hide.

Jijia felt a great fire rising within him: he wanted to curse someone or even kill someone. This woman was irrational

– didn't she know he was helping her? If the conflict didn't get resolved today, those two men would be forever fighting over her and her small tent would know no peace.

'You really don't want either of them to die?'

'Of course not. Do you think I'm like you, as careless with people's lives as if they were sand or grass?'

'Am I some sort of demon to you?' Jijia's eyes blazed again. He took a step forward and glowered at Yongxi.

'Bah, a demon is a hundred times better.' Yongxi lifted her head and stared at him as she waited for the whip to fall.

Looking at her stony face, a strange new thought suddenly came into Jijia's head. It seemed this woman considered him to be beneath her; she was behaving as if he was a piece of grit, a grain of sand that she wanted to keep from getting into her eyes. What if the grain of sand were to land on her? The thought brought a cold, malicious smile to his lips. 'If you are determined that neither of them should die, we can arrange that. There is a way. But I'm not sure you'll agree to it.'

Seeing his chilly smile, Yongxi couldn't stop herself from trembling. This demon who would kill without batting an eye… who knew what kinds of torturous ideas circled in his head?

'If you're not interested, then forget about it. Let one of them die. Once one of them is dead, you'll be safe.' Jijia gave a faint smile and laughed carelessly. He turned and raised his hand, preparing to shout the signal to begin.

'No, I don't want either of them to die,' Yongxi shouted fearfully. 'Tell me, what's the alternative?'

Jijia turned his head and, paying no heed to what was happening, and without changing his expression or letting his heart race, said quietly but clearly, as if this was all just part of the plan, 'Be my woman.'

'What?' Yongxi looked at him in shock, thinking she'd misheard.

'What?' The men stared at their boss in surprise, also thinking they'd misheard.

'If you become my woman, Qiangba won't dare bother you again. As for that man, he can live.'

Yongxi rolled her eyes. 'You're so sure Gongzha will die?' she said uncooperatively.

'He's called Gongzha?' Jijia pretended not to see the look of amazement on his men's faces. He kept his eyes on Yongxi, speaking softly as if he was reasoning with an intransigent child. 'If Qiangba dies, things will be even worse for you and your grandmother. My companions are not very reasonable men; they're not going to watch their comrade die and do nothing about it, are they? Even if I help you, I can't watch them every day, and once my back is turned, they may come and find you and take their revenge.' Jijia raised his voice when he said this and added threateningly, 'Isn't that right, brothers?'

The other men knew perfectly well that even if Qiangba died, they wouldn't seek revenge. The grassland rules were clear: if a dispute was to be resolved with a fight and that fight was fairly won, that was the end of it, no matter who died. Even so, the men all nodded vigorously and shouted, 'Of course, boss, of course we'd take revenge.'

'Alright, I agree,' Yongxi shouted in despair; she couldn't bear to hear any more.

Jijia smiled and glanced at the man to his right. In tacit understanding, the man galloped off, shouting, 'Don't fire! The woman belongs to our boss. You don't need to fight!'

'What?' Qiangba turned round, his eyes as large as a yak's. 'What did you say? She's our boss's woman?'

'Our boss has taken a fancy to her, so she's our boss's woman!'

Qiangba noted his comrade's serious tone and glanced back at his boss, who seemed to be embracing the woman and smiling contentedly. He had no choice but to shoulder his gun and reluctantly ride back, his head low.

Yongxi's eyes were full of loathing. As Jijia stared into them, he kept his expression neutral, even though he was laughing inside. 'I have to go. I'll come and get you when I've taken care of my affairs. And don't forget that you agreed to be my woman. I don't like the idea of other men living in my woman's tent.' He leapt onto his horse. 'I'll come and visit you in ten days.' And with that, he whipped his horse and led the posse away. They disappeared into the distance in a flash.

The wilderness became peaceful again. Several white clouds hung from the blue curtain of the heavens. On the distant sand dunes, antelopes gazed curiously at their surrounds. Herds of yak and sheep nibbled lazily at the grass.

Yongxi's life was now quite different to what it had been. Gongzha took on all the work she used to do, so most of the time now she did nothing but churn butter or untie her plaits and redo them. What she wanted was a dependable man who could support a tent. Someone like Gongzha. Someone who would only have one woman in his heart and who would stay at his own pasture.

She sat on the sandy ground holding a small lamb, watching the figure of the man busying himself in the sunlight, a smile on her lips. How wonderful it would be if things could always be like this!

Gongzha reapplied mud to the lamb pen, fixed the holes in the tent where the wind blew in, cleared the area around the pasture, and scared away the lone wolves that were eyeing the flock. When everything was finally in order, he began to pack his things, although he didn't have much to pack. His clothes doubled as blankets, his riding boots were already on his feet, his gun was leaning next to the stove, and the powder was in its leather bag; he only had to mount his horse and then he could go.

He was worried about how to tell them he was leaving. The old woman and Yongxi had been very good to him, and his heart, which had been wandering for so long, had been touched by their warmth. Particularly Yongxi, and she'd hinted several times that Granny also hoped he might stay. It wasn't that he misunderstood what staying would mean; it was that his heart was already full, and he had no way of emptying it and filling it with a new life. He thought that if Cuomu had still been with him, he'd have felt so blessed, he wouldn't have considered taking even a single step away from their tent.

When the sun rose, Gongzha shouldered his gun and stood out on the plain staring in silence at the distant mountains, his brown horse at his side.

Yongxi was churning butter in the large wooden churn, one stroke up and one stroke down, occasionally lifting her head to look at the solitary Gongzha. The sight of his sad, lonely silhouette pained her. Was she being selfish keeping him there? His heart was not in their tent; what good was keeping his body there? She should let him go. He belonged out there in the vast wilderness. She could only hope that one day, when his body was weary and his legs weak, she would hear his steps outside her tent once again.

So that night Yongxi wrapped up the butter in a sheep's stomach, placed a freshly whetted knife in Gongzha's sheath, and said, 'Go. Go and do what you need to do.'

Gongzha nodded gratefully.

The next morning, as Gongzha was leading his horse away, the old woman came rushing out and put a leg of dried yak meat on its back. 'Child, when you are tired, come here to rest.'

He nodded.

Yongxi stood by the side of the tent, her narrow shoulders shivering in the wind. Despite all her efforts, he was still determined to leave. Would she ever see him again? Men who wandered never made plans. And even if he did return, it wouldn't be to this small tent in No Man's Land.

Gongzha mounted silently, cantered a few steps, then looked back.

The old woman had placed her hand on her forehead to shield her eyes from the sun. Yongxi was standing in front of the tent, rolling her plaits back and forth in her hand; she too was watching him. The black sheepdog was by her side, staring at the man on horseback. A light blue thread of smoke floated up from the small tent that had warmed his heart; it too was basking now, in the rays of the sun.

He whipped his horse and sped away. The pasture became as peaceful as a painting from ancient history.

16

Two Beijing Jeeps sped towards Tibet's northern wilderness. Feng's mood rose and fell as sharply as the mountains around her. Normally when she went on holiday she chose a scenic spot and went exploring – or, to be more accurate, she went touring. She sat on a luxury bus, followed the tour guide's little flag, made a charming pose once they reached the spot, and took a few commemorative photos in which the people looked more lovely than the spot itself. She was used to being in a city packed with cars and people, but here they met almost no one on the road. She'd expected there not to be many people, but she hadn't expected there to be no trace of human life for kilometres on end. She found the vastness hard to process. The sky, the mountains, the grassland and the occasional temple that flashed by seemed like a scene from a fantasy movie; it was almost too beautiful to be real.

To get to Shenzha from Lhasa, they had to go through Shigatse's Namling County. There was no public road to speak of: in the valley, everywhere was a road and nowhere was a road, so you simply had to trust your instincts and follow other people's tyre tracks. Happily, none of Feng's companions were in a hurry, so finding 'the right road' was not important. They were a troop of idle, curious children for whom the grassland was like something out of a dream.

On the first night they stayed in a small roadside rest-house in Jiacuo. They were so exhausted, they just ate some snacks and went straight to bed. The smell of yak butter on her blanket made Feng's stomach roil and the sound of her companions' snoring stopped her from falling sleep. She missed her mother's cooking, she missed her bright office, and she missed the gleaming lights of the big shopping malls. She even felt fondly towards her boss, strict task-master though he was.

She didn't know what time it was, but she couldn't sleep. She crawled out carefully from under her blanket and in the moonlight put on her shoes and windcheater and went outside. The moon shone bright and pure, and several fires were burning out on the plain. The people around the fires were speaking softly in Mandarin. Feng walked over to where four men were standing around a fire chatting.

'If I can pay off my debts by the end of the year, I'm going to go back home for a visit. I haven't been home in two years. My son won't even be able to recognise me.'

'You've only been away two years – I haven't been home for four. When I left, my daughter was only in year eight, and now she's almost finished senior school.'

'Maybe things will be a bit easier next year. Right now, going home is too hard – you have to spend more than ten days on the road.'

'It would be great if they built a railway.'

'How would you even start building a railway in a place like this?'

'Hard to say. But maybe one day the higher-ups will make the decision.'

'Ever since Old Deng went on his southern tour, the economy's really picked up – everyone and his mother has gone into business and is making money for himself.'

'Once I've finished this contract, I'd like to start my own trucking company. Driving for other people just doesn't bring in enough, especially when you've got a wife and children back home to support.'

Feng walked over and sat down beside them, stretching her hands out to warm them at the fire. 'Are you going to Shenzha? What's in your trucks?'

'We're taking gold-mining equipment to Shenzha.'

'Tibet has gold?' Feng said in surprise. She only knew Tibet as a wilderness that stretched for thousands of kilometres, an impoverished land, a place populated by Tibetans in unusual clothing, and benevolent monks. Apart from that, she knew nothing about it.

'There are lots of valuable resources here, it's just hard to get at them. The altitude's too high and there's not enough oxygen. We've been here for years and we still pant when we're walking.'

'What's the pay like, working here?' Feng asked.

'A bit better than elsewhere in China. If you drive fast, you can support a wife and kids, no problem,' one of the men said, laughing. 'Though a lot more people have come to do business here this year – Lhasa's filling up fast.'

'You're all from elsewhere?'

'Yes. I'm from Sichuan, those two are from Hunan, and he's from Shandong,' the small man next to Feng replied. 'Where are you from?'

'Shanghai. I'm on holiday.'

'Oh, you city people! What can these empty mountains possibly have for you?'

'What's Shenzha like? Is the scenery along the road nice?'

'The scenery's nice enough, it's just too short on oxygen, and there's nothing to eat and nothing to buy.'

'There's a beautiful hot spring up ahead. It's in a valley, less than twenty kilometres up the road from here,' another man said.

Feng continued chatting with them and they told her all about what Tibet had been like when they first came and what it was like now. They were proud to have seen with their own eyes how the place was gradually changing.

'You know, when I first came here, you couldn't even find a public telephone in Lhasa. And the restaurants only served food three times a day, at meal times – you couldn't get anything during the rest of the day.'

'Yes, and they used to cook with a blow torch – it sounded like a war was going on.'

'Showering was even worse. Whenever someone from back home came to Lhasa on business, if they stayed at the Friendship Hotel, we'd all go there to have a shower. Having a hot-water shower felt like being on holiday.' The Shandong man sitting opposite her laughed. 'It's much better now – you can come here on holiday. Back then, people called us crazy even for coming to work here.'

'Really?' Feng smiled, her face glowing in the firelight. Her heart had never felt so light. She couldn't remember the last time she'd had such a relaxed and spontaneous chat with someone – her work was all-consuming, and even just going out to eat with her old schoolfriends always required a lot of forward planning.

'Yes, really! It might be hard to imagine, but when we first started working in Tibet, not even the Potala Palace had locks on the door – no one stole anything. You could leave a bicycle anywhere and no one would take it. Life's improved a bit, but there are thieves now too.'

'One of the downsides of economic progress is that people get corrupted,' Feng said. 'Although when you compare Tibet with the rest of China, people here seem much more honest.'

The man next to her chuckled. 'That's true enough. I've never heard of a trucker being ripped off by his employer, for example – at worst, we just might get paid a bit late sometimes.'

It was rare for the truckers to meet a woman on the road, much less a beautiful city woman who spoke their language, so they were happy to share with Feng what they knew about Tibet. Feng herself was thrilled. In her diary, she wrote: *I never knew that people could speak so openly with each other, share their ideas so honestly. Being away from the city and all its bustle makes it easier for me to be myself. If I'm upset, I can say so. When I'm tired, I can sit down and rest; no one's watching to see how long I sit for, no one's pushing me to work harder...*

During their second day on the road, they stopped often – whenever they were passing through particularly beautiful scenery. Feng eagerly snapped photos: she'd already used up nearly half of the twenty rolls of film she'd brought with her.

'No problem. I still have at least fifty rolls – I can lend you some,' Haizi, one of her fellow travellers, said. Haizi was from Hangzhou. He was a reporter on a weekly photography magazine in the south and had been sent to Tibet on assignment.

Through his lens, Haizi focused on Feng sitting by the river. She was leaning over as she played with the water, and her long hair, braided into a single plait that reached her waist and was tied with a silk handkerchief, swung slightly as she moved. Her jade-white wrists rose and fell in the clear spring water. She had a gentle air about her that could stop people in their tracks.

He went over to her. 'Do you like Tibet?' he asked.

'I like it, but it doesn't suit me. And you?'

'The same. I don't mind coming here to take pictures, but it would be too hard to live here.'

'Let's go!' Agang called. 'We have to make it to Shenzha today.' Agang was a warm-hearted person, as simple as a child. He'd been travelling around Tibet for many years, riding his bicycle everywhere. He was very familiar with the roads and made a good guide.

Feng stood up and automatically brushed herself off, even though there was no dirt on her. She was used to sitting on expensive leather chairs and assumed that sitting on rocks or sand would make her dusty. But if that were the case, would brushing herself off with her hands make her clean?

Shenzha's county town was very small, so small that there was only one street. The car stopped at the side of the road while Agang and Haizi went with Feng to find Gongzha's work unit. They were disappointed to learn that Gongzha had resigned and gone back to his old home. As they were exiting the courtyard on their way back to the car, a Tibetan women of undiscernible age ran out. Her Mandarin had a strong local accent. 'Wait a minute, are you looking for my older brother?'

'Gongzha is your older brother?' Feng asked.

The woman nodded, blushing, and stared at her toes in embarrassment. 'I just heard that you were looking for him?'

'You're Gongzha's sister?' Feng asked gently.

'I'm called Lamu, and Gongzha is my older brother.'

'I'm Zhuo Yihang's classmate – he says that Gongzha's his uncle?'

'Yihang? I remember him. When I was little, he came to our grassland.' Lamu looked at Feng and laughed happily. 'Have you just arrived? Why don't you come and stay at my house?'

Feng glanced at Agang. He was the leader and of course she needed to take the rest of the group into consideration.

'There are lots of us. Is there room for all of us at your house?'

'There's room, there's room! Our house is very big.' Lamu was innocently eager; she just nodded energetically without asking how many people there were.

'Why don't we go and have a look? If there isn't room, we'll think of something else,' Agang said.

'Good! Good!' Lamu nodded. Without further ado, she took Feng's hand and led her into the courtyard.

Lamu's house was right at the back of the courtyard. It was a two-storey Tibetan-style home and each room was large and light. An old lady sat quietly on the veranda sunning herself.

'This is my mother; she's not well,' Lamu said. She walked over to her and said, 'Ama, we have guests; they're Yihang's schoolfriends. Do you remember Yihang? He used to send you medicine. He's Dr Zhuo's son.'

The old woman turned slowly and looked at the three young people, a flicker of recognition passing across her face. 'Ha ha, Dr Zhuo,' she murmured.

Yes, this was Dawa, the onetime beauty of Cuoe Grassland, now a grey-haired old lady. Time had treated her in the same way it treated everyone; no matter how beautiful or ugly, how rich or poor, in the end everyone got white hair, a bent back, shaky legs and missing teeth...

Perhaps the words 'Dr Zhuo' stirred some memories in Dawa's brain. She looked at Feng and suddenly said, 'Cuomu, is Gongzha good to you?'

Feng cast Lamu an inquiring look. She didn't understand Tibetan and didn't know what the old lady was saying.

'Ama, she's not Cuomu, she's a friend of Yihang's. You've forgotten, Auntie Cuomu died a long time ago.' Lamu didn't explain to Feng immediately but settled Dawa first. She tipped two pills out of a bottle and handed them to her mother. 'Take your medicine, Ama.'

Dawa swallowed her pills obediently, then turned away, stared out at the sun and fell back into her own world.

Lamu covered her with a blanket, and said, 'Mother's brain isn't quite right, although she still remembers Yihang's father. Let's go, I'll take you to see the rooms.'

So the tourist group moved into Lamu's house. They made their own food, washed their clothes, and sang and danced when they were happy. Lamu buzzed around taking care of everyone, smiling happily and singing the herders' songs that she'd learnt growing up. After Sister Cuomu died, her mother had fallen ill again, and her older brother had stopped smiling; though he'd continued to take care of the household, he remained very distant. Her three other brothers lived in the encampment. They had their own families to take care of and couldn't come to the county town very often. So Lamu and her mother were usually the only ones there, watching the rising of the lonely sun and the solitary setting of the moon.

Agang and Haizi followed the lively Lamu everywhere with their cameras, but Feng preferred to stay still. When she wasn't out and about, she sat with Dawa on the veranda. She didn't speak, just helped the old woman with her blanket and gave her her medicine when she needed it.

Sometimes when the wind picked up or the sun set behind

the mountains, Dawa would mumble to herself or cry out in distress. Feng couldn't understand her but would look into her eyes and smile, gently patting the veiny backs of her hands. Then Dawa would quieten, and, staring into the distance, would slip back into her own world again.

Lamu said that Feng would make a good doctor because her mother was as well-behaved with her as she was when the doctor was around. Lamu and Feng shared a room and the two of them often talked late into the night. Lamu told her all about how beautiful the grassland was and about the mysteries of Mount Chanaluo; she talked about the pranks Zhuo Yihang had played when he was a child and about Dr Zhuo's medical skills.

But mostly she talked about her brother and Cuomu. To Lamu, Gongzha was the best man in the world, and the love he had for Cuomu was the kind of love that every woman on the grassland dreamt of.

Wasn't that every city girl's dream too? Feng's heart began to churn as she listened to Lamu. When she heard that Cuomu had been mauled to death by a bear and that Gongzha had carried her to the funeral platform himself, she wept. She was sad that such a beautiful romance had not ended happily. Through Lamu's stories, the gun-toting wanderer crept into her heart.

When Agang heard that there was a lake like the Dead Sea in No Man's Land, he came back and raved about it, loud with excitement one minute and quietly intense the next. 'We must go and see it, it's Tibet's Dead Sea. If you throw someone in, they'll float – they can't drown.'

Hearing that, everyone else became enthusiastic too, and they began to get their luggage together, preparing to leave Shenzha the next morning. They were all excited about going to No Man's Land in search of the 'Dead Sea'.

As they were leaving, Dawa suddenly came down from the veranda, grasped Feng's hand and mumbled something.

'Mother says you must come back and bring Brother with you,' Lamu said. 'She's confusing you with Auntie Cuomu again. Will you come back, Auntie Feng?'

'Take good care of your mother, Lamu. I will definitely come back and see you all.' Feng took Dawa's thin, frail body into her arms and patted the old woman's back comfortingly.

When the car set off, Dawa chased after it, calling, 'Ah, ah.' With her grey, dishevelled hair and tottering gait, she seemed so weak and helpless. Feng felt quite upset. In their week together, she'd developed a fondness for the sometimes silent, sometimes crazy old lady.

The weather out in the wilderness was changeable. One minute it was so clear, you could see for thousands of kilometres, the next a great wind would blow, and hail would come pattering down, carpeting the ground in no time at all.

Then the fog came down, obscuring both the nearby lake and the distant mountains. They could see neither the road ahead nor the road behind them. The two cars, originally quite close together, became separated. The atmosphere in Feng's car grew tense; even Agang, who was normally very lively, stopped chatting.

Feng began to get nervous. Even though she was in her mid twenties, this was the first time she'd encountered such extreme conditions. The wild wind brought icy bullets that clattered against the car windows. The windows were not very robust and seemed as if they might break at any time. A cold gust of wind penetrated a tiny crack somewhere and chilled them to their bones. Was it safe in the car? In the face of nature at its craziest, their little metal box seemed like a small skiff out on the ocean.

Feng was afraid. In her heart, she called out to the bodhisattva, to God, Laozi and Allah, praying in her confusion. She even promised herself that if she got out of this alive, she would never come back to Tibet.

Then, what they'd hoped would not happen, happened. The car shuddered a few times and ground to a halt. The driver got out and looked at the engine. He shook his head and sighed, then asked everyone to get out of the car and help push. After two torturous hours, the car still showed no signs of starting.

They had no idea where the other car had gone.

To lose your way in northern Tibet was a terrifying thing. You could travel a whole day and on the second day discover that you were back where you'd started. Which wasn't so bad, actually – at least you knew where you were. Far more terrifying was going out at night and discovering, when the sun came up, that you recognised nothing around you and that everything looked the same, in all directions.

Everyone looked at Agang, hoping he could come up with something. He was the only one with experience of living out in the wilds, after all. Agang talked to the driver and confirmed that the car could not be fixed. They were in the hinterlands of No Man's Land and could not rely on someone coming along and helping them. 'We can't just stay here and wait to die. We'll have to get out of this ourselves,' Agang said.

Leading the way, Agang shouldered both his bag and the bag of a girl called Han and set off into the wind and the snow, leaving the car behind. The other four, including the driver, followed him.

They had no idea how long they'd been walking for or even in which direction. The needle on Agang's wrist compass wavered constantly, swinging back and forth so much, it upset them to look at it. 'There may be a mine near here that's making it deflect,' Agang said, giving them a look that was far from confident.

They had a discussion and decided to carry on along the mountain valley. But heaven and earth seemed to have fused into a single murky gloom behind the fog, rain or snow (it was hard to say which), and it was impossible to tell what was sky, what was land or where the mountains were; everything looked the same, in every direction.

The bitter wind continued to howl and the hail continued to fall. Feng drew the hood of her windcheater tightly around her head and gripped its cords. Her backpack got heavier and heavier and she felt as if her legs were filled with lead. Each step forward required an enormous effort.

Han began to cry, her tears sounding even more desperate in the wind and snow.

The day grew darker and it got harder to see the person in front or behind. Agang occasionally called the others' names and told jokes to encourage everyone. When at one point he called Feng's name loudly but no one responded, he got frightened and yelled even louder, 'Feng, Feng, where are you? Feng, answer me! Feng…'

Haizi also began to call loudly, then Han joined in tearfully, then so did everyone else…

But only the wind screamed back.

The weather in northern Tibet was like a child's face: if it decided to be clear, it cleared instantaneously. It took just a second for a blizzard to vanish and turn into a beautiful day, and the speed of the transformation was truly astonishing to anyone not used to it.

When the storm had passed, everything returned to normal beneath blue sky and white clouds. The mountains were still intact and the grass was still soft – so soft, it was like walking on a woollen blanket. Just a few hailstones remained, even though moments before they had filled the sky and tumbled in every direction. The air had become extraordinarily clear and cool and there was the merest hint of a breeze. Lakes near and far sparkled a deep blue, merging so perfectly with the deep blue sky, it was impossible to tell where the one ended and the other began. Up there on the unpopulated plateau, heaven and hell were just one tiny step apart.

A valley ran from east to west, its green grass like a mattress and its flowers like a colourful blanket spread on top.

Occasionally a large flock of sparrows flew up twittering from among the flowers, then settled again.

Feng had already walked for two days in this beautiful place. She didn't know how far she still had to go, nor did she know how much longer she could last. She continued mechanically, following the course of the valley, desperately hoping to meet someone – even a sheep would do. Alone in the middle of the desolate wilderness, carrying her bag and with very little left of the chocolate and sweets that had been sustaining her so far, she had now used up every last drop of enthusiasm. Was she going to die out here? She lifted her head and stared at the scorching sun above the mountain peak. Its rays had already dried her lips so severely they'd cracked, and her face had started to peel. Her legs felt as heavy as cement beams.

She sat forlornly by a dark blue pool. She needed to drink and she needed to regain her energy. But to what purpose? She might as well be on different planet. Which way should she go? Every direction looked the same to her. She began to curse Zhuo Yihang. If it hadn't been for him, she could have been sitting in a fancy café right now, holding a cup of warm coffee, reading or daydreaming.

Feng pulled out the chocolate and stuffed a piece into her mouth. She didn't dare eat too much; she had fewer than five pieces left, and other than that there was only a bag of candied fruit and two packets of biscuits. How long could she survive on that? As she felt the chocolate in her mouth slowly melt and disappear, tears flooded down her face.

Helpless. That was the only word Feng could think of to describe her situation. Who could ever understand how she felt unless they'd been in the same situation, with no one around for fifty or perhaps even five hundred kilometres. It was terrifying, and no amount of mesmerising scenery could change that.

When she'd cried herself out, Feng stood up. The sun was burning her face, but all around her there was not a tree she could go to for shade, not even a moderately tall blade of grass.

In that environment, almost every plant had to cling to the ground to give it a chance of survival.

As she stood beside the rippling lake, she screamed, suddenly and repeatedly. Her helpless, despairing cries spread across the wilderness, then disappeared into the nothingness.

The wind picked up, and the surface of the lake began to get choppy. That meant it must be the afternoon. After two days of walking, Feng had gained some experience. The mornings were always gentle and beautiful, but as soon as the sun passed the mountaintops, the wind would pick up and it would either snow or hail.

She lifted her water and drank a few mouthfuls. Luckily, there were lakes all over the grassland and there was no shortage of water. If there'd been no water either, in that barren place of no people and no food, she might not have even survived a day.

She might as well keep walking. If she didn't walk, what else would she do? She couldn't just sit there waiting to die. She picked up her bag and headed towards the colourful meadow, each step a trial.

In that extraordinarily beautiful, vast and lonely place, her solitary figure looked so piteous and helpless.

When the wind and snow came again, the sky darkened.

The tiny yellow tent on the west-facing slope made a poignant sight.

Feng lay inside it, gazing absently at the roof. She could sense her life slowly slipping away. Little by little, her body was getting lighter and her vision was becoming blurred. The strange thing was, she wasn't in any pain.

She thought about her mother and how she always looked so tired and stressed. Whenever Feng went home, her mother spent most of the time talking about how house prices had gone up again and how she wanted to upgrade from their sixty square metres to somewhere double the size. She would talk about how she wanted to put aside some money to help her son, who was about to graduate and start working. Or she would ask when Feng and Yang Fan were going to get married, and if they couldn't help the family a little afterwards. Feng's mother was very discontented with the way her life had panned out, blaming everything on the fact that she'd brought up two children by herself with no help from her good-for-nothing husband. But things wouldn't be like that for Feng. And if she died here, in this place as close to the heavens as it was possible to be, however much her mother complained, she couldn't come and get her.

Feng thought about Yang Fan too. Their love was like a marathon: the wedding date was often discussed and often postponed, because whenever he was close to coming home, he always had more pressing commitments, always said, 'We have plenty of time, let's wait a bit longer, give ourselves the chance to build a good foundation for our life ahead.' Then they'd wait a year before they brought up the subject again, and so it went on. The cycle of uncertainty had made Feng's heart numb. She started to see their wedding date as an entrancing mirage: beautiful but unreal.

She thought about Zhuo Yihang, her best friend, a man who was like a brother to her. He'd often spoken to her of Tibet, of the Potala Palace in Lhasa, of the Guge Kingdom in Ngari. He said that Tibet was heaven, the last pure place on earth. Now she was lying on the pure ground he'd described, waiting for the last moment of her life.

It was alright; it would be alright to go like this. When she thought about going, Feng was surprised to find herself smiling. She would never again have to work day and night writing interminable reports, never have to worry about whether her dress would clash with her co-worker's shirt, never have to see her mother's hurt expression, never have to remind herself to say, 'I love you.'

With the end now in sight, Feng had never felt so relaxed.

Was the snow outside very thick? Looking at the odd shape

of her tent, Feng thought it must be. Had the wolves come too? As a lonesome howl sounded in her ear, she was surprised she wasn't afraid. In idle moments in the past, when she'd wondered how she might meet her end – through illness, or in a car accident, a plane crash or a boating disaster – she'd never imagined she might die on the Qinghai–Tibet Plateau in the jaws of a wolf.

The howls began to sound one after the other. Even before dawn broke, the strange cries of the vultures started up too. Wolves, vultures – they were the most sensitive creatures on the grassland; they could always tell when something was about to die, ready to snatch their food at the first opportunity.

The sun had not yet risen and a half moon still hung over the mountain. As its clear rays hit the snowy, silvery ground, it gave off a pale, cold light. On this ominous morning, how long could the lonely tent last?

17

After Gongzha left, Yongxi's life reverted to how it had been before: milking, herding and churning, with one day much like the next. In the infinite wilderness that was No Man's Land, there were plenty of yaks, bears and wolves; the one thing in short supply was men.

She couldn't get out of her head the image of Gongzha's departing figure against the plume of dust kicked up by his horse. She had so wanted him to stay, so wanted to help wipe the sadness from his face, the depth of which, in spite of her efforts, she still didn't understand. She knew he wouldn't be coming back.

Distracted by her thoughts, Yongxi had failed to notice that her yak herd had grown to include two enormous wild yaks. She did see, though, that four of her female yaks had wandered off. She tossed her plaits over her shoulders, took out her slingshot and hurled a stone in their direction.

Two yaks in the centre of the herd suddenly lifted their heads. Their round eyes fixed on Yongxi, their backs stiffened, and she could tell they were about to charge. She was startled. Wild yaks! How could there be two wild yaks in among her herd?

Knowing she had no time to lose, she leapt onto her horse, yanked the reins and headed for a nearby slope to get a better view of the herd in the valley. She frowned. The dog kept darting over to the herd and barking, but the wild bulls were unperturbed. They didn't even look at him, just pawed the ground and raised their heads ready to chase him when his barks annoyed them. The dog ran off and the wild bulls returned to the herd.

The domesticated bulls could only look on as the two massive wild bulls made a play for their mates. Yongxi, too, could only look on. Like most people, she was too scared to try and chase them off; usually the herders just had to wait until the mating season was over and the bulls left of their own accord. Yongxi's main concern was that the wild males would drive away the domesticated bulls. Yaks had long legs and when they were determined to go somewhere, there was really no way of stopping them.

Just after noon one day, Yongxi was nestled in a grassy dip when she heard the dog barking with unusual urgency. She raised her head and, as feared, saw that the two wild bulls were leading four of her domesticated females up the slope towards the snowline. She quickly grabbed her meat bag and mounted her horse. With a crack of the whip, she and the dog chased after them.

She was no match for those two enormous creatures; all she could do was circle round in front of them and try and drive them, along with the four females, back to the herd. The bulls were not at all concerned by the girl so bravely trying to block their way. They simply lifted their heads, bellowed and charged. The females trotted along unhurriedly behind them, occasionally nibbling on the blades of grass poking up through the light covering of snow on the mountainside.

As the wild bulls led the females further and further away, Yongxi got so upset, she wanted to cry. If she had a man, today's tragedy would never have happened. She shouted for the dog to pursue them and cut them off. The sun was fierce and its rays scorched her forehead. She wiped away her tears, whipped her horse, and resumed the chase in defiance.

Just then, a figure on horseback appeared on the snowy mountain ridge and fired a shot at the two bulls. The bulls could afford not to fear Yongxi because they'd understood that she couldn't do anything to hurt them. But a person with a gun was different. At the sound of the gunshot, the two bulls spread their legs and tore off in a different direction, without giving a second thought to the females behind them.

The domesticated females did not run. When they heard the shot, they simply looked up with momentary curiosity, then returned to their grazing. The dog immediately charged forward and encouraged them back down towards the rest of the herd, barking and leaping.

The man who'd fired the shot had his back to the sun, so Yongxi couldn't see who he was. Perhaps he was from one of the tents in the area, had come out hunting and just happened to have been in a position to help her? She reined in her horse and waited for him to gallop over.

When eventually she could see his face, she saw that he wore an evil smile. It was Jijia.

'You…! What are you doing here?' Yongxi said, furious.

'I came to see you, of course. I told you I would, didn't I?' He grinned, seemingly unconcerned by her reaction.

'Why would you need to come and see me? I'm doing fine – what is there to see?' Yongxi threw him a cold stare. She would have loved to have thrashed that smug smile off his face with her whip. If it hadn't been for him, Gongzha would still be in her tent. What had she done to deserve this?

'You're my woman – you're supposed to be happy when your man comes back.' Jijia took a couple of steps forward and seemed surprised.

'Your woman…?' Yongxi said. 'You're dreaming!' She turned her horse and sped down the mountainside.

'You are my woman – I'm serious,' Jijia said. But Yongxi didn't hear him.

He watched with narrowed eyes as she disappeared into the distance. She really was quite something – the only woman on the grassland who saw him as nothing special. Other women were either so frightened of him, they trembled as soon as they saw him, as if he were some sort of demon, or they flirted with him, hoping he'd become a regular visitor to their tent.

Jijia took up the reins and dashed after her, his horse's hooves kicking up a cloud of snow.

When she got back to the pasture, Yongxi took out the teapot and prepared to make tea. Jijia was only minutes behind her. Seeing her outside her tent, he jumped off his horse, swept her into his arms and, without thinking, covered her lips with his. Something stirred deep in his heart. The sweet taste of her soft lips kindled an almost insatiable desire and he squeezed her even more tightly, wanting to merge their two bodies into one.

He only released her when he felt he was about to run out of air. He was surprised to see Yongxi's eyes were wide with distaste, as if something horrible had happened. He'd only kissed her – did she really need to be that frightened? He patted her oval face. 'Can't you just enjoy it a little, woman?'

'Aaaahhh!' Yongxi finally recovered herself and jumped back with a yell. She darted into her small tent and pulled the flap tight shut.

As Jijia unconsciously licked his dry lips and tasted the sweetness of her mouth again, he couldn't help but smile. He polished off a cup of tea, then lifted the shiny silver pot to pour himself another.

He'd come there without telling anyone. His comrades probably thought he'd gone to pay his respects to the Buddha. Whenever he completed a deal, he either made a pilgrimage to Mount Kailash or one of the sacred lakes, or he went to the temple to meditate. Sometimes he took two or three men with him, sometimes he went by himself. This time he'd gone by himself, and his journey was not for the Buddha but for a woman deep in the wilderness.

Jijia watched as the fireball sank behind the mountaintops. Stripes of orange light streaked the ground. It had been a long time since he'd sat so quietly and watched the sun set. He was always busy: busy killing, busy making money, busy drinking, busy sending people out to find the next herd of Tibetan antelopes to poach. And so the cycle continued, leaving him with neither the time nor even the energy to sit and watch the setting sun.

Simply sitting there quietly beside a tent, contemplating the peaceful scene in front of him, was surprisingly enjoyable. If he had a woman and then a couple of kids, and if he raised a herd of yaks and sheep, he would no longer have to live in fear, would no longer have to live life on the run. A smile floated across his lips. She couldn't be sleeping, surely – why was it so quiet in there?

He walked over and opened the tent flap. She was sitting napping on a cushion, her head bobbing and her shoulders slumped. Hearing a noise, her head jerked up, and when she saw it was Jijia, fear flashed through her eyes. In a split second, she grabbed her knife, slashed at the fabric behind her, ripped a large hole in her tent and climbed through it. Her movements were as nimble as a rabbit's and Jijia watched dumbstruck from the doorway. He didn't know whether to laugh or cry at the hole through which the wind now howled.

What kind of woman was this, that she was as clever as a fox? He crawled into the tent, stuck his head through the hole and saw Yongxi standing outside staring at him, ready to run in an instant. He smiled kindly, the sort of smile he usually reserved for small children. He had no idea that on his face such a smile just made him look more malicious. 'I'm not going to eat you. What are you running away for?'

Yongxi continued staring at him, her right hand clasping her knife, terrified he was about to rush at her. 'Get out of there. It's my tent.'

'Fine, fine. It's your tent. You come back in – I'll get out!' Jijia withdrew his head, backed out of the tent and walked round towards her. How was he to know she would hop back in through the hole?

Looking at the spot where she'd been standing only a moment before, he sighed and shook his head. Then he took out his whip and walked over to the yak herd. The herding dog was also clever; it knew Jijia knew its mistress, so it cooperated with him. Together they drove the yaks to a small valley out of the wind; then the dog lay on the ground and watched to make sure the yaks didn't head off again. Jijia took a piece of dried meat from his bag, petted the dog's head, and threw it the meat. The dog gave a low growl and licked his hand.

Yongxi, meanwhile, had crawled to the side of the tent and stealthily pulled the flap open a crack. When she saw Jijia looking her way, she snorted and let the flap fall back into place.

Late that night, Yongxi, wrapped in her blanket, was frightened awake by a swishing sound outside her tent. A silver needle was weaving in and out of the fabric in the corner where she'd slashed the large hole. Clearly, Jijia was outside fixing it. Her heart couldn't help softening a little; she could see that he was a meticulous man. But she made no sound, and let him suffer on the outside.

Jijia had never imagined that one day he might establish a tent and share his life with a woman. But as he sat under the star-filled sky, it suddenly occurred to him that it would be a fine thing to watch over this herd of yaks and this tent. It was a scary thought, so he stole another look at the small tent. Only when he heard the quiet, even sound of Yongxi's breathing did he turn back and continue to look at the starry sky and dream.

At night, Gongzha usually just looked for a grassy hollow out of the wind. With his *chuba* wrapped around him, the chill didn't bother him.

Once, ten minutes after midnight, he heard the lone howl of a wolf not far off. At first he assumed that it had found food and was calling its comrades, so he thought nothing of it. But the wolf's howl became louder and louder, especially as daybreak approached. He also saw a flock of vultures circling overhead. Vultures were the sign-bearers of the grassland. Wherever they appeared, something below had died or was about to die.

Although the wolf howl repeated, this was not a sign for attack. Although the vultures circled, they weren't descending. This was unusual; it meant that their target was still alive or at least was still exhibiting some signs of life. Wolves would not waste their energy on an unnecessary fight, and vultures would not prey on a living creature.

What kind of animal was about to die – ass, yak, antelope? Gongzha was curious. He looked at the sky. It was already turning red in the east, so he opened his *chuba* and stood up. He whistled for his horse, took up his gun, mounted, bag in hand, and galloped off to where the vultures were circling.

From quite a way off, he could see the small yellow tent on the mountainside and the wolves circling it. He was shocked. This was the depths of No Man's Land and he hadn't seen a human being for many days. What was a city camper's yellow tent doing there? He raised his gun and shot one of the wolves that was in the middle of howling. Seeing that the horseman speeding towards them had a gun, the other wolves fled, legs splayed, and disappeared in a flash over the ridge.

When Gongzha reached the tent, he leapt off his horse, pulled down the zip of the door flap, and saw that a Han woman was lying there in a sleeping bag. Her face was deathly white and several large bubbles were forming at her lips. He called to her twice, but she didn't reply. She didn't even move. It seemed she'd fallen unconscious from altitude sickness. Gongzha crawled into the tent and felt her nose. She was still breathing faintly. He searched in his *chuba* for a small bottle, poured out two sugar tablets and stuffed them into her mouth. Then he went outside, scooped up a handful of snow, melted it and fed it to the woman.

He knelt by the door of the tent and looked out. The tent had been pitched halfway up the mountain facing west, but the wind was strong and it wasn't a good spot. He carried the woman out in her sleeping bag and laid her on the ground. Then he strapped her tent and her bag onto his horse and mounted with the woman in his arms. He wanted to find somewhere on flat ground for her to rest.

When they got to a valley, Gongzha laid her down on the grass, put up her tent, spread out his sheepskin *chuba* inside it, then took her out of the sleeping bag and wrapped her in it. Next he took a bottle from her backpack, found a spring and fed her some water. Once her breath had become less ragged, he left her in the tent and laid her sleeping bag out in the sun.

In the afternoon, Gongzha went in to look at her. Her colour had improved and he fed her two more sugar tablets.

Feng was muddled that whole day. In her dreams she was sometimes in Shanghai and sometimes on the grassland, and she thought she might be dying. Later, she tasted something sweet seeping into her parched mouth. She didn't know what it was, but she swallowed it instinctively.

After that she was soaring; she seemed to be in a warm embrace, like when her mother had held her as a child. And then? Then it was as if her body was somehow unwrapped and she was lying on something as soft as clouds.

And after that... After that she couldn't remember anything!

When she woke, it was already the morning of the next day. Her finger twitched, then twitched again. Her body slowly shivered, then shivered again. All of the bones in her body hurt, but the pain told her that she was still alive, that she hadn't become food for either the wild wolves or the starving vultures out in the wilderness. She wanted to sit up, but she didn't have the strength. She opened her eyes and took in everything around her.

She was still in her little yellow tent. She was still alive. She hadn't died. Feng flicked her eyes back and forth. She didn't know if she should think herself lucky or if she should cry bitter tears. She was alone and out in the wilds – she might be alive right now, but what about tomorrow, and the day after that?

Just then, someone unzipped the tent flap. A bearded man appeared outside and, using rather basic Mandarin, asked, 'Awake you? How feel?'

'Was it you who rescued me?' Feng's tears fell uncontrollably. Another human being at last!

'Yesterday morning found you. Unconscious you, altitude sickness had, ate my medicine, sugar tablets.' His word order in Mandarin was sometimes incorrect. He didn't smile but lowered his head, came into the tent and half knelt by her side. He shook two black tablets out of his medicine bottle, propped her up with one hand, put the tablets in her mouth, helped her to a couple of mouthfuls of water from the bottle next to her, then supported her as she lay back down, and covered her with the sheepskin *chuba* again. 'Your sleeping bag not let air out. Can't use here.'

When he finished, he turned to crawl back out.

'Wait,' Feng called softly. She was afraid he might leave and not return. She'd already gone several days without speaking to anyone and she was longing to talk to another human being. 'What's your name?'

'Gongzha.'

'Gong... Gongzha?'

Gongzha didn't understand why Feng was so surprised by his name. He looked at her inquiringly.

'Do you have a friend called Zhuo Mai? With a son called Zhuo Yihang?'

Gongzha stared at her in surprise. 'I do, yes. You know them?'

Feng's tears began to flow again. Zhuo Yihang had told her to go and find Gongzha, promising that he would introduce her to the real Tibet, would show her how people lived up on the plateau, take her to see wild animals in their natural habitat. She had certainly had a taste of the real Tibet, not to mention its animals in their natural habitat – enough to almost cost her her life.

Gongzha felt quite helpless. He was more afraid of seeing women cry than of many things; when women cried, he never knew what to say. 'You... what you fear is not. You are not that sick. Not accustomed to here is your body. Once you have medicine, you fine.'

'I'm a schoolfriend of Zhuo Yihang's. It was he... He's the one who told me to come and look for you.' Feng was racked with sobs; the trauma of her experience was finally catching up with her. 'He said you would take me to see the wild yaks and the Tibetan antelopes. I went to your house in the county town and I saw your sister Lamu and your mother Dawa.'

'You saw Lamu?'

'Yes. We all stayed at your house for quite a few days.' Feng was sobbing now, overcome with distress.

'You all? But I only see you!'

'Our car broke down and it was snowing and we got separated.'

'Where did it break down?'

'I don't know. I don't know which road.'

'We need to find them. They danger have.' Gongzha looked at Feng with an earnest expression on his face. 'Meat more eat, you heal faster. Tomorrow find them go we.'

Feng dried her eyes and nodded. When Gongzha saw she'd stopped crying, he closed the tent flap.

That night, Feng felt a little better. She dressed and climbed out of the tent. Gongzha was nearby, roasting some kind of meat on a stick over a fire; its delicious aroma filled her nose. When he saw Feng, he cut off a chunk and passed it to her.

Feng accepted it and took a bite; her mouth was flooded with flavour. 'What meat is this?'

'*Guagua* chicken.'

'Wild chicken?'

'Yes. Mountain opposite are many. Hit a few.' Gongzha rotated the stick over the flames while adding twigs and yak pats to the fire. 'Zhuo Mai and Yihang, well?'

'Yihang is alright; his business isn't doing badly, but his father passed away.'

'Zhuo Mai... is dead?'

'Yes, he died two months before I came here.' Feng looked up at him. 'The meat's burning!' she said hurriedly.

Gongzha was distracted, thinking about Zhuo Mai, remembering him with his guitar, how the skinny young Han doctor used to sit there singing to the moon. They were about the same age – how could he have left this earth? He hadn't even realised the stick of meat in his hand had caught fire. He snatched it out of the flames and glanced at it. The meat was charred, so he tossed it away and began roasting a new chunk over the flames.

'You and Uncle Zhuo must have been good friends?'

'When he was in the army, he often came to the grassland to take care of the herders.'

'When I was little, Uncle Zhuo often told us about Tibet. He loved eating Tibetan mushrooms best. He'd asked some friends to send him some, but he died before they arrived.'

'How did he die?'

'Heart disease. A doctor told him his heart had become acclimatised to the high altitudes of the plateau and that he would have to adjust his lifestyle now that he was back in the city. But he just carried on working as hard as ever, almost as if he wanted to die. He didn't look after himself at all.'

Gongzha didn't respond, just stared into the fire. Last year, Zhuo Mai had written to him and promised that once he retired he would come back and visit the grassland. He'd also said that his work unit was based very near Shida's and that the two of them often went drinking together and talked a lot about life on the grassland. He'd envied them then, old friends together, laughing about their shared past. How nice that must have been. These days, Gongzha had no one he could talk to, and even if he had, no young person could possibly understand what life had been like for him and his friends.

'Zhuo Yihang said that he lived on your grassland when he was young?' Feng said, trying to find something to say.

Gongzha nodded. 'He was very young then. Wherever Zhuo Mai went, he went too.'

Feng gazed at Gongzha's face in the firelight. She thought for a moment, then asked, 'Why did you come here?'

'I came to find a bear.'

'Kaguo?' Feng said, remembering Lamu's story.

'Lamu told you?' Gongzha handed her the roasted meat.

'Yes.' Feng nodded. 'You should eat too.'

'I'm eating this,' Gongzha said, using his knife to put a hunk of raw, bloody meat into his mouth. 'You Han like to eat cooked meat.'

As Feng watched him nonchalantly sawing at the meat and wolfing it down enthusiastically even though his knife was streaked with blood, she suddenly felt terrified. What kind of person was this? He seemed so wild. Her stomach began to heave and she hurried away from the fire and threw up what she'd just eaten.

'What is the matter? Feeling uncomfortable, are you?' Gongzha went over and handed her the kettle.

'I'm fine.' Feng waved him away, took the bottle and gulped down several mouthfuls.

That sudden burst of fear had petrified her and she scurried straight back into her tent. Zhuo Yihang had told her that Tibetans ate raw meat, but she'd thought he'd meant the wind-dried yak and mutton like they served at the Tibetan restaurants in Lhasa, or like they'd had at Lamu's house; when you dipped it in hot pepper, it wasn't that bad. She certainly hadn't imagined that Gongzha would eat meat that was still dripping blood.

Gongzha returned to the fire. 'You want more meat?' he asked, raising his voice a little, a smile playing on his lips.

'No!' Feng shot back immediately. She buried herself in the lambskin *chuba* as if Gongzha might want to eat her too.

In the middle of the night, Feng heard Gongzha singing a Mandarin song over and over again.

'Today I must go to a faraway land
When we parted you said, "Please don't forget me."
Our promise hangs high in the sky
Those white clouds, those stars, that moon
Bear witness to our promise that in the next life we
    will meet again
And never forget each other.

'Beautiful shepherdess, I love you
No matter how the world changes, you are forever in my
    heart.
Beautiful shepherdess, your laughter echoes under the blue
    sky
And deep in my heart.

'Oh, give me a tent
I want to take your hand and live together free of pain.
Oh, give me some land
I want to dance with you there, slowly and forever.

'Shepherdess, sweet shepherdess
When will you return and make our love run smooth?
My greatest hope is not to be separated
Has our love in this life already scattered?
Could it be that loving you brings only despair?
Every day without you is a tragedy.'

The waning moon hung over the empty, never-ending wilderness and the silhouette of its mountain peaks. The stars glittered in the sky. Beneath them lay a solitary tent, the glow of a dying fire and a song of ageless sorrow.

Nyima County was the first place to see the sun set and the first to see the moon rise; it was the place nearest to the heavens and furthest from the sea. It was the highest point on the roof of the world. Rongma was the most remote town in Nyima County and the closest to No Man's Land. It comprised just a few mud-brick homes with dirt roads running between them and was usually very quiet, as quiet as the old yaks lying by the outside walls, too lazy even to look up. Occasionally an old lady might come out of one of the houses carrying a water bucket as she emerged into the light, a babbling grandchild or a lamb following behind.

But today the quiet little town was bursting with energy. A big crowd of herders in old sheepskin *chubas* had assembled in the large, simple courtyard in front of the county government office. A man in a police uniform emerged from a squat building and addressed them. 'Please, everyone, make as much effort as you can over the next two days and search again carefully. We cannot let that young woman die in the wilderness.'

Agang, Haizi and the others had come to Rongma to report Feng missing.

The herders lowered their heads and bowed their agreement. They split into their pre-arranged groups, collected their horses from the entrance and headed off.

Beyond that range of mountains lay No Man's Land, and every herder feared it.

The midday sun beat fiercely down on the browned earth.

The two people and the horse walked slowly.

Gongzha was in front, leading the horse; his *chuba*, the bags of dried meat and the backpack were strapped onto the horse's back. Feng followed behind, wearing Gongzha's leather hat. It was a bit big for her, and she had to push it off her face occasionally. She carried the gun in her right hand, its forked stand dragging in the dirt and tracing two meandering lines through the dust.

They needed to cross the snow mountain.

'How much longer do we have to walk?' Feng asked listlessly.

She fiddled with some strands of hair around the brim of the hat and raised her head to look at the sun.

'About two hours.' Gongzha wound the reins around his hand twice so that the horse would stand closer.

'Can we rest for a bit? I'm so tired.'

Gongzha glanced back at her. 'Not yet,' he said lightly. 'We need to cross the mountain before the sun reaches its full height, otherwise it will be too warm and there might be an avalanche.'

'My face hurts.' Feng pushed up her sunglasses and shook the snow from her leg.

'Your skin's peeling. It'll be fine in a few days.'

'I'm peeling? Really?' Feng unconsciously touched her hand to her face.

Gongzha didn't reply.

'It'll be so annoying if it tans unevenly,' Feng complained. 'How will I face people when I get back?'

'Oh, you Han women! What's more important: your life or your face? Look around the grassland – all the women have patches on their faces. That's the gift the sun gives our women. Having that gift is what makes her a grassland woman.'

'The gift the sun gives to your women? That's interesting.' Feng laughed. 'But the problem is that I'm not a grassland woman. I'm from Shanghai, a large, sophisticated city. I couldn't possibly walk into my office building wearing the sun's gift.'

Gongzha glanced back at her in amusement. 'Your work involves your face?'

'There's no direct connection, but it would affect my mood.'

'The place you're from sounds strange.'

'Maybe you just don't like beautiful women?'

'As long as they're healthy, I'm happy!' Gongzha said.

'Healthy like your grassland women, with their deeply tanned skin and sun-scarred faces, who laugh loudly when they're happy? No, Gongzha, Shanghai wouldn't tolerate that sort of woman. What Shanghai requires is fashionable, cultivated women.'

Gongzha stayed silent. Shanghai – that was a world he didn't understand. Zhuo Mai used to say that you could buy anything there for money, except for the love he sought. Gongzha thought about how his own love had floated off with Cuomu's spirit to Shambhala. What about Zhuo Mai's love? He had never married. His love must still be on the grassland.

'No Man's Land is so vast,' Feng said, searching for something to talk about, 'how will you find Kaguo?'

'Eagles drop feathers when they fly overhead; bears leave prints when they walk,' Gongzha replied.

'But this place is so big!'

'I'm a hunter. I know the kinds of places bears like to go.'

'But even if you kill your bear, it won't bring Cuomu back.'

Hearing Feng's comment, Gongzha stiffened, stood straighter and lengthened his stride, ignoring Feng as she scampered along behind him, huffing like a cow.

Feng regretted her words as soon as she'd said them. Cuomu was a very deep wound in Gongzha's heart and she should have kept well away. How could she have exposed his hurt like that? She hurried after him, yelling, 'I'm sorry, Gongzha, I didn't mean to say that.'

The two of them walked on in silence after that. The only sound in the vast wilderness was the crunch of their feet on the snow.

Finally they came to a pass. Fresh, cool air rushed in on the wind. Beneath them, at the foot of the mountain, a valley stretched into the distance. Because it had snowed the day before, mist was still rising off it, and a blanket of vividly coloured flowers extended in all directions, laid down between the mountain and the valley. A small, misty lake occupied the centre of the valley, like a piece of fine jade hanging just so on a young woman's pale neck.

Feng widened her eyes in excitement and shouted, 'It's gorgeous! Is this really No Man's Land? I've never seen such a beautiful place, Gongzha. Look at that lake – how can it be that beautiful? Heaven put the most stunning scenery on earth where almost no one can see it – it's so unfair!'

Gongzha narrowed his eyes and gazed down at the base of the mountain, but he didn't say anything. A gust of cold air blew his long hair behind him.

'Are you still angry? I've already told you I didn't mean to say what I did, but let me apologise again. I'm sorry.' Feng looked at him, standing expressionless on the snowy ground with the reins in his hand, and she very deliberately made a deep bow, all the way to ninety degrees.

'I'm not angry.' Gongzha looked away. 'Let's go!' And he led the horse onwards.

Feng stuck out her tongue and made a face behind his back. His words really were precious like gold dust.

When they got to the shore of the small lake, Gongzha unloaded the supplies off the horse, took off the reins and slapped the horse's rump, leaving it to walk away swishing its tail.

He took up his gun, looked around and saw that there were several deer in the distance. 'There are quite a few dried yak pats around,' he said. 'You collect some.' Then he walked off with his gun in a different direction.

Feng stared after him in incomprehension. Was he going hunting? But the deer were in the other direction! She took off her windcheater and put it on the ground. Wearing only her grey polo-neck sweater, she began to collect yak pats. In the last few days, she'd learnt quite a few things about wilderness living from Gongzha, including how to distinguish between the pats of wild and domesticated yaks.

Feng carried some pats back, threw them down next to their luggage, and then went back to gather some more. She had soon collected quite a large pile and saw that she had enough. She sat down on the black pebbles of the shore and turned to watch Gongzha in the distance. He'd crouched down and was slowly making his way along a low ridge towards where the deer were playing, stopping every few steps. The deer occasionally looked up cautiously at him, but when they saw that he wasn't moving, they lowered their heads again. Feng didn't dare laugh; after all, he was an experienced hunter and must know what he was doing.

A shot sounded and a deer fell to the ground. The other deer immediately fled.

A short while later, Gongzha returned, carrying the deer. Feng went smiling to meet him and helped with the deer's hind legs. 'Your aim was spot on, Gongzha! You really are a crack shot.'

Gongzha smiled thinly. He laid the deer down on the shore, got out his knife and began to skin it. He made an expert job of it and in barely any time had cleaned off the meat. Then he used the flint hanging from his waist to strike a spark and light some oily paper, which he held to some dry grass he'd collected. After he'd piled on the yak pats, the fire slowly began to take hold. Once the flames were hot enough, he pulled out the bag of salt he always carried, put it to one side, speared the meat on his knife and roasted it, adding salt every so often. When he'd finished, he handed the meat to Feng, whose mouth was watering. She took it and stuffed it into her mouth like a ravenous wolf.

Finally, Feng patted her belly and shook her head, saying, 'I don't want any more! If I eat another mouthful, I'll explode. You go ahead and eat.'

Gongzha stopped the roasting and began cutting off hunks of raw deer meat and putting them straight into his mouth, not even adding salt.

Feng willed her roiling stomach to settle, but her brow furrowed. 'Do you always eat meat that way?' she asked. After the first night, when she'd thrown up from watching him eat, she'd got into the habit of going elsewhere during his meals, but now she'd got to the point where she could watch, albeit with discomfort. It had been a painful process.

'Meat is supposed to be eaten this way,' Gongzha said, putting another piece of raw flesh into his mouth.

'But... it's very unhygienic!'

'Unhygienic?' Gongzha looked at her with amusement. 'The meat grows on the deer and is protected by skin – how could it not be clean? If you remove the meat and put it into water, you're adding any bacteria that are in the water; and when you roast it, you're adding ash. It's only unclean after it's been exposed to different pollutants. That's what your Dr Zhuo himself said.'

Feng thought about it. There was a logic to what he said. Fresh meat was clean to begin with but became unclean as soon as it passed through human hands.

'When you eat it like that, with no flavouring, does it taste good?'

'Meat has a naturally good flavour. If you add other things, it doesn't taste good.' Gongzha's Mandarin had got much more fluent in these last few days and he now rarely made mistakes with his word order.

'You're... you're just like one of the wild wolves!' Feng suddenly said, looking at Gongzha's full beard and his eyes deep as lakes.

Gongzha laughed and wiped his mouth. 'A wild wolf... I suppose so. Look around you – there are no humans out here, but a wolf can live quite well.'

Feng looked at Gongzha and her heart fluttered. This wild man represented a real challenge to her way of looking at things, and even to the way she led her life. Were the things she had always taken for granted really so unassailable? Like that you couldn't eat raw meat, or that you couldn't touch food unless you'd washed your hands, or that only a pale face wearing a lot of make-up was beautiful? She even found him handsome. Did a man need to be in a suit and nice shoes and wearing a few drops of cologne to make him attractive? How could this tanned and dusty man who ate raw meat, expressed happiness when he felt it and kept silent when he did not, *not* be attractive?

Gongzha withdrew his gaze from the wilderness and saw that Feng was staring at him. 'What is it? Did I say something wrong?'

Feng beamed, then blushed and turned her eyes to the rippling surface of the lake. A pair of wild geese were chasing each other across it. 'No. Quite the opposite.' She didn't know why, but when he looked at her, her heart raced.

18

Deepest No Man's Land. It had no name and no sign to identify it. The entire region looked pretty much the same: there were blue skies, snow mountains, plains, lakes.

As the sun shone warmly upon it, all was still and quiet, so apparently lifeless that it hardly seemed part of the human world.

Gunshot! A battery of gunshots. Gunshots that seemed inappropriate in such a tranquil place.

'You two go over and block the right side. If a single antelope gets away, you'll lose a finger,' Jijia said icily to the two men next to him. They were standing on a slope, watching the now surrounded antelope herd below.

The men acknowledged him and turned their horses to the right. They fired two shots, driving the antelopes who were straying back to the holding area.

Jijia stared contentedly at the frightened, bleating animals. A cruel smile hung on his lips: it was as if he was watching an enormous pile of gold accumulating in front of him.

A male antelope suddenly darted out from between the two horses on the right, its long horns dancing in the sun. Jijia opened fire. *Ping!* The antelope didn't even get twenty metres before it fell to the ground, blood bubbling from its neck.

Jijia rested his gun on his shoulder and fixed the two horsemen below him with a chilly stare. The men looked up with bleak faces; when they met Jijia's gaze, they blanched, and large beads of sweat appeared on their foreheads. They slowly drew their knives, a cold light glancing off the blades, and their little fingers fell into the dust with a thump.

Jijia twitched the corner of his mouth in satisfaction, shivered and looked away. Holding his gun in one hand, he fired the first shot at the antelopes desperately seeking a way out of the poachers' ring. That was the signal for the real slaughter to begin.

Without missing a beat, the men positioned on the surrounding slopes took aim and let off a volley of gunfire. As the shots popped and sizzled like so many frying beans, the entire herd fell. Not a single Tibetan antelope escaped.

The cloying stench of blood drifted on the breeze and vultures began to circle overhead.

Three baby antelopes bleated beside the body of their dead mother, tragic and helpless. Jijia lifted his gun and nonchalantly fired at one of them. It tumbled onto its mother's body before it could make another sound, its large eyes still wide open.

The men cheered with excitement and the air was shrill with wild whistles as they cantered their horses back and forth. For a brief time, that bloody valley in the depths of the northern Tibetan wilderness was as terrifying as hell.

The wind picked up, and the sand began to whirl and dance in vortexes.

As the evening sun reddened the sky, two figures stood staring at the blood-soaked ground and the litter of skinned antelope corpses.

'How can they be so cruel? These were living creatures!' said the woman in the yellow windcheater, her long hair streaming out behind her.

'Human greed knows no limits.' The bearded man watched as the rays of the setting sun lit the skinless antelopes; his face betrayed no emotion.

'And no one cares what they do?'

'I hear the government is drafting a law to protect wild animals. When I was small, there were many herds of Tibetan antelopes on the grassland. Now there are fewer and fewer.'

'Ohhh...' The woman walked over to the two baby antelopes; their frail bodies were trembling and they looked around with fear-widened eyes. 'Can we take them with us?'

The man nodded, took one and walked off, the woman following behind.

In another valley with mountains on three sides and a lake on the fourth stood a scattering of tents. Several horses rambled between them, occasionally lowering their heads in search of one of the rare blades of grass. The place looked beautiful because of the mountains, tents and horses, but it also looked odd because there was no sign of human activity.

Several yak-skin boats were travelling across the lake, getting closer and closer. When it became clear that the men in them had cheerful expressions on their faces, the women came darting out of the tents.

'They're back! Do you know how many they killed?'

'According to Qiangba, they got quite a large herd.'

'This time I'm going to get my man to buy me a pair of gold bracelets. Tell Yangji to quickly stew some meat – the men will be starving.'

Another woman poked her head out of a small tent, and a lovely graceful young girl followed close behind. The woman was Yangji, Ciwang's daughter, from Cuoe Grassland, and the girl was her daughter. The girl had her mother's face and Shida's eyes.

Yangji glanced at the far side of the lake and then at the shore, where the men and women were laughing excitedly together. She frowned, turned and walked over to one of the large tents. Inside, a great pot was steaming on the sizeable stove. She threw several yak pats onto the fire, then ladled the boiling tea water into the tea churn. Taking several large lumps of butter from a bamboo basket, she dropped them into the churn and began to mix the tea. She did all of this with practised hands and an expressionless face. She'd been doing that sort of work for a long time.

Everyone on Cuoe Grassland had assumed Yangji was dead, likely eaten by wolves. Shida, feeling responsible, had left the grassland out of guilt, unable to forget her. Yangji had indeed encountered a pack of wolves when she fled the grassland in the middle of the night all those years ago. She lost her way and stumbled into No Man's Land. But, luckily, Jijia had rescued her just in time. He'd taken a crew into that area to kill antelopes and had heard the wolf howls. Because Yangji had no desire to return to Cuoe Grassland and see Shida, she'd gone with the shadow hunters back to their encampment and became their cook.

A few months later, she gave birth to a daughter on the sandy shore of the lake. When she saw how much the child resembled a certain person, her tears rained down. She looked at the pale blue water of the lake and told the old woman who'd helped deliver the baby, 'I'll call her Dawacuo. I hope she'll be as beautiful and healthy as the moon and the lakes.'

So Dawacuo was born in the wilds of No Man's Land. No one knew who her father was and no one cared. Dawacuo turned out just as her mother had hoped: she was healthy and strong and grew more beautiful every year. All the men and women in the encampment liked her, not only because she was the first child born in the shadow hunters' encampment, but also because she was pretty and lively, the sort of child people couldn't help but be drawn to.

Becoming a mother gave Yangji the courage to carry on living. She patched up her injured heart and put all her energy into bringing up her daughter. She had grown from a girl into a woman and from a woman into a mother. She had, as it were, lost two layers of skin. No longer the wilful herding girl of Cuoe Grassland, she was now a tanned, middle-aged, labouring woman.

Laughing loudly, the men in the boats threw the ropes to the women who'd gone down to welcome them home. Once ashore, they playfully rubbed the cheeks or breasts of their women, then strode into the large central tent, sat down on the cushions and waited for the women to serve them *baijiu*. Raising their glasses, they toasted one another and knocked back their drinks.

Yangji and three other women brought in platters of steaming meat, set them on the table and stuck small knives into the flesh ready for the men. The men began to eat, cutting off large hunks, tearing them into smaller pieces and cramming the meat into their mouths, fat dripping down their chins.

Jijia sat at the head of the table on a chair piled high with antelope wool. A woman put a platter of lamb ribs in front him. He didn't move, just downed one glass of *baijiu* after another. A strange emptiness engulfed him after every slaughter. The sight of fresh antelope blood splattered all around always gave him a wild thrill, but that was invariably followed by a long period of aimlessness.

The blue sky bore not even the wisp of a cloud, and the sun was strong enough to bake a person dry. On the side of a craggy slope, big-bellied Kaguo was flipping over stones in search of mice.

A gun barrel was protruding through the jumble of broken rocks and Gongzha was squinting through its sights. There were three dots and a line in his crosshairs, and at the centre was Kaguo's hefty body. He placed his finger lightly on the trigger, ready to pull.

'Gongzha! Gongzha!' Feng stood barefoot on the plain below and yelled loudly up at him, holding four pink eggs.

Hearing the noise, Kaguo didn't linger; she shook herself a couple of times, then disappeared into the rocks on the slope. Gongzha raised his head impatiently and shouldered his gun. Since he'd met Feng, the rhythm of his life had been disrupted. This was the third time she'd scared away Kaguo.

'I'm sorry, Gongzha, it's all my fault.' When Feng saw Gongzha coming silent and glowering down the slope, she knew she was in trouble again. 'I didn't know you'd seen Kaguo. I'm so sorry. I thought you were hunting for food and I wanted to tell you that there are a lot of eggs over there so you don't need to hunt today because we can boil them.'

It would be better to take Feng back to the town before trying to hunt down Kaguo, Gongzha thought, keeping his head low. They'd been making slower and slower progress the last few days. First Feng would say she was tired, then that she was hungry, which wasted more and more time. Yesterday, beside a pretty little lake, she'd said that her head really hurt and she needed to rest for half a day. And then she'd spent the time playing energetically with the two baby antelopes by the lakeside. So much for her terrible headache.

'Don't worry about it. I'll get her in the end,' Gongzha said. He glanced at the eggs in her hand. 'Those are from a ruddy shelduck. There's a hot spring nearby and the water's very hot.'

'Let's go and cook them then!' Feng was delighted. She called loudly to the two little antelopes, who were standing a short distance away. 'Baobao, Beibei, come back here! Let's go!' They bounded happily over.

'They're called Baobao and Beibei?' Gongzha looked at the two scrawny grey antelopes in surprise. Giving them names as if they were pets in the city was really quite inappropriate.

'They are! And they already recognise their names.' Feng slipped on her shoes and followed Gongzha, who was carrying the luggage. The old horse followed Feng and the two antelopes walked beside her. 'The taller one is called Baobao and the shorter one is called Beibei.'

When they got to the hot springs, Feng found a small pool and put the eggs in it. Then she slipped round to the other side of a travertine outcrop and found a larger pool. 'I'm going to take a bath,' she said loudly. 'I feel dirty.'

Gongzha set the horse loose and sat cross-legged against the outcrop holding his gun. He closed his eyes and began to collect his thoughts.

Feng extracted her make-up bag from her backpack, stripped quickly and slipped into the warm water. In truth she wasn't really that dirty, she just didn't want to miss the chance to relax in the pure water of a hot spring out in the wilderness.

She lay at the edge of the pool, the warm water gently lapping over her. Her heart was suddenly full of an unnameable feeling. Looking at the clouds like puffs of cotton in the blue sky, her thoughts turned to what her colleagues in Shanghai would be doing right then. Zhuo Yihang would probably be sitting in that terrifyingly large office of his, wearily rubbing his forehead and planning some star's new album. And Yang Fan? He'd be leafing through a thick stack of notes, racking his brain about how to present tomorrow's pitch. She wondered if, after so much time off, she'd ever be able to readjust to normal working life again.

Baobao and Beibei lay by her side, occasionally nibbling her shoulder. The tickling sensation made her giggle.

Gongzha sat with his legs crossed, chewing on a blade of grass. As he rested his back against the rock, he lost himself in the white clouds moving slowly across the sky. Hearing Feng's giggles from behind the rock made him smile. In the few days they'd spent together, he'd come to like this city girl. She was always scaring off his game, but she had a good heart; she kept begging him not to kill Kaguo because she was pregnant or asking him to wait until she'd had her cub; and if they came across an ass that had fallen into a gully or an antelope that had been blinded in a sandstorm, she always wanted to try and save it. It didn't matter what sort of environment a person found themselves in, if they had a good heart, it would always shine through.

Gongzha scanned the surrounding mountains. They might be able to reach Rongma tomorrow. There were people there, and cars. Feng could finally return to her world. And him? *Cuomu! Oh, Cuomu...*

A little while later, Gongzha picked the eggs out of the hot pool and set them down on the ground. 'They're done.'

Feng got out of the water, dressed, and walked over barefoot. She sat down next to Gongzha, picked up one of the eggs, tapped it on the ground, peeled off the shell, and handed it to him.

He took it, and in a single bite the egg was gone.

'There are ten in total, so that's five each, to make it fair,' Feng said. She peeled one for herself and took a small bite. For a brief moment her mouth was full of the egg's light flavour. 'I've never had such a delicious egg – did you say they're from the ruddy shelduck?'

'Yes. There are a lot of waterfowl by the lake and at this time of year their nests contain plenty of eggs.'

'If I'd known they were this good, I'd have taken more.'

'If you want more, there are plenty around.'

'Really? Alright, if I see any more, I'll collect them and we can boil them and take them with us.' Feng smiled happily before peeling another and stuffing it in her mouth.

Gongzha also peeled one and put it in his mouth. 'You won't be able to eat them after a few more days.'

'Why not?'

'They've already started to develop. If you opened it and found a duckling inside, would you still eat it?'

'No!' Feng turned her head away. 'Can't you say something a bit more appetising?'

Gongzha laughed. 'Eat up, we need to get going. We should reach Rongma tomorrow.'

'Rongma, that's the town closest to No Man's Land?'

'That's right. Once you get there you'll be safe.'

'I'll be safe?' Feng said to herself as she looked at the towering mountains in the distance. 'I can go home – back to Shanghai?'

'Once you get to Rongma, you should look for the town cadres and they'll help you find a way to get back to the county town.'

'Alright.' The thought of being back in the big city she knew so well made Feng happy. She couldn't wait to stroll along its wide, neon-lit streets, couldn't wait to drink a large glass of German stout, couldn't wait to luxuriate in a spa and doze off with a moisturising mask on her face. 'Let's go now!' she said. She put the rest of the eggs in her pocket and went over to pick up the luggage.

Gongzha saddled the horse and strapped on the bags. Then they set off, taking the two antelopes with them.

After passing through two valleys and crossing a fairly low snow mountain, Gongzha said, 'By midday tomorrow, we should be there.'

'Tomorrow midday, I'll be safe?' Looking at the grassland around her, Feng felt a sudden pang in her heart.

'Mhm.' Gongzha took the luggage off the horse and unpacked it, then quickly set up Feng's tent. 'We'll stay here tonight and set off again tomorrow as soon as it's light.'

Feng nodded and threw her sleeping bag into the tent. Gongzha picked up his old gun and walked off.

She was going home. She was finally going home. Feng lay on the grass in front of her tent and mumbled to herself as she looked at the nearby snow mountains. When she got back to the city, the first thing she was going to do was buy an enormous pile of fruit: apples, pears, grapes, watermelons… Then she'd go out for an expensive French meal, its food as delicate as flowers, so romantic and aesthetically pleasing. Her stomach had really suffered out here.

She turned over, stood up, went into her tent and dragged out her bag. She tipped everything out onto the grass, rolled up each item of clothing tightly, and put her cleansers and other make-up back into their little bag. In among her things was a small gold Buddha she'd got on Barkhor Street. She picked it up. She'd got it from a Swedish man called Nadal whom she'd met on her wanderings around Lhasa. The two of them had gone to a bar and he'd got blind drunk. When he'd finally stumbled out of the bar, he left a small white cloth bag on the table. Feng had looked inside, found the Buddha and chased after him, but he'd already disappeared into the swirling crowds. Frustrated, she'd kept the Buddha with her, hoping she might run into Nadal again and be able to return it. But she hadn't had time to go back to Barkhor Street before coming to northern Tibet.

She stood the little Buddha in the grass. It looked and smelled ancient and would make a nice addition to a shelf of antiques; it was a shame it was so small. She didn't look at it again, just closed her bag, picked up her dirty socks from the grass and walked over to a nearby stream to wash them.

Gongzha came back dragging a small deer. When he saw the Buddha in the grass, he froze. He bent to pick it up and turned it this way and that, squinting at it. When he saw a delicate ¤ scratched onto the Buddha's outward-facing palm, his face darkened. He was sure it was one of the Buddhas he'd brought down from the cave complex on Mount Chanaluo.

When Feng came back carrying her clean socks, Gongzha greeted her with a sombre face.

'What's wrong? Didn't you hit anything?'

'This Buddha, where did you get it?'

'I met a foreigner on Barkhor Street; he got drunk and left it behind. What about it?'

'A foreigner dropped it?'

'Yes. He said he paid 20,000 yuan for it. There were about five of them, apparently. I think he was tricked; if they really were antiques, he shouldn't have paid less than 100,000 yuan for one of them.' Feng laughed and laid her socks on the grass.

'It is real!' Gongzha said, sitting down cross-legged.

'What?' Feng turned her head in surprise.

'It is real,' Gongzha repeated in a low voice. 'This is one of the Buddhas from the temple near my home, Cuoe Temple.'

'You... you mean it's a real... antique? A cultural relic?' Feng went over and took the Buddha from his hand. She looked at it from every angle but could see nothing remarkable about it.

'That's right. Look at the symbol on its palm. That symbol is special – no outsiders know anything about it.'

'What does it mean?'

'Kaguo's forehead has the same symbol.'

'Kaguo the bear?' Feng asked cautiously.

Gongzha nodded and his face twitched with pain.

'I'm sorry, Gongzha. Don't... don't think about it, alright?'

Gongzha kept silent and looked at the mountains, trying hard to control the pain in his heart.

Then, for the first time ever, he told an outsider about the cave on Mount Chanaluo, about his hatred for Kaguo, and about the learned Living Buddha Zhaduo. Finally, he said, 'This symbol might be the symbol of an ancient clan of our grassland; the elder of that clan was skilled at taming bears.'

'Wait, wait, Gongzha. Did you say that the English writing on the cave wall said "Sven Hedin"?' Feng asked in surprise.

'Apparently, yes. That's what Zhuo Mai said. Afterwards we went to ask our clan elder about it; his father had actually rescued a foreigner called Sven Hedin many years before and led him out of the grassland.'

'My goodness, it really is a small world! Nadal, the Swede I met, he said his grandfather was called Sven Hedin and that he'd been to Tibet and had gone to No Man's Land.'

Gongzha was speechless with amazement.

'He also said that the Cuoe Temple Medicine Buddha was a real treasure and very finely crafted. His grandfather told him that he had to find a way to get it.'

Gongzha looked at Feng, shaking his head, and for a while could not respond. 'I brought this Buddha out of the cave myself and gave it to Basang, the monk at Cuoe Temple. How could it have got into Nadal's hands?'

'It's obvious, isn't it? Basang must have sold the Buddha to Nadal,' Feng said. Cultural relics and antiques were worth a lot, and the chance to earn a big stash of cash could have a transformative effect on a person. Feng had seen that a lot in her business life.

'Basang... sold the Buddha?' Gongzha looked at Feng in shock. How could he have done that? Basang had told him he was a disciple of the living Buddha; he loved the Buddha so much, used to pray morning and night – how could he have done such a thing?

'Antiques like this are very valuable now. There are people who spend their whole time scouring Barkhor Street for a lucky find, people from all over, from other parts of China and even from overseas. They buy a statue and take it back home to resell, whether or not they believe in the teachings of the Buddha. Some people are just a lot more interested in the beautiful world of the here and now than in the world to come that they can't see.'

'He sold the Buddha?' Gongzha couldn't get over it. It was incomprehensible. Even though he himself wasn't a devout Buddhist, he knew that to the believers on the grassland, images of the Buddha were incomparably holy. They usually venerated such images and protected them – how could one of them take the Buddha's image and exchange it for money? He'd never heard of such a thing.

'He's not selling the Buddha, he's selling the Buddha's image!' Feng took in Gongzha's serious expression and didn't know whether to laugh or cry.

'It represents the Buddha!' Gongzha said, looking at the statue.

'That's true. For those of you who believe, of course he represents the Buddha. But, Gongzha, for people who don't believe, it's just a very valuable object, something they can make a lot of money out of.'

'But Basang is a monk – he was one of the living Buddha's disciples.'

'But the living Buddha isn't here any more, there's no one to control him.'

'But Basang...' Gongzha tried to make sense of what he'd just learnt. In the space of a minute, it had all become very confusing.

The Buddha's disciples would sell his image for money? If that was true, how could the light of Cuoe Temple's Buddha ever shine on the grassland again?

Feng looked sideways at him. 'Did you know Basang from before?'

'No.' Gongzha shook his head.

'Did anyone on your grassland know him?'

Gongzha thought and then shook his head again. 'I never heard of anyone knowing him.'

'That makes sense. Gongzha, I think it's safe to say that this person is almost certainly an imposter.'

'An imp... imposter?' Gongzha was even more surprised to hear that, so surprised that he couldn't even speak clearly. Before the Cultural Revolution there'd been a lot of monks at the temple, many of whom he hadn't known.

'Yes. Think about it – if he really had been Living Buddha Zhaduo's disciple, how come no one knew him? And...'

'What?' Gongzha saw that Feng was hesitating and looked at her inquiringly.

'I can't say for sure, it's just a feeling...' Feng said. 'But from what you've said, Basang is quite old and has difficulty walking. How could he have taken the Buddhas to Lhasa to sell? I think he must be working with someone – and probably not just one person. They must have known you'd go and look for the Buddhas, which is to say they must have known you had a good relationship with Zhaduo, so they used the fact that the government had started righting the wrongs of the Cultural Revolution and they made Basang pretend to be a monk and come back to the grassland to trick you.'

'Then... what if I hadn't found the Buddhas?'

'If you hadn't found the Buddhas, they wouldn't have lost much,' Feng said. She could sense the thread of a thought twitching in her mind, but she couldn't quite grasp it. 'But if I'm right, would they really have gone to all that trouble just for those little Buddhas? They're only worth a few ten thousand yuan. I'm not sure... It can't be that straightforward. Let me think...'

Gongzha stared at the woman in front of him, quite stunned. Everything she'd said ran counter to what he'd always believed, and yet he instinctively felt that there was truth in her words. And the consequences of that were alarming.

As he lay dying, Zhaduo had made one last request of Gongzha. Had Gongzha lost the chance to fulfil that one request?

Feng was still furiously rubbing her forehead; her brain was whirring. 'So... the Medicine Buddha. Didn't you say that the Medicine Buddha was the temple's most precious treasure, and that Zhaduo gave it to you? I think it must have been that statue they were really after.'

Gongzha looked at Feng again. 'They were really after this...?' From his *chuba* he took out the Buddha bundled in yellow cloth, unwrapped it and set it on the grass.

Feng looked at the Buddha in amazement. It was exquisite, a work of extraordinary beauty. Its colour was not pure black but rather the deepest of blues, like the depths of the sea or the heart of a sacred lake. It gleamed, too, as bright as Venus.

The Buddha's expression was so serene, it matched everything she'd imagined about him. As she gazed at the statue, she couldn't help being entranced; it made her heart and spirit feel so peaceful. She didn't dare stare at it for too long, for fear that her mind would empty. She reached out, quickly wrapped up the Buddha again, and thrust it back into Gongzha's hands.

'Until we've resolved this, you can't tell anyone you have this statue, Gongzha,' she said, 'otherwise your life might be in danger. Not everyone is as honourable as you. There are people who will stop at nothing if there is money to be made. Also, didn't you say that Lobudunzhuo—'

'Luobudunzhu, not Lobudunzhuo.' Gongzha didn't know whether to laugh or cry.

'And what do you think of this Luobudunzhu? Didn't you say he'd pursued and harassed Living Buddha Zhaduo? I think that must have been because of this statue. Of course, I'm only guessing, and I don't have any evidence, but I think you should be careful.'

Gongzha thought about the time, long ago, when he, Cuomu and Shida had upset Luobudunzhu's plans to follow Zhaduo with his gang of men. And he remembered how Luobudunzhu and his men used to circle Zhaduo's small tent. He couldn't help but nod.

'I still don't understand what their connection is with Nadal.' Feng shook her head. 'It can't be coincidence – there must be something else there.'

'Once I've taken you to Rongma, I'll go back to the grassland and see how things are there,' Gongzha said, packing away the Medicine Buddha.

Feng picked up her small bronze Buddha and put it into Gongzha's *chuba*. 'Take this back with you too; it belongs to the grassland.'

'You don't want it?'

'I can't take it.' Feng giggled. 'It's too valuable and I'm too greedy. If I were to take it, I might not be able to resist selling it.'

Gongzha laughed. 'I thought you wanted to get rich!' Feng had prattled on endlessly about how she would buy a villa in the Shanghai suburbs or a fancy car when she got rich.

'I don't dare. It's a Buddha – if I sell a Buddha, I might get struck down!' she said jokingly. She pushed her stray curls behind her ears and stood up. 'So, Mr Gongzha, what about that meat? I'm starving.'

Gongzha stood up too, carried the deer in one hand over to the stream, got out his knife and skinned it. Then he brought out the salt bag and gave it to Feng, who was almost drooling in anticipation. He sliced the haunch into thin strips and passed some to her.

Feng sprinkled on some salt, stuffed a slice into her mouth and narrowed her eyes in blissful appreciation. 'It's really good. I never knew raw meat was this tasty.'

'You're not afraid of turning into a barbarian?' Gongzha

looked at her with a pleased expression and put a piece of meat into his own mouth.

'Who said eating raw meat was barbaric? Don't the Japanese eat raw fish? And that's a famous dish!' Feng dipped another slice into the salt and ate it.

'You really are an unusual woman!' Gongzha said. He cut off another piece of meat and passed it to her.

Feng sat up straight. 'Does that count as praise?' she asked in all seriousness.

Gongzha looked at her spirited eyes and turned his head away. Cuomu used to have eyes like that. *Cuomu…* His heart hurt quietly.

'Are you blushing?' Feng said. 'Gongzha, would you ever come to Shanghai?'

'What would I do there?' He tossed a deer bone into the distance. 'The city's too big. I'd get lost.'

Feng laughed uproariously. 'You're so funny, worrying about getting lost. But I won't lie to you, Gongzha, I get lost in the city too.'

'When you see Yihang, don't forget to tell him that he's always welcome back on the grassland.'

'I won't. Yihang really respects you. He's often told me that you're the best hunter on the grassland.'

'Haven't you seen that for yourself? I've been that close to Kaguo three times and still haven't killed her.'

Feng blushed. 'I'm sorry, Gongzha. That's my fault.'

'It doesn't matter. I still have time – she can't stay on the run forever.' Gongzha passed her some more meat.

Feng dipped it in salt and put it in her mouth. 'But you really are a good hunter. You have so many principles: not killing a pregnant animal, not killing an animal with young, not killing anything strong.'

'A hunter without principles isn't a hunter, he's a murderer.'

'You're right. Like those people who slaughtered the antelopes with absolutely no sense of shame; they'll end up killing every last antelope in Tibet.'

'You have a pretty strong sense of right and wrong.'

Feng giggled. 'Is that another compliment?'

Gongzha noted the pleasure on her face and narrowed his eyes. 'Is praise really so important to you?'

'Of course.' Feng frowned. 'Who doesn't like hearing kind words?'

She took Gongzha's knife, pulled the napping Baobao and Beibei towards her and began scratching something onto their horns.

'What are you doing?'

'I'm scratching their names. Otherwise next time I won't recognise them.'

Feng laughed as she tightened her grip on the necks of the squirming antelopes. With a straight face, she admonished them. 'No sudden movements! My hands aren't used to doing this, so if you move suddenly, I might cut your throats.'

Gongzha shook his head and laughed drily. Then he sprinkled some salt on the leftover meat and stashed it away.

After Feng was finished with her name-scratching, she sighed and stared contentedly at her handiwork. 'Hmm... not bad. Now, wherever you go, I'll be able to recognise you.' She patted the antelopes on the back and watched them bound off. Then she followed Gongzha back to the tent.

The evening sun was already slanting over the plain, and the mountains glinted gold. Feng stretched out her legs and leant back with her hands behind her head. As she watched the sun set over the grassland, she let her mind wander. Gongzha stood beside her, gazing out into the wilderness. Baobao and Beibei were next to the old horse, staring fixedly at them.

Below them on the grassland, a fox was digging into a mouse hole, a stream of dirt flying out from between its hind legs. Every so often it raised its head to survey its surrounds. In the light of the evening sun, its red fur blazed like leaping flames. A herd of wild asses was grazing not far off, two foals gambolling at their mothers' sides. Their carefree attitude made Feng envious.

'It's gorgeous, isn't it?' she said lightly.

'Mhm.'

'I'm going to come back to the grassland, Gongzha.'

'Mhm.'

'Will you be pleased to see me?' Feng said quietly.

'I...' Gongzha paused for a moment and then said, 'I'll be pleased to see you.'

'I will always remember these days we've spent together, Gongzha. I have so much to thank you for – not just for saving my life, but also for the wonderful experience these past few days have been for me.'

Gongzha stayed silent.

The sun set, and the wilderness fell quiet.

Feng lay in her sleeping bag listening to the sounds of the night. She couldn't sleep. Gongzha had found a grassy hollow out of the wind and she pictured him in it, wrapped in his sheepskin *chuba*, holding that strange old gun, his eyes shut. Perhaps that great beard of his would be tinged with frost? And his long, wild hair, would it be stirring in the breeze? What sort of expression would he have on his face, she wondered. No, there'd be no expression – it would be impassive.

Feng turned over and faced the other side of the tent, her thoughts racing. Tomorrow they would say goodbye. Would he remember her? Maybe he wouldn't. His heart held only one woman, and that was the long-departed Cuomu. To him, his time with Feng was just a strange episode during his travels in the wilderness; she was a guest who'd strayed briefly into his world. To leave was to say goodbye forever. What would be the point in remembering, for either of them?

Tomorrow she would be out of the wilderness; she would be safe. Logically, she should be happy. Why was her heart suddenly full of inexpressible sadness?

She went back over the last ten days: her initial terror, her despair, her relief at being found by Gongzha, and how her survival instinct had made her cling to him as if he was some sort of life-raft. She thought about watching him eat raw meat, how disgusted she'd been to start with and how she'd got used to it and was now eating it herself. He'd taken her to see wild yaks, had taught her to identify animal tracks and to use plants to tell direction, and he'd told her what to do when she encountered wolves or bears. She'd almost forgotten about the hectic city, forgotten about her tubes of make-up and her enormous stack of files; she'd even started to think that a permanent life in the wilderness could be quite desirable. To live there, to be with Gongzha, to watch the sun set and the moon rise, to mark the passage of the four seasons...

When she caught herself thinking along those lines, she was scared. A red wave washed across her cheeks. How could she possibly live out here, like a herder, wearing a sunburnt face and a heavy Tibetan robe, driving the livestock out every morning and back home every night, growing old before her time?

She turned over again. Would such a life be so bad? One tent, one column of smoke. She would stand in the evening sun, shading her eyes with her hand, watching for the figure of her returning man. If there was love, surely a quiet life would not be lonely? No, when she thought about it, it would not. There would be yaks, and sheep, and a man. When she pictured the returning man, it was Gongzha's bearded face that appeared before her. It was a lovely picture, a picture that made her heart sing.

Feng sat up suddenly, pulled down the zip of her sleeping bag, put on her windcheater and left the tent. The night was calm and the clear cold moon shone low over the plain, like quicksilver.

Feng looked around and discovered Gongzha lying to one side in a nest of short grass, Baobao and Beibei huddled beside him. She crept over and crouched down next to him. Baobao and Beibei opened their eyes and glanced at her, then shut them again.

Gongzha had the classic face of a grassland man. His skin was as rough as a lump of ancient rock, his lips were worn and slightly cracked, and his nostrils were large. His dark, bushy eyebrows were like sharp swords and his forehead had two deep wrinkles like two mountain ranges. His beard was unkempt, ragged and dirty. He'd pulled his *chuba* up to his neck and some of its greying wool stirred gently in the wind.

Feng quietly leant down and kissed his forehead, then scrambled up and bolted back to her tent, zipped up the flap and sat inside commanding her racing heart to be still.

In the moonlight, Gongzha half opened his eyes, directed his gaze at the little yellow tent and stared at it with calm seriousness.

When their two figures appeared on the mountain pass above Rongma town, the people on the plain below could barely contain their excitement. Their shouts of encouragement in Mandarin and Tibetan filled the sky.

'You really won't come down with me?' Feng asked in a hurt voice as the two of them stood there.

'No,' Gongzha said. 'You go on down, they're waiting for you.' He handed her her backpack.

'Don't worry, as soon as I get to Lhasa, I'll report the case. I won't let Nadal take your precious Buddhas away.'

'Mhm.'

'Yihang says he wants to bring his father's ashes back to Tibet.'

'Mhm.'

'I know you're as comfortable in the wilderness as you are in your own home, but please do be careful out here.'

'Mhm.'

Feng picked up her bag and started making her way down the slope. Her legs felt as if they weighed several hundred kilos. The two antelopes whinnied and followed her. Feng knelt down, petted their heads and spoke to them quietly. They looked round at Gongzha, then bounded back to him.

Feng looked at him too, wrinkled the corners of her mouth, turned and continued down.

Her travelling companions embraced her and spun her in circles, everyone talking at the same time, wanting to know what had happened and how she'd managed to survive out there for so long.

Feng glanced up at Gongzha astride his horse on the mountain pass. He was just turning to leave. A string of five-coloured prayer flags fluttered beside him, the sky so blue, the clouds so soft. His silhouette seemed as smooth as a *mani* prayer stone. A sharp pain pierced her heart.

'Gongzha...' she suddenly screamed, her voice tearful, 'I'll miss you!'

The figure on the horse straightened his back at the sound but did not turn round. A moment later he hunched low again; then his horse shot off like an arrow from a bow and disappeared over the ridge.

Beneath the blue curtain of sky, on the brown mountainside, only the prayer flags remained, flapping wildly.

19

Feng returned to Shanghai, returned to her former life.

Her days were hectic. Every month she received a handsome salary, then indulged in a shopping frenzy at a famous mall. To everyone who knew her, she was a model businesswoman, someone who took her position and job seriously. But even though she kept on getting promoted, her boss's approving gaze and her colleagues' envious stares were no longer enough.

'You've become a shopaholic – something's not right.' Zhuo Yihang was helping carry some of her many bags from the mall to the car park.

Feng briefly stopped walking but quickly recovered herself.

When they found the car, Zhuo Yihang opened the door then loaded her purchases into the boot. Feng got in and put on her seatbelt. She sighed, then quietly asked Yihang, who was about to start the car, 'Will you ever go back and live in Tibet?'

'That's the plan. Next year, or perhaps the year after, I want to go to Lhasa and buy a house to retire in.'

'Retire? You?' Feng rolled her eyes.

'Aren't you the one who's always going on about how living here reduces your life expectancy? So I'd like to find somewhere that will extend my life expectancy. Tibet's the first place that comes to mind.'

'Tibet…' Feng's gaze rested on the quivering leaves of the roadside trees. Could she ever forget Tibet? That plateau and that man were never out of her head for long. She longed to be back there, yearned for it with an intensity that was deeply personal and heartfelt, but returning there was out of the question, an impossibility.

She had to keep saying to herself, 'Forget about it, forget about him. Tibet's not your sort of place. This bustling city with its swarms of cars and seas of people, that's where you belong.'

At 8 a.m. sharp one morning, three years after her return from Tibet, Feng was sitting in her bright, spacious office. As she stared at the enormous pile of papers that needed to be signed, approved or revised, her eyes clouded over. Was this really the life she wanted? A large work of calligraphy by someone famous hung on the wall and a crimson leather sofa stood to the side. No one ever sat on the sofa for more than two minutes; it was little more than window dressing – window dressing for the company's image, and window dressing for her empty heart.

There was an orchid on her marble side table, a stem extending from amid its elegant leaves. A bud was bursting into bloom and its delicate fragrance filled the room. But Feng didn't look at the orchid; instead she gazed out through the floor-to-ceiling window. The sky was grey; was there more rain coming? She frowned. When would the sky be blue again? When would white clouds float across it? If there were no tall buildings or concreted areas, would sparse grass grow there like it did in northern Tibet? Would it wither and then spring up again? Feng imagined it, then laughed at herself and withdrew her gaze.

A light, extremely polite knock sounded at the door. It was a standard knock, neither loud nor soft, but courteous.

Feng frowned again. If it were Gongzha, he'd probably hammer on the door as if he were setting off a cannon. Or he'd just push it open and come straight in. When she realised she was daydreaming again, she laughed wryly and called a polite, 'Come in!'

Her secretary came in wearing a standard work outfit and a standard professional smile. She put a sheaf of papers in front of Feng, leafed through them to the signature line on the last page and placed the pen in Feng's hand. 'These are the minutes of this morning's meeting.'

Feng barely even looked at them before scrawling her large signature across it.

The secretary smiled and left, shutting the door carefully behind her.

Feng was alone in her empty, sterile office once more.

She forced herself to go through the papers on her desk. At midday, her secretary quietly opened the door and glanced in. When Feng didn't even look up in acknowledgement, the secretary shook her head and placed the boxed lunch she'd bought on Feng's desk. Feng threw her a smile of thanks, then dropped her head again.

When she was finally done, Feng put down her pen and stretched; her shoulders were a little sore. She pressed the buzzer and her secretary quickly knocked and entered.

Feng motioned for her to take away the documents neatly piled on the desk.

The secretary noticed the box of now congealed food and said worriedly, 'If you carry on working as if your life depended on it, will your body be able to take it?'

'It doesn't matter,' Feng said. 'Take that design plan for Century City to the boss's office.'

'Okay!' The secretary went out, then returned soon after with a cup of hot coffee and took away the cold boxed lunch.

Feng lifted the cup and took a sip. She frowned. All of a sudden she'd lost the taste for Jamaican coffee; what she really wanted was a drink of north Tibetan spring water: fresh, cool and bursting with sweetness. When she realised she'd begun daydreaming again, Feng stood up, picked up her bag, walked out of the door and took the lift down to the car park.

There was a crossroads not far from the office complex. She had no particular direction in mind, so she chose a road at random, just as she had every day previously.

The trees on either side of the road had been neatly pruned and the flowerbeds planted in intricate patterns. Shanghai could be beautiful. The flowers were fragrant and the birds soared and sang. Zhuo Yihang had already invited her several times to go for an outing to the suburbs, a chance to relax; he said it was the perfect season for a stroll. But when she thought of those manmade vistas, those hand-crafted stone paths, Feng had little interest.

For three years, day after day, she had missed Tibet, missed the wild, unsophisticated highlands, missed that rough, uneducated man. The two of them had said nothing, done nothing, but she'd been unable to let him go ever since.

She couldn't carry on living like this, could she? It's the weekend, Feng thought. I'll go out with Yihang and his friends.

She found a large shop and ransacked it from top to bottom, buying a huge stack of things to take back to her parents' house. They'd bought the house last year and Feng had paid quite a bit towards it; it was one hundred and twenty square metres and her mother was finally satisfied.

'Why did you buy so much? We've still got one bottle,' Feng's mother, a classic city woman, asked from the kitchen door, holding up a bottle of shampoo.

'Take your time,' Feng said, as she unpacked the vegetables into the fridge. She took out a box of uncooked mutton rolls, casually ripped it open and stuffed a couple into her mouth. The meat's rich flavour filled her mouth and crept into her heart.

'Why are you eating raw meat again?' her mother shouted, appalled, as she snatched the box out of Feng's hand.

Without looking at her mother, Feng quickly walked out of the kitchen, through the living room and onto the deck. She could hear her parents in hushed discussion behind her.

Gongzha's life continued as before. He searched for the bear and periodically returned to visit his mother.

Baobao and Beibei had grown up. Now that they were no longer dependant on him for their survival, Gongzha decided to let them go. He was standing beneath the blue sky on the brown slope of a small rise in a valley surrounded by towering peaks. A herd of male antelopes was grazing nearby. They were almost the same age as Baobao and Beibei: not yet mature but already living on their own. Baobao and Beibei saw them, but their hooves seemed to be weighed down and they hesitated.

'Off you go!' Gongzha finally stood up, his *chuba* tied around his waist and his hair brushing his shoulders. Even though the antelopes had stayed with him, after Feng left it was if they'd lost their souls. 'You should go too. Go and find your peers; don't keep following me.' He purposely didn't look at them as he said this. He'd got used to having them around and he was reluctant to have them leave so suddenly.

Baobao and Beibei hesitated a moment and then trotted down into the valley. When they turned back, there was no one there, only a golden, shining slope.

Gongzha had seen no trace of Kaguo for a long time. He decided to climb to the top of Tajiapu to look for the chain that Yongxi had mentioned. There was the same large black boulder, the same strange symbol. As Gongzha felt the sable chain, his mind churned. Two identical chains, two identical boulders, two identical ⌘ marks: Tajiapu, Chanaluo – so distant, but connected.

He walked round the peak but found nothing else of interest so he went down the mountain again.

An idyllic farm in the suburbs of Shanghai. A narrow, shady, gravel path, willow branches gently waving beside it.

This really was a beautiful time of year. The breeze and the sun were both just right, and all sorts of flowers were competing to display their colours. Over the weekend, some friends had got together to find somewhere lovely to play cards, chat or otherwise while away a day. Originally, Feng had been one of them; in the past, she'd been a tireless arranger of such events. But today, she didn't know why, she didn't have the heart for it.

She and Zhuo Yihang strolled along the gravel path. When Feng frowned and sighed yet again, Yihang turned to her and said, hoping to make her laugh, 'Your mother called me. She said you'd eaten almost an entire box of raw mutton and she wants me to get you to go to the hospital for a check-up. She thinks you've got some strange disease.'

Feng rolled her eyes. 'You're the ones with the strange disease.'

'You must know how strange it looks for you to eat raw meat here. You don't want people to think you've gone feral, do you?' Yihang was only half joking.

'Why's eating raw meat so bizarre? Cooked meat just doesn't have any flavour – why should I eat it?'

'My dear friend, this is Shanghai; don't forget you're a sophisticated woman.'

Feng shot him another look. 'Fuck you. Can't you say something to make me feel better?'

'Alright, alright, alright. Here's something to make you feel better: last night I talked to Yang Fan, and he's really coming back this time.'

Feng stopped in her tracks and sighed lightly. 'Does that mean I have to go to America?'

'You need to think about that. Yang Fan's coming back next month. Once you're married, you can't carry on living separately forever.'

'I... Do I really have to marry Yang Fan?'

'Feng, what's wrong with you? You've been together for how many years? Your personal Eight Years' War of Resistance is almost over! You've done enough complaining in the past about how little attention he pays you – all he cared about was studying, then all he cared about was his job, he never cared about your feelings – and now he's coming back to marry you, but you look unhappy. What's that about?'

'I don't know, Yihang. I'm really conflicted.'

The two of them were standing on a rocky ledge beside a stream and as Feng stared at the lilies blooming on the water, tears clouded her gaze.

'Even after three years, you still haven't forgotten him...'

'What?' Feng turned and looked at Yihang in surprise.

'My Uncle Gongzha, of course. What, you won't admit it?'

Feng was silent. A moment later, two teardrops the size of beans rolled down her face. Yihang knew her so well.

'Why don't you go and find him?'

'Find him?' Feng was shocked again. 'What about Yang Fan?'

'He'll find himself another pretty woman soon enough. Don't forget, he's a returning PhD student and a top man on Wall Street. Women ten times better than you will be making eyes at him,' Zhuo Yihang said, half joking and half in earnest.

'But... what about my parents?' Feng's eyes were gleaming, but she was still hesitant.

'Your parents are only in their sixties, they're in good health, and, anyway, your brother's here, isn't he? What's there to worry about? Besides, you'd only be moving to northern Tibet. It's quite a way away, true, but it's still in China. And transport's so much better now, you can fly to Lhasa in three hours.'

As Feng looked at Yihang, her eyes brightened and it was if the cloud that had settled over her face for days had been blown away. She gave him a spontaneous hug. 'Thank you, thank you, Yihang. Thank you so much. You don't know how miserable it's been, thinking about Tibet all the time – while I'm reading work reports, while I'm shopping, even while I'm eating.'

'I just hope Yang Fan doesn't kill me when he gets back.' Yihang gave Feng an affectionate shove and chuckled. 'Wait till I come back to Tibet, then you'll need to slaughter a yak for me.'

'Yes, yes, yes – and ten sheep,' Feng said, her smile like a flower in full bloom.

'It sounds like you really want to marry him,' Zhuo Yihang prodded. 'You need to prepare yourself. I spoke to Lamu and apparently Gongzha recently went back to No Man's Land to take revenge on that bear. Cuomu really is rooted deep in his heart – there may not be room for you.'

'Don't worry, once this beautiful woman has made up her mind, there's no escaping her! He can hunt the bear and I will hunt him.'

Out in the vast, desolate wilderness, the sky was still blue and the earth still brown. And there was still that figure with his gun and his horse...

> 'The stars in the sky
> Are like Brother's eyes
> Watching Sister's silhouette.
> The butter lamps ablaze all night
> Cannot see your eyes, Brother,
> As they fall inside the tent
> To light up Sister's heart.'

He sang the lament in a voice full of heartbreak.

He was walking into the wind. That was the hunter's way: he could smell what was ahead of him without revealing himself to his prey. Two days earlier he'd caught sight of Kaguo at the entrance to a valley, but before he could pick up his gun, she'd disappeared into a ravine. Gongzha had followed.

Gongzha and Kaguo had been playing this game of chase for so long; sometimes it seemed as if it would go on forever, at other times it felt like the end was drawing near.

That night, Gongzha slept in a hollow on a slope overlooking Yongxi's winter pasture. He wrapped himself in his *chuba*, leaving only his eyes exposed, as desolate as the stars in the sky. Yellow butter lamps glowed in the tent below. To the wanderer, they represented a kind of unreachable warmth: a home; a home with children and a woman. Gongzha didn't dare go near Yongxi again. He was afraid of getting lost in the warmth of those lamps. Yongxi was like a sister to him and he didn't want to alter that relationship.

In the middle of the night came the sounds of a quarrel from the tent at the base of the mountain.

'You're the child's mother, but I'm his father – why won't you come with me?' said the man's voice.

'The child is a seed that you forced into my body; I birthed him because I had no choice. You can have us with you if you leave the shadow hunters and promise to stop your killing,' said the woman's voice.

'Yongxi, don't be like this, alright? If I were to leave, what would happen to my men?'

'They managed fine before they had you, didn't they? You say you love us, Jijia, but you don't treat us with respect. You continue with your demonic behaviour – how many innocent lives will you take this year? Do you think the Buddha will forgive you? Retribution will come calling one day. I won't have my son growing up to be like you and ending up as a criminal, imprisoned by the government.'

'Can't you be a bit less harsh, woman? They lay traps for me everywhere, but I still manage to have a good life, don't I?'

'You sneak around, here and there, day and night, more cautious than a wolf – what sort of life is that? Would you dare take your son to Lhasa even once?'

'Yongxi—'

'The child and I will not go with you. We don't need your money. I have hands and feet and I can bring him up myself.'

After a while, Gongzha heard the sound of a car rattling off into the distance.

Jijia and Yongxi already had a child? When was it he'd last seen Yongxi? It must have been when her grandmother had passed away. He stood up and made his way down the mountain.

As he reached the side of the tent, a knife came hurtling out at him. 'I told you to fuck off! Don't come and bother us again.'

Gongzha picked up the knife and opened the thick tent flap with a smile. 'Do you really hate him that much, Yongxi?'

'Brother Gongzha!' Yongxi got up, embarrassed, from where she'd been sitting holding her child beside the stove.

'What's this, your son's already got so big and in all that time you couldn't find someone to bring me a letter?' Gongzha sat down with a smile. He drew out a red fox-skin from his *chuba* and handed it to her. 'Consider this a meeting gift from this uncle to the child.'

'But this is the present you'd promised Cuomu – you can't just give it to anyone,' Yongxi said, hurriedly setting the child down and pushing his gift away.

'Well, she has no use for it now. Take it, make the child a hat.' Gongzha laid it on a nearby cushion.

'Then... thank you, Brother Gongzha.'

Gongzha accepted the butter tea Yongxi passed him, drank a large mouthful, then raised his head to ask, 'What's wrong with you and Jijia?'

'I told him to leave the shadow hunters, but he won't listen. It's not like it used to be. Before, no one cared when people killed antelopes, but the government has outlawed it now. The last time I went to the county town to shop, there were propaganda posters everywhere. It's especially Tibetan antelopes: they're some kind of Class 1 protected species now and you can be sentenced to death for killing even a single one, let alone the hundreds he's been responsible for. But he won't listen to me, no matter how much I try. He says there's no faster way to make money, and he's right about that – he's even bought himself a car now. But the child and I, we worry for him every day.'

'You really should try and get him to stop the slaughter. There are fewer and fewer antelopes on the grassland these days, and if he keeps killing them like this, they'll become extinct.'

'What's it to you whether they become extinct or not?' Jijia's low growl suddenly sounded outside the tent. 'What are you doing coming to my tent and stirring up my woman?'

Gongzha immediately stood up and left the tent.

Yongxi followed with the child.

Jijia was standing there in the moonlight with ten or more men. They glared at Gongzha with animosity. Three white off-road vehicles were parked by the broken wall. Next to them stood a haughty-looking long-haired woman dressed in black and playing with a slingshot.

'Why have you come back?' shouted Yongxi furiously.

'You've got it all wrong, Jijia,' Gongzha said lightly, noting the flames of anger in his eyes.

'What have I got wrong? It's you that's been caught visiting my woman's tent and yet you have the gall to say that it's me who's in the wrong?' Jijia was waving his arms and bellowing, as if he'd caught them in bed together. 'I know you're fearless, Gongzha, but in this wilderness, no one touches my woman.'

Gongzha gave a dry laugh. 'Yongxi and I were just talking.'

'And still you persist in telling me I'm wrong! You really fucking aren't a man of the grassland.'

Jijia had a gun in his hand. Luckily, Gongzha dodged quickly, and the bullet hit the ground and ploughed up a line of earth instead.

Yongxi flew into a rage. In two steps she placed herself in front of Gongzha and stood glowering at Jijia, who was preparing to fire again. 'Jijia, if you shoot again, kill me.'

'Get out of the way!' Jijia roared, waving his small machine gun wildly. 'You dare to throw sand on my head? That's going too far! Comrades, keep shooting until he's dead.'

'Don't you dare.' Yongxi swiftly pulled a small knife from her belt, held it against her neck, and fixed Jijia with her eyes. 'If anyone dares to open fire, I'll kill myself.'

'Yongxi!' Jijia was shocked into sudden silence. He stamped his foot in fury and yelled, 'You... Why are you so good to him?'

'He's my brother – he carried my grandmother up to her sky burial. You say you love me and the child, Jijia, but apart from frightening us, what have you done for us?'

'I've told you, I can't help myself. Can't you... can't you give me a little more time?' Jijia said carefully, his voice quieter now. He didn't dare look Yongxi in the eyes. Had this woman been sent by Buddha to torture him? Why did she hate him so much?

'Haven't I given you enough time already? It's been three

years, Jijia. The child is walking already, but still you delay. Fuck off. Don't come here again. I don't want the child to have a demon for a father, and I want a demon for a husband even less!'

Seeing Yongxi's icy expression, Jijia exploded like thunder. Brandishing his gun in fury, he yelled to his men, who were looking on in amazement, 'Fire! Fire! I'm ordering you to fire! Kill her wild man!'

Jijia's men looked at one another. How could they open fire? He had to be joking. Everyone knew that this woman was their leader's most cherished treasure. If Yongxi even so much as nicked her neck with the knife, knowing Jijia's temper, he'd probably set about killing them all once he'd recovered himself.

When Gongzha saw this, he whistled and his old horse trotted over. He mounted, cracked his whip and disappeared into the waves of moonlight striping the wilderness.

The tension disappeared with Gongzha's horse and things quieted down immediately. The woman standing by the car watched contemplatively as Gongzha's figure vanished into the distance.

'You still haven't put down the knife!' Jijia seemed to suddenly come to his senses. He took a few quick steps forward, grabbed Yongxi by the arm, forced the knife out of her hand and threw it to the ground.

Yongxi wrenched herself free of him, kicked his leg, picked up the child and went back into the tent.

Jijia rubbed his leg in pain but neither followed her nor moved away. He turned round and saw that his men were covering their mouths and screwing up their faces to keep from laughing. They went sombre in an instant. 'Fuck off, all of you!'

And with that, the men who wanted to laugh but did not dare piled happily into the cars and rolled off in a trail of smoke.

20

Feng stood in front of that familiar small courtyard once again, an enormous pack on her back, a welter of feelings in her heart.

Lamu wasn't there, but silver-haired Dawa was sitting in the sun on the veranda, looking at Feng and smiling.

'Dear Ama!' Feng walked in and went across the courtyard and up to the veranda. She put down her bag, knelt in front of Dawa and took up her bony hand. 'I've come back.'

'Cuomu, where's Gongzha?' Dawa asked as she stroked her face.

Feng didn't understand Tibetan, but she understood Gongzha's name. 'He's gone hunting,' she said. She looked at her watch and picked up the nearby bottle of medicine. It was the medicine she'd sent. She shook out two pills and put them in the old woman's palm, then poured a cup of hot water and lifted it to Dawa's mouth. 'He'll be back very soon. You should take your medicine, Ama. Look, the sun's almost over the rooftop.'

Dawa swallowed the medicine obediently.

'Auntie Feng, is that you? Auntie, auntie, it really is you! Yihang called to say you were coming, but I thought he was tricking me.' Lamu raced in like the wind, a small girl toddling behind her. She hugged Feng and smiled happily.

Feng stood up. 'You have a toddler already, Lamu?'

'Yes. I got married the year after you came. My daughter is over a year old now.' Lamu laughed and picked up Feng's bag. 'Come on, let's go to your room. I got it ready a long time ago.'

Feng followed Lamu, carrying her little girl in her arms.

When they got to the second floor, Lamu opened one of the rooms. 'This is Brother's room, but I've cleaned it up. You can stay here.' She put the bag on a blue cushion by the window, then sat down and pulled Feng down to join her. 'Auntie, are you really going to look for my brother?'

'Yes. I want to find him.' Feng dragged over the bag and began taking out her things.

'But, Auntie, do you know where he is? No Man's Land is so big...'

'Don't worry, I'll find him.' Feng pictured the little antelopes they'd rescued, and the lakes and snow mountains, and a smile rose in her eyes. Let the dust from those memories settle. She would find him and take care of him; they would share one life and one world.

'Why don't you just wait for him here? It'll be the same in the end. Men always come back when they're tired,' Lamu said, a little worried. 'You can't speak Tibetan – it's too dangerous for you to go to No Man's Land by yourself.'

'But who knows when he'll be back? Don't worry, Lamu, this time I've come prepared.' Feng produced a bulging plastic bag. 'This is medicine for your mother; it's all Chinese medicine and should be good for her body. You need to give it to her at the right time.'

'Don't worry, Auntie, it's fine. You get some rest, and I'll cook you some yak meat.' Lamu took the bag and stood up. She hugged Feng again, then took the child by the hand and walked out.

As the house fell still, Feng's heart churned.

Her decision had been a sudden one. Her parents didn't understand it, but having seen her so morose for such a long time, they could only agree. They'd prepared clothes for all seasons; she had two pairs of leg warmers and five pairs of woollen socks. She had duly booked her tickets and arranged a car for when she arrived in Lhasa. She'd been anxious each step of the way. It was only when she finally reached the small county town in the depths of northern Tibet and saw Dawa's grey hair stirring in the breeze on the little veranda that she calmed down. She had finally arrived, she was finally a little closer to him.

Could it be that she was living in a fantasy world? Gongzha had never said anything to her; he had never even looked at her with meaning or affection. But she had begun to love him, to miss him day and night with a yearning that could not be healed.

Feng sat on the cushion and looked around the room. It was large and empty, with a Tibetan-style roof; the walls were clean and white. On one side were three Tibetan-style couches covered in wool cushions for people to sit or sleep on. There was a bed by the window and a table with a vase and a plastic flower in it.

Lamu had said that this was his room. Where did he sleep when he stayed here? On this side or that side? Feng rubbed the carefully made wool cushion next to her. Her eyes were wet and a wave of longing enveloped her. Gongzha, Gongzha, these last three years, have you missed me?

Feng settled in.

To get to No Man's Land, she had a lot of organising to do. Thankfully, there'd been many changes in the past three years and the remote grassland had finally got public roads and electricity. All the towns had telephones, and it was no longer necessary to give ten days' notice for a meeting and still not have everyone show up.

Feng and Lamu walked slowly down the street in the county town. The dilapidated low-rise houses and the roads that used to leave cars caked in dust were now a thing of the past; they'd been replaced by Tibetan-style apartment buildings and smooth concrete streets.

'It's changed such a lot.' Feng scanned the shops on either side of the road. 'The last time I was here, there were only low-rise mud-brick houses. I didn't expect to find apartments here, and the roads are much wider now, too.'

'The cadres supporting Tibet did it; they've built a hospital, too. Now they're fixing the encampment at home; the government is paying half, and we're paying half.'

'This won't become a second Lhasa in another ten years, will it?' Feng said a little dejectedly.

'Wouldn't that be good!' Lamu smiled at Feng. 'Auntie, I dream of going to live in Lhasa.'

'It might be good, but the grassland atmosphere would be lost.'

'Oh, you city people, you want life here to stay as it is and for us not to change anything – it's not fair.'

'Ha ha, it does seem a bit unfair.' Feng laughed, slightly embarrassed. 'Lamu, how did your Mandarin get so good? The last time I was here, you were getting quite a few of your tones wrong.'

'You don't know about that?' Lamu said in surprise. 'A lot of cadres came to help Tibet, all of them Han. And that inspired a wave of other Han people to come and do business in our county. That Sichuan restaurant over there is run by a man from Chongqing, and there are shops selling fresh produce, shops selling dry goods, public baths, barber shops – we have everything now. I learnt my Mandarin from them.'

'Is it easy to rent a car?'

'Yes, yes; there are plenty of cars now. Quite a few herders have cars, which makes moving pastures much easier – they don't have to come all the way here to rent them.'

'Can you help me find a good car and a driver who speaks Mandarin?'

'No problem,' Lamu replied quickly.

She arranged a car that night: a six-cylinder Mitsubishi for three yuan a kilometre, which was a very good price.

She also got someone to take a letter to her home encampment asking after her brother. Gongzan wrote back saying that Gongzha had been there a fortnight earlier but had left again and that people had seen him in Yongxi's area of No Man's Land.

Lamu wanted Feng to wait – her brother might come back at any time – but Feng couldn't wait. As soon as she heard news of Gongzha, her heart grew restless and would not be settled.

Lamu could only let her go. She stood by the side of the road and lectured the driver, Junsang. 'Brother, you must bring my auntie back in exactly the same shape as she is now, do you hear me? She cannot lose even a single strand of hair, otherwise I'll never forgive you.'

'Not a problem. We're only going to find your brother, aren't we?' Junsang replied loudly. 'I come from No Man's Land, I'm familiar with that area.'

'Alright, then you should be off. Auntie, when you find my brother, tell him that Ama is still waiting to hold his children.'

Feng looked at Lamu with a small smile. They said their goodbyes and she set out.

In keeping with her plan, they went first to Gongzha's home, Cuoe Grassland, where he'd grown up. Since she was preparing to marry him, she wanted to better understand the man she would be spending the rest of her life with. Besides, she was curious about the landscape that had produced such a rough, noble and single-minded man.

As she walked beside the lake, Feng gazed at its rippling surface and at the ancient snow mountain reflected in it, pure and beautiful. Black tents of different sizes were scattered across the plain by the lake like stars, plumes of smoke rising from them. The wild asses in the distance and the sheep driven by the herders cracking their whips were perfect additions to the scene. As she imagined spending the rest of her days in such a picturesque place, Feng's heart swelled with happiness. The grieving Gongzha would no longer be simply a floating presence in her heart – he would be hers for real. She was set on him, whether he was in agreement or not. It was just a matter of venturing into No Man's Land one more time. Just one more round of challenges. As long as she could bring him home, she could endure any amount of hardship.

In honour of his special guest, Gongzan carefully selected and killed a nine-year-old yak, made blood sausages and had his woman stew the bones.

They spoke different languages? No matter. Their backgrounds were different? That didn't matter either. As they sat by the lake, cutting meat and miming details about their lives, their laughter rang out clear across the water.

Gongzan used his hands to indicate a section of his leg, pointed to the white off-road vehicle, then picked up a rock and mimed setting it down. Feng laughed loudly and nodded; she understood that he meant he would save one of the yak's legs and put it on the roof of their car.

That night, Feng got drunk. It was her first time. She saw the family around her through a haze, waved her hands and give them all a thumbs-up. Gongzan and his brothers were also quite drunk. They put their arms round one another and began singing herders' songs, their voices echoing across the grassland. Their songs attracted others, and one by one people came to join them, bringing *baijiu* or meat.

Feng didn't know who started it, but at some point everyone began singing a familiar song.

'Today I must go to a faraway land
When we parted you said, "Please don't forget me."
Our promise hangs high in the sky
Those white clouds, those stars, that moon
Bear witness to our promise that in the next life we will
    meet again
And never forget each other.

'Beautiful shepherdess, I love you
No matter how the world changes, you are forever in my
    heart.

Beautiful shepherdess, your laughter echoes under the blue
*   sky*
And deep in my heart.

'Oh, give me a tent
I want to take your hand and live together free of pain.
Oh, give me some land
I want to dance with you there, slowly and forever.

'Shepherdess, sweet shepherdess
When will you return and make our love run smooth?
My greatest hope is not to be separated
Has our love in this life already scattered?
Could it be that loving you brings only despair?
Every day without you is a tragedy.'

21

No Man's Land: a nameless valley. Gongzha was cantering through it, letting his horse go where it pleased; his fox-skin hat was pulled down over his eyes and he was humming a little ditty. He was quite tired, so he pulled on the reins, jumped off, unloaded his bag and threw it to the ground. Then he sat down with his legs crossed, pulled out some meat and began to slowly hack off chunks to eat. There was a large herd of wild yaks not far off, some of them grazing and others butting heads; this was clearly their domain and seemed to have been that way forever.

Within moments, the distinctive crack of a whip split the air and a black figure appeared in the distance. Gongzha lifted his head and narrowed his eyes watchfully, but he didn't move. What was a lone rider, and a lone female rider at that, doing out in the wilderness so far from any other sign of human life?

The black horse rode straight for Gongzha. At a quiet sound from the woman, it reared and stopped almost directly in front of him.

Gongzha didn't even blink; he just looked on calmly.

'You're Gongzha?' the woman on the horse said in a haughty voice, pointing her whip at him. She wore a black leather hat, her wool robe was edged with gold, and her multiple plaits were fanned out across her shoulders.

Gongzha nodded.

'You're looking for the bear that mauled your woman to death?'

'How do you know that?' Gongzha said in surprise, a shadow of emotion crossing his face.

'Yongxi told me. The bear known as Kaguo, with a white circle on its forehead?'

Again, Gongzha nodded.

'I know where she is. Come with me.' Without even giving Gongzha a second look, the woman in black redirected her horse, cracked her whip and sped off, her long plaits streaming out behind her.

Gongzha chucked away his meat, put on his bag and leapt onto his horse.

The two horses clattered through the valley; neither rider spoke.

They'd been riding at a swift gallop for about three hours when a lake appeared in front of them. The woman in black reined in her horse and turned to Gongzha. 'Kaguo is in a mountain cave on the opposite side of the lake from here; she gave birth to a cub three days ago.'

Gongzha thanked her, took up his reins and prepared to set off along the lake shore.

'The lake is huge,' the woman called after him. 'If you go that way, it'll take you more than ten days' riding to get to the other side.'

Gongzha turned his horse back round and shot her a questioning look.

'Do you even know where to find Kaguo's cave?' The woman shook her head, jutted out her chin and gave him a mocking glance. 'And the shadow hunters' base is in the valley opposite. If you accidentally stumble in there, do you think Jijia will let you out alive?'

Gongzha looked searchingly at the woman, a string of questions circling in his head. She had appeared so suddenly, she was wearing a black robe and a brimmed hat, and her Tibetan accent indicated that she was an outsider, perhaps from Ngawa in Sichuan. Who was she and how did she know he was looking for Kaguo?

As he took in her black leather robe and proud eyes, he suddenly remembered that on the night he and Jijia had clashed, there'd been a woman standing by the cars. 'Are you... one of the shadow hunters?'

'Yes and no.' She laughed, neither confirming nor denying. 'I'm called Sega. I want you to remember that name.'

Gongzha couldn't help laughing at her imperious tone. 'Alright. I've remembered it, Sega.'

Sega cracked a smile, showing a row of white teeth. With a light tug of the reins, she steered her horse in a different direction, then glanced back and said loudly, 'Jijia is looking everywhere for you; if he finds you, I doubt you'll survive. I've got a boat ready in one of the bays on the lake, but first we need to hide the horses in another valley.'

Gongzha followed her without hesitation and they left the horses in the secluded valley, free to roam where they liked. Gongzha took his gun with him – as long as he had that, he would have food. From the valley they continued to a concealed spot on the lakeshore where Sega had stashed a yak-skin boat. She jumped in and Gongzha pushed the boat off the pebbly bottom, then began paddling them across the lake.

Sega sat in the back watching Gongzha, her arms propped behind her against the sides of the boat. 'There aren't any spies around here, don't worry. But there are a lot of Jijia's men in the valley where Kaguo is. When we get there we'll need to be careful.'

Gongzha glanced back at her. 'You know this place well?'

She smiled but didn't reply.

They landed in a sheltered cove, hid the boat in a reef and began to climb into the mountains. After they'd crossed two mountains, mountains that were neither large nor small, and a river valley, they came to a narrow pass of red rocks.

Sega crouched behind a large boulder and motioned for Gongzha, who was behind her, to do the same. Then she pointed upwards and said quietly, 'There are people up there.'

Craning his neck, Gongzha saw that higher up the pass there was a man in a leather *chuba* carrying a gun and pacing back and forth. 'What should we do?'

'They change guard every three hours. But even when they do the changeover, it'll be hard to get past them.'

'Is this the only route through?'

'There's one other, but it's harder,' Sega said quietly. 'You can get in via the mouth of the valley, but the guard there is very sharp – you'd definitely be spotted.'

'Then... there's no other way?'

'No.' Sega gave him a faintly derisive smile.

Gongzha didn't speak again, just picked up his gun ready to go forward.

Sega pulled him back. 'What are you doing?'

'I have to find Kaguo. If it's a choice between fighting a lone wolf or a pack of wolves, I choose this lone wolf,' Gongzha said, staring up nonchalantly at the pass.

'Do you really love Cuomu that much?'

Gongzha's face twitched. Then he said in a low voice, 'I cannot let my woman die unavenged.'

'Fine. I like men with principles and strong feelings.' Sega flashed him a smile that was like the unfurling of a mulberry flower. She stood up. 'Wait here. I'll get you through.'

'How will you do that?' Gongzha asked uneasily.

'Don't you worry about it. Stay here quietly, and don't move until I signal.' She glanced at him, crouched down in the shadow of the boulder and made her way to a spot about ten metres away. Then she stood up straight, deliberately stamped her boots and began to sing a herding song in a loud voice.

The man guarding the pass turned towards her when he heard her singing. In local dialect, he asked, 'Sega, what are you doing here?'

'Brother Qiangba, I'm chasing a fox. It came this way, but then I lost it. It's good you're here – help me look for it.'

'I'd be happy to help you look for it, Sega, but I'll be in trouble if the boss finds out I'm not at my post.'

'Don't worry about it! This is such a wild place, too wild even for birds – how could anyone get through here? Brother Jijia's too jumpy. Besides, he's fast asleep and won't be coming up here for a while.' Sega had scrambled up to the pass and was now standing in front of Qiangba, pointing at him with her whip. 'Or is it just that you don't really want to help me, Brother Qiangba?'

'No, no.' Qiangba shook his head and unslung his gun. 'Let's go. I'll help you find the fox.' He took a couple of steps and then glanced back. 'Is the boss really asleep?'

'Let's go. He was snoring when I left.' Sega gave Qiangba's back a shove and headed off, waving to Gongzha below as she went.

Gongzha laughed. He waited until they'd vanished behind the rocks on the slope, then sprang up and stealthily made his way across the pass.

He found himself looking down at a modestly sized river valley bounded by mountains on three sides and a lake on the fourth. A number of large tents were scattered across the valley floor. Jijia really did know how to choose a spot. The valley was easy to defend and hard to attack: Jijia could shoot down anyone who tried to come in and trap anyone who tried to leave; if all else failed, he and his people could take everything over the snow mountain behind them and disperse.

Kaguo was extremely clever to have chosen this place and to use Jijia's security to protect herself from Gongzha. Bears were no less intelligent than people.

As he rounded a bend, Gongzha saw Sega playing with her whip, leaning on a rock and smiling easily.

'Like I said, Kaguo is in this area. But you can only hunt her at night, once all the lights in the valley have gone out. During the day you'll have to stay hidden, otherwise the shadow hunters will know you're here, you'll be trapped, they'll find you, and there'll be trouble for me, too.'

Gongzha nodded. 'Thank you.'

'I'll bring you some food, don't worry. There's a spring on the mountain behind us – I've seen Kaguo drink there many times.' Sega smiled. She was still leaning against the rock and seemed to be laughing even when she wasn't.

'After I left, was Yongxi okay?' Gongzha asked.

'Oh, you care a lot about her,' Sega said with a crooked smile. 'Don't worry, Jijia might look like a leopard, but as soon as he gets anywhere near Yongxi, he turns into a sheep.'

Gongzha thought back to that moonlit night when Jijia had assumed he'd slept with Yongxi and brought his men to attack him. He gave a bitter laugh.

Sega stood up but didn't look at him again. 'There's a cave round the side of this boulder; you can stay in there. I'll find time to come and visit you. Remember, don't let anyone down there see you.'

Gongzha nodded.

Sega laughed, then turned and went down the mountain.

Gongzha walked around the boulder and found that there was indeed a cave. He bent down to go in and saw a thick wool blanket at the back and a bucket full of spring water beside it, together with a little bag of *tsampa* and some dried meat.

With such a safe and warm spot to stay in, Gongzha fell to dreaming almost immediately.

Sega returned to the encampment singing and carrying a large bunch of wild onions. She ran into Yangji coming out of a tent with a plateful of delicious-smelling fried buckwheat bread. When Yangji saw Sega, she smiled. 'Where have you been, Sega? You're so late back, and the boss has been looking all over for you.'

Sega stopped and handed the onions to Yangji. Then she took a piece of bread from Yangji's plate. 'Why have you made this? Has the wolf stopped eating meat and become vegetarian?'

'Oh, that mouth of yours! When the boss hears you, you'll be in for it again,' Yangji said smiling.

'What does the boss want me for?' Sega asked through a mouthful of bread.

'Haven't you heard? Jijia went out this morning and came back with his and Yongxi's child. When the boy couldn't find his mother, he started crying and making a fuss, so Jijia told me to make some fried bread for him. As the child's only ever eaten meat, he thought the bread might calm him down.'

'He stole the child?'

'He's the child's father – how can you say "stole"? Although it's true he didn't get his mother's permission.'

Yangji continued on to Jijia's tent and Sega followed her. Even from a distance they could hear the child's heartbroken cries. 'Ama! I want Ama! Ama...!'

'Tajiapu, darling, don't cry, be good. Aba has asked someone to make you something delicious, alright? Don't cry. Your *ama* went to look for some yaks; she'll be here in a few days. Be good, okay?'

Yangji and Sega opened the tent flap to find Jijia trying to keep hold of the child, who was squirming and flapping his hands and feet non-stop.

Dawacuo came in with them, carrying a small fox. 'Tajiapu,' she said, 'do you want some dried apricot? I'll make the fox play with you, would you like that?' She took the boy from Jijia and put him on the wide cushion, then set the fox down in front of him. 'Look, isn't it fun? I raised the fox myself. It's very smart. It can catch mice. Wait a bit and I'll take you out to play, alright? There are lots of people picking fruit.'

The little boy's eyes were glistening with tears, but when he saw the fox, he stopped crying and stretched out his hand to grab it. The fox was so scared, it dived right back into Dawacuo's *chuba*. Dawacuo grimaced at Sega and Yangji. She pulled the fox back out and put it on the cushion again, then lay down looking at Tajiapu. She picked up his little hand. 'Is that fun? Come on, you can pet it. That's right, pet it like this. It won't bite.'

Tajiapu started to focus on the fox and giggled as he grabbed its bushy tail.

Just then, Jijia, who had snuck out of the tent, put his head back in. As soon as the child saw him, he opened his mouth wide and began to wail. 'Ama! I want Ama...!'

'Go on, Brother, go and have a drink with the others. As soon as this little boy sees you, you child-stealer, he starts thinking of his mother.' Sega walked over and pushed Jijia's head out of the tent. She closed the flap and turned back. 'It's alright, the thief has gone. Darling, do you like the little fox?'

The child continued to cry, but nodded.

'If you stop crying, I'll get someone to catch one for you – how about that?' Sega bent down and smiled, scrunching up her face.

Tajiapu was in the middle of howling 'I want...' but when he heard that, he kept '... Ama' inside and instead turned his tear-streaked face hopefully towards Sega.

'That's better.' Sega sat down, picked him up and wiggled his nose. 'Let's wash your face and eat the bread, and then we'll go and catch a baby fox, okay?'

The little boy nodded.

Dawacuo raced out, smiling, and returned quickly with a bowl of water. She used a wet cloth to clean the little boy's face. 'He really looks like Uncle Jijia, Ama,' she said to Yangji as she watched the freshly cleaned child obediently eat his buckwheat bread.

Once he was done, Dawacuo took him by the hand and led him outside, carrying the fox.

Sega walked to the tent doorway, lifted the flap and scanned the area. There was no one in sight. The glare of the sunlight hitting the sand hurt her eyes a little.

She dropped the flap, looked at Yangji and said, 'I saw Gongzha.'

'What?' Yangji stared at her, thinking she'd misheard.

'Keep your voice down,' Sega said quietly and gestured outside. 'Yes, Gongzha... The Gongzha from your home encampment. Your friend Cuomu's man.'

'Whe... where?'

'The first time was at Yongxi's. The boss thought Gongzha had visited Yongxi's tent and he wanted to kill him. Later I heard Yongxi say that your friend Cuomu was mauled to death by a bear and that Gongzha has been trying to get his revenge ever since.'

'Cuomu was mauled to death by a bear?' Yangji muttered, leaning on the small table and staring at Sega. As she thought about her childhood playmate, she couldn't stop two streaks of tears from running down her face.

Sega and Dawacuo walked along the lake shore. Dawacuo was holding Tajiapu's hand and Sega was carrying her gun. A flock of wild ducks had recently come to the lake and as Sega hadn't touched her gun in a long time, she was keen to satisfy her urge to shoot something.

Jijia stood at the entrance to the big tent watching the three figures with a contented smile. He turned back inside, bottle in hand, poured himself a drink, then knocked it back.

Sega made Dawacuo take the little boy off to play. She set up the forked stand for her gun, lay down and squinted at the ducks on the sand. As the gunshot rang out, one duck fell and the others squawked and flew away. She laughed, then raced over to collect it.

'Dawacuo, get your mother to fry this tonight.'

'Okay. Your aim is getting better and better, Auntie!' Dawacuo took the wild duck and giggled.

'There's nothing else to do all day in this wretched place but practise. But I'm still not as good a shot as you – in fact, there's probably not even two men who can match your skills. You're lucky, having your Uncle Jijia as a teacher.'

Sega picked up the gun, walked to the edge of the lake, set up the stand again, lay down and fired a second time. She hit another duck and the water slowly became stained with blood. It wasn't that she wanted to eat wild duck, she was just bored and looking for something to do.

'My mother says women shouldn't play with guns. She says if

we get too wild, we won't find a man, so recently she hasn't let me shoot anything.' Dawacuo pursed her lips.

'Your mother is dead wrong. We women of the wilderness, we don't spend our days planting barley or weaving blankets – we spend our time fighting off wolves. If we didn't know how to use a gun, what would happen when the wolves came?' Sega fired another shot. This time she didn't hit anything.

By the time there were five dead ducks floating on the dark blue surface of the lake, Sega had lost interest. She put down the gun and glanced up at the mountain where Gongzha was hiding, a smile hovering on her lips.

Gongzha. The first time she heard that name was from Yangji. All Yangji had said was that he was her good friend Cuomu's man. He was in the army, he had never visited another woman's tent and he treated his woman like a precious treasure. When Yangji talked about Gongzha and Cuomu, there were traces of envy in her voice: any woman who found such a faithful man would not have lived in vain, she said.

Later, when Yongxi was about to give birth, she had a sudden fit of rage and kicked Jijia out of the tent. He couldn't get near her, so he sent Sega to be with her at the birth. Sega remembered that night well. Yongxi had taken herself out onto the plain, to a spot out of the wind. Sega squatted by her side and wiped the large drops of sweat off her forehead. According to grassland legend, children could not be born in the tent, otherwise a bloody disaster would follow. As she lay there racked by labour pains, Yongxi had repeated the unfamiliar name: Gongzha. He was the most important man in her heart, she said, but they were not meant to be together. His heart belonged to Cuomu and there was no room for another woman.

Ever since that night, Sega had longed to meet Gongzha and be the one to take up residence in his heart.

She returned her gaze now to the shimmering lake.

The first time she'd seen him for herself was outside Yongxi's tent, when he'd stood there in front of the raging Jijia. Gongzha had been calm, unfazed by the undeniable danger of the situation. That cool head, that ability to stay detached, and that air of melancholy – in a flash, Sega had fallen for him. After they'd got back to the encampment, she'd taken Jijia's black horse and without a word to anyone had sped off in the direction she thought Gongzha might have gone in.

Luckily, Kaguo had come to their area. Luckily, she'd found Gongzha.

As she pictured that bearded face and those sad eyes, a smile drifted up to Sega's lips again. She would convince him; she would make him forget that woman who'd already gone to Shambhala. Then, in the depths of the wilderness, they would build a tent and a family together, hunting and herding for the rest of their lives.

Sega sat there until the sun had set, then carried Tajiapu back to the tent. That night she couldn't sleep. She feared hearing a gunshot, feared that Gongzha would kill Kaguo and leave, feared that when he killed Kaguo, Jijia would find him. She lay there tortured by her fears until daybreak.

While she was busy looking after Tajiapu, Sega couldn't get away to see Gongzha. Even though she'd left Gongzha enough meat for two days, she was still worried about him.

When she saw that the child was playing happily with Dawacuo, Sega went to the kitchen tent pretending to look for something to eat. She waited for the two other women to leave, then called Yangji over and said quietly, 'Gongzha is on the mountain!'

Yangji's hand flew to her mouth in astonishment and she stared at Sega with wide eyes. Then she collected herself, walked swiftly to the tent flap and scanned the outside to make sure there was no one within earshot. 'When did he get here?'

'Two days ago. I brought him here. He wants to find Kaguo and get his revenge.'

'Are you crazy? Surely you know that Jijia's got men looking for him everywhere. He says Gongzha visited Yongxi's tent.'

'He's wrong. Gongzha and Yongxi haven't done anything.'

'I know that. Gongzha's heart still belongs to Cuomu, otherwise he wouldn't be searching for Kaguo like that. But you shouldn't have brought him here – it's too dangerous.'

'Don't worry, he's fine. I hid him in a cave. Dawacuo knows which one; she's been there with me before. I can't leave the encampment right now, so you and Dawacuo will have to think of a way to take him something to eat.'

Yangji nodded.

'Tell him that he cannot go outside under any circumstances, but I'll find a way to visit him,' Sega said. She heard Tajiapu crying and hurried out to him.

Yangji watched Sega's departing figure and sighed. She emptied the wild onions out of the basket and threw them all into the stove. After she'd watched them burn, she prodded them with a stick a few times and threw some yak pats on top to cover them. Then she scooped up some stewed and dried meat, wrapped it in a handkerchief and put it in her *chuba*. She went out of the tent and in a deliberately loud voice shouted for her daughter. 'Dawacuo! Dawacuo...!'

Dawacuo came running over, the little fox perched on her shoulder. 'What is it, Ama?'

'We're out of onions. Come with me up the mountain and help me dig some.'

'Yes, Ama.' Dawacuo followed behind her mother. When she saw Sega watching them with Tajiapu in her arms, Dawacuo gave her a sly wink and Sega smiled back.

Gongzha sat near the mouth of the cave, occasionally sticking his head out for a quick look around. He'd spent the previous night prowling round the mountain, but Kaguo hadn't emerged either to hunt or to drink. Gongzha was confident Sega wouldn't have brought him to the mountain under false pretences – she had no reason to trick him – and anyway he'd found quite a few traces of Kaguo's presence. He just needed to be patient; Kaguo would appear eventually. Every experienced hunter knew that patience was essential. It was simply a question of whiling away the time and wearing down your prey; as long as the hunter's patience was greater than that of his target, there was every chance of success.

So Gongzha was in no hurry. Whenever he felt tired during the daytime, he slept, and after he woke he sat by the mouth of the cave, watching the tents below and daydreaming. He knew that when he did finally see Kaguo, he wouldn't be able to resist firing at her, and he also knew that his gunshot would alert Jijia, the man who thought Gongzha had visited his woman and who longed to have Gongzha in his crosshairs. Gongzha wasn't afraid of fighting it out with Jijia, nor was he afraid of Jijia himself; he just didn't see the point of it. Jijia's hands were dark with the blood of illegally killed Tibetan antelopes and the government would deal with him.

When he heard two sets of footsteps approaching, he drew his head back inside the cave and picked up his gun from where it had been leaning against the cave wall.

'Is this it, Dawacuo?'

'Yes, Ama. Auntie and I often come here. There's a woollen blanket inside that I stole off Uncle Jijia.'

A woman stuck her face inside the cave and called softly, 'Gongzha! Gongzha…!'

Gongzha put down his gun and poked his head round the rock wall that he'd been hiding behind. 'You are…?'

'I'm Yangji! Don't you recognise me?' Yangji came in smiling.

'Yangji?' Gongzha stared at her, not quite believing his eyes. 'You weren't eaten by wolves?'

'Who said I was eaten by wolves?'

'That's what everyone on the grassland thinks. They found your headscarf all bloodied.'

'I did run into some wolves, but I wasn't eaten; they rescued me,' Yangji said with a smile. She pulled out the meat from her *chuba* and set it down on a nearby rock.

'Why didn't you go back to Cuoe Grassland?'

'What would I have gone back for? The skies are the same blue wherever we are.' Yangji pulled over her daughter. 'Dawacuo, this is your Uncle Gongzha.'

Dawacuo smiled shyly at him. 'Hello, Uncle Gongzha.'

'Lovely young lady, why do you have a fox with you?' Gongzha asked.

'I raised him,' she said with a smile. 'His mother was killed and he was very sad. I fed him yak's milk and meat. Uncle Gongzha, Auntie Sega says you've come to take revenge on Kaguo. When you do, can you please not kill her cubs but give them to me to raise instead?'

'You know Kaguo too?'

'Of course. I often see her. She has two cubs and they're exactly like her, with the same white rings on their foreheads.'

'Alright.' Gongzha laughed. 'Uncle will spare the cubs and give them to you.'

'It's a deal!' Dawacuo was very excited, and she slapped her palm against Gongzha's. 'I promise to take good care of them and I won't let them bite anyone.'

'Dawacuo, go outside and gather some wild onions,' Yangji said. 'Ama has things to discuss with Uncle.'

Dawacuo did as she was asked.

Yangji sat down and began filling Gongzha in on everything that had happened to her. She asked him about life back on Cuoe Grassland. He told her that her mother had cried every day after she'd disappeared and that she'd blamed Yangji's father, who eventually got so fed up with her mother that he vanished too. Yangji wept when she heard that.

Gongzha didn't know how to comfort her. Thinking about their childhood, remembering how they'd all collected yak pats and played in the lake together, remembering those who'd died and those who'd left, he felt sad too.

After quite a while, Yangji wiped away her tears and looked up. 'Look at me! I've been gone more than ten years and my child is almost grown. I never thought I'd see anyone from home again.'

'Dawacuo is Shida's daughter?'

'Yes. I left the grassland because I thought there was no future for me there. I didn't expect that I'd be rescued or that I'd deliver her. Shida... his children must also be nearly grown-up by now?'

'Shida went to college and stayed on in the city to work. Last I heard, he's coming back to the grassland to get a divorce.'

'He wants a divorce? Why?'

'That's what his older brother said. Shida left the grassland very suddenly. Everyone was saying that you'd been eaten by wolves and Shida was broken-hearted. He didn't want to stay on the grassland, so he decided to take the college entrance exam and leave.'

'Oh...' Yangji sighed. 'When I think back to that time, it's like it's a dream.'

'Don't you want to go back and see Shida?'

'Forget it, Gongzha. Shida and I couldn't be together back then and we can't be together now. He's been to college and is a national cadre. What am I? I'm not even a herder. I'm just the poachers' cook – how could I be with a national cadre? Luckily, I have a daughter. Dawacuo has a good head on her shoulders and with her as my companion, I'm happy enough.'

After Yangji left, Gongzha sat on by himself in the cave. Meeting her had been so strange and unexpected – he felt like he was in a dream. He had never imagined that Yangji might be alive still, let alone that they'd meet in a mountain cave in No Man's Land. What other surprises lay in wait for him? Where would he be tomorrow? These were not really things people could control. *Cuomu, if only you were here, we would be happy... Cuomu...* Gongzha's eyes were red.

*

Bears were most active at night; it was then that they came out to drink and to hunt for food. Gongzha had found the only spring on the mountain and he knew that for as long as Kaguo stayed on the mountain, she would always need to come there for water. If he waited patiently and did nothing to scare her, he was certain he'd see her one night.

He lay on a pile of broken rocks near the spring, as still as a leopard preparing to pounce. Two bharals came to drink, followed by some antelopes and some deer, but there was no sign of Kaguo's silhouette in the moonlight. Gongzha quietly picked up his gun and headed off.

Age-old enemies could sense one another, Gongzha thought as he made his way back to the cave. Had Kaguo detected his arrival on the mountain? After so many years of being pursued, her sensitivity to danger had got sharper. Could Kaguo pick up his presence on the breeze just like he could smell her musk on the wind?

As he approached the cave where he'd been hiding, he heard a rustling sound from inside. There was meat in the cave, and any wild animal on the mountain – fox, wolf or even bear – would be able to smell it. He lifted his gun off his shoulder.

When he reached the cave, there was a figure moving around inside it, and he heard Sega's voice. 'Gongzha!'

'Yangji said that you were watching Jijia's child – how did you get away?' Gongzha hung up his gun by the mouth of the cave. He saw that Sega was wearing a red robe with otter-skin collar and cuffs. Her hair was freshly washed and sat gleaming on her shoulders. She'd lost some of her swagger and seemed gentler, beautiful.

'Tajiapu is sleeping. I told Dawacuo to watch him and sneaked off. How are you? Did you see Kaguo?' Sega began to tidy up. She laid the sheepskin blanket she'd brought on the ground and threw the discarded bones out of the cave. 'Come in, I've brought you some good things to eat.'

'What sort of good things?' Gongzha smiled a little and stooped to come into the cave.

Sega opened the bamboo basket beside her, took out the food and set it on a rock between them.

'Yak's tongue, blood sausage and *baijiu*?' Gongzha sat down cross-legged and looked with astonishment at the things laid out on the rock.

'They just brought some back – I stole two bottles.' Sega picked up one of them, bit off the cap, and handed it to Gongzha. 'Yangji said that you liked *baijiu*.'

Gongzha took it and downed a large mouthful. 'Thank you, Sega.'

'Just for this bottle of *baijiu*?' Laughing, Sega grabbed the bottle, took a large swig and handed it back to him.

'Thank you for bringing me here to find Kaguo. And for Yangji. She came yesterday. If it wasn't for you, I'd still be thinking she was dead.'

'What of it? Yangji's been alive all along.' Sega took a piece of tongue and passed it to him, then bit into some herself. 'As for Kaguo, after all these years, it's obvious you're not going to be able to move on until you've had your revenge.'

Gongzha didn't say anything, just took another slug of *baijiu*. It was a long time since he'd last had any alcohol – out there in the wilderness, he had no way of getting any.

Sega shrugged off one sleeve of her *chuba* and tied it round her waist, revealing the white dress she was wearing underneath. 'Drink up,' she said, smiling. 'There's another bottle, to make sure you get enough to drink tonight.'

'From your accent, I think you're not from here, are you, Sega?'

'I'm from Ngawa. I joined the poachers' posse after my mother and father died. Brother Jijia and his men found me on a road somewhere. I'd fainted and luckily they came across me while they were out hunting and rescued me.'

Gongzha nodded. 'Don't you want to go back to Ngawa?'

'What would be the point? I don't have family there. Besides, no one cares whether women like me live or die.' She passed Gongzha a piece of sausage.

'Don't say that, Sega.' He lifted the bottle and took another mouthful. 'You need to live well. A beautiful woman like you should find a man to spend your days with. Staying with the poachers is not a long-term plan.'

'I agree. I want to find myself a man,' Sega said pointedly.

Gongzha gulped down the rest of the *baijiu*, put the empty bottle to the side and wiped the corner of his mouth, not yet satisfied.

Sega passed him the second bottle with a smile.

Gongzha smiled his thanks. The atmosphere in the cave grew strained; neither of them knew what else to talk about. Gongzha knocked back the *baijiu* in swift gulps. Sega kept passing him meat, taking the occasional sip herself.

By the time all the *baijiu* had been drunk and all the meat eaten, the moon's rays were slanting into the cave. That night, the moonlight seemed a little different, the wind a little softer.

Sega pushed away the rock they'd been eating off, looked at Gongzha leaning against the wall in a drunken haze, and blurted out, 'Gongzha, be my man – don't go looking for Kaguo.'

'What?' Gongzha opened his eyes and stared at her in surprise.

'Be my man,' Sega repeated clearly. 'Let's set up a tent together: you can hunt and I'll herd.'

Gongzha sat up. 'I have a woman, Sega.' He swayed a little, but he spoke with conviction.

Sega looked at him straight. 'What grasslander commits themselves to just one woman? And anyway, Cuomu isn't here any more, she's gone to Shambhala; let me take care of you in her place,' she said passionately.

'No, no, no...' Gongzha swayed again. His head had begun to hurt. 'You're a good woman, Sega. Find a man who loves you. I already have Cuomu. I will never forget her, no matter where she is – in Shambhala or on the grassland, she will always be in my heart.'

Sega looked at him and flushed. How could he be so stupid? The woman was dead and yet he continued to yearn for her.

Could he really sacrifice his whole life for a dead woman? She knelt down in front of him, patted his chest, looked into his reddened eyes and said, 'Gongzha, Cuomu isn't here any more. You need to start living again. You need to find another woman and set up a tent. Cuomu is in the past. You still have tomorrow, and a long life thereafter.'

'Don't you understand, when Cuomu died, so did my future.' Gongzha shook his head and stumbled back against the wall, his face dark. 'When she left, she took my heart with her. When you've lost your heart, what else is there to do but wander?'

Sega shook her head in defeat. She wanted to scream, wanted to scratch him and kick him. But she didn't. She just turned and scrambled out of the cave.

The moonlight was stark and lonely, just like her heart.

Abruptly she turned round and went back inside, but Gongzha had already fallen asleep, slumped against the cave wall. He repeatedly called, 'Cuomu! Cuomu!' and his face was wet with tears.

A familiar shape flitted past the mouth of the cave. Gongzha woke suddenly, as if he'd sensed it in his dream.

Kaguo!

Without thinking, and in a single swift move, he snatched his gun off the wall, crouched down and fired at the lumbering figure.

The *ping* of the gunshot lingered for a long time in the quiet night.

The tents at the foot of the mountain erupted in sudden commotion: torches and butter lamps began to light up, and then came a chorus of human shouts and neighing horses.

People began to race up the mountain.

'You...' Sega darted over. When she saw that Gongzha was hunched down and about to pursue Kaguo with his gun, she ran over to stop him. 'Don't follow Kaguo. You need to find somewhere to hide – and quick! I'll work out the rest.'

Gongzha glanced down at the troop of dancing torch beams and very unwillingly retreated into the cave.

Sega berated him a bit more, then went down another way.

22

Everyone heard the gunshot, but no one knew where it had come from.

Jijia grabbed his gun and scanned the surrounding snow mountains. He gestured at the man beside him and barked, 'You! Stay here with three others, organise the women and make sure we're ready to decamp at a moment's notice. Everyone else, split into three groups and search the mountains, one group on each side of the encampment. I want you to be so thorough, even a rabbit couldn't get through.'

'Yes, boss!' The men raced off.

Sega came in all dishevelled, looking as if she'd been frightened awake, and holding Tajiapu sound asleep in her arms. When she saw the group leaders preparing to take their men up into the mountains, a worried expression came over her face; she turned and took the child away.

Yangji was already in Sega's tent, pacing back and forth, wrapped in a shawl. As soon as Sega returned, Yangji quickly took Tajiapu, laid him on a cushion and covered him with a blanket.

Sega gripped her hand in desperation. 'What do we do now, Auntie? What will we do if they find Gongzha?'

Yangji patted her hand and said quietly, 'Let's see how things play out. There's no point getting upset.'

But Sega was in tears. 'The mountain is only so big – they'll find that cave very soon. He's just one man, how will he fend off so many?'

'Don't worry yourself. Have a seat.' Yangji was actually frightened to death herself, but she still comforted Sega. 'Dawacuo, make your auntie some tea.'

Dawacuo poured a glass of tea for Sega and then went to look out of the door.

Sega held her glass and stared at Yangji, tears streaming down her face. Even the most heroic woman would lose control seeing the man she loved in such danger. To care was to be distraught. 'Auntie, it's all my fault. If I hadn't brought him here, he wouldn't be in this mess.'

'How is it your fault? Gongzha is desperate to find Kaguo. He would follow her no matter where she went. Don't cry; it won't do you any good to cry. Dawacuo, go and see what's happening outside.'

Dawacuo went out and came back shortly after. 'They're still looking. Uncle Jijia sent lots of men to guard the road out and others are searching around the lake.'

Sega looked at Yangji and burst into tears again.

Just before dawn, the sound of gunfire came from the mountain. Sega and Yangji immediately rushed out of the tent.

Jijia, who was halfway up the mountain on the left, laughed coldly and shouted into the darkness. 'Gongzha, come out! Why are you hiding in the rocks like a sparrow instead of soaring through the sky like an eagle?'

Gongzha replied calmly from somewhere on the mountain. 'I'm a hunter, Jijia. Hunters have to be patient.'

'I've been looking for you everywhere. You really have some nerve, stealing into my lair like this. It seems you and I have some kind of shared destiny. Why don't you come out and show us your face? Let my comrades see the great hunter, the man so hated by the wolves.' He fired a shot up the slope. The bullet hit a rock and sparks flew in all directions.

'I'm here to look for Kaguo, Jijia. The Buddha knows what you've done and there are people on the grassland who will deal with you.'

'Are you afraid? You dare to come into my lair, but you don't dare show yourself? What kind of grassland eagle are you? Comrades, he looks down on us; he thinks we're poachers. Why don't we go up and invite this brave hero down?' Jijia laughed darkly and waved his hand towards the peak.

The men crouched down again and resumed their search up the mountain.

A shot rang out. Someone called back, 'Over here, Brother, he's over here!' As soon as the man finished shouting, another shot rang out and the same man fell to the ground. 'Argh, my leg. You bastard! He's shot me in the leg – come and get me!'

Everyone rushed to where he'd fallen.

Yangji and Sega stood at the foot of the mountain, staring up anxiously. They could just make out a lone figure flitting around close to the peak, with others in pursuit.

Every so often an injured man was helped down the mountain. 'He's a really good shot, that man – definitely a match for the boss,' Qiangba said as he handed over one of his wounded comrades to the waiting women. 'No one but Gongzha would dare come into No Man's Land with just a gun and his horse, that's what the boss said. He's tough, for sure – he answered as soon as the boss called out to him.'

'What will Brother do?'

'What can he do? Our orders are that no matter what happens, Gongzha can't be left alive, otherwise our base will be in danger.'

'I don't think Gongzha is the kind of coward who'd squeal on us to the government.' Sega glanced at Qiangba and flashed him a smile.

'We don't know whether he would or not, Sega, but we can't risk it. As the boss says, it's better to be wrong ten thousand times than to have just one regret.' And with that, Qiangba headed back up the mountain.

As it slowly started to get light, the sun daubed the horizon red. Men began coming down the mountain one after the other, wanting meat, *baijiu* or water.

Jijia came down at about noon. He propped his reddened eyes open, looked in on Tajiapu, rubbed his forehead as if his heart hurt, then went back to his tent. He changed into light clothes, put on his black leather hat and took out an automatic pistol.

'Brother, Brother...' Sega burst out.

Jijia looked at her worried face and smiled. 'Take good care of the child, Sega, and don't worry, Brother will be fine.'

'Brother... you're... really going to kill him?'

'We've lived here for many years now – we don't want to have to move just because of Gongzha. Besides, he's your brother's enemy.'

'I... I'm afraid...'

Jijia patted her shoulder comfortingly, thinking she was worried for him. 'Your brother is here, Sega. There's nothing to be afraid of. Don't worry, he's just one man.'

'No, Bro... Brother, I... I'm afraid Auntie Yongxi... she... she... she won't forgive you!' As soon as the words were out, Sega regretted them. Everyone knew Jijia hated Gongzha because of Yongxi, and bringing Yongxi into this was like throwing oil onto the fire.

Jijia's face darkened, his eyes flashed and he turned and strode off towards the mountain.

Through the following hours they heard occasional shouts from the mountain and occasional gunshots. In the afternoon, Qiangba came down with ten or more sheep-gut water bags to refill. 'The boss got him.'

Sega was in the middle of ladling out the water. When she heard the news, she dropped the bag into the water and stared at him.

'What's up, Sega?'

'You... Who did you say was hurt?' Sega looked fixedly at him and spat out every word.

'Don't worry, your brother's fine.' Yangji came over and gave Sega's clothes a tug. Then she turned to Qiangba. 'Look at her, she's been worried about her brother since last night – she barely slept. Sega, hurry up and get Qiangba the water; they're waiting for it up on the mountain.'

'You scared me, Sega. From the expression on your face, I was starting to think you were Gongzha's woman.' Qiangba laughed. He took one of the water bags and hung it from his belt. 'I meant that Gongzha got hit by the boss. There's no one like the boss, is there! I've never seen a shot like him. Although our friend Gongzha is pretty good – he'd have made a useful addition to our posse. Shame!'

As soon as Qiangba left the tent, Sega collapsed onto the ground. Yangji quickly helped her over to a cushion, then poured a cup of tea and passed it to her. Sega drained it, thumped down the cup, stood up resolutely and snatched up her gun ready to head out.

Yangji held her back. 'What are you doing?'

'I'm going to rescue him.'

'You're going to rescue him? Aren't you just following him to his death?'

'I don't really care.' Sega looked at Yangji. 'I can't watch him be killed, Auntie. He's my man. If he dies, I want to die with him.' There was a new determination in her voice.

'Who says he's going to die?' Yangji took Sega's gun and forced her back onto the cushion. 'Sit down, we need to give this some more thought. There has to be something else we can do.'

Sega sat. Her heart felt as if it had been clawed by a cat. She grabbed hold of the cup beside her and hurled it across the floor in frustration.

Yangji paid no attention to Sega. Instead, she gazed at the flames leaping in the stove and the meat turning as it cooked. Dawacuo kept working the bellows, and the yak pats burnt fiercely. Tajiapu lay in her arms, chuckling as he watched the little fox. The flames from the stove lit up his face and his cheeks glowed red.

'I have a plan, Sega.' Yangji glanced at the two children and her voice trembled a little.

Sega darted over to her. 'Auntie...'

Yangji put her mouth to Sega's ear and quietly explained her plan. Sega nodded repeatedly, and a little smile finally appeared at the corners of her mouth.

The day grew dark. The moon slowly rose in the sky.

The three men who'd been left behind to take care of any emergencies in the encampment felt there was nothing to worry about now that they knew Gongzha was on his own and wounded, so they went up the mountain to join in the fun. The women didn't go up with them; they stayed down below, chatting among themselves.

No one knew how the fire in the tents behind them started. They just heard Sega shouting and then Yangji.

'Fire! Fire! Come and help us put it out!'

'Who could have started it? What about the children? Tajiapu, where are you?'

'Dawacuo? Dawacuo!'

Gongzha was hiding behind a boulder, his sheepskin *chuba* tied around his waist, his shoulder wet with blood. He'd been plotting his escape when he suddenly saw flames rising into the sky. Then he heard Jijia shouting orders. 'Three of you go and watch the pass; everyone else go back down to fight the fire.' Guns in hand, the men who'd been hunting him flew back down the mountain.

Gongzha had no idea what was going on, so he poked his head out to have a look.

'Uncle Gongzha! Uncle Gongzha...'

A figure appeared to the right of the boulder; it seemed to be carrying a child.

'Dawacuo, what are you doing here?'

'We've come to rescue you!' Dawacuo flashed him a clever smile.

'This is no time for games, Dawacuo. Hurry back and find your mother.'

'Ama sent me up here. Uncle Gongzha, this is Uncle Jijia's child. Auntie Sega says that you're to take good care of him and not hurt him.'

'Jijia's son?' Gongzha pictured the little boy in Yongxi's arms, sturdy as a calf.

'Yes. He's called Tajiapu. He's sleeping now. Are you hurt, Uncle Gongzha?'

Gongzha twitched the corner of his mouth, forced out a smile and said, 'Uncle is slightly hurt, but it's fine.'

'Let's go to the cave; there's medicine there. Before, when Auntie Sega was learning to shoot, she came up here to hunt. If she hit an animal that was too small to keep by mistake, we helped it get better and then let it go.'

Gongzha glanced at the flames down below and then at Dawacuo. He finally understood. Clutching the right side of his chest, he followed Dawacuo back to the cave, took off his *chuba* and made Dawacuo hang it over the cave mouth. He used his flint to light some oily paper and sterilised his knife. Then he bent his head and cut open his chest; blood streamed down his copper-coloured skin.

Dawacuo took off her headscarf and helped mop it up. 'Does it hurt, Uncle Gongzha?'

Gongzha gritted his teeth and pulled out the bullet. It clanged as it fell onto the stony floor of the cave. 'No.'

Dawacuo pulled a paper bag from a crevice in the rock, sprinkled some medicinal powder on Gongzha's wound, then wrapped it in a clean cloth she'd brought.

Tajiapu lay quietly on Dawacuo's *chuba*, breathing evenly.

Dawacuo filled a wooden pail with water, cleaned the blood off Gongzha's chest with a small cloth and helped him pull on his clothes. When he saw her looking tearful, Gongzha smiled and said, 'Dawacuo, why doesn't Uncle sing for you?'

'Alright.' Dawacuo took down the *chuba* from the cave mouth and covered Gongzha with it. With Tajiapu still fast asleep, she sat down and leant against Gongzha.

Gongzha gazed out at the bright moonlight and sang softly.

'Today I must go to a faraway land
When we parted you said, "Please don't forget me."
Our promise hangs high in the sky
Those white clouds, those stars, that moon
Bear witness to our promise that in the next life we will
    meet again
And never forget each other.

'Beautiful shepherdess, I love you
No matter how the world changes, you are forever in my
    heart.
Beautiful shepherdess, your laughter echoes under the blue
    sky
And deep in my heart.

'Oh, give me a tent
I want to take your hand and live together free of pain.
Oh, give me some land
I want to dance with you there, slowly and forever.

'Shepherdess, sweet shepherdess
When will you return and make our love run smooth?
My greatest hope is not to be separated
Has our love in this life already scattered?
Could it be that loving you brings only despair?
Every day without you is a tragedy.'

In the morning, Jijia came charging murderously up the mountain with a band of men and horses. He rampaged all over the mountain, occasionally firing into the air. 'Gongzha, Gongzha, what sort of man are you? Not only do you set fire to one of our tents, but you steal my son too?'

The gunshots frightened the child awake. When Tajiapu opened his eyes and saw that he was not in his familiar tent, he began to wail.

Gongzha stood up, clasping his wound, took up his gun, and walked out.

Dawacuo quickly picked up Tajiapu and put him in Gongzha's arms. 'Auntie Sega said that if Jijia sees you holding him, he'll let you go. I know you're hurt, Uncle Gongzha, but we can't do anything about that just now – try and hold on a bit longer.'

Using a child as a shield was against Gongzha's principles. He wanted to put Tajiapu down, but the little boy was still bawling and Dawacuo was pushing him from behind. He had no option but to go out there with the child in one hand and his gun in the other.

Jijia was standing less than fifty metres below him with a gang of men. They all looked up in surprise when he suddenly appeared with Tajiapu.

'Tajiapu, darling, Aba's here; there's no need to be afraid.' When Jijia saw his son flailing and screaming in Gongzha's arms as if his guts were about to burst, he hurriedly ordered his men to hold back. 'Don't open fire. I'll kill anyone who hurts Tajiapu.' Then he cursed Gongzha. 'You'd use a couple of kids to protect yourself, Gongzha? You spineless creature, you're feebler than a blade of grass on the plain.'

Gongzha gave a bitter laugh. He glanced first at the child bawling in his arms and then at Jijia. 'Yongxi had this child for you, and you still doubt her? Don't you understand what sort of person your woman is, Jijia? Come, take your son back down. I might not be a soaring eagle, but I have eagles' wings in my heart. How could I use a child to protect myself? Come, take your son.'

Hearing this, Jijia's eyes grew wide. He stared at Gongzha in disbelief. 'If you weren't intending to use him as a shield, why did you steal him?'

'Steal him? When did I steal—' Gongzha was about to say that the children had run up the mountain themselves, but

Dawacuo tugged on his clothes from behind. He recovered himself and hurriedly said, 'I was simply afraid that your son would be killed in the fire, so I brought him and this little girl up here.'

'So I'm supposed to thank you for saving my son?' Jijia laughed coldly. 'You think I'm three years old?'

Gongzha laid the child on the ground, squatted down, pulled Dawacuo forward and said, 'Take him over there.'

Dawacuo took Tajiapu's small hand very unwillingly and slowly made her way down the slope.

Gongzha stood up. 'Jijia, why don't we settle this matter the grassland way?'

Jijia rushed over, picked up his son and handed him to his men. When he turned to face Gongzha, there was a look of appreciation in his eye. 'It seems you're a decent man after all. So, what will it be?'

'Man to man. No guns. Knives.'

'That's not fair. You're wounded. Let's use guns, it's faster.'

Gongzha nodded and lifted up the old gun beside him. Jijia shook his head. 'That gun of yours is too heavy; use this one.' He took a smaller gun off one of his men and threw it to Gongzha.

'We'll go by the old rules: a single shot each. Let fate decide.' Jijia stood on a rock and raised his hand.

Gongzha also raised his hand.

The two men stood there in the morning light staring at each other, faint signs of frustration on both their faces.

Gongzha's frustration was that his opponent was Yongxi's man. No matter how evil Jijia was, it shouldn't be up to him to take his life. In all Gongzha's years of hunting, his gun had never taken a human life.

Jijia's frustration was that Gongzha had unexpectedly given his son back. He'd thought Gongzha had stolen Tajiapu and was going to use him as a hostage. He saw that Gongzha's chest was bandaged and that blood was seeping through the white cloth, yet Gongzha stood there proud and quiet. Jijia admired that kind of man, a true grassland man: dripping blood not dripping tears, prepared to lose his life but not to lose face.

The wind moaned. Two old geese flew past, squawked and disappeared into the distance. The silence intensified, as in the moment just before an explosion. If there was a gunshot, one man would fall.

A sudden hysterical shout rose up from the foot of the mountain and surprised Jijia so much he almost dropped his gun. 'Jijia, you stole my son! If you kill my brother, don't you ever expect to enter my tent again!'

Yongxi. If only she'd come earlier or later – why did she have to turn up exactly at this moment? Jijia was a respected figure in the wilderness, how could he be so frightened of a woman?

Very impatiently, very reluctantly, Jijia put down his gun, lowered his head and said disappointedly, 'Go, Gongzha. The bear you're looking for left this area yesterday. She went to the other side of the lake.'

Gongzha looked at Jijia, who a moment ago had stood there fearlessly, about to risk his life, but now seemed as miserable as a patch of frostbitten grass, and he couldn't help laughing. This really was a case of one person having power over another. He brought his palms together in grateful thanks, nodded to Jijia, picked up his gun and headed off towards the mountain pass. The sound of his lusty singing drifted back on the wind.

23

As Feng watched the grassland flashing by, getting wilder and increasingly remote the deeper in they drove, she grew more and more unsettled. But this was No Man's Land after all, not some Shanghai backstreet. She'd set out so hastily – what if she didn't find him? What if when she did find him, he didn't want her?

She sighed inwardly. Given that she had made the decision to go looking for him, what was the point of overthinking it now? As for whether or not he would want her, she'd worry about that when she found him.

Gongzha: placid by nature but also capable of intense feelings. She had never missed someone so much, had never missed a place so much. Everything about the Tibetan wilderness was beautiful, and he was somewhere in this heavenly place, somewhere in this boundless vastness.

Rongma was right on the edge of No Man's Land and the last place to get supplies. Feng took the advice of her driver Junsang and agreed to stay there a couple of days to rest and stock up on food. Two days was not a long time, but to Feng, who was longing to spread her wings, it seemed like two years.

She remembered Rongma very clearly. She had said goodbye to Gongzha on the mountain pass above the town. At the time, she'd thought she would never come back, would never see him again. Standing in the town now, she felt an incomparable sense of familiarity. Even the afternoon dust and the filthy street dogs seemed almost familial; it was as if she'd never left. She walked confidently as she meandered down the empty street. A little lamb trotted by and Feng knelt down to let it lick her palm. The warm feeling on her hand felt just like Gongzha's gaze. When she was ill, being in Gongzha's care had felt like that. Where under this blue sky was he? Which white cloud was hiding him, which mountains were sheltering him?

As if in a dream, she made her way to the hot springs, marvelling at the lovely red-rock valley unfolding in front of her. Beneath the blue sky and white clouds, the glistening travertine had formed all kinds of shapes, and the clear, steaming pool shone like a beautiful piece of jade. Red, white and blue pools were scattered across the slope. A stream wound its way through the pale yellow travertine, babbling cheerfully over red and green pebbles polished smooth and shiny by its flow. She picked one up and held it in her hand. It was cold, and as she rubbed it she felt a deep sense of calm. The grass on either side of the stream was a lush, dark green, and further up the slope some lost sheep were gazing down at her.

Feng stood on a ledge and saw that there were three levels, each with its own particular beauty. She was on the highest tier, where steam swirled across the surface of a hot-water lake and a small spring gurgled alongside. Some of the nearby springs had water, others were dry patches of ground that quivered and pulsed. To one side stood a stone incense burner that looked like it hadn't been used in a long time, and above the steaming lake a string of five-coloured prayer flags fluttered gently in the wind. These were the only manmade things in sight and they lent a Buddhist air to the land and the water.

On the second tier was a small pool fringed by slabs of black stone. Hot water streamed down the slope from the plain above and in places a yellow flower protruded above the flow, waving towards the sun. The springs on the lowest tier were fed by a stream, its silver waters like a little parasol. The entire place was like a dreamscape. Feng stood there captivated by the sight of such striking beauty in the wilderness, quite forgetting where she was.

Just then a Tibetan woman emerged from the valley opposite. Tall and slender, with tanned cheeks and heavy eyebrows, she was dressed in a black robe and wore her long hair braided into countless tiny plaits; her large eyes shone like the light of the sun.

When she saw Feng, she stopped in surprise, then smiled, revealing two rows of white teeth. She continued to the edge of a small pool, took off her robe, walked into the water and began splashing herself. Seeing Feng staring stupidly at her, she laughed and said in Sichuanese-accented Mandarin, 'Aren't you going to bathe?'

Feng watched as the woman carried on splashing herself and giggling as the water caressed her butter-coloured skin. In a flash, Feng's body began to itch, as if tens of thousands of tiny insects were crawling all over her. All those days on the road had made her weary, and her long hair had sand in it and stuck to her back like a board.

She walked over, took off her clothes and entered the pool. As her body sank into the warm, clear water, she felt relaxed in a way she'd never experienced before.

The woman laughed. 'Your skin is so white, it's like milk.'

'Yours is also very nice, like butter.' Feng looked at her smiling face and added, 'I'll help you undo your plaits.'

'Alright!' the young woman replied and came over, turning her back towards Feng.

Feng lifted up a handful of her small plaits and began to slowly undo them. She laid the pieces of red coral and turquoise that were threaded through the plaits at the edge of the pool. 'Your hair's so long! Black and slippery like silk.'

'It's never been cut,' the woman said. 'Your hair is also beautiful, so curly. Where are you from?'

'Shanghai. Have you heard of it?'

'Yes. It's very big, isn't it?'

'It is. Lots of cars and people.'

'Are you here on holiday?' The woman dunked her hair in the water and began to scrub it; it drifted lightly in the ripples.

'I...' Feng leant back against the edge of the pool and stretched out her legs. Underwater, her skin looked as smooth and white as jade. She folded her arms behind her head and gazed up at the slowly moving clouds; as she did so, that bearded face floated out from among them. She laughed, blushing a little, and said lightly, 'I've come to find my spouse.'

'What's a spouse?' the young woman asked, turning to Feng with a smile.

'A spouse is what you would call a man.'

'Oh, you've come to find your man!' She smiled again. 'Your man is very lucky to have married a woman as beautiful as you!'

'Am I beautiful? No, you're beautiful. As beautiful as this plateau.' Feng smiled, sat up and helped the young woman rub her back. 'Do you have a man?'

'Yes. But he's not here now, he's always off with his gun somewhere. I'm getting ready to go and look for him.' The woman blushed, her fingers unconsciously running over her full breasts. Where was he? When would that man stop wandering the wilderness with his old gun and his old horse and come to permanent rest in her tent?

Feng looked at the woman, so lost in her imagination; her entire face was a picture of blissful rapture. This was a woman sunk deep in the river of love – only a woman with love and longing in her heart would wear an expression like that.

'You must have felt blessed when you were together,' Feng said, as she and the woman rested against the side of the pool.

'Yes. I like being with him. He's a real man, not afraid of anything. That's the sort of man I like, the sort that makes a woman feel safe. What about your man? Is he good to you?'

'He is. The last time I was here, I'd got so lost, I almost died, and it was him who saved me and led me out of No Man's Land. Those days that we were together were the happiest of my life. He taught me how to tell the direction and how to identify the tracks of different animals. We even rescued two little antelopes, called Baobao and Beibei, though unfortunately I couldn't take them back to Shanghai. They must be grown up now – I wonder if they'll recognise me?'

'If you've come this far to find him, surely he'll be moved?'

'I don't know. Although...' Feng pictured the shocked expression on Gongzha's face when he finally got to see her and she couldn't help smiling.

'Men...! If you kept them locked up at home all day, they'd feel stifled. But no matter how far they run, women like us will always catch them in the end.'

'When I find him, I'm not going to let him go off wandering by himself again. I want to be with him – where he goes, I'll go too,' Feng said. As she imagined never being apart from him again, she laughed happily.

'Yes, I'm the same. I don't want to leave my man either. Just wait till I catch him – I won't let him leave. Ha ha ha...'

Feng laughed too and the two women chatted on until the sun began to sink in the west. They were interrupted by the shrill sound of a whistle from a distant mountaintop; looking up, they saw several faint male figures near the summit. Feng automatically clasped her clothes to her chest. The other woman stood up unconcernedly, beads of water hanging from her buttery skin. She stuck her fingers in her mouth and issued a piercing whistle in reply. Then she picked up her black robe, put it on and fastened her belt. She looked at Feng and said sincerely, 'Hey, I'm going. Do you want me to help you find your man?'

'Thank you, but no. I believe the Buddha will help me find him.'

'Alright then, I'm off.' She bent down and quickly ripped away the clothes Feng had been holding in front of her chest. Feng shrieked and slipped back beneath the water.

'If you ever need any help in No Man's Land, you can come and look for me; my name is Sega.' She laughed loudly, threw Feng's clothes down beside the pool and ran off towards the valley she'd come from.

Feng laughed too. As she watched Sega get further and further away, her long, damp hair flying out behind her, Feng suddenly came to her senses and called out, 'Hey, Sega, have you seen a man looking for a bear in No Man's Land? He's called Gongzha!'

But all she could hear by way of response was the vanishing sound of drumming hooves.

When Feng was satisfied that the men on the mountain peak had also disappeared, she climbed out of the water, put on her clothes and left the valley.

That night Feng stayed at the government guesthouse, in a mud-walled room of around twenty square metres containing a scattering of iron and wooden bedsteads. A floral drape hung from the ceiling, but it had clearly not been changed for many years and looked like it would rain dust at any minute. It wasn't such a bad set-up, though; certainly preferable to sleeping outdoors, as she had on other nights, in sheep pens or by tumbledown walls. Compared with that, being out of the wind in a place with four walls and a roof was a luxury.

Junsang slept in the car as usual. He said he needed to watch over it because of all the supplies they were carrying.

Very early the next morning, someone in a herder's outfit turned up and said that his brother had seen Gongzha in some valley, although he couldn't say exactly where. Junsang told Feng to wait in the town while he went and found out more. Feng wanted to go with him, but, mindful that someone needed to keep an eye on the car, she stayed put. She reminded herself that she was now in Tibet and that Gongzha was only just ahead of her, in some unknown place; she would see him soon – the Buddha did not play tricks on those with a sincere heart.

There was a well in the courtyard and local residents came by frequently to draw water. Feng leant over the side of the well and stared at her reflection, reimagining it with the bearded man reflected alongside her. She had no control over her emotions: her longing was like a spider's web and she was the insect trapped inside it, unable to free herself however hard she struggled.

A silver-haired old woman arrived carrying a deep wooden bucket on her back. When she saw Feng, she smiled compassionately.

Feng smiled in return and turned to help her. She lifted the bucket off the woman's back, tied it to the well rope and helped her fill the bucket. Then she copied the old woman and placed the bucket strap around her own forehead to bear the weight on her back more efficiently. The old woman watched Feng but made no objection, only helped Feng push her long hair out of the way. Then she took Feng's hand and they walked out of the courtyard together.

When they arrived at her home, the old woman called her granddaughter and said something in Tibetan, pointing to the mountain behind the house.

'Granny says the bearded man you're looking for was here several days ago,' the little girl said in halting Mandarin. 'He carved a picture up there.'

'He carved a picture?' Feng couldn't quite imagine that. Gongzha's large hands were adept at handling a gun, but could they draw as well? The idea was highly entertaining.

'Yes.' The little girl nodded earnestly. She pulled Feng outside, pointed at the nearby mountain slope, and said, 'Up there. There are lots of pictures on those rocks.'

'Can you take me there?' Feng asked, giving the girl a pleading look. Just the words 'the bearded man you're looking for was here several days ago' had been enough to make her heart leap.

'Granny says she'll watch the car for you,' the little girl said, and pulled Feng outside.

The crushed stones that littered the ground gleamed darkly in the sunlight. Feng looked at her outdoor sports watch; it was three in the afternoon. In northern Tibet, this was when the sun was at its strongest. She pulled up the hood of her windcheater and fastened it tight around her forehead. She didn't want Gongzha to not recognise her, and a woman had to look good for the one she loved. But when she thought about that some more, she realised it didn't matter. During their days together, she'd been so ill, she'd almost died; her face had peeled and her lips had been chapped. He'd already seen her at her worst, and surely she looked a lot better than that now?

The mountainside she'd thought looked so near actually took two hours to climb. 'It seemed so close, but it's three kilometres away.' Feng's watch tracked distance; she could hardly believe it.

'Many things here look near but take a long time to reach,' the little girl said.

'That's true enough.' Feng nodded, gazing up at the snow peaks and mountain ranges in the distance. The air in northern Tibet was crystal clear, which made it seem like you were looking through binoculars the whole time because you could see things in such detail. 'Where are the pictures?'

'On these rocks!' The little girl pointed at the boulders scattered across the slope.

'On the rocks?' Feng dipped her head and began to search.

The mountainside was covered in broken rocks, large, small, thin and thick, their surfaces burnt black by the sun. There were quite a few ancient rock engravings on the larger ones. Rock engravings? When Feng realised what she was looking at, she got very excited. The pictures were simple outlines etched with stones and all of them depicted scenes from the lives of ancient peoples: herding, making tea, hunting, and singing and dancing.

Feng picked up a stone and tried scratching a rock herself. The rock was very hard; it wasn't easy to leave a mark. She could tell it had been very difficult to make these pictures. No wonder they were still visible, despite having endured thousands of years of wind and rain.

'Where are his pictures?' Feng was stooping down to examine each one.

'Here.' The little girl squatted in front of another rock.

Feng flung down the stone in her hand and hurried over. Sure enough, there was an image on the rock. It had obviously been engraved with a knife. In the middle were two Tibetan antelopes, with two people alongside them. Below were engraved four characters: *Bao bao, Bei bei.*

'Baobao, Beibei...' Feng murmured, kneeling down. Those were the antelopes they'd rescued; they had to be quite big by now. Were they still with him? *Gongzha, Gongzha, where are you? Do you know I'm here? Do you know I've come thousands of kilometres to find you?*

Her tears flowed. When they hit the rock, they dried in an instant.

She pulled out her Swiss army knife and used all her strength to carve her words:

> *I still remember my first glimpse of you,*
> *Your face weathered by wind and frost.*
> *The grass was young, the flowers bloomed,*
> *The clouds were light, the wind was soft.*
> *I want to take your hand and never part,*
> *I long to see my love set deep in your heart.*
> *My heart is steadfast,*
> *The sky is my witness, and so is the earth,*
> *My love endures*
> *Though days and months may pass.*

'Is he the one you're looking for, Sister?' the little girl asked as she watched Feng finish.

Feng nodded, wiped away her tears, and raised her head with a satisfied smile. Gongzha the tough mountain man had a soft side. He hadn't forgotten her – why else would he have engraved that picture?

She had never felt so happy. She stood up and impetuously hugged the little girl. 'It's him, it's him. Gongzha. He's the only who knows Baobao and Beibei.'

'Is Gongzha your man, Sister?'

'Yes, he's my man,' Feng said firmly and with absolute certainty, as if she were telling the whole world.

When the girl saw Feng's smile, she smiled too. 'There are lots more paintings over there, Sister, do you want to have a look? Granny says they were all drawn by the Buddha and are very interesting.'

Feng nodded and picked her way through the rocks, holding the little girl's hand.

That part of the slope was covered in broken black rocks. There were ancient rock engravings on almost all of the bigger ones. The rough outlines had obviously been made by something with a small circular point; some were deep, some were faint. The clumsy execution had a kind of ancient beauty.

Feng looked at one and took a photo. If she got the chance, she'd try and get an archaeologist to come out and have a look. Sparsely inhabited though the area was, it certainly wasn't lacking in evidence of human activity.

On one of the rocks, she saw a troop of horsemen fighting. In the next picture a group of women were walking, and she could tell from the slant of their bodies it was an arduous journey. Yaks, asses and horses were all carrying bundles. In the third she saw a herding scene; there were many Buddhas above it.

'Are they moving pasture?' Feng asked.

'No, Granny said this shows the Nacangdeba and the Jialong of Cuoe Grassland fighting. When the Nacangdeba knew they couldn't win, they sent the women and children to hide in No Man's Land.'

Cuoe Grassland? Gongzha's home territory? The thought flashed through Feng's mind, but she turned her attention to the pictures. Gongzha had mentioned that battle, as well as that mysterious cave. The Nacangdeba had had no choice but to leave, and the women and children were the grassland's last hope. She thought of the Buddha the Swiss man had left behind, which Gongzha had said belonged to Cuoe Temple. She'd reported it in Lhasa and had later heard that the police had found the Buddhas and returned them to the temple.

As Feng looked at the rather large Buddha in the middle of the engraving, it suddenly seemed familiar. It reminded her of the blue-black Buddha Gongzha carried with him, that Medicine Buddha of unknown material. There was another circle below the image, with some intricate lines in the middle. In the centre lay two people with their torsos raised, as if they were swimming. On either side of them were two yaks and two sheep. Yaks and sheep swimming with people? Feng was taken aback. Those ancients really did have vivid imaginations.

They descended the mountain to find Junsang waiting for them. He had a herder with him called Cirensangzhu, or Sangzhu for short. Sangzhu had seen Gongzha a week ago when he was in No Man's Land searching for a yak.

'Where was he?'

'He was in a valley. This is the map I drew.' Junsang drew a notebook from his *chuba*. 'Going by what he said, it's not far from Yongxi's pasture.'

'Yongxi's pasture? There's pastureland in No Man's Land?'

'Yes, sure, No Man's Land has good pastures, though not many people live there. I think I remember that Yongxi had a grandmother, and they've always lived in No Man's Land.'

'Have you met her?'

'I met her once when I went looking for a yak.' Junsang closed the notebook and put it back in his *chuba*. 'I'm afraid I won't be able to find the place myself, so I've asked Cirensangzhu to take us.'

'Good, good.' Feng nodded her approval. 'When do we leave?'

'Tomorrow morning.'

'Good.' Feng was delighted and nodded at Cirensangzhu. Then she reached into the car, pulled out two packets of chocolates and gave one to the little girl and one to Sangzhu.

Sangzhu took his, copied the way the girl unwrapped one of the chocolates, and put it into his mouth. He quickly frowned and spat it out, giving the rest of his bag to the girl. The other three laughed loudly.

Feng couldn't sleep a wink that night.

She'd thought about Gongzha day and night for the last three years and had even convinced herself that seeing him again was nothing more than a pipedream. So she was surprised to discover that now she was so close to finding him, she was nervous. It felt a bit like having been away for a long time and getting apprehensive at the prospect of returning home.

When she realised that she wasn't going to get to sleep, Feng got up and began to organise her things. She took everything out of her bag and repacked it. But when she checked the time, not even an hour had passed. She shook out her sleeping bag, rolled it up neatly, and put it in her bag, but that used up only twenty minutes. Now what could she do? She stared out at the bright moon, sighed, got up and went outside.

The moonlight was strong – it was almost as bright as day. It was only in Tibet that Feng realised there was truth to that phrase. She walked down the stone stairs and saw that someone was lying in the courtyard. It was Sangzhu, the herder who was to be their guide. He lay snoring on the sandy ground, wrapped in his sheepskin *chuba*. Feng didn't find that at all strange. When they were in the wilderness, Gongzha had slept that way every night. He said grasslanders saw the earth as their bed and felt unsettled when they didn't sleep on the ground.

She tiptoed out of the courtyard and sat on a boulder outside. Some wild dogs who were nosing through the nearby rubbish heap for scraps stared at her and barked a couple of times but didn't come over.

In front of her stretched a white salt lake. In the past, herders from all over the north Tibetan grasslands used to come there to collect salt. But now they didn't need to, because processed salt came in on the Sichuan–Tibet and Qinghai–Tibet highways. As people lost interest in natural salt, the once busy salt lake quietly slipped out of the herders' lives.

The grey snow mountain loomed in the distance. Without the sun glinting off it, it looked soft and lovely. The stars were clear and bright and seemed as if they'd been stitched into the sky with just the right distance between them.

Resting her elbows on her knees, Feng cupped her chin in her hands and stared out into the night. She wondered if, somewhere out in the wilderness, Gongzha was sitting like her, sleepless and stargazing.

It was hard to wait until seven o'clock. If she'd been in the city, the streets would already have been bustling with people. But in this frontier town, it was as quiet as if it were the dead of night. Feng couldn't take it; every minute seemed as long as a year. She went back to the courtyard and woke up Junsang.

Junsang climbed out of the car, rubbing his eyes. He woke up Cirensangzhu and then started the car so it could warm up.

Cirensangzhu stood up reluctantly, walked groggily to the well, drew a bucket of water and washed himself splashily. When he was finally more awake, he put his *chuba* on the roof of the car. Junsang gave him two biscuits; Sangzhu tucked them away, took out some dried meat and began to eat it.

When the people living round the courtyard heard the car running, they all got up to see them off. After two days together, they were all quite reluctant to say goodbye. The little girl who'd taken Feng to see the rock engravings came out with her grandmother and they gave Feng a box of curds. Feng refused them – she didn't want them – but the old woman didn't care and put them in the car. The town cadre brought some dried meat; another auntie brought some steamed *momos*. Feng was so moved that her eyes welled with tears.

When they got to the pass above the town, Feng made Junsang stop the car. She stood there, in the place where heaven and earth met, gazing at the fluttering prayer flags, listening to them snapping in the wind. As she walked, the flags brushed across her body and face.

She remembered him that day, how he'd turned away amid a scene much the same as today's. The wind had been just as strong and the flags had fluttered just as wildly. He'd said he could only take her that far, that she would be safe there.

Her body had been safe, but she'd left her heart in No Man's Land.

A goshawk swooped down suddenly and Feng instinctively brought her palms together to greet it. Spontaneously and for no reason, she howled at the mountains: 'Gongzha...'

As her cry echoed through the mountains, tears began to pour down her face. She was lost in a sea of memories and her body had become as weak as clay.

> *'I have climbed to the highest of places, just to find you,*
> *I have travelled over mountains and rivers, in search of*
>   *you.*
> *Oh, eagle, where will you fly?*
> *Have you seen the one I love as he wanders,*
> *Has he grown thin, has he grown weary, is he hurt?*
> *Please tell him I am here, under the white clouds,*
> *Hoping to follow him as he wanders,*
> *To follow him wherever he roams.*
> *Let love calm the pain,*
> *Plant love in your heart,*
> *Let there be two hearts in one tent,*
> *So that, no matter where they wander, they will find their*
>   *way home.'*

24

Gongzha was making his way through an unnamed valley, accompanied only by his horse and his gun. He was used to being alone, on his own in the wilderness, a lone wolf on the wild plateau. It was where he belonged; he could be himself out there.

He stopped every so often to dismount and look around. The smell on the wind and the marks on the ground told him whether or not he was going in the right direction. A hunter used a hunter's methods, whatever he was searching for.

Kaguo, you will not escape, Gongzha repeated to himself as he narrowed his eyes and scanned the mountain ridges ahead of him. The wound in his chest hurt faintly. He reined in his horse and jumped down. Spreading his *chuba* on the ground, he sat down cross-legged, undid the bandages and examined the wound. It was red around the edges. Gongzha frowned. It wasn't good that it had become infected; he needed to find a doctor and get it treated. He surveyed his surroundings. He wasn't far from Rongma and could be there in two days at most.

He ate some dried meat and then got back on his horse. He needed to hurry to Rongma – he didn't want to die in the wilderness. There was a clinic there, and his injury needed attention.

He got to Rongma around noon the next day and went straight to the clinic. The doctor on duty was a young woman who'd only recently graduated. She looked at his wound in surprise, then quickly cleaned and drained it, and hooked him up to an intravenous drip.

Gongzha sat squinting on a cushion.

'Is your name Gongzha?' The doctor sat by the window cutting her nails, occasionally raising her hands to the sunlight to inspect them.

Gongzha glanced at her and nodded.

'Your woman has gone to No Man's Land to look for you.' Seeing Gongzha's stunned expression, the doctor was suddenly curious. She laid her nail clippers on the table and turned towards him with renewed interest. 'What made you choose a Han woman?'

Gongzha stared at her, even more bewildered now. *What had made him choose a Han woman?*

'You're a lucky man – not only is the Han woman you married very beautiful, she's also so devoted, she's gone all the way to No Man's Land to find you.' The doctor laughed. Seeing a little girl with a backpack walking by, she stood up, waved at her, and called out, 'Pumu, come in here a minute. Didn't you take that Han lady to see the rock engravings? Her man is here now.'

The little girl came in, leant against the door and stared at Gongzha and his IV drip. 'Are you Uncle Gongzha?'

Gongzha nodded.

'Auntie's gone to look for you. Did you see her?'

'Feng's gone to look for me?'

'After Auntie saw the picture you carved, she cried and cut lots of words into the rock, and then the next day she left.'

'She's gone to No Man's Land? With who?'

'By herself, in a rental car. And with a herder called Cirensangzhu. Cirensangzhu said he'd seen you near Auntie Yongxi's pasture, so Sister took him with her to find you.'

When Gongzha heard this, he yanked out the IV needle and stood up.

'Hey, hey, your wound is infected.' The doctor jumped up hurriedly. 'If you don't finish the IV, you'll die.'

'Give me some anti-inflammatory medicine,' Gongzha said, pressing the needle wound on the back of his hand. 'I'll take it on my own. It's not important.'

'You really have so little regard for your life?' The doctor turned, took two packets out of a drawer and handed them to Gongzha. 'Two tablets, three times a day. Don't forget, no matter what.'

Gongzha took the packets, popped out two tablets and put them in his mouth. He swallowed them without water and stashed the rest inside his *chuba*. He rubbed the little girl's head as he went out of the door, then strode out of the courtyard.

His horse was tied to a rock by the entrance. He leapt onto it, cracked the whip and sped off to the mountainside with all the engravings.

Once there, he stood beneath the blue sky and its white clouds, the afternoon sun beating fiercely down. As he gazed at the words carved above his picture, waves of emotion rose in his heart.

> *I still remember my first glimpse of you,*
> *Your face weathered by wind and frost.*
> *The grass was young, the flowers bloomed,*
> *The clouds were light, the wind was soft.*
> *I want to take your hand and never part,*
> *I long to see my love set deep in your heart.*
> *My heart is steadfast,*
> *The sky is my witness, and so is the earth,*
> *My love endures*
> *Though days and months may pass.*

Even if Gongzha's Mandarin had been worse than it was, he would still have understood what the words meant. His chest tightened. How could she be so stupid? She knew full well how dangerous No Man's Land was, but she'd rushed in anyway. If she were to get caught in an avalanche or run into a pack of wolves, what would she do? His stomach churned at the thought. He jumped back onto his horse, whipped it savagely and tore down the mountainside and off into the boundless wilds.

He reached Yongxi's pasture on the third day.

Yongxi was carrying a lamb. The little boy Tajiapu, whom Sega had given him as a hostage, was beside her.

When she saw Gongzha, Yongxi set down the lamb and called out to him with a smile. 'Brother Gongzha, how's your wound?'

'It's much better.' He leapt off his horse, led it over and lifted Tajiapu onto its back. 'Jijia agreed to give the boy back?'

'He didn't dare refuse.' Yongxi's face was sombre. 'If he hadn't given my son back, I would have forbidden Jijia from ever visiting my tent again.'

'You used that as a threat?' Gongzha teased. 'Aren't you afraid he'll visit other women? There are lots of women at his encampment.'

'Let him try and I'll destroy him,' Yongxi said with a fierce look on her face and a hand on her hip.

'Well, Jijia is still a grassland man. Who would have guessed you'd have such power over him? It's Buddha's justice.' Gongzha took off his *chuba* and laughed. 'You're really not going to move to his encampment? It's dangerous here for a woman and child on their own.'

'I'm not going. That posse is like a pack of wolves and there'll come a day when the Buddha punishes them.' She opened the tent and let Gongzha in. When he'd sat down, she poured him some tea. 'Have you come because you need something, Brother?'

Gongzha rubbed his nose. 'Have you seen a Han woman, Yongxi?' he asked a little uncomfortably.

'Do you mean Feng?' Yongxi opened the stove.

'You've seen her?' Gongzha leapt up, then sat down again awkwardly when he saw Yongxi smiling at him.

'Is she really your woman?'

'How could she be? I already have a woman.' Gongzha lifted his teacup to hide his face.

'You can't live like this forever. You have to have a woman to have your children and take care of your tent and your horse.'

'Yongxi...'

'She said you saved her life and that you were the one who led her out of No Man's Land. Is that right?'

Gongzha nodded.

'So she fell in love with you and pursued you all the way from Shanghai to No Man's Land. If I were a man, I'd be impressed. She was here four days ago. I thought you were still over at the valley that Jijia mentioned, looking for Kaguo, so that's what I told her and she set off the next day.'

'Still with two others?'

'No, by herself. Their car ran out of fuel and they left it in the valley over there. Cirensangzhu needed to get back to his yaks, and Junsang went with him to get a rescue car. Feng couldn't wait. She rode off on my horse in the middle of the night – to find you, I assume. But don't worry, when Sega heard that, she went off after her. Sega knows the area; Feng should be fine.'

'Why did Sega... go after her?'

'After you got shot, Sega went everywhere looking for you. She ran into me when I was searching for Feng and asked me what was the matter. I told her about you and Feng, and she told me not to worry; she said she'd already met Feng and would bring her back.'

Gongzha couldn't stay sitting down any longer. He put down his teacup and strode out of the tent with his gun.

Yongxi ran after him. 'Brother, your *chuba*!'

Gongzha took it and hung it off the back of his horse, nodded to Yongxi, climbed onto his horse and disappeared in a cloud of dust.

Beneath blue skies, a woman in a yellow windcheater cantered across a wilderness so vast and bleak that even the distant snow mountains and the lower, closer hills seemed diminished. If it hadn't been for the blue lake and the lazily grazing wild asses and yaks, Feng might have thought she'd travelled back into some unknown ancient era.

Hadn't Yongxi said it was only a two-hour drive along the lake to get there, and yet she'd already been riding a whole day and still hadn't arrived. Perhaps she'd gone the wrong way? No, she'd kept close by the lake. And hadn't Yongxi said the valley was very easy to recognise because of its red rocks? Well, there hadn't been any red valleys so far. Feng scanned her surroundings and began to get nervous, afraid she'd got lost again. But the rippling lake in front of her reassured her that this was the right direction.

When she felt the earth beneath her horse's hooves getting soft, Feng took up the reins and guided the horse slightly uphill, away from the marshy ground. Gongzha had told her that these marshes were treacherous; once you got sucked in, there was almost no chance of getting out alive.

She glanced at the sun; it would soon be sinking behind the mountains. She dismounted, found a place out of the wind, took off her backpack and put up her tent. She didn't dare travel by night for fear of getting lost, like last time.

She took her water bottle down to the lake. She knew from Gongzha that not all the lakes in No Man's Land had potable water but that it was safe to drink from any lake with animal tracks by the water's edge. Feng spied a flock of waterfowl on the lake and gulped down a few mouthfuls. In ten short days, Gongzha, she said to herself, you turned me into something of a northern Tibet expert – did you know that? See, I know what water to drink, where to put up my tent, what I can snack on. But now I would really like to find you and let *you* collect my drinking water, cut my meat for me and help me put up my tent.

She gazed out at the calm waters in front of her; the lake seemed to go on for ever. The birds chased each other, cavorting freely. This was the most beautiful season in northern Tibet: the grass was lush and wild flowers of all kinds grew as if in competition with one another, determined not to miss the growing season, their one chance to flourish.

Could it be that people were like that, too?

Feng sighed and stood quietly gazing at the reflection of the snow mountains in the lake. How beautiful it was there! If she hadn't experienced it for herself, she would never have believed such a lovely place existed on earth. A place so far removed from the bustle of the world; a place with no human sounds and no fire smoke; a place with nothing in it but the sky and the earth, the thump of her heartbeat and her endless longing.

It wasn't until the birds on the lake began one by one to swim back to their nests in the marsh that she noticed the black clouds coming in over the mountain peaks. Even so, she thought nothing of it, just turned and headed back towards her tent. She knew the skies would clear again in a few minutes. Northern Tibet was like that: raining one moment, hailing the next, and back to sun in the blink of an eye.

She hadn't yet reached her tent when she saw a black horse speeding along the lakeside; the rider, a woman in black, looked familiar.

The woman sprang off her horse as soon as she saw Feng, and Feng smiled at her. It was the woman she'd bathed with in Rongma. 'What are you doing here, Sega?' she asked.

Sega stared at her, a distinctly antagonistic look in her eye. 'You're looking for a man called Gongzha?'

'I am. How did you know? Have you seen him?' Feng was delighted to have met someone she knew in such a lonely place.

'You are not his woman!' Sega shouted, gesticulating angrily. 'His woman died a long time ago.' Her eyes blazed as if they would spout fire. 'Cuomu's gone. Gongzha's future is his own – no one can take it from him.'

Feng stared back in confusion. What was wrong with this woman? Gongzha's former woman was dead – what did that have to do with her? 'What's the matter with you?'

'Go home! Go back to your Shanghai. Gongzha is mine, and no one can take him from me.'

'Gongzha is your man?'

'Yes, Gongzha is my man. Go home! Go back to Shanghai.'

'No, Gongzha isn't your man. If he was, he wouldn't have carved that picture of Baobao and Beibei and me and him onto that rock. That was our story, our secret. Gongzha isn't yours; you're definitely wrong—'

'Are you leaving or not?' Sega was losing patience. This was No Man's Land and she was a she-wolf of the wilderness. Would a she-wolf let another she-wolf steal her mate without a fight? No, she would not.

'No, I'm not leaving,' Feng said adamantly. 'Unless Gongzha tells me himself that you're his woman, I won't go.' She bent to pick up her water bottle and slowly continued walking towards her tent.

'You...!' As Sega glared at Feng's back, a murderous expression came over her face. She whipped the knife from her belt and raced after Feng, shouting, 'Are you leaving or not?'

Feng didn't look back; she continued walking at a slow pace and her voice remained firm. 'I'm not leaving. I have to find him.'

'Fine – you won't leave!' Sega spat hatefully. In a frenzy, she stabbed Feng in the waist. Blood streamed out.

Feng was momentarily dazed, then she turned to Sega in disbelief. 'You...!'

Sega waved her knife defiantly, splattering blood onto the black pebbles. It began to hail. Hailstones pinged off the knife blade. Sega glowered furiously at Feng. 'I'll make you leave – go back to your Shanghai! There's no man of yours here. He's mine! No one can take him from me – not Jijia, and not you!'

'No, Gongzha isn't yours.' Feng pressed her hand against the place in her side that was gushing blood. Her face was white and she was unsteady on her feet. 'If he really was yours, you wouldn't have come here and said all those things to me. I won't leave. Even if I have to die trying, I will at least die as close to him as I can get.'

'Alright, if you won't leave, then die,' Sega shrieked, brandishing her knife. She plunged her blade into Feng again, into her left shoulder this time, then yanked it out, her eyes red, her brain in a whirl.

'He doesn't love you at all!' Feng said, her whole side now bloodied.

'It's true, he doesn't love me. I won't let him love you either.' Sega glared at the tottering Feng, her mind seething with hatred. She rushed over with her knife and savagely stabbed Feng in the chest. Fresh blood spouted, splattering Sega's face and body.

'I still love him, and I will find him even if it kills me,' Feng said. Then everything went black, and she fell, frightening the water fowl, who flew up squawking from the lake.

The hail suddenly stopped, and the sun came out again.

Feng lay on the ground, her blood staining the pebbles. The sun warmed her a touch and she wanted to stand up, to move her fingers, but she had no strength, just like the last time she was in No Man's Land. Was she going to die? Was she really going to go like this? That would be fine; she could die here, at least she was close to him. And it would put an end to her eternal longing.

Sega glanced at the fallen Feng, laughed wildly and hurled her knife into the lake. Then she dashed down to the water and began to scrub herself: her hands, face and clothes all had blood on them – how could there be so much? Despite all the scrubbing, she still couldn't get clean. She kept splashing water on herself, rubbing and crying. 'I didn't want to kill her, but she wouldn't leave. Oh Buddha, forgive me, a demon came into my head and I couldn't control myself. Buddha, you must forgive me, I didn't want to kill her. Truly, I didn't mean to...'

She turned and, catching sight of Feng lying on the shore, wailed and ran up the bank as if she'd gone crazy.

As she ran, the ground beneath her got so soft, she began to sink into it. She could no longer lift her feet. She suddenly realised that the black mud all around her was full of bubbles. It was slowly swallowing her.

Sega thrashed around in a panic, which made her sink even faster. She stared up at the sky and cried out, opening her blood-shot eyes wide, 'Oh, Buddha, is this your punishment to me?'

Feng lay nearby, muddled, facing death. She was at peace. She'd stopped thinking about Gongzha or Shanghai and was just waiting quietly for death to arrive. She turned her head to watch the birds that had returned to the lake; they were still happy. In her next life, she wanted to be a bird, a bird in No Man's Land. She would be free, free of love, free of the troubles love brought.

Who was that crying out? Was it the woman who'd stabbed her? Why hadn't she left? When she died, there would be no one to steal that woman's man. Feng moved her heavy head, shifted her gaze, and focused.

The woman was struggling frantically in the marsh in front of her, waving her two arms helplessly, unable to grab at anything.

The mud was making a terrifying gurgling noise.

The woman was sinking into the marsh!

Feng forced herself to concentrate and her survival instinct made her raise her head and use all her strength to call out to Sega. 'Don't move! You'll just sink faster.'

She heaved herself up and slowly crawled towards her tent, leaving a crooked trail of blood in her wake. She had no idea how long it took her, but she got there eventually. Painfully, she pulled a handful of thin white ropes from her backpack. They were guy ropes for her tent. She couldn't use her left arm, so she used her teeth to knot them together. Then she crawled over to the horse, held onto its leg, and slowly pulled herself upright. She tied one end of the rope to the saddle and tried several times to mount the horse, but she was too weak and kept flopping backwards. Frustrated, she grabbed the reins with one hand, the saddle with the other, and walked down towards the marsh. She stumbled every few steps but got back up again every time.

She was going to die anyway.

By the time she'd crawled as close as she could to Sega, Feng looked as if she was entirely made of blood. She picked up a stone, tied the rope around it, and called to Sega, 'Catch the rope.' Then she hurled the stone with all her might.

The stone landed about a metre in front of Sega; she stretched out her arms but couldn't reach it, which only made her sink faster.

Feng quickly yanked the rope back in, gathered her strength once more, and hurled the stone again.

This time it landed to Sega's right, but she still couldn't reach it.

Feng pulled the rope back in and tried a third time. This time, it landed right in front of Sega. Sega quickly untied the rock and wrapped the rope around her wrists.

Feng began to crawl backwards with the rope. When she reached her horse, she steadied her foot against a small heap of earth, leant back and used the horse to drag Sega out. The horse strained with all its might, neighing, and bit by bit pulled Sega out of the mud.

When Sega finally reached safety, she freed herself from the rope, raced over to her own horse, ripped off her mud-soaked robe, ran into the lake and washed all the mud off herself. Then she raced back to Feng's side.

Feng had fallen unconscious. Sega didn't even try to wake her, she just grabbed Feng's arms, lifted her onto her own shoulders and carried her back to her horse. She laid Feng on the ground, searched through her bag, found a white vest, tore it into strips and used those to bind her wounds. She searched through Feng's bag again and changed her out of her damp clothes. Then she tied Feng onto the horse and climbed up after her. Holding Feng in her arms, she cracked the whip and the horse clattered off towards the adjacent valley.

*

Gongzha sped away from Yongxi's pasture, following the lakeshore.

'Gongzha, I'll miss you!' Feng's heartfelt cry at their last parting sounded in his ears and would not fade.

He didn't dare ride too fast for fear of missing any traces of her. Sega was a determined woman; she was like a female yak when she was angry, stirring up trouble without a thought, like when she'd given him Yongxi's child as a hostage with no heed for the consequences. He didn't want either Feng or Sega to get hurt. They were both good women, and both had their qualities. It was just that their qualities were not ones that, as a wanderer, he had any use for.

When he saw the little yellow tent, Gongzha's heart leapt with joy. He whipped his horse and galloped over, but all he found inside it was a sleeping bag. He stood up and surveyed the area. The sight of the crooked black trail on the ground scared him. Squatting down in disbelief, he lifted a handful of sand to his face; the stench of blood filled his nostrils. Then he saw Feng's backpack and its scattered contents, and the dried blood on the pebbles on the shore.

Finding the muddied robe nearby, Gongzha was confused. It was the one Sega usually wore – why would she have left it there, and why was it covered in mud? Then he saw the depression in the marsh and the traces of someone having been dragged out.

'Feng…!' Gongzha yelled repeatedly, but his only response was the echoes that bounced back from the mountains.

He jumped back on his horse and tore off towards the hidden valley. There was no time to lose.

The wind picked up and began to tumble the sand and the stones.

Sega thundered into the encampment, gripping Feng tight and yelling, 'Auntie Yangji! Auntie Yangji, come and help me! Dawacuo, go and call Brother Qiangba to my tent and tell him to bring the medicine kit.'

'What's going on?' Yangji came out her tent. Seeing a blood-ied woman on the back of Sega's horse, she was momentarily stunned. Then she quickly put down the bowl she was carrying and hurried over to help Sega lift the woman down.

'What happened?' Jijia also emerged from his tent. When he saw Feng, he was shocked. 'Where did this woman come from?'

'Don't ask, Brother. She has nothing to do with you hunters,' Sega said, and she and Yangji carried Feng to her own tent.

Qiangba and Dawacuo followed them in. Qiangba stared at Feng's wounds with wide-eyed surprise. 'How did she get hurt so badly?'

'What do you care? Just get a move on and patch her up,' Sega snarled. 'And if you don't save her, if she dies, I'll make you pay with your life!'

'And if I do save her, what's my reward?' Qiangba shot Sega a suggestive look.

Sega glared at him. Qiangba quickly controlled his smile and told Dawacuo to bring hot water and *baijiu*.

He carefully cleaned the blood from around the wound, then doused it with the alcohol.

Feng was confused. She was suddenly in a great deal of pain, so she opened her eyes and instinctively yelled out. When she saw that there were lots of people standing around her, some in fox-fur hats, some in sheepskin hats, and some not wearing hats but with their hair in topknots, she thought: am I in heaven? Why do the people in heaven look like the people on the grass-land? She looked around and finally her gaze came to rest on a familiar pair of eyes. There was no hatred in those eyes any more; rather they were suffused with apology and concern. Had Sega died too? That was good: they'd both died and wouldn't have to compete with each other any more. But Gongzha would be so lonely!

'Don't worry, everything's going to be fine,' Sega said. 'Qiangba will make you better.' She held Feng's arm, which had been shaking from the pain.

'We... haven't... haven't died?' Feng looked into her eyes. They really were beautiful eyes, round and sparkling. Was Sega worried about her? Did Sega not hate her any more? Was she no longer prepared to kill in order to get her man?

'You're not dead. We're both alive. Qiangba is looking after you; don't worry.' Sega smiled, and finally the tears fell. 'Feng, I'm sorry. I was crazy, I didn't know what I was doing.'

'Don't worry, Sega. I understand.' Feng smiled and wanted to lift her hand and wipe away Sega's tears, but she didn't have the strength.

'Where am I?'

'No Man's Land! You get better first, and then I'll help you find him.'

'Thank you, Sega.'

'Right then, everything's taken care of.' Qiangba lifted his head, took several tablets out of his *chuba* and gave them to Sega. 'Give her the first one tonight when the stars come out, and the next one four hours later. Tell your friend not to make any sudden moves or the wound will reopen. If after three days it hasn't got infected, she'll be fine; if it does get infected, even the Buddha won't be able to save her.'

Sega explained this to Feng in Mandarin, and Feng nodded. Sega and Yangji caressed Feng soothingly. Dawacuo brought in some beef broth to help the medicine go down, and then Feng fell into a deep sleep.

Sega made Dawacuo watch over Feng in the tent and she and Yangji went out.

The two women sat facing one another by the lake.

'Did she really come to find Gongzha?' Yangji asked.

'Yes, Auntie. Do you know how far Shanghai is from here? Thousands of kilometres.' Sega picked up a rock and played with it.

'Then what are you going to do?'

'Wait till she's healed and then help her find Gongzha.'

'You're really going to give him up?'

'What choice do I have? Besides, she saved my life. My life in exchange for the love she yearns for; that's how it goes.'

'Ah...' Yangji sighed. 'Gongzha is a lucky man.'

'It's fate. Auntie Yongxi once told me that if something isn't in your destiny, no matter how hard you try and get it, it will never be yours. I didn't believe her at the time, but I believe her now.'

Yangji squeezed her hand, not knowing how to comfort her.

Feng slept straight through until the afternoon of the following day. When she opened her eyes, she saw that a young girl with long plaits was napping by the side of her bed, a small fox perched on her shoulder.

When it saw that Feng was awake, the fox began to yelp. The little girl turned her head, smiled and said something in Tibetan. Feng responded with a blank expression, so the girl laughed, pointed to her stomach and made an eating gesture. Feng smiled and nodded. The little girl carefully helped Feng sit up, brought over a cushion to support her and then carried over a bowl. She began to feed her with a small spoon.

When she'd got through half the bowl, Feng shook her head to show she was full. The little girl put down the bowl, brought over some medicine and cool water from the side, and fed that to Feng.

Sega came in. When she saw Feng was awake, her eyes were full of guilt.

Feng smiled. 'I'm feeling much better. Thank you, Sega!'

'It was me who hurt you in the first place, and you still thank me?' Sega laughed and sat down beside the couch. 'It's a shame I'm not from the city.'

'But you saved me in the end. You didn't abandon me to the wilderness and the wolves.' Feng gave Sega a half smile. Sega was wearing a sky-blue Tibetan dress, her freshly washed hair lay damp on her back, and she didn't have any jewellery on. She looked clean and cool, totally different from when they'd first met. 'You have a good heart, Sega.'

Sega grinned. 'I did think about throwing you to the wolves,' she said in fluent Sichuanese-accented Mandarin, 'but then I decided it would be a waste to let such a beautiful woman get eaten, so I brought you back here instead.'

'That's okay; you went down the wrong path, but then you changed course. I forgive you.' Feng pretended to look stern.

The two continued chatting in the same relaxed vein, the rancour between them slipping away. It was neither woman's fault that they both loved the same man, nor was it either woman's fault that they both sought his love in return. The fault was heaven's for having planted the seed in both their hearts, for letting it grow, and for allowing it to leaf and flower when there was only a single ray of sun.

Feng's wound slowly began to heal over. She was able to move a little bit if she forced herself. She taught Dawacuo some simple Mandarin and the two began to communicate with gestures.

Feng pointed outside and said, 'I want to go outside and sit in the sun, Dawacuo.'

'Hurt!'

'Don't worry, I'll take it slowly.' Feng pushed off the thick woollen blanket and swung her legs down.

Dawacuo hurriedly helped her put on her shoes, then supported her as she tried to stand. When she was finally up, Feng gave a deep sigh. Just taking the tiniest step forward caused tremendous pain in her chest and shoulder. She clutched her chest and began shuffling out of the tent one step at a time.

On the sandy ground outside, a group of people were cleaning bloody antelope pelts. When they saw Feng and Dawacuo, everyone raised their heads.

They were killing sheep, that was Feng's first thought. But then she saw several antelope heads scattered across the ground. They weren't killing sheep – they were cleaning the pelts of Tibetan antelopes. Poachers! The word flashed through Feng's head like a thunderbolt; it made her dizzy, and she had trouble standing. Could they really be poachers? These herders in the depths of the wilderness who'd so kindly helped a stranger back to recovery in their encampment, how could they be cold-blooded poachers?

When Yangji saw Feng's deathly white face, she hurried forward and blocked her path. She said quite a bit to Dawacuo and seemed to be scolding the girl for bringing Feng outside. Feng shook her head at Yangji, trying to signal it wasn't Dawacuo's fault and that it was she who'd wanted to come outside.

Yangji clucked disapprovingly and accompanied Feng back to the tent.

Feng dutifully sat on the cushion. 'Is Sega not here?' she asked Yangji.

Yangji couldn't understand Mandarin, but she understood the name 'Sega'. She made the gesture for picking plants, trying to convey that Sega had gone looking for medicinal herbs.

Feng laughed. With Dawacuo's help, she slowly lay down and closed her eyes. Yangji realised she wouldn't be doing any more talking and beckoned Dawacuo out.

Feng didn't sleep. She couldn't erase what she'd just seen from her mind. Tibetan antelopes had been identified by the government as endangered and were a Class 1 protected species. She'd known there were people in No Man's Land who rode the profit wave and killed antelopes despite the law, but it was still shocking to actually see it.

Sega returned that night, with two snow lotuses in her hand.

'I searched for a long time before I found them. What do you think?' She held the lotuses under Feng's nose. 'Don't they smell nice?'

'Thank you, Sega.' Feng smiled. She scanned the tent and on seeing that there was no one else there, said, 'If I ask you something, Sega, will you give me an honest answer?'

'Ask. I promise I won't lie to you.'

'The people outside, what are they doing?'

'Have you heard of the shadow hunters?'

'I heard Gongzha mention them. Are you really... poachers?'

'Feng, this is No Man's Land. We're as much a part of the wilderness as the antelopes. The antelopes depend on grass to survive; we depend on the antelopes to make money. There's nothing wrong with that.'

'But they'll become extinct soon.'

'No, they won't, Feng. Most of our ancestors hunted antelopes, and they're still here. Besides, antelopes and wild asses compete with our yaks for pasture and the pastures are getting smaller; there just isn't enough room for all of them.'

'But the antelopes are a Class 1 protected species and it's illegal to kill them. Don't you know that what you're doing is wrong?'

'That's a city law, it has no relevance in the wilderness. For us, if we need money to buy tents, guns or livestock, we see nothing wrong in killing a few antelopes. Let's not talk about this. When you're better, I'll take you to find Gongzha – don't concern yourself with things here. But I should warn you: don't tell those people outside that you know Gongzha. He's Brother Jijia's sworn enemy and if Brother were to find out, I'm afraid things might not go well for you. Do you understand?'

Feng nodded.

'Good. I'll go and find Yangji and get her to boil up the medicine, and then she'll come and change your bandages.' Sega smiled, took the snow lotuses and left.

Out in that great wilderness, the shadow hunters didn't need to sneak around under the cover of darkness. They knew that no one would come searching for them by themselves, and if a group of strangers were to suddenly appear out there, it would be very obvious, giving the poachers ample time to disappear, stash their guns, change their clothes and hide anything that might implicate them. Those wild, bloodthirsty men could turn into sheep-driving herders in an instant.

The change in the law had so far had no effect on the ongoing conflict between the poachers and those who opposed them. But Jijia had recently ordered his men to keep a close guard on the lake so that no one could get in or out. He was expecting the government to make a move sometime soon.

Feng's wound improved every day. She could now slowly move her arm, turn her body, and even walk a little. However, no matter where she went, there was always a pair of eyes watching her. At first, Feng thought people were concerned for her, worried she might knock into something, but as time went on, she realised that wasn't it at all. Whenever she strayed too far from the encampment, someone would come and ask her to go back. Their tone was always polite, but even though she didn't understand what they said, she knew there was no room for argument.

As the days went by, Feng grew curious, and she began to pay attention to her surroundings. She worked out there were two ways into the encampment. One route wound through the mountain valley and took a little longer. The other involved crossing the lake in a boat. Both routes were overseen by guards and both sets of guards were changed at dawn. It would be impossible for anyone to get in without the guards noticing.

'If there aren't any surprises, you'll be well in a month,' Sega said as she carefully removed the bandages on Feng's shoulder and peered at the black scabs. 'Qiangba says you have to be careful when you move around. If the wound reopens, that'll be a problem because we haven't got anything to stop the bleeding here.'

After her bandages had been changed, Feng held Sega's hand and said earnestly, 'I don't blame you for what happened, Sega. Love is a private thing that you can't share with anyone. I understand.'

Sega hugged Feng and wept. 'Don't worry, I'll help you find him.'

Feng looked her in the eyes and nodded.

Qiangba came in carrying a bowl of medicine. He handed it to Sega and picked a wayward blade of grass out of her hair. Sega pushed his hand away impatiently.

It suddenly occurred to Feng that if Gongzha had a woman like Sega, that wouldn't be such a bad thing.

That night, she stood at the entrance to the encampment watching Sega race her horse back and forth along the lakeshore, her long plaits flying. The mountains shimmered and trembled in the rippling surface of the lake.

Sega gave a loud whoop and twisted theatrically in the saddle: her arms hung loose, one of her feet left the stirrups, and in a flash she'd bent down and scooped a toad off the ground.

Feng was envious. Only women who'd grown up in the wind and rain of the grassland could be that free. Sega was a true galsang flower of the plains, and only an eagle soaring high could be worthy of such a flower.

Without warning, an image flashed into Feng's mind of Gongzha and a woman roaming through the mountains and across the plains, past herds of asses, antelopes and yaks. Feng couldn't see herself in that picture. Perhaps she really was just a guest there, someone who came, had a look around and then left.

25

A gentle breeze drifted across the grassland and the clouds were very white and soft. The lake shimmered like a bolt of blue silk unfurled across the wilderness.

Dawacuo and Feng sat on the shore, staring at the distant peaks.

Where in those mountains was the wanderer? When he stopped to rest, was it with anything like the longing that plagued Feng?

Feng thought about everything she'd been through on her journey to this point; she'd endured a lot, and all because she cherished the prospect of finding him and being with him. But again she thought, was northern Tibet really the place for her? It was such an alien environment and such an alien way of life, could she really go with him on his wanderings?

Sega, ray of sunshine that she was, seemed to love Gongzha as much as she did. Why else would she have taken her knife to Feng? Was Feng fighting against fate? Loving someone and then having to give them up was torturous, she understood that now. She hadn't even decided whether to give him up and her heart was already in pain. If she did give him up, would it cost her her life? Sega's smiles these days were forced, but she still kept Feng company; could Feng stand to see Sega's sorrow deepen?

The blood, the crazed eyes, the bubbling marsh, the swerving trail of blood, the hail, the waves lapping against the lake-shore… and then Sega clasping her tight as they galloped home. Despite Sega's deep hatred, in the end she'd treated Feng with kindness. She'd come to her senses and rescued Feng from the brink of death.

Experiencing all of that had caused Feng to doubt her own quest. Was she right to continue trying to get what she wanted regardless, just because she was in love? Could she stand there and watch another woman suffer? Sega lived there; the grassland was her home. And she loved him. Rationally speaking, her attitude to life made her a much better partner for Gongzha.

The thought of giving up, of letting him go, made Feng miserable and she began to cry silently. Her search had brought her so far, she'd been through so much and often with such little hope of success. To leave now, to return home and go back to square one – what a depressing thought that was.

'Feng! Feng…!' Sega was shouting to her from a distance, flying in on a brown horse, her gun slung across her back. 'I've got news of your man!'

'He…' Feng stood up quickly, but the sudden movement sent a spike of pain from her wound and she sat down again fast.

Sega drew up in a cloud of dust and sprang off her horse; she was holding a bunch of herbs in her hand. She threw her whip onto the saddle and looked at Feng excitedly. 'He's not in that mountain valley, Feng. I went to find Yongxi and she said Gongzha knows you've come and he's looking for you. I told her that when she next sees him, she's to tell him I'll bring you over as soon as you're well.'

Feng nodded and gave a tight smile.

'What's wrong? Aren't you happy to hear that?'

'Sit down, Sega.' Feng patted the rocky ground beside her. 'Let's talk.'

Sega shot Feng a questioning look, then glanced at Dawacuo. Dawacuo shook her head to show she knew nothing about it.

Feng gazed out at the vast blue lake and her tears rolled silently down. She took a deep breath and swiped them away. Oh, unsteady heart – how could it be so weak? 'Sega, I think… I don't really belong here. Once I'm better, I'm going to go back to Shanghai.' As she spoke, her heart felt as if it had been slashed with a knife.

'What are you saying, Feng! You've come so far to find him, and you've been through so much, but now that you're almost there, you want to go back?' Sega stared at her with incomprehension.

'My home is in Shanghai, I've lived there since I was little. I can come here to travel, Sega, but to live here... I don't think I could adjust.' Feng forced out a smile and turned to look at Sega. 'I'm not like you. You've lived on the grassland since you were young and you understand life here. You and Gongzha would make an ideal couple. Him and me, we'd be as alien to each other as this wilderness is to me.'

'No, you wouldn't – you shouldn't worry about that. As long as you're together, you'll get used to each other over time. Look at me, I'm from Ngawa, but I do fine here, don't I?'

'That's because you've been living this life since you were young. I've thought it over, Sega, I'm not right for this place. I should make my home in Shanghai.' Feng took another deep breath and blinked back the tears that threatened. 'You and I are friends, aren't we? You're welcome to visit me in Shanghai anytime.'

'Feng, you...' Feng's decision had caught Sega off guard. She was not someone skilled at interpreting the hearts of others and she had no way of understanding the thousands of thoughts going through Feng's mind. For herself, Sega always said what she was thinking and never hid her feelings.

'It's decided. Once I'm well again, you'll see me out of No Man's Land, okay? Since our brush with death, we're like sisters now, and when one sister leaves, the other has to see her off, right?'

'Of course I'll see you off. I'll take you to the county town,' Sega said, but she was still doubtful. She looked searchingly into Feng's face; she had no idea why Feng had changed her mind so fast.

Dawacuo looked at Sega as if she'd just remembered something. 'Auntie Sega, Ama's been looking for you everywhere. I think there's something she needs to tell you.'

'You and Dawacuo go back,' Feng said. 'I'll stay here a bit longer.'

'Fine!' Sega stood up and led her horse away. 'We'll come back for you in a while.'

Feng nodded and watched them walk off. The tears she'd held back finally ran down her face, pattering like raindrops on the rocky ground and slowly rolling away.

'Gongzha has already got past two of our guard posts, boss,' one of Jijia's men reported with a bow while Jijia sat drinking in his tent. 'What shall we do – open fire?'

'No need. Just keep watch at the pass. Remember, don't hurt him. Tie him up and bring him to me,' Jijia said without raising his head. He kept his gaze fixed on the cup in his hand, and a cold smile crept across his face. He was thinking about the layout of the pass. It's quite some man who can get past two of my guard posts, he thought, but if he can get through the third, then my life's work has been for nothing.

The guard bowed and left.

Jijia drained his cup, wiped the corner of his mouth and exited the tent. He stood on the empty sand of the lakeshore, contemplating the cloud-wrapped peaks. Those mountains were his guardian spirits; when he had the mountains and the wilderness around him, he could not be threatened. No Man's Land in all its vastness was his heaven, the place where he could roam freely. Here, and only here, he was like a king; here, he was master over the land and could change his mind as he pleased; here, the fastest antelopes fell at his feet, and his men looked at him with respect. The thought made him swell with pride.

It was the ecstasy of the kill that made him keep picking up his gun. It never occurred to him that he was committing a crime. People and animals had battled for survival out there since the beginning of time: the weak versus the strong, that was the law of the wilderness. When people were young and weak they were seen as prey by the animals; when they grew up, it was their turn to kill. No matter how many directives the government issued against hunting wild animals, Jijia just laughed at them. If they stopped hunting, the animals would multiply and where would the herders pasture their livestock then?

He was clearing the way for the herders to live a good life. Jijia liked to think about this when he was resting. If there were no antelopes or wild asses competing with the livestock for pasture, every tent could raise fifty per cent more livestock than they did now. When that day came, when there was an abundance of yaks and sheep and every household was wealthy, there'd be no need for people like him to hunt antelopes and sell their fur for money.

He did feel guilty sometimes – not for killing the antelopes, but for all the times he'd promised Yongxi he'd disband the shadow hunters but hadn't done so. Yongxi... She was a woman unlike any other on the grassland. She didn't worship him, wasn't afraid of him. At any time, she could threaten him with her whip and banish him from her tent. She was a wild one and he couldn't do without her: every time she drove him away, he vowed never to return, but he couldn't help himself. He pictured her holding the child, her brows furrowed, glaring at him and ordering him to leave, and a smile flitted across his face. She was his woman, the only woman he would ever have.

As these thoughts went through his head, his hatred of Gongzha intensified. Gongzha had dared to visit his woman's tent. That was a clear case of disrespect, and disrespect was one thing Jijia would not swallow.

Just then, the unmistakeable sound of a gunshot rang out from the mountain.

All the women came running, eager to find out what had happened. Even Feng came tottering out of her tent, supported by Dawacuo; she looked inquiringly at Sega, and Sega avoided her gaze.

A man was flying down the mountainside. When he got to

Jijia, he said something in a low voice. Jijia nodded, his face expressionless, then turned and went into his tent.

Sega and Yangji glanced at one another, and hurried back to Sega's tent. Dawacuo brought Feng in.

'Go and find Yongxi,' Yangji said, looking at Sega. 'Only Yongxi can stop this.'

Sega nodded and was about to go out when they all heard shouting. Dawacuo ran out to look, then hurried back in. 'Ama, they've brought Uncle Gongzha back, and he's tied up; they're in Uncle Jijia's tent.'

Feng didn't understand most of what Dawacuo said, but she was very familiar with the word 'Gongzha'. 'What's going on?' she asked, staring concernedly at Sega's back.

Sega straightened her shoulders and wrestled with whether to tell her or not.

'Tell her!' Yangji said quietly. 'After all, if he's been brought here tied up, she'll know soon enough.'

Sega nodded and turned to Feng with a sombre expression. 'Don't worry. We'll find a way to sort this out.'

Feng's heart sank at the sight of Sega's serious face. Had something happened to Gongzha? Had that gunshot been something to do with him – had they killed him? Feng forced herself to stay calm and said quietly and concisely, 'Is he here?'

Sega nodded.

Feng was trembling now. 'Did you lot catch him?'

Sega nodded again, then shook her head in distress: Feng's 'you lot' was misplaced – Gongzha's capture had nothing to do with her. But Feng didn't see the distinction, and Sega couldn't face explaining her connection with the shadow hunters all over again. Besides, the most important thing was that Gongzha had been caught. He'd come for Feng, but Sega didn't care. She wanted to save him. She had to save him.

'Why?'

'Brother thinks Gongzha visited Yongxi's tent, so he wants to kill him.'

'That's impossible. Gongzha's heart has room only for Cuomu,' Feng said sharply.

'But Brother doesn't understand that. He thinks Gongzha has disrespected him, so—'

'No, Gongzha wouldn't.' Feng looked at Sega. 'Aren't you one of them, Sega? Can't you go and say something to Jijia? Gongzha's loyal, he's not like other men, and he certainly wouldn't do anything with Yongxi.'

Gongzha's loyal, is he? Sega thought angrily to herself. Even though he's obviously let you into his heart and has risked his life for you, despite knowing the dangers? 'Feng,' she said, 'Jijia rescued me, that's all; he won't listen to me. And if Yongxi were to come to Gongzha's defence again, that would only make him even more suspicious. Even so, she's our one hope; she's the only one Brother will listen to.'

'What if you married Gongzha? Wouldn't that stop Jijia being so suspicious?' Feng said earnestly.

'I can see what you're thinking, Feng, but that's not going to happen. Gongzha would never agree to it. His heart has room only for Cuomu and for you.'

'No, Sega, his heart has room only for Cuomu. I'm just a woman from another ethnic group whose life he saved, just like he saved the lives of those lambs and foals.' Tears welled up in Feng's eyes. 'If you go and get Yongxi now, I'm afraid they'll have killed Gongzha by the time you get back. Let's go and tell Jijia now that Gongzha is your man and that you're going to get married soon, then he'll stop being suspicious of him.'

'Feng...'

'There's no time to lose, Sega. You have to act quickly if we're to save him.' Feng stood up and took Sega's hand. 'Come on, I'll go with you.'

Sega looked at Yangji. Yangji nodded. 'This might be the best way.'

So Sega allowed herself to be dragged out of the tent by Feng.

Jijia was sitting at the back of the large white tent, his feet propped up on the table, the tips of his boots quivering slightly, a brown leather whip by his side. The shadow hunters were gathered round him, some standing, some seated. In the centre of the tent stood Gongzha, bound with wetted leather straps, a man to either side of him. A few women had poked their heads round the door.

'The eagle of the grassland has flown down to our little valley again. We really are fortunate.' Jijia raised a glass to toast Gongzha, a hollow smile on his face.

'I've told you before, Jijia: I'm not here on your account.'

'I know you're not here for me. Jijia is not nearly important enough to merit a visit from the eagle of the grassland. You've come for a woman, have you not?'

Gongzha nodded. He thought Jijia knew he was looking for Feng.

Jijia thumped down his cup, swung his feet off the table and stared into Gongzha's eyes. Gongzha's calm, unwavering gaze made him very uncomfortable. He stood up, brandished the whip and cracked it across Gongzha's naked torso, leaving a bloody welt.

Gongzha frowned but continued staring calmly at Jijia, whose face was now twisted with explosive rage. 'I've heard that you go to Mount Kailash every year, Jijia, to wash away your guilt. Do you really think the Buddha will fall for that? What you've done on the grassland is enough to guarantee you'll never reincarnate.'

'In this valley, I am the Buddha – no one can cross me,' Jijia snarled, whip in hand. He walked over to Gongzha and stood in front of him, a cruel smile on his face. 'You might be a good shot, but you're still a man and you won't escape me now. At first, I didn't want to kill you. I let you go last time because you chose not to use my son as ransom; I thought you were a good man. But now that you've sneaked up on us again, well, I'm sorry, but that changes things. No one's ever managed to get in here uninvited before, you're the only one, and for the safety of my men, I can't let you leave here alive. My men and I give you our apologies.' Jijia twisted his mouth at the two men next to Gongzha. 'Drown him in the lake. It'll be cleaner and easier.'

'Yes, boss!' The men grabbed Gongzha's arms and prepared to leave.

'Wait!' The tent flap flew back and Feng and Sega burst in. Yangji followed, pulling Dawacuo along with her.

Feng hurried straight over to Gongzha. When she saw the injury to his chest, her heart hurt so much she began to cry.

'I'm fine. This wound is nothing to a wanderer like me.' Gongzha smiled. Seeing Feng standing unharmed in front of him was a huge relief. As long as she was safe, that was all that mattered. He could let go of his worries from the past few days.

'Why did you come here?'

'Yongxi told me you'd come to No Man's Land, so I came looking for you, and when I saw the blood by the lake, I was worried about you and followed you here. I'm so glad to see you're alright.' Gongzha smiled again, downplaying the danger. 'When all this is over, you should go straight home. This is no place for you.'

Feng nodded, then raised her head, tears streaming down. 'You're such an idiot! You must have known they'd kill you, but you still came?'

'I was afraid something had happened to you,' Gongzha said quietly. 'It's fine; don't cry. There's something I need to tell you. Can you come a bit closer?'

'What?' Feng looked into his face.

'Come a bit closer. Little lady, there's something I need to tell you.' Feng's doubtful expression was almost enough to make him laugh. Could it be that this woman who'd abandoned her whole life in order to come and look for him was now afraid of standing too near him? 'Pretend we're friendly and come and lean on me.'

Feng hesitated but eventually did as he asked.

Gongzha dropped his head, put his mouth to her ear and whispered quietly. To the others they looked like a pair of lovers reunited after a long separation.

'Your destiny appears to be full of women, Gongzha,' Jijia commented sarcastically.

Feng raised her head, looked into Gongzha's eyes, and nodded.

Gongzha smiled and said to Jijia, 'I've said what I needed to. Let's go.'

The two men began to push Gongzha towards the door again.

'No!' Sega cried. 'Don't kill him, Brother.'

Feng held onto Gongzha and screamed. 'No!'

'Brother!' Sega didn't look at Gongzha. She fixed her eyes on Jijia and said quietly but firmly, 'I didn't want to say anything, but now that things have gone this far, if I don't say something, it'll be too late and you won't be able to undo your mistake.'

'This is men's business, Sega. It's got nothing to do with you.' Jijia turned to the two men, who were looking to him for instructions. 'Why haven't you left yet?'

They began to drag Gongzha out again.

'No! No! Gongzha...!' Feng yelled wildly. She ran over and began to pull at Gongzha. A couple of people came up and grabbed her wrists, yanking them out to the side, but that made Feng scream, and blood began to ooze from her shoulder and chest.

'Feng!' Gongzha stared at the blood in surprise and started struggling against the men's grip. 'What happened to you? Where are you hurt? Why are you bleeding so much?'

'Don't worry about me, I'm fine.' Feng smiled, her face as white as paper. 'I'm fine. It's just a bit of blood. Don't worry, there's nothing the matter.'

'Sega, help her bandage up her wounds, would you, please? I'm begging you – please.' As Gongzha looked at Feng's blood-less face, a great fear the like of which he'd not felt in a long time spread through him: he was terrified she'd collapse like Cuomu had and would never get up again. The thought of going through such heartbreak again was unbearable, and in that moment Gongzha realised he no longer saw Feng simply as a chance acquaintance whose life he'd saved. Feelings for this woman had crept into his heart, put down roots and blossomed without him noticing. He'd come to the poachers' encampment to rescue her with no consideration for the danger he was putting himself in, and he'd persuaded himself that this was merely him doing the right thing by Feng, who had after all come a long way on his account. The truth was, it was his heart as much as his principles that had made him come, he just hadn't wanted to admit it, had been afraid of admitting it.

'Feng...' Sega pulled open Feng's clothes to have a look. The wounds on her chest and shoulder had split open and blood was seeping out.

Feng bit her lip, trying to endure the waves of pain coursing through her. 'Don't worry about me, Sega. Hurry and talk to Jijia like we discussed.'

Sega nodded, turned to Jijia and said clearly, 'Brother, Gongzha is... is my man!'

Jijia stared at her in shock. 'What did you say?'

The other men also gawped at her, wide-eyed.

'Last time, when Gongzha was here looking for Kaguo, you sent your men up the mountain to surround him. It was me—'

'Sega!' Gongzha yelled, interrupting her and turning to face her. He wasn't going to allow Sega to sacrifice herself for him. He knew that Yongxi was only one small reason for Jijia wanting him dead; far more important was that Gongzha knew the location of the shadow hunters' secret camp. 'I have never loved you – stop imagining things. My heart only has room for Cuomu.'

Sega's expression changed at his words. It was if thousands of needles had been stuck into her heart. She'd tried to save him, and this was how he responded? She turned round, fixed Gongzha with her eyes, and said in Mandarin, 'No. You're lying. Your heart doesn't only have room for Cuomu; it has *her* in it too. Why else would you have followed her here?' Sega was a woman too, a proud woman of the wilderness. She'd never been disrespected like that before. Even if she were ever to lie in Gongzha's arms, seeking pleasure from his body, it was obvious he'd always be thinking about another woman. It was a tragedy. How could she have loved him? She needed to forget this heartless man.

'Not true. I don't love either of you. Neither you nor Feng can replace Cuomu. My heart was given up long ago, when Kaguo killed Cuomu. You're a good woman, Sega, but we're not destined to be together. Get Feng out of No Man's Land – please, I beg you.'

'I thought you said Feng means nothing to you? In which case, what does it matter to you whether she leaves or not?' Sega laughed sarcastically. 'You're not speaking from the heart, Gongzha. When a grassland man loves someone, he truly loves them and nothing can stand in his way. This is just death you're facing, right? If you two were to die together, you would have Buddha's blessing upon you!'

'Get her out of the wilderness, Sega, I'm begging you!'

'You're begging me? You're begging on her behalf, but still you say you don't love her? Are you a man or not, Gongzha? You love her, but you don't dare admit it!' Sega began to cry, but her words were clear.

'I'm not going anywhere,' Feng said firmly, straightening herself and gripping Gongzha's bound wrists. 'I think Sega's right, Gongzha. I gave up everything to come looking for you, and I don't want to leave you again. If you're going to die, let's die together.' She shot him a significant look, remembering his whispered words from earlier. 'We'll let that statue of the Buddha rest beneath the earth forever – perhaps that's the Buddha's will, after all.'

'You... Don't do this, Feng. You don't deserve to die for the sake of a wanderer like me.'

'Whether you're worth it or not should be up to me to decide, right?' Feng looked into Gongzha's eyes and smiled. 'I've never forgotten you, Gongzha, not once in these last three years. Not a day has gone by without me thinking about you. The time we spent together was the happiest period of my life. I wanted to come and find you, and the prospect of being with you kept me going through my darkest days. I love you, Gongzha. In this world, in this life, you're the only man I've ever loved and the only man I've wanted to spend my life with. So I came to find you. I didn't worry about the ferocity of the sandstorms or the length of the journey – I didn't care about any of that, I just wanted to find you. And now that I have finally found you, how could I even think of exchanging you for a Buddha statue? To me, you are my Buddha, my master. Without you, I have no reason to live.'

Her words brought Gongzha to tears. A wanderer like him could still have a love like this! He tilted his head to look at Feng and smiled. 'You don't regret loving a wanderer who doesn't even have a place to pitch his tent?'

'If I regretted it, I wouldn't have come.' Feng placed her hands on his shoulders and without waiting for him to react bit him lightly on his cracked lip. 'I'm your woman now. Grassland women don't need their men to protect them from the wind and rain, they just want to stand shoulder to shoulder with them and fight alongside them, advancing and retreating together. I think I can do that.'

'Alright.' As he gazed into Feng's questioning eyes, his heart softened. 'We'll go to Shambhala together. Today,' he said loudly. 'And in the next life, I will be a good man to you.'

Feng's face lit up and she rested gently against Gongzha. He dropped his head and lightly rubbed the top of hers with his chin.

As she watched the thwarted lovers finally come together, Sega was moved to tears. She turned and said to the shocked Jijia, 'Are you really going to put these two to death, Brother? If you do, not only will Yongxi and I hate you for the rest of your life, but Buddha will certainly not forgive you.'

Jijia returned to his seat and collapsed into it. A war raged in his heart. Should he have them killed or let them go? If he had them killed, like Sega said, she and Yongxi would hate him forever. If he let them go, would this base that he'd worked so hard to establish still be safe? He glanced at the people around him, his face clouded with uncertainty.

Sega stepped forward. 'Relocating wouldn't be that hard, Brother. There are many places on the grassland to set down a wanderer's tent. But if you have them killed, we'll never be at peace.'

'Think of your son, boss. Let them go,' Yangji said.

Dawacuo chipped in. 'Auntie Sega's right, Uncle Jijia. Let them go.'

'Let them go, boss.'

'We can just find a new site, boss.'

Jijia drank a mouthful of *baijiu* and set the cup back on the table. 'Very well. Let them go. We'll move tonight.'

Sega let out a deep exhalation and hurried over to untie Gongzha's bonds.

When Gongzha's hands were free, he caught hold of Feng, who'd uttered a great sigh and was about to fall over. He sat down, held her in his arms and pulled opened her clothes. He was shocked by what he saw. He drew out a small bottle from his *chuba* and shook some medicinal powder onto the wound.

'Qiangba! Qiangba...!' Sega shouted, realising that Feng was about to faint.

Qiangba walked over reluctantly and Sega grabbed his wrist. 'Help her! Quick!'

Qiangba knelt down to examine Feng's wounds. He rubbed his forehead and shook his head. 'There's nothing I can do, Sega. She's lost too much blood, I'm afraid...'

'What rubbish!' Sega shouted, pulling at his robe. 'I thought you said you were an amazing doctor? Think of something, quick!'

'She was on the mend, Sega, but the wounds have reopened and she's lost too much blood. There's really nothing I can do.'

Gongzha scooped up Feng and walked out of the tent. His old horse was waiting on the sand outside and Gongzha gently laid Feng across the saddle and then got on himself. One of the men handed him his gun and Gongzha whipped the horse and sped off.

Some way beyond the encampment, he stopped his horse beside a hollow, brushed away some sand and dug out the Medicine Buddha from its temporary hiding place. Then he remounted.

They'd not gone five kilometres when he heard hooves pounding behind them and a voice calling, 'Gongzha, wait!'

Gongzha pulled the reins into his chest and turned to see Jijia speeding towards them on a black horse. He didn't say anything, just stared at Jijia in silence.

Jijia rubbed his nose and looked a little embarrassed. 'Ahem... Well... If you take the valley up ahead and then ride east for three days, you'll come to a sacred lake. A group of Buddhist ascetics live beside that lake, including one called Samu who's an expert in traditional medicine. Maybe he... maybe he can... heal your woman.'

As soon as his words were out, Jijia redirected his horse and tore off as if he was fleeing for his life.

Gongzha watched him flying into the distance. 'Thank you!' he bellowed. Then he turned back and urged his horse on towards the valley Jijia had described.

On a distant peak, Sega sat on her horse watching all of this. In her black robe and set against the blue sky she looked like a statue: mournful and solemn.

26

A herd of antelopes had arrived at Yongxi's pasture. There were about a hundred of them. Tajiapu tugged his dog's tail and gambolled across the plain in hot pursuit. The antelopes weren't afraid of them; they just raised their heads occasionally to look at the boy and the dog, then went back to their grazing.

Yongxi was mending the tents.

It was a peaceful scene: humans, livestock and wild animals co-habiting without bothering one another.

One of the male antelopes began moving towards Tajiapu. Yongxi stood up and was about to shout a warning, when she realised that it had no intention of hurting Tajiapu, it was simply looking at him quietly.

Tajiapu stretched out his hand and the antelope came slowly towards him. It licked Tajiapu's palm. Tajiapu giggled. Then he called, 'Ama! Come here, he has a picture on his horn!'

Yongxi went over and saw that there really was something carved onto its horn. She remembered Gongzha telling her that he and Feng had rescued two antelopes and that Feng had used a knife to engrave their names. Could this be one of the pair they'd rescued? She reached out and scratched the antelope's neck. No wonder it wasn't afraid of people, if it had grown up around them.

She stroked its smooth back and tried calling it. 'Baobao.'

The antelope didn't move.

She took a step back and called again. 'Beibei, come here.' This time the antelope walked slowly towards her.

Yongxi hugged its neck and laughed loudly. 'You're called Beibei? By the Buddha, you really are called Beibei. How lovely that Gongzha and Feng's little darling has grown so big. Why don't you stay here at my pasture and let me look after you.'

Beibei looked up at Yongxi with large, trusting eyes.

'You agree? Good, good. Come on then, Beibei. Come with me.'

Yongxi took her son by the hand and returned to the tent, trailed by one dog and one long-horned antelope. It was a unique picture: a solitary herder woman in the depths of No Man's Land, her son and their dog, now accompanied by an antelope. But this was the northern Tibetan wilderness, where all manner of strange things could happen.

Gongzha was carrying Feng through a valley thick with snow, his horse following behind.

Feng kept slipping in and out of consciousness. When she was conscious, she babbled to Gongzha about how her wounds hurt, her wrist hurt, her feet hurt, her head heart, she was hungry, her back was sore; she loudly recited all of the ways in which she was uncomfortable or might become uncomfortable. She figured that seeing as she'd suffered so much during her quest to find him, she should make him worry a bit now. If she was going to die, she needed to give him something to remember.

So, whenever she was awake, she complained.

Gongzha worried very cooperatively. Whenever she cried out, he stopped, examined her wounds and then wrapped her in his arms, frowning, trying to do everything he could to make her a bit more comfortable. He was not a great talker, so he channelled all of his concern into the hand that held her wrist or the worried expression on his face. Every so often, Feng would give him a peck on the lips, and that made him glad. The more time he spent with her, the deeper into his heart she travelled. Loving someone meant serving them with all of your mind and all of your heart – that was not how Gongzha had been brought up, it was just something he understood with the core of his being.

Most of the time, however, Feng was unconscious, saying and doing nothing. The deathly pallor of her face and the feverish heat of her skin terrified Gongzha. He kept worrying that she'd never wake up again, that she would go far away, like Cuomu had, and leave him on his own again. Life on his own was so lonely.

As long as Feng wasn't crying out in pain, Gongzha trudged on day and night, desperate to get to the lake Jijia had told him about and to find the doctor, Samu.

On the afternoon of the third day, Feng's temperature shot up so much, it was as if she was on fire. Gongzha was too scared to have her stay on the horse for fear that she wouldn't be able to take the jolting, so he carried her himself. It was a huge effort to trudge through the snow with Feng in his arms, but he hoped the snow might at least help cool her a little.

When he finally came to a summit and looked down to see stone houses scattered around a steaming lake at the foot of the mountain, his face ran with hot tears. It had to be the valley of Buddhist ascetics Jijia had told him about. He skidded down the mountainside as fast as he could, with Feng in his arms.

The people who lived at the foot of the mountain were wrapped in swathes of cloth that left only their eyes visible. When they saw Gongzha, covered head to toe in dust like a wild man and carrying a woman in his arms, they stopped and looked him up and down with curiosity.

'Please, where is Elder Samu?' Gongzha asked the person closest to him.

The man pointed to a house on a peak across the valley.

'Gongzha, why are they wrapped up in all that cloth?' Feng asked quietly, having suddenly returned to consciousness. 'And look at the symbol on their chests – it's the same as the one on the Medicine Buddha.'

Gongzha glanced at the elder in front of him and suddenly noticed the white ♉ on his chest.

'They... they...' Feng coughed as soon as she started to speak. The injuries to her chest and shoulders sent hot, sharp pains shooting through her. She stopped and waited for the pain to subside before continuing. 'Lots of them have it, Gongzha. Maybe... maybe they're... con... connected to that cave you went to.' She gave a sudden shriek. 'There are scorpions on the ground, Gongzha! Masses of scorpions!'

Gongzha glanced down to see a huge scorpion about to crawl onto his boot. The people around him yelled out in panic and fled. He raised his boot and kicked the scorpion into the distance, but the sudden movement disturbed Feng's wounds and made her wince and cry out. 'It hurts! It hurts so much, Gongzha. Why are there so many scorpions here? Look, in that crevice, on that bush, they're everywhere. Do you think that's why the people here cover themselves up so much, because of the scorpions?'

'Don't do any more talking now, Feng. Samu lives just over there. He'll help you get better.'

Feng smiled. Her man might appear very cool on the surface, but a great fire raged in his heart. In the past, he'd not found anything to allow his fire to catch, but now she was the kindling. The thought brought a smile to her face. Once she was better, they would go to Cuoe Grassland together, set up a tent, bring back his mother Dawa, make a home, have two children and grow old alongside each other.

When Gongzha saw her looking at him with a flushed face and a mysterious smile hovering on her lips, he knew exactly what she was thinking. When she was awake, her brain never stopped spinning out strange ideas. 'Could you not just let your mind rest for a while?'

'You... know what I'm thinking?' Feng smiled. She wanted to lift up her hand, but that would stretch her wound and cause even more pain. She frowned. With so many people around them, she was embarrassed to yell out.

Gongzha saw that and immediately understood that her wound was hurting again, so he picked up the pace. 'Don't move any more.'

'Do you know what... what I was just thinking about?' Feng wasn't that interested in finding Samu because she didn't believe Jijia would have given them the right information. Scheming poacher that he was, why would Jijia have wanted to help Gongzha of all people, the man who only hours before he'd wanted to kill?

'What were you thinking?' Gongzha asked obligingly. He knew she'd keep asking if he didn't reply.

'I was thinking that once I can walk again, we should go back to Cuoe Grassland, put up a tent by the lake and bring your mother back. What do you think?'

'You... you're really not going back to Shanghai?'

'No. Even if you drove me away, I wouldn't go back,' Feng said, a serious expression on her face.

'I'm old enough to be your uncle!'

'I know. Doesn't Zhuo Yihang call you uncle? From now on, that little boy Zhuo Yihang will have to call me auntie, won't he?' Feng found the idea of jumping a generation ahead of Yihang highly satisfying. She couldn't help laughing, but the laughter brought on another burst of searing pain.

'You...! You're just as much trouble as Baobao and Beibei,' Gongzha said as he carried her along the curve of the lake.

A few elders were floating on the lake and seemed totally at ease, as if the gentle waves were soft woollen cushions supporting their bodies. The lake was fringed with pure white sand and then a ring of black pebbles, as if the lake had been given a black and white frame. Beyond it, the ground was mostly sand and rocks, with occasional bushes and clumps of grass. Antelopes and asses wandered about.

At the top of the mountain stood a solitary house facing the sun. Its stone walls made it seem as if it was almost sinking back into the landscape, and from each corner hung a string of prayer flags printed with well-known scriptures. The most unique part of the house was its windows: rather than being square, they were in the shape of a ☼; the centre was empty and the circle and its four radial lines were white.

A man entirely swaddled in red robes, with only his eyes visible, was coming down from higher up the mountain. When he saw Gongzha, he looked startled, turned and hurried back up the mountainside, quickly disappearing around a curve in the path. But neither Gongzha nor Feng had noticed him, they were so focused on the stone house in front of them.

Gongzha raised his hand and knocked on the low wooden door, which also bore the mysterious ☼ symbol.

The door creaked open to reveal a ruddy-cheeked, silver-haired elder. Around his neck was wound a length of red cloth, one end of which hung down his chest. Many Buddhist ascetics dressed that way: when they meditated, they attached the loose end of the cloth to something high up, so that if their head drooped and they nodded off, the cloth would tug them awake. Ascetics lived a life far removed from worldly distractions; they spent their days immersed in the vast canon of Buddhist doctrine and literature, researching and pondering.

'Excuse me, does Teacher Samu live here?' Gongzha asked courteously.

The old man placed his palm on his shoulder and nodded.

'My woman is injured and we're hoping you can help make her better.'

Samu noted the streaks of blood on the front of Feng's jacket and opened the door a little wider. Gongzha carried her inside and Samu motioned for him to lay her on a cushion on the floor. Then he gestured for Gongzha to undo Feng's clothes.

When Samu saw Feng's wounds, he frowned. Her shoulder, waist and right breast had become seriously infected and inflamed, and some places had already started to fester. He handed Gongzha a wooden bowl, followed him outside and indicated the steaming lake below; he meant for Gongzha to quickly fill the bowl from the lake. Gongzha nodded and strode off.

Samu returned to the house. Taking a cloth bag out of a cabinet, he pulled out some stone knives, some small wooden rods, a yak-horn needle, some lengths of thread and several bottles of different shapes and sizes. From one of the smaller bottles he shook out some powder as white as jade into a bowl.

Gongzha returned with the hot water and Samu poured some over the powder. When the water had turned purple, he dropped the stone knife, horn needle and thread into it to soak. Then he took a soft red cloth out of the cabinet, handed it to Gongzha and made a scrubbing motion near one of Feng's wounds. As Gongzha duly dampened the cloth and carefully washed away the blood, Feng ground her teeth at the excruciating pain; drops of sweat as large as beads broke out on her forehead.

Gongzha sighed heavily: washing the three wounds clean was quite a challenge.

Samu glanced at Feng's deathly pale face, selected one of the bottles from his collection, took out a black medicine ball and put it in Feng's mouth. Soon after, Feng slowly shut her eyes and went to sleep.

Samu now set about cutting open the infected areas with his thin stone knife. He pressed the pus out of the wounds then used the horn needle to sew them closed. After that, he spread red ointment over them and covered them with bandages. By the time he'd finished, the sun's rays had already begun slanting into the stone house.

Samu picked up a pen, wrote a few sentences on a piece of paper and passed it to Gongzha:

There is an empty stone house at the foot of the mountain. You can stay there, but don't go wandering: there are poisonous scorpions everywhere and you need to be careful. If you're stung, there's no medicine that can save you. When the Rigel star rises, take your woman out to where the hot springs are in the lake and let her soak in them for two hours each night, then come back up and change the bandages. Once she's better, please leave immediately and do not speak of this place to anyone.

Gongzha realised that Samu must be a hermit and therefore didn't speak. He brought his palms together in gratitude, then carried the sleeping Feng out through the door.

Inside the stone house were a couch, a chair, a pan, a pot and a stove. Hunks of wind-dried yak meat and mutton hung from the walls and there were stone pots full of *tsampa*.

Gongzha laid Feng on the couch and covered her with his *chuba*. Then he sat beside the couch, held her hand and watched her face as he silently replayed her words in his head: 'I've never forgotten you, Gongzha, not once in these last three years. Not a day has gone by without me thinking about you. The time we spent together was the happiest period of my life. I wanted to come and find you, and the prospect of being with you kept me going me through my darkest days. I love you, Gongzha. In this world, in this life, you're the only man I've ever loved and the only man I've wanted to spend my life with. So I came to find you. I didn't worry about the ferocity of the sandstorms or the length of the journey – I didn't care about any of that, I just wanted to find you. And now that I have finally found you, how could I even think of exchanging you for a Buddha statue? To me, you are my Buddha, my master. Without you, I have no reason to live.'

Every one of those words carried such power, and Gongzha was deeply moved. It made him more determined than ever that she should come to no harm; he'd already done her enough damage.

The woman he loved had gone far away, but he'd never stopped loving her. When he calmed himself and looked at Feng, Cuomu appeared. Cuomu always kept him company when he was at peace; over the years, she'd become part of him, part of his body and his soul.

When Gongzha saw that Feng was sleeping peacefully, he gathered up an armful of clothes and went down to the lake to wash them. Further up the mountainside, a gaunt face appeared at the ☿-shaped window of another stone house. As Gongzha washed the clothes, the face stared at him with hate and fear.

Feng was still sleeping when Gongzha returned to the house. He spread the clothes out to dry on a boulder outside, then boiled some water and ate a little *tsampa*. He sat down by the couch again and took Feng's hand. Watching her face deep in sleep, he felt a familiar sense of peace. It was as if Cuomu was lying next to him, calm and still.

The moon rose. The night sky beyond the window was like water and the stars were brighter than ever. Unfamiliar insects raised a chorus of sounds, rendering the tranquil night extraordinarily lovely.

Gongzha quietly waited for Feng to wake up. When the Rigel star rose, he would do as Samu had instructed and take her down to the lake.

He felt her fingers stirring and smiled as her eyes slowly opened. 'You're awake? How do you feel? Are you still in pain?'

'Yes, but a bit less than in the past few days.'

'Samu said that each night, once Rigel has risen, we're to soak your wounds in the lake for two hours and then change the dressings. It will help you heal quickly.'

There was no one by the lake.

A crescent moon hung over the mountain ridge.

Gongzha carefully removed the *chuba* Feng was wrapped in, lifted her into his arms and waded into the hot-water lake. When he was in deep enough, he sat down, leant Feng against him, put one arm round her and used his other hand to bathe her wounds.

When the water came into contact with her injuries, Feng frowned and moaned.

'Does it hurt? Does it hurt a lot?' The sight of Feng's deathly white face made Gongzha wince in sympathy.

'It's fine.' When the pain had faded a little, Feng forced a smile. 'It's fine, I can put up with it.'

'Doing this for me – is it worth it?' Gongzha murmured, stroking her cheek.

'Even if I had the chance to go back and do things differently, I'd still make the same choices.' Feng rested her head on his shoulder. 'A life without you in it would be no life; I might as well be dead.'

'I might as well be dead,' Gongzha repeated softly. What if he hadn't joined the army, if Ama hadn't needed looking after, if he'd not been so set on seeking revenge – how different would his life have been then? *Oh, Cuomu, if only I'd got to you just a bit earlier; if only I'd brought you here, to this lake, you would have recovered too.* He pictured the terror on Cuomu's face and it was as if she was right there in front of him. *Oh, Cuomu...* He dropped his head.

She sighed gently, lifted her chin and pressed her lips tightly against his.

A shiver passed through Feng's body, as if a feather had lightly brushed the deepest recesses of her heart. After all that she'd experienced, this moment was more beautiful than anything she could have imagined. This solitary man, so like a wild wolf, was the one she'd chosen. No matter how unlikely a couple they seemed, no matter that other people thought she was crazy, she had no regrets. She loved him and she wanted nothing more than to be with him.

It was a night to be lost in the moon and the stars. The waves lapped lightly against the lakeshore and a white mist shrouded the two lovers. But Gongzha quietly whispered Cuomu's name and an enormous rift seemed to open before Feng's eyes.

Off in the distance, the hum of scriptures being recited drifted out from one of the houses and slowly circled in the air. Together with the gentle slapping of the water against the shore, it kindled ineffable emotions in the pair of troubled lovers, further inflaming their hearts and making their feelings even more complex.

After ten days, Feng's wounds started to heal. With Gongzha supporting her, she began to leave the stone house and go for little walks to have a look around.

'I think this place must have some connection to the cave you told me about. It's a pity none of them talk,' Feng said from the path as she stared at a white ☐ on a large black boulder.

Gongzha kept silent, mulling over something.

'There's a secret somewhere here. This place definitely has a secret.' Feng turned and caught a flash of crimson as a monk darted behind a yellow cluster of thorn plums. 'That person... it's like he's watching us. I see him every time we come out.'

'Who? Where?' Gongzha looked around in surprise.

'Behind that bush with the yellow flowers.' Feng gestured with her chin towards a bend in the path. 'I've noticed him lots of times, but as soon as he sees me looking, he always hides.'

Gongzha saw that there was an indistinct figure behind the bush and was about to walk over to him, but Feng pulled him back. 'Don't rush over. Didn't Samu tell us not to go wandering? We don't understand anything about this place, so let's just observe for now and discuss it later.'

Gongzha glanced at her and nodded. Feng always stopped him from rushing in at the key moment. He took her hand and held it in his, as gently as if he were holding a baby rabbit. He had no idea how Feng's hands could be so soft; it was almost as if they had no bones. They were warm, too, and he'd grown to love that.

The more time they spent together, the better he understood her qualities. She could be strong and independent, but she could also be weak and dependent; and sometimes she was petulant, tearful and complaining not on account of her injuries but purely because she wanted a hug. She was very curious and very determined. The more he got to know her, the more he appreciated her warmth, and the more he was reminded of Cuomu's warmth, Cuomu's determination and Cuomu's softness.

His days were spent peacefully now, not continually on the move through the wilderness, and whereas before his heart had been lonely and full of hurt, it had now come back to life, thanks to Feng's strong affection, and was stirring once again. But the stirring had made his longing for Cuomu even more intense, and he wanted her badly.

Gongzha and Feng sat on the grassy slope looking at the lake, Feng resting her head lightly on his shoulder, and Gongzha holding her hand.

'How beautiful it is. Wouldn't it be nice if it could always be like this, just you and me,' Feng murmured.

Gongzha squeezed her hand and said nothing. She had given up her life for him, and he would use his life to protect her and stop any harm from befalling her ever again.

As they sat there, they heard a commotion coming from the foot of the mountain, and people began calling loudly for Teacher Samu.

Samu appeared at his door, followed by a disciple carrying his medicine bag, and the two of them shot straight down the rocky slope, ignoring the path they usually used. Gongzha and Feng had no idea what had happened, but they went over to have a look anyway.

In front of a stone house on the left, a band of Buddhist ascetics stood pressed together in such a tight knot that even the wind couldn't get through them. Gongzha pulled Feng to the side and they saw that an elder was lying on a cushion. His hand had gone black. Samu squatted on the ground and jabbed it with his needle. Black liquid spurted out and splattered on the ground.

Samu silently cleaned the needle and then stood up. He sighed, made it clear that the elder should be taken away and then impressed upon Gongzha and the others that they should be careful: the elder had been stung by a scorpion. He returned to his house, his back as crooked as a weak bow.

As they made their own way home, Gongzha gripped Feng's hand tight, his eyes fixed on the ground for fear a scorpion would scuttle out.

'This place is infested with them – why don't the ascetics just move somewhere else?'

Gongzha shook his head. Even though he'd become friendly enough with the ascetics during their time there, and even though he was intensely curious about the place, he was afraid of asking them the wrong question. The last thing he wanted was to offend Samu and make him unwilling to treat Feng. Deeply curious though he was, Feng's recovery was more important.

'Dr Samu! Dr Samu...!' Feng energetically pushed open the door to Samu's little house, a bunch of yellow, white and purple flowers in her hand. She'd grown fond of the silent, compassionate elder. Yesterday she'd forcibly taken his dirty cushion and monk's robes down to the lake to wash them.

Samu had just finished meditating. When he saw Feng, his expression brightened and his eyes smiled. This girl was not at all like the wilderness girls: she was spirited and wild, forever coming up with strange new ideas. For example, she'd gathered up all the broken and discarded bottles from outside and put water in them, and now every day she placed a bottle with a wild flower stuck inside it on the windowsill near where he meditated, bringing a touch of life to the dark room. She'd washed his medicine bottles and arranged them neatly so he didn't have to search everywhere for them, and she'd also put all his scriptures and ritual instruments in a cabinet together so he could find them easily when he needed them.

Feng took the flowers from the day before out of the bottle and threw them out the door. Then she put in the new flowers and stepped back to admire them.

'They really do look lovely – this girl is so creative!' said Samu.

Gongzha stood behind her, covering his mouth, wanting to laugh but not daring to.

Afterwards, Feng sat on Samu's meditation cushion, her legs crossed, and asked pointedly, 'Old Mr Samu, aren't you going to thank me?'

Samu didn't understand what she was saying, but he could understand her expression. He smiled and stroked her hair. Then he took a medicine bottle out of the second cabinet on the right.

Feng pouted but bared her wounds with Gongzha's help.

Samu pressed lightly round each of her wounds and smiled with satisfaction. He spooned out a dollop of the sticky substance and began spreading it gently on each wound, but before he'd finished applying it to her shoulder, Feng screamed and fainted.

'Feng! Feng...!' Gongzha was terrified. He snatched her up and patted her face.

Samu was also stunned. He gazed in astonishment at the bottle in his hand, lifted what was left of the paste on the spoon to his nose and sniffed it. He was so shocked that he forgot he'd taken a vow of silence. 'Why does it smell like scorpion venom? Impossible, this is impossible!' He sniffed again, then pushed open Feng's eyelids and her now dark purple lips to take a closer look. He shook his head. 'It's over. It's all over!'

'What is it? What's wrong with her? Why has she suddenly gone purple?' Gongzha gazed in horror as Feng's face went puce. He felt as if the sky was falling in.

'She's been poisoned. There was poison in the medicine and it was from the most venomous scorpion in the wilderness,' Samu said, looking at Gongzha with frustration.

'How could there be poison in the medicine? You used it before without any problems.'

'I don't know what happened either, but someone must have poisoned the bottle while I was out.'

'What can we do? What should I do?' Gongzha stared at him in desperation, clutching Feng close.

'Take her down to the lake and wash her wounds, then press down hard on the wounds until you see fresh blood coming out of them. Don't worry about hurting her. I'll go and find my master and see if there's anything else we can do,' Samu said quickly. He rushed out the door and began hurriedly heading up towards one of the higher peaks.

With Feng in his arms, Gongzha slithered so fast down the mountain, it was as if he was flying. He ran straight into the lake, ripped opened Feng's shirt and supported her in the water. Then he started to press down on the wound on her shoulder. The shattering pain brought Feng back to consciousness. She screamed and struggled, feet and hands flying. 'No, Gongzha! It's killing me, it's really killing me!'

Gongzha used his arms to hold her still, his hands still pressing on her wound; black blood spurted out, staining the lake water.

'It hurts! It really hurts, Gongzha! I really am in pain – stop pressing it, okay? Let's just stop the treatment – we'll just leave and go back to the grassland. It hurts too much...' Feng screamed and at one point even bit Gongzha.

Gongzha ignored her and kept pressing on the wound. Bean-sized drops of sweat and tears rolled off Feng's purple face and slid into the lake. She gave one final scream, then fell unconscious.

All Gongzha could think about was pressing down with all his strength. A thousand voices shouted in his head, 'Don't let her leave you, don't let her go like this.'

The foul-smelling black blood continued to pour out of her.

As her face got darker and darker, he really felt as if the end of the world was nigh.

'Buddha, I beg you, save her. If this is some kind of punishment for her, let me bear it instead, don't torture her any more.

'Samu, Samu, where are you? Hurry up and come! Hurry up and save her!

'Feng...! Feng, my woman, open your eyes and look at me. Haven't you spent years waiting for me, don't you want to come back to the grassland with me? Open your eyes and let me take you back to the grassland!'

'Aaaaah!'

As Gongzha's crazed howl filled the air, two crimson figures slipped quickly down the mountainside towards him. It was Samu and an elder whom Gongzha didn't know. They hurried straight into the lake, paying no heed to their robes getting wet, and immediately bent over Feng's floppy form, the older man pulling up her eyelids and lifting her crow-black fingers. He sighed deeply, shook his head at Samu, and turned back towards the shore.

'Master, is there really nothing you can do? Think again, please! We can't watch her die like this. We've never had any of our patients die, Master.'

But the old man didn't turn round; he just walked on, his back hunched and his steps agonisingly slow.

Samu looked at Gongzha, who was still pressing down on the wounds, and said bitterly, 'You can stop that now. There's nothing more we can do.'

'No, that can't be right. She wouldn't leave me like this. It can't be right...' Gongzha continued pressing, tears rolling down his tanned face, tears that were all the more pitiful and unexpected because of who he was: the strong man of the wilderness, a man who'd lived with wolves for companions and hadn't batted an eye; a man who always stayed calm in the face of danger. But now, seeing that he was about to be abandoned by his beloved all over again, he was distraught, riven with despair.

Was heaven playing with him? Was the Buddha sleeping?

'Take her back to the stone house, Gongzha. Let her go in peace.' Samu couldn't stand to watch, so he turned to walk away.

'Is there really nothing we can do? I thought you were the

best doctor in the wilderness, Samu?' Gongzha shouted. 'There must be something else you can try.'

'She's taken in a poison that doesn't have an antidote. Unless the Medicine Buddha appears, there's nothing we can do,' Samu said. 'My master taught me everything I know. He's never come down the mountain before, it's always been me that's treated people, but today he came down and even he couldn't save her. There is truly nothing to be done.'

'The Medicine Buddha? The Medicine Buddha! I've carried his image with me every day, but where is he now? He won't even protect my woman. What good is he to me?' Gongzha yelled in despair. He yanked Zhaduo's statue of the Medicine Buddha out of his *chuba* and hurled it onto the broken stones by the beach. It landed with a clang.

Samu scrambled after it. He picked up the Buddha and looked around in amazement, laughing loudly.

'What are you laughing at?' Gongzha said unkindly.

'Your woman can be saved, my son!' Samu said with a huge smile. 'Your woman can be saved. And not only can she be saved, everyone else can be saved too – all of us who live here!' He raised the statue high.

'You're crazy!' Gongzha stopped listening to him, picked up the unconscious Feng and carried her up the bank.

'Really, I'm telling you, she can be saved, the girl can be saved,' Samu repeated over and over, and with great excitement. Then he shouted towards the houses on the mountain, 'Come out, all of you. The Medicine Buddha has appeared! We no longer have to fear the scorpions!'

People started pouring out of the houses in twos and threes. Men, women and children were running down to the lakeside. When they saw the Medicine Buddha in Samu's hand, they knelt together on the bank and began continually prostrating themselves.

'They... what are they doing?' Gongzha asked.

'It's a long story. Let's go back to the house first. We need to move quickly if we want to save her.'

Raising the Buddha high, Samu passed through the crowd and returned to the house at the foot of the mountain. Everyone followed him. When they looked at the Buddha, their eyes flashed with a fervent light.

Samu's master was waiting for them in front of the house, along with three elders. When they saw Gongzha, they put their palms together and bowed. Gongzha didn't understand why they were treating him with such respect, but he was certain they had a strong connection with the Medicine Buddha. Because he had Feng in his arms, he couldn't make the palms-together gesture in return, so he simply nodded at them.

Once Gongzha had gone inside, one of the elders made a sign with his hand. Those waiting outside sat down and watched the stone house quietly.

Gongzha laid Feng on the couch, covered her with his *chuba* and turned to Samu, who gave him a reassuring smile. 'Don't be afraid, child. She will be saved.' As he spoke, he handed the Buddha to his master. 'Master, it is for you to open!'

Master Zhamu took the Medicine Buddha with both hands and placed it on a shelf. He looked directly at it and prostrated himself three times. Then he stood up, took the knife that Samu handed to him, traced the edge of that strange ⌺ with the knife and prised it up.

The ⌺ snapped open and revealed a small hole in the back of the Buddha, out of which the old man carefully lifted two pieces of paper. He unfolded them and examined them carefully. Tears sprang from his eyes.

The other elders wept too.

'This piece of paper contains the formula. We're only short of one ingredient. I'll send someone to get it.' Master Zhamu rolled up the two slips of paper and put them into his monk's bag. Perhaps because he'd not spoken for a long time, his voice was a little raspy and uneven. 'Take her to my house for now.'

Samu nodded and Gongzha scooped up Feng and went out with the old man.

When the people sitting on the sandy ground outside saw them come out, they all stood up and watched them silently, preparing to prostrate themselves in front of the Buddha image.

Master Zhamu lifted up the gleaming black statue. 'Go back home for now. We need to save this woman first. Come out again when the stars have risen and we will venerate the Medicine Buddha!'

The people did as he'd instructed and stood hand in hand watching them make their way up the mountain.

'It's been many years since anyone was allowed into my master's house,' Samu said as he walked beside Gongzha. 'Even though he taught me medicine, that was all done elsewhere.'

Gongzha hesitated, then finally asked, 'You... what kind of people are you?'

'The last soldiers of Nacangdeba!' Samu said proudly.

'The last soldiers of Nacangdeba? There are some of you still living?'

'You know about the Nacangdeba?'

Gongzha nodded. 'I've been to that cave.'

'That explains it... Is that where you found the Medicine Buddha, in the cave?'

'No, Living Buddha Zhaduo gave it to me.'

'No wonder he never came back,' Samu muttered to himself.

'He's dead now,' Gongzha said. He thought back to that extraordinary period, when people had tried so hard to outdo one another with their political zealotry, when everyone was so unsettled and no one felt safe. Ama's eyes, Danzeng's wounds, Ciwang's arrogance, Zhaduo's calmness – all of that was now long in the past. It was like when the spring rains came to the grassland and turned the ground to mud, erasing all scars. 'Living Buddha Zhaduo came here?'

'Yes, many years ago, when he was very young. He came to No Man's Land to pick medicinal herbs. He was caught in an avalanche and Master saved him.'

Gongzha thought back to what the clan elder had told him all that time ago, about how a plague had come to Cuoe Grassland and Zhaduo had gone to No Man's Land with some disciples to look for herbs to cure it; but they got lost in a snowstorm. Things were suddenly starting to make sense to Gongzha, and he was about to ask for more detail when Samu announced that they'd arrived. 'This is where Master Zhamu practises; no outsider has ever been allowed here before.'

It was a solitary peak, and it contained just a single courtyard house. Two snow-white dogs were crouched by the door, the fur on the backs of their necks bristling as Samu and Gongzha approached. Master Zhamu signalled to them and the dogs obediently lay down again. Then he gestured Gongzha and Samu inside and indicated that Gongzha should lie Feng on the cushion by the window.

Zhamu produced a small bag wrapped in yellow silk and drew out several black needles of differing lengths and some thin blades. He told Samu the name of a herb, and Samu went out to search for it.

Then Master Zhamu turned to Gongzha. 'Help me hold her still; don't let her thrash about.'

Gongzha nodded and sat on the cushion as instructed, holding Feng against his chest.

Zhamu took up a black, razor-thin knife. 'Before the antidote is given, I need to release all the poisoned blood.'

Gongzha nodded again. He knew from Living Buddha Zhaduo that letting blood in this way was an ancient practice of traditional Tibetan medicine. It involved making an incision at a specific spot with a specially made blade in order to release the bad blood. Tibetan medicine held that when someone had been poisoned or had become ill, there was a particular stage when the good blood and the bad blood in their body would separate. If you drained the bad blood and kept the good, the patient would recover. But if you did the blood-letting before the good and bad blood separated, not only would the patient not be healed but they'd be subject to a secondary illness. An experienced doctor would check the nasal cavities, mouth and anus. If the blood was fresh, then it was good blood. If there were white bubbles or it had become yellowed, then it was bad blood. If the good and bad blood weren't mixed together, that meant it was time to do the blood-letting.

Zhamu used the knife to make a small cut in Feng's nostril, and a stream of rotten-smelling black liquid flowed out. He dipped his finger into it and wafted it under his nose. Then he quickly lifted her right leg and supported it on his own leg. He made small incisions on the front of her calf and her thigh, and more black liquid streamed out.

Feng's face appeared lifeless and she lay unmoving in Gongzha's embrace.

Feng herself felt extraordinarily light, as light as a feather; the slightest exhalation and she would float into the sky. The sun was so beautiful, with its thousands of golden rays, and her entire body was bathed in its radiance, inside and out. She heard Gongzha softly calling her and felt his tears dripping onto her face. She wanted to tease him: you're so tough, you can stare down a pack of wolves without blinking, so how come recently you've been crying at the slightest thing?

Then, suddenly, without any warning, all of the pain came clawing at her: her shoulder hurt, her chest hurt, her leg hurt. Everything swirled in her head: Shanghai, the grassland, Zhuo Yihang, Sega, Jijia, Gongzha...

'Oh, it's killing me, I'm going to die from the pain. I can't stand it, Gongzha. Gongzha, I can't stand it!' She wept, shouted and struggled.

Gongzha didn't know how to comfort her. She carried on struggling, even though she was dripping with sweat, and Gongzha felt her pain as if it was his own. 'You'll get through this, Feng. Buddha will make sure of it. You'll get through this, Feng, I know you will.' Apart from continually wiping the blood off her and holding her flailing arms, there really was nothing else he could do.

Zhamu glanced at Feng's face and began using strips of cloth to bind the cuts he'd made. 'It's good she's awake. She took in so much venom that she can only last another four hours now, after the blood-letting, before the poison in her system starts taking hold again. May the Buddha allow Samu to return soon.'

Gongzha didn't know what to say. If he could, he would have given his life to bring Feng peace.

Zhamu watched Feng slowly settle down, then he picked up the Medicine Buddha and went to another room.

Gongzha held Feng in his arms and leant back against the cushion, covering her with his *chuba*. As he stared out at the sky-blue lake, he began to sing, without even realising it.

'Today I must go to a faraway land
When we parted you said, "Please don't forget me."
Our promise hangs high in the sky
Those white clouds, those stars, that moon
Bear witness to our promise that in the next life we will
    meet again
And never forget each other.

'Beautiful shepherdess, I love you
No matter how the world changes, you are forever in my
    heart.
Beautiful shepherdess, your laughter echoes under the blue
    sky
And deep in my heart.

'Oh, give me a tent
I want to take your hand and live together free of pain.
Oh, give me some land
I want to dance with you there, slowly and forever.

'Shepherdess, sweet shepherdess
When will you return and make our love run smooth?

My greatest hope is not to be separated
Has our love in this life already scattered?
Could it be that loving you brings only despair?
Every day without you is a tragedy.'

He sang with great feeling.

'You won't leave me, will you, woman?' he murmured softly to the sky, oblivious of the tears running down his face. One deathbed farewell was enough for any man.

Feng smiled at him through her tears. 'Promise me,' she whispered, 'that whatever happens, whether I live or die, you'll take me back to Cuoe Lake. If I live, I'll be with you, but if I die, I still don't want leave you.'

'You're not going to die. Samu's gone to prepare the antidote. Do you remember the Medicine Buddha, the one I've carried with me everywhere?' Gongzha held her closer. 'They found the formula for the antidote in his belly. You're not going to die.'

'If I do die, Gongzha, just take me to the grassland you love so much. Don't give me a sky burial; bury me by the side of the lake. I want to always be with you.' Feng stroked his face.

Gongzha gazed into her eyes and his tears flowed uncontrollably. 'I promise we'll never be apart again. Wherever I am, you'll be there with me. I'm not leaving you ever again and I'm not going to make you wait for me ever again.'

Feng smiled, and it was a contented smile.

27

In the flat-bottomed river valley out of the wind, the air was warm and the grass plentiful. At dawn, when the sun had only just shown its face, its golden rays shone low and gentle over the rocky wilderness. It had rained the night before, and the air was clear, the colours even more vivid than normal, lending an extraordinary beauty to the distant snow mountains and the nearby lakes.

Yongxi darted out of her tent, fastening her dress as she walked. The rhythm of her days echoed the rhythms of the barren earth beneath her feet and the mountains encircling her; the sun above and the shadows below were her timekeepers. She didn't need to think about what to do when; her brain automatically directed her hands and feet.

The yaks were round the other side of the tent, lying scattered in ones and twos across the sandy ground. The dog was with them, stretching, its face to the sun; it barked casually twice, and the yaks lumbered to their feet one after the other, dislodging a small flock of sparrows, who rose into the air in a whirr of wings.

In recent days, many antelopes had arrived at the valley to have their young, and their prints were all over the riverbank. Vultures circled high overhead and a lone wolf drifted in the distance – sure signs that the first antelope calves had been born. Antelopes gave birth rapidly and as soon as the baby's fur had dried, the calf could stand up and walk around.

Just as the antelopes came to the valley each year to give birth, Yongxi came each year to pasture. When she saw the mass of hoofprints, she was delighted, as if a friend she hadn't heard from in a year had suddenly returned. She stood with her back to the sun and smiled happily at the sunny slope busy with large-bellied mothers and their newborn calves. Despite the effort it required to get there, they came back year after year because the valley was far from human interference and the safest of hideaways.

Yongxi never tired of watching the calves being birthed or seeing the mother antelopes again, that bit older each year. Sometimes she thought she and the antelopes were fated to be together. They met once a year and parted soon after, the antelopes heading off with their young, she driving her yaks, each going their separate ways. The following year, without prior arrangement, they reunited in the same place.

The male antelopes keeping watch from the heights turned to look at Yongxi, the contours of their bodies accentuated in the morning light, their long horns resplendent. On the western slope, newborn calves bounded and romped, exploring their world with curiosity. The young antelopes born the year before were much quieter, either grazing quietly alongside their mothers or raising their heads and looking nervously around.

Antelopes were easily startled and even the tiniest disturbance could cause them to scatter as if their lives depended on it. During the breeding season it was dangerous: a pregnant female could lose her foetus if she ran too quickly, and if the whole herd was startled, newborns could be trampled in the stampede. Yongxi was careful to watch her band of old friends quietly, a reassuring smile on her lips.

The antelope Beibei and the dog wandered over and stood to either side of her.

After a long while, Yongxi withdrew her gaze, undid the long rope that tethered all the yaks together, and signalled for the dog to drive them towards the river valley. She went back to her tent, helped the newly wakened Tajiapu put on his tunic and boots, and set him on the ground. Then she began to boil tea water. Beibei was lying beside the tent and Tajiapu darted out and began to play with his long horns.

It was a quiet morning, like every morning. Yongxi got on with her usual chores, humming a grassland love song as she went.

Ping!

Yongxi didn't even raise her head – she thought Tajiapu was throwing stones. But the sounds kept coming, one after the other, until the air was thick with them.

They were gunshots – a barrage of gunshots.

Yongxi stopped humming, dropped the butter-tea churn to the ground with a clang and raced outside. She didn't even pause to set the churn upright; its contents emptied onto the stove and extinguished the flames with a sizzle.

A group of gun-wielding men had appeared on the surrounding slopes, seemingly out of nowhere, and were laughing wildly and shooting at the antelope herd.

Within moments, the herd stirred like a pot of boiling water, and antelopes tore off in all directions, fleeing for their lives. Some were in the middle of giving birth, with a calf's back leg or even half their body poking out, and even they began to run for their lives. The calves that had just been born couldn't run, either because their legs weren't yet strong enough or because they didn't know how, and they bleated in agony as thousands of desperate hooves trampled over them. The ones who died quickly were lucky; those who had their legs or backs broken could only bleat piteously.

Beneath the orange rays of the sun, one antelope after another closed its eyes in agony. The cloying stench of blood was everywhere. It was tragic.

Yongxi waved her arms and ran forward, yelling, 'No, Jijia, I beg you, don't shoot, don't kill them!' Tajiapu toddled behind, bawling.

Too late.

The three surrounding slopes were littered with fallen antelopes of all sizes. Those that hadn't yet died cried out forlornly. Those that had managed to escape the circle of gunmen kicked up a trail of dust and disappeared into the distance.

Above the solitary black tent, a line of blue smoke continued to rise, a strangely beautiful sight amid such insanity.

Yongxi rushed up the nearest slope. At the sight of all the antelope corpses, her legs went weak and she fell to her knees. Tajiapu waddled up behind her, pulling at her clothes and crying; Beibei stood beside them.

Another gunshot rang out, and a bloody hole opened in Beibei's neck. Before he could make a sound, he started rolling down the slope.

Yongxi ran after him, grabbed one of his horns in one hand and made a futile attempt to stem the spouting blood with the other. Before she even had time to call his name, Beibei, the most trusting of antelopes, closed his eyes forever.

Yongxi glared up at the sky and raged. 'Buddha, why don't you destroy these demons?' Her voice, ragged with grief and anger, echoed across the wilderness.

Just then, a white off-road vehicle careered to a halt nearby, dragging dust behind it. The gunmen rushed over excitedly.

'We did it, Brother, we did it!'

'This is the biggest kill we've had this year, Brother!'

'We hit it lucky, boss! It was a huge herd.'

'You're too late, boss, there were too many of them. We didn't have time to wait for you.'

When Yongxi realised that it was Jijia who was getting out of the car, she leapt up, raced over, snatched a gun from one of the men, and fired off a volley of bullets.

Jijia was terrified; he jumped back into the car, slammed the door and hunkered down. The bullets rained against the car door.

The men who'd been riotously happy moments before didn't know what was happening. They were so frightened, they stood stock still to the side, not daring to fire back.

When Yongxi had emptied the gun, she dropped to the ground and wailed, hammering the earth with her fist. Tajiapu rolled down from higher up the slope in terror, crawled to his mother's side and gripped on to her arm, his face streaked with tears. The herding dog raced back from the mountain valley opposite, howling.

The sun pierced through the clouds, but the valley would not be warm again.

The evening sun was slanting through the window, but Samu was still not back from gathering herbs.

Master Zhamu stood on the bare ground in front of his house, his crimson monk's robes fluttering in the wind, his sleeves billowing to one side. The people going about their business down below couldn't help looking up at him, and there was admiration in their eyes, for Master Zhamu was their most respected and revered elder. He was the only one not bound by the mysterious laws they all lived by, but he adhered to them anyway. He had willingly and rigorously adopted the laws their ancestors had passed down so as to be an example to the rest of them, a model for how to live a quiet, ascetic life.

As their ancestors had lived, so he lived, and so would their descendants live. Zhamu had never considered changing and had never needed to change. Their life there was good – it was always peaceful there, in their haven far removed from the outside world. Every so often a lost outsider or two would stumble by, and then he and his clanspeople would do as the Medicine Buddha had decreed and try everything they could to save them before inviting them to stay or leave.

Zhamu and his clan venerated the Medicine Buddha. When the last of the Nacangdeba soldiers had discovered this Shambhala of the wilderness and sent their wives, sons and daughters there, they made them swear that they wouldn't leave until the Medicine Buddha reappeared on earth. The Medicine

Buddha had always been the protecting spirit of the clan and the Nacangdeba soldiers had found this lovely place in the depths of No Man's Land under his guidance. Generation after generation, the clan chose the most suitable person to keep the secrets that had endured for so many years.

Samu was Master Zhamu's disciple; Zhamu had seen in him a noble and generous spirit, so he'd taught him everything he knew about traditional Tibetan medicine. When Zhamu had to meditate, Samu could continue healing people. Deep in thought, Zhamu watched the path through the valley. The sun was sinking in the west, but the path was still empty. The place where the plant grew was neither far away nor high up; Samu should have been back long ago.

Master Zhamu began to feel uneasy. For the first time in his life, he felt that something terrible was about to happen.

The waters of the lake were as calm as ever beneath the gauzy white mist, and the stone houses built into the mountainside glowed a pale gold in the setting sun, looking as ancient as if they'd been present when heaven and earth were separated. But the ascetics' valley had never been as lively as it was that day. There were lots of people swimming in the lake: adults, children, elders and women were all floating freely. Others were doing their washing by the rocky shore, beating their clothes and splashing water playfully over one another. The sound of singing spiralled out from the scattered houses, the notes rising and falling rhythmically.

A column of dust rose at the far end of the valley. Then a horse appeared. A figure lay slumped on its back, seemingly about to fall off.

When Zhamu saw the crimson monk's robes, he called to two disciples who were standing nearby and the three of them sped down the mountain. When they reached the horse, they helped a bloodied Samu dismount.

'What is it? What happened?' Zhamu asked anxiously.

'I'd just finished gathering the herbs and was about to come back,' Samu said with difficulty, 'when a boulder suddenly came rolling down from above me. I couldn't dodge it, so I got hit.' He drew the herbs out of his *chuba* and handed them to Zhamu.

Zhamu glanced at them and passed them to his disciple. Samu had lost a lot of blood and his vision was cloudy; Zhamu pulled out a bottle of medicine and put a tablet in Samu's mouth. 'Help him home!'

A line of people carried Samu back to Zhamu's house on the peak.

When Gongzha saw them returning, his eyes brightened; then he noticed the state Samu was in and said in surprise, 'What happened?'

'A little accident; it's nothing.' Samu forced out a smile. 'I brought the herbs back. Master, please.'

Zhamu nodded, and ordered his disciples to bind Samu's wounds. He went into another room and began preparing the antidote himself, in the manner prescribed by the formula.

Feng consumed the medicine and almost immediately began to vomit violently and continuously. As she drifted in and out of consciousness, she kept feeling as if there were drops of water on her face.

That night, neither Master Zhamu nor Samu slept. They came in and checked on her periodically and when at last Zhamu saw that Feng's vomit had finally turned a pale red, he sighed with relief. Turning to Samu, he said, 'I need to go out. You oversee the making of the antidote. And remember, don't let anyone go near that room.'

Samu nodded.

On the second day, the purple in Feng's face began to slowly recede. On the third day, her skin began to look normal again. On the fourth day, Feng finally began to feel hungry.

Gongzha made *tsampa* porridge and held her in his arms as he fed it to her little by little. Feng swallowed slowly. After she'd eaten half a bowl, she shook her head to indicate that she didn't want any more. Gongzha put down the bowl and used his sleeve to wipe the corners of her mouth. He had no words to describe the joy in his heart.

Feng leant into his body and turned to face him. His beard had grown much longer and his eyes were more sunken. She knew he hadn't been able to rest for days, so she lightly stroked his cheek and said, 'Why don't you lie down for a little while? I'm fine.'

'It doesn't matter. Do you want to sleep a bit more?'

'I've slept for many days and my body aches; I'd like to lean on you for a little while.' Feng put her hand in his palm. 'Have you not slept at all?'

'I couldn't sleep. Seeing you awake one minute and unconscious the next, I was afraid.'

'Afraid I would be like Cuomu and die suddenly?'

Gongzha nodded.

'You know what, when I was on my way to find you, I worried the whole time about what would happen to me if you didn't want me, if you ignored me...'

Gongzha's eyes prickled. He squeezed her hand. 'Silly woman!'

'When I can walk, can we go back to Cuoe Lake?' Feng said quickly, looking at Gongzha lovingly. 'I can't wait to be your bride.'

Gongzha stared down at her earnestly, trying to hold back his tears. A moment later, he lowered his head and kissed her eyelids.

The valley of the ascetics had cast off its usual demeanour and the air was filled with laughter and cheerful chatter.

Monks walked around with buckets of the antidote and brushes of dried grass, sprinkling the liquid everywhere, in front of each stone house and along every path. The scorpions that habitually scuttled all over the place took one sniff and immediately retreated into the nearest rocky crevice, never to be seen again.

Carrying new clothes and herbs for bathing, the ascetics went down to the lake in twos and threes, chatting and laughing. They ripped off the long robes they'd been wrapped in, exposing their pallid bodies to the sun after years of having kept them bundled up. They felt clean and cool in a way they never had before and smiled delightedly as they rushed into the warm water.

The youngsters splashed each other, chased each other and playfully shoved each other, examining one another's bodies with interest, occasionally patting or gripping a friend's flesh. When they'd finished bathing, they strode confidently to the bank, rubbed themselves with the antidote, then reverently picked up the clothes they'd left neatly rolled up and put them on. Their bodies had never felt so free. The wind gently stirred their sleeves and blew on their skin like the gentlest of breaths. They felt so light on their feet, it was as if they might take flight at any moment.

Feng and Gongzha stood in front of their stone house, watching the joyous goings-on in the vast, misty lake. A young man in plain cotton clothes came along the path carrying two wooden buckets; when he saw them, he smiled and brought his palms together in gratitude to Gongzha, saying, 'Teacher Samu asked me to bring you these. Please rub the antidote on your bodies after you've bathed, then you won't have to worry about the scorpions.' Then he took one of the buckets and sprinkled the liquid all around the house.

'Respected guest, thank you for bringing our Medicine Buddha back and allowing us to bathe in the sunshine once more. You won't know this, but we've never once sat out in the sun.'

'Why not?'

'Because of the scorpions. If you got stung, you died – everyone knew that. So we protected ourselves as best we could by wrapping ourselves up as tightly as possible, from the moment we were born; even so, people have still died. But now all is well; the Buddha has returned, so we have a way to avoid the scorpions and we don't need to be afraid of them any more.' The young man had a broad grin on his face.

'With this many scorpions, why didn't you move away?'

'Move away?' The young man looked at him strangely. 'We're the last soldiers of Nacangdeba, we have sworn to follow the orders of the Medicine Buddha and watch over Princess Gesar's jewels, which are hidden with King Gesar's treasure. How could we move away?'

'Watch over Princess Gesar's jewels?'

'Yes, respected guest, our ancestors have lived here a long time, watching over Mount Tajiapu. Even though the Medicine Buddha was lost, no one ever left.' The young man smiled again, brought his palms together once more, bowed and left.

'What were you talking about? What's this stuff for?' Feng asked urgently, pulling at Gongzha's sleeve.

As Gongzha explained, Feng tilted her head to one side and said, 'Some of what he said definitely sounds right. One: there are lots of poisonous scorpions here and they once had an antidote but they lost it. Didn't you say they found the formula in the belly of the Medicine Buddha? Two: these ascetics venerate the Medicine Buddha and they lost your statue. But I don't understand why it would reappear on your grassland? Three: they made a solemn vow not to leave because they wanted to guard Princess Gesar's jewels. That's made up, I think: the legend of King Gesar's treasure is just a fairy tale, so how could the princess's jewels exist?'

Gongzha rubbed her head and smiled indulgently. He picked up the bucket. 'Should we go down to the lake now, or after the moon's risen?'

Feng blushed. When she'd been unconscious, he'd taken her to the lake countless times to soak her wounds, which meant their naked bodies had touched, but that was because she hadn't been able to move of her own accord. She dropped her head and said in a voice as quiet as a mosquito, 'After dark, please.' Then she turned and went inside.

Gongzha gazed after her retreating figure in astonishment; he had no idea why she'd suddenly blushed.

When the moon came up, Gongzha carried the bucket and Feng followed him.

It was quiet around the lake. The banks of black pebbles gleamed like black pearls at the water's edge and the bright moon lit the mist that hung above its surface and drifted with the waves.

The hot springs gurgled and a strong smell of sulphur filled the air.

Gongzha took off his clothes, threw them on the ground and walked barefoot into the water. When he saw Feng hesitating on the bank, he said, 'What is it? Come on in, it's not cold.'

'You... um... could you turn around?'

The sight of Feng dipping her head and looking at him out of the corner of her eye made Gongzha's head reel as if he'd been hit with a hammer. In the days since they'd been reunited, he'd watched her struggle between life and death, had supported her, held her and even kissed her, and through it all he'd felt nothing but sorrow. But this sidelong glance of hers electrified him; it was like he'd been struck by lightning. He whipped his head round and stared straight at the lake, his body as rigid as a statue.

Feng slowly stripped off her windcheater and snow-trousers. She glanced down at her long underwear and thought about taking that off too but didn't have the courage. She stepped barefoot into the water, kept a few centimetres distance between herself and Gongzha and sat down.

Their expressions were rather stiff and neither of them dared speak first, so they just sat there aimlessly splashing water over themselves. The atmosphere was more strained than usual, so much so that they could hear each other breathing.

Feng's wet underwear clung to her wounds and itched uncomfortably; she pulled at it every now and then, sometimes turning to glance at Gongzha's naked torso. He sat there looking serious, his long, damp hair reaching to his shoulders, his eyes deep-set and unfocused. His left hand occasionally sprinkled water on his broad torso, drops of water rolling down his solid chest.

Cuomu used to frolic with him in Cuoe Lake; they'd been so carefree then. Year after year, when he returned on annual leave, he'd tickle her in the water and she'd laugh the same clear laugh. It would always be Cuoe Lake's most beautiful sound.

Gongzha looked mysterious and sensual in the moonlight and there was so much strange tension between them that Feng could barely breathe. She slipped down into the water, stretched out and floated on the surface. The stars gleamed, and the moon, partially hidden behind a cloud, gazed down on the tortured pair.

Feng's change of position dissipated the tension and Gongzha let out a long breath, locking his gaze onto Feng's floating form. He watched her bob up and down with the waves, her long hair as soft as satin in the water, her fingers occasionally tugging at her thick underwear, which seemed to be making her uncomfortable.

He stretched out his legs on the black pebbles. When he saw her counting the stars like a child, he laughed; it was a game Cuomu had often played. This was the happiest he'd seen Feng in the past few days and that made him happy too. But there was something missing. If Cuomu had been there, everything would have been much better. *My Cuomu, are you lonely in Shambhala?*

Feng's body suddenly began to twist unnaturally, and her hand grasped at the empty air. 'Gongzha, my leg...'

'What is it?' Gongzha rushed over, held her hand and noted the creases on her brow. 'Are your wounds hurting again?'

'No, it's my leg. My right leg seems to have cramped.'

Gongzha held her right ankle and rubbed it for a few moments. 'How's that? Any better?'

Feng grunted, moved her right leg a bit, and felt much better. 'Those clothes of yours are too thick,' Gongzha said, and, without caring whether she agreed or not, he grabbed her by the waist and stripped off her long underwear.

Feng closed her eyes and held still. As skin brushed against skin, the tension returned. But, freed of her cumbersome underwear, she could feel every hair on her body dancing with pleasure in the warm water.

He laid her lightly on the water again and caressed the wound at her waist. 'Does it still hurt?'

'It doesn't hurt, but it itches.'

As she watched his eyes roam over her body, she blushed even more. Things felt different tonight: the hand he laid on her waist had some kind of magic in it and his touch was like a raging fire, spreading an intense heat through every cell of her body. She closed her eyes and moved gently with the waves, her lashes trembling occasionally, betraying the turbulence in her heart.

Moonbeams pierced through the clouds and streamed down onto the lake, rendering the mist hanging over the water even more ethereal. To Gongzha, Feng seemed like a celestial maiden, like a spirit who'd just descended to earth, pure and beautiful, unsullied. His Cuomu had been like that.

Feng's body grew warm in his embrace. She slowly lost her self-control, circled her arm around his neck and pulled him closer. Gongzha's body was trembling with desire; he drew her to him. Her low gasps and murmurs filled his ear and he realised he wanted her, there and then.

He placed one gentle hand around her waist, letting her body move lightly in his arms, and the other on the wound at her shoulder, the only scar still faintly visible. Carefully, his exploring hand slid slowly down to her erect nipple (it was cool out there on the moonlit lake), which he covered with his warm palm, watching her eyelids flutter. She quivered and her soft lips opened slightly with nervous anticipation. Gongzha's heart thumped. He put his arm around her under the water, gently lifted her up and pressed her into him, then he slowly covered her cold, trembling lips with his and softly kissed her.

The moonlight was like water, the mist was thick, the lake lapped gently against their entwined forms. They gazed at each other, their eyes travelling over one another's faces.

Gongzha felt Feng's body heating up, its gentle movements transmitting information that made his heart leap, and when he felt his own body swell suddenly, he didn't know quite what to do.

He scooped her up and set her down on a rock by the spring. Then he lay down and stared into her eyes, and she stared back.

He kissed her eyes, her nose, her lips; he heard her happy sighs, felt her twist and gasp faintly in his embrace. Under the light of the moon, the woman on the black rock looked beautiful, so beautiful she made his heart hurt.

He gently entered her. Her light cry of pain sounded like a signal to continue, so he surged onwards, not thinking of anything else.

The moonlight was like silk, and the lake lapped gently against the rocks.

Feng endured the thrusting of the man on top of her. She forgot her pain, she forgot her body even existed; only her heart was present and it was consumed with him. In the moonlight, beside the misty spring, amid Gongzha's growls the word 'Cuomu' crashed out and echoed in her ears.

She didn't say a word.

Gongzha lifted himself off her, washed her tenderly, then walked with her to the bank, where he rubbed her all over with the scorpion antidote and wrapped her in his *chuba*. Feng dipped a small towel in the antidote and rubbed him all over. When she felt him becoming erect and his muscles tightening, she blushed. Although she was a mature woman, this was the first time she'd actually been with a man. Gongzha's fingertip drifted across her face, exploring her eyes, her delicate cheeks; when it reached her soft lips, it stopped.

He gripped her by the waist again, threw the towel in her

hand into the bucket, held her close, and with a look that was both dazed and tortured, said, 'Don't ever leave me again, woman. Don't put me through that torment again.'

Feng bit his shoulder and tears rolled down from beneath her lashes. She didn't know whether he was taking to her or to Cuomu. Her heart was torn, but she was also happy. At the very least, he had accepted her, and eventually he would love her as he had loved Cuomu.

Gongzha dressed quickly, picked up her windcheater and snow-trousers, pulled her by the hand and asked gently, 'Shall we go back?'

Feng nodded and followed him like an obedient lamb.

Two days later, everyone in the valley stood together outside Master Zhamu's house, staring expectantly at its tightly closed door.

Two clear bells rang out and the door creaked open. Four young monks emerged, wearing new crimson robes draped over their shoulders and carrying the traditional long horns used in Buddhist ceremonies. They stood on either side of the door. Four elders followed, carrying other ritual musical instruments; they took up position in front of the young men, obliging them to take a step back.

A ceremonial yellow parasol filled the doorway: the imperial canopy.

Young and old knelt on the ground, their foreheads pressed to the sand.

Finally, a crimson robe appeared beneath it, advancing slowly into the light until Master Zhamu was revealed. He moved with dignified majesty, his hands bearing a silk-covered tray. In the centre of the tray stood the blue-black Buddha Gongzha had brought. Samu followed behind, his expression solemn.

Generations had waited for this moment. The hope sustained by those generations was realised in that moment.

The ceremonial horns rang out and the other instruments struck up.

Everyone intoned the mantra of the Medicine Buddha together: *'Tayata Om Bekandze Maha Bekandze Radza Samudgate Soha.'*

The horns cleared the way, the canopy began to move, and Master Zhamu bore the Medicine Buddha along the mountain path. Samu followed, drawing Gongzha in with one hand and Feng with the other. Everyone else came on behind, fervently reciting scriptures. Their prayer wheels flashed as they spun in the sunlight.

The lone stone building on the mountaintop dazzled with its white walls and crimson edging. Its courtyard had been repaired, the weeds pulled and the broken rocks removed. The once desolate place, abandoned to the mice and unvisited in years, was now so clean, it made people nod approvingly.

The vermillion door adorned with a white ☐ slowly opened to reveal delicately crafted banners hanging from the ceiling. Butter lamps along the walls emitted a wavering light.

Master Zhamu entered the hall to the solemn lowing of the long horns. His attendants took away the tray and Zhamu lifted the Medicine Buddha high with both hands. He bowed, kept his arms raised, stepped forward quickly, still bowing, and placed the Buddha on a white jade throne; then he stepped back three paces. En masse, the assembled crowd brought their hands together in supplication and touched them to the crowns of their heads, then to their foreheads, then to their hearts; then then prostrated themselves flat on the ground.

Gongzha and Feng did likewise, with sincerity, prostrating themselves five times. This was a physical ceremony, but it was also a baptism for the spirit: pressing heart and body to the ground, lifting your thoughts to the sky, forgetting the world and yourself.

When they had completed all the rites, Master Zhamu turned round to face the crowd. Holding a long *khata* in his outstretched arms, he bowed deeply to Gongzha and hung the ceremonial scarf around his neck. Then he held Gongzha's face in his hands and pressed his forehead to Gongzha's. 'Thank you, my child. May the Buddha bless you with peace and health. *Tashi delek.*'

Gongzha brought his palms together and bowed deeply in return.

The monks unfurled a crimson cape and draped it over Zhamu; on the back was printed a white ⌀. With their support, Zhamu ascended the glinting, gold-plated throne in the centre of the hall and sat down cross-legged upon it. He looked around at the crowd, composed himself, rang the bell softly, and prepared to lead his people into communion with the Buddha.

Gongzha quietly ushered Feng out of the hall, and they sat down together on a rock on the edge of the cliff. As they stared down from their vantage point, they could see the mysterious ⌀ on many doors, windows and prayer flags, and even on the stones and incense burners by the side of the path.

Feng pointed to the ⌀ on the rock next to them. 'Did you notice, Zhamu's cape had the same symbol.'

'I did. I'd never heard of the Medicine Buddha having a connection with that symbol before. Shall we ask Samu about it if we get the chance?'

Feng nodded and slipped her hand into Gongzha's. Gongzha squeezed it and turned to look back towards the hall. He didn't have a clear view of what was going on inside, but he could hear the recitations. Wave after wave of intoned scriptures rolled out, accompanied by the rhythmic ringing out of the instruments. This was a truly pure environment; his spirit had been cleansed.

The recitations stopped suddenly and four monks took tea into the prayer hall. A while later, Samu emerged along with some disciples carrying a teapot and bowls. When he saw Gongzha and Feng, he came over, beaming, poured some tea and offered it to them in the formal way, with both hands. Gongzha and Feng jumped down from the rock, accepted the tea and drank deeply. The disciples refilled the tea bowls and set them down on the rock.

'Teacher Samu, we... we... have something...' Gongzha put his palms together and looked at Samu. He wanted to ask him about the story of the ♉, but he didn't know how to begin. When he'd first arrived there with Feng, seeking their help, Samu had warned them not to wander around and not to tell anyone about the valley. The reason he'd said that was because he didn't want outsiders intruding on them. Gongzha worried that by asking Samu he might be breaking a taboo, which would not be good.

'Did you want to ask about this symbol?' Samu pointed unconcernedly at the marking on the rock.

Gongzha nodded.

'It's a long story!' Samu glanced up at the sky, saw that the sun hadn't yet reached the tops of the mountains and thought the ceremony in the temple had ended rather prematurely. The story of their valley had indeed once been highly secret, but now that the Medicine Buddha had returned, the long-held taboo no longer pertained. 'Come with me.'

Gongzha and Feng looked at one another and followed him down the mountain.

When the three of them reached Samu's small house, Samu sat cross-legged on a cushion and motioned for Gongzha and Feng to do the same.

'We are the descendants of Nacangdeba. Legend has it that the first clan elder of the Nacangdeba was abandoned by his parents and raised by bears. That bear, which must be the ancestor of your Kaguo, had a white circle on its forehead, and that circle became the symbol of the Nacangdeba. As for the battle with the Jialong, although it seemed like the Jialong won, in truth, no one won. You've been to the cave on Mount Chanaluo and you know that the Nacangdeba warriors killed themselves because they had no food or water and refused to become slaves. But actually, one person survived, and that person was the clan elder's son, Cinuo. He was only twelve at the time, but he joined the soldiers nonetheless. When the others were preparing to end their lives, he happened to be elsewhere, playing with two bear cubs. He lost track of time – he was still a child, after all, and children always love to play. He only discovered the tragedy in the cave when he came back for food. He was terrified. He didn't dare go down the mountain on his own, so he stayed in the cave, surviving on the mother bear's milk and the leftover *tsampa*. After a couple of months, he finally followed the bears out of the cave complex, taking with him the Medicine Buddha and *The Epic of King Gesar*, only to find that Cuoe Grassland, which had been overrun by the Jialong, was now empty.'

'How come?' Gongzha asked in surprise.

'Plague. A plague had decimated Cuoe Grassland, which was hardly surprising, if you think about it. When the Jialong won their battle with the Nacangdeba, they slaughtered many yaks and sheep for their celebrations. It was almost May, the warmest season on the grassland, and the Jialong were so exultant at their success that they forgot to clean up the battlefield, which would have been littered with many corpses. When the plague appeared, there was little they could do. The clan elder of the Nacangdeba was an expert in traditional medicine, but he'd died in the cave. When Cinuo saw that everyone on the grassland had died, he didn't dare stay. He knew the clan had sent the women and children to a place near Mount Tajiapu, so he found his way there.'

'But how did the Medicine Buddha get lost again?'

'That happened later. After Cinuo came to No Man's Land, he underwent a long and difficult training and became the most successful of doctors. Because he'd seen two clans wiped out in battle, he swore never to get involved in another war and he had his disciples swear that they too would lead an ascetic, restrained existence for the rest of their lives. Because Cinuo had been able to tame bears since he was a young boy, he still kept company with them after he came to No Man's Land. But as for how the Medicine Buddha was lost, I'm not very clear about that. I've only heard the elders say that Master Cinuo saved an injured herder and that when the herder was healed and left, he stole the Medicine Buddha and *The Epic of King Gesar*, and the antidote to the scorpion venom was lost with them.'

'But now Yongxi is the only one who stays by Tajiapu Snow Mountain.'

'It's been over a hundred years and the grassland has undergone huge changes. The land is more sandy and stony than it was, and the grassy areas have turned to wilderness. People had no choice but to find someplace new. Some went back to Cuoe Grassland, some went to the scared Dangreyong Lake in Wenbu, and some went to the area of No Man's Land near Shuanghu.'

'And you all are...?'

'We are a group of ascetics who venerate the Medicine Buddha. Master Cinuo was Zhamu's master. When Master Cinuo left Cuoe Grassland, he made a vow: not to engage in war, to turn his heart to the Buddha, to make the Nacangdeba experts in the study and practice of traditional medicine, and to let the children of different clans grow up healthy in the compassionate love of the Medicine Buddha. Most of the clanspeople left, but a few stayed on to live under his guidance and remain here forever.'

'And why was that?'

'The statue of the Medicine Buddha is an ancient treasure left by King Gesar. In the Buddha's body are hidden two secrets. The first is the formula for the scorpion venom antidote. It's said that the Medicine Buddha left that himself. This place is teeming with scorpions; if there was no antidote, there'd be almost no way to survive here even if you wanted to. You saw yourselves when you came how everyone kept themselves wrapped up tightly. Despite that, every year there'd always be several people who got stung and died. But now that we have the antidote we don't need to fear the scorpions.'

'And the other secret?'

'It's said that it had to do with the jewels of Princess Gesar. Although that's only hearsay; no one's ever seen them.' Samu smiled drily. 'I've heard Master Zhamu say that the map to the princess's treasure is on the Medicine Buddha's body itself. Although even if you did have the map, the treasure's in an ice cave and the secret to opening the ice cave is in a book.'

'A book?'

'Yes, the book that tells the story of King Gesar. It's written in gold ink.'

'Is it this one?' Gongzha pulled a package wrapped in yellow silk from his *chuba* and passed it over.

When he opened it, Samu's eyes widened in excitement; he immediately turned and ran off to the hall.

Gongzha smiled after him, then followed him to the hall, holding Feng's hand. The crowd parted as they passed, smiling at them and clasping their palms together in respect.

Master Zhamu was looking at *The Epic of King Gesar*. When he saw Gongzha and Feng, he ordered his two disciples to help him descend from the throne. Smiling softly, he pressed his palms together and bowed deeply.

Gongzha smiled appreciatively and bowed deeply in return. Feng bowed too.

Several disciples stepped forward with long, ceremonial *khatas* in their hands; one by one, they hung them round Gongzha's neck in the traditional display of respect and gratitude. The rest of the crowd followed suit, placing the ritual scarves around his neck one after the other. The silk scarves fluttered, and face after smiling face gazed up at Gongzha and Feng.

It was an otherworldly scene: a dim temple hall, strings of prayer flags suspended from the ceiling, flickering butter lamps, crimson-clad figures, drifting spirals of incense, and the Medicine Buddha set high on the altar looking silently on...

28

At the foot of the great snow mountain stood a little red hill, one peak flapped with prayer flags strung up the year before, above a pile of broken stones used as an occasional incense burner. Feng and Gongzha were on the hill, gazing down at the water lapping gently against the lakeshore. As they sat there deep in silent thought, from far down the valley they heard the howl of a bear and a person screaming in fright.

It didn't matter where he heard it, Gongzha never failed to recognise that sound. It was that same howl that had fuelled his decade of wandering, a howl he couldn't wipe from his mind, the howl that had separated him from his beloved Cuomu and sent her to Shambhala.

Gongzha raced down the slope and back to the stone house, dragging Feng with him. Grabbing his gun, he whistled to his old horse, which was grazing by the lakeshore, leapt on it, pulled Feng on after him, cracked his whip and hurtled towards the other valley. Some of the other ascetics were already speeding in the same direction.

In that nearby red-sand river valley, a brown bear with a white circle on its forehead was bellowing in maddened fury as it chased a man dressed in crimson, its howls reaching to the heavens. The man, who had somehow managed to escape the bear's paws several times, was shrieking, 'Save me! Someone come...!' But there was nothing the onlookers could do except shout back.

Gongzha leapt off his horse and helped Feng down.

When the man saw Gongzha, it was like he'd seen his saviour

star. He limped towards him, dragging a broken leg, shrieking and crying. 'Gongzha, save me! It's me, Ciwang – Ciwang from Cuoe Grassland. I apologise to you; I apologise to Dawa. Oh, Buddha, have mercy on me. Gongzha, save me, I beg you, save me!'

'Ciwang…!' Gongzha was startled but immediately began setting up his gun-stand on the ground.

He took aim at Kaguo and was about to pull the trigger when a great shout came from behind him. 'Don't shoot! Don't hurt her!'

Gongzha glanced back to see Master Zhamu and Teacher Samu rushing down from the red cliff, three disciples following behind. When they reached Gongzha, they lay down beside him.

'Don't shoot!' Zhamu said. Pulling out a white conch shell, he blew a low-pitched, horn-like call.

When the bear heard the sound, she looked surprised, stopped chasing Ciwang and sat dazed on the ground.

Gongzha lifted his gun again, but Samu restrained him with a hand on the shoulder. 'She isn't the Kaguo you're looking for,' he said gently. 'This cub was born last year. Look carefully at the circle on her forehead. It's wider than Kaguo's, isn't it?'

Gongzha looked intently. Even though the bear was about Kaguo's size and had a white circle on her forehead, Samu was right: the circle was much bigger than Kaguo's.

Zhamu advanced slowly, still blowing on the conch shell, his robes billowing red against the green grass, blue sky and white clouds. The bear continued to sit quietly. Ciwang stayed crouched to one side, in shock.

When Zhamu reached the bear's side, he placed his palm on her head, looked into her eyes and spoke to her quietly. The bear's eyes clouded over. She slumped to the side, put her head on her front paws, closed her eyes and began to snore.

'Master Zhamu is a true son of Master Cinuo,' Samu said, 'the only one trained in the art of bear-taming.'

Two ascetics carrying lengths of rattan appeared, hurried over to Zhamu, pointed to Ciwang and spoke quietly. Zhamu nodded and turned to Ciwang with a deeply pained expression on his face.

'When you got lost and ended up near here, it was Samu who found you on his way home from picking herbs. It was Samu who rescued you, who took you on as a disciple and taught you traditional medicine. Why did you hurt him?'

Squirming under Zhamu's severe gaze, Ciwang yelled, 'It wasn't me! It wasn't me who wanted to hurt him. It was him – he made me do it!' He pointed in the direction of an elderly monk in tightly wrapped robes. 'He made me follow you all – it was him, it wasn't me!'

'You're lying,' the elderly monk shot back. 'If you tried to hurt the teacher and the Buddha punished you, what's that got to do with me?'

'It was you! You made me put the scorpion poison in the medicine bottle. You said that if the woman died, Gongzha would leave and the story about me hurting Dawa would never come out.'

'You're lying.' The old monk's eyes glinted coldly at Ciwang. He pulled out a knife and was about to rush him, but two young monks held him back and pinioned his arms.

'I'm lying? As soon as you got here, you found me and told me you were sure that these people were the descendants of the Nacangdeba and the guardians of King Gesar's treasure. You told me that when we found the treasure, we could go back to the grassland and buy all the pasture and livestock we liked. You made nice with Master Zhamu, because you thought he knew where the treasure was. But you were wrong, because the Medicine Buddha was lost, so the secret of King Gesar's treasure was lost too. Then Gongzha turned up and you thought he might have the Medicine Buddha. So you told me to poison his woman, because you knew he'd bring out the Medicine Buddha if he had it, to save his woman.' Ciwang was shrieking now, his eyes bulging, his spit flying in all directions.

He rushed up to the gruff old monk. 'And everything happened as you predicted: I put the scorpion poison in her medicine and Gongzha brought out the Medicine Buddha. You were afraid that Samu was on to us, so you followed him when he went to pick herbs and pushed that boulder over the cliff, hoping to crush and kill him. But it only grazed him and made him more suspicious, so you tried again, saying that Samu would be picking herbs here today and that I should drive the bear here so he would be mauled to death. What you didn't know was that they have a special relationship with those bears. As Buddha is my witness, this man made me do everything, it has nothing to do with me!'

'You're lying! You did all those evil things yourself. Don't put the poisoning on my head.'

Samu looked at Ciwang and addressed him with pity in his voice. 'Should you not reflect on your own part in this? I began to suspect you when the scorpion poison suddenly appeared in that medicine bottle. My treatment room is usually locked tight and I always check it thoroughly for scorpions before I use it. How could one have got in? And there was only venom in the bottle, no actual scorpion, so the venom had been put in there deliberately. The only person other than my two disciples to come near the treatment room that day was you. I raised those two disciples myself; they're orphans and I trust them completely. But your ego is too big. From the start, you wanted to learn medicine from me as quickly as possible so you could return home and make money from it. That I could understand: you'd been part of that world for many years and it would take time to change your way of thinking. I hoped that under my guidance you would begin to see things differently, but instead you strayed further and further away, particularly after this man arrived. The two of you spent all day gadding around together, not reciting scriptures or studying, just looking everywhere for clues to the whereabouts of King Gesar's treasure. Oh, you lost creatures, if only you'd taken the time to think about what you were doing. Buddha has shown you the path, why do you turn away from it?'

'The reason I wanted to study and return to the grassland as soon as possible was not for money but because I wanted to heal Dawa. I never intended to make her crazy. She was nasty to me and she threatened me; she said that Gongzha would deal with me when he came back on annual leave, so I was terrified and I knocked her unconscious with a rock. How was I to know she'd wake up crazy? I've had nightmares every day since – I see demons everywhere, coming to chase me down.'

Ciwang knelt on the ground and tugged at Samu's robe, babbling and weeping. 'Master, I truly didn't do any of this on purpose – it was him. After he came here, he kept telling me that if we could only find the Medicine Buddha, we could locate King Gesar's treasure and then we'd be able to have any woman we wanted. I did these horrible things only after hearing his evil talk. Forgive me, Master.'

'The person of whom you must ask forgiveness is not me, it's him,' Samu said, pointing at Gongzha.

Ciwang crawled over to Gongzha and prostrated himself repeatedly in front of him, palms clasped, tears running down his face. 'I was wrong, Gongzha. I'm sorry about your mother – a demon poisoned my heart. Buddha has already punished me: he made me go without sleep every day; as soon as night fell, he sent demons to catch me and bite me. I couldn't stand it, so I left the grassland. But I still haven't found peace; your mother still comes into my dreams, haunting me with that cold laugh of hers.'

He smashed his head against the rocky ground, and there were traces of blood in the dust on his forehead. 'I was wrong. I apologise to your family: I apologise to your mother, I apologise to your father. I won't go back to the grassland and I'll carry on with my medical practice. I'll be a good person from now on.' He looked up very contritely at Gongzha. 'You were a PLA soldier and a government cadre, Gongzha. You're a good man, forgive me...'

Gongzha stood there remembering how his father had been

tied to the tent pole and how his mother had suffered unbearable pain for so many years. He lifted his foot and kicked Ciwang as far as he could, then turned to find his gun.

Feng held him back. 'He's been punished enough, don't you think, Gongzha? His leg's been mauled by the bear, and it's obvious he's suffered a lot these past years. That was a unique time – neither people nor animals acted rationally – and you can see he's been in torment ever since. Look at him, he's like a mad old man. Forgive him, Gongzha.'

Gongzha held Feng's gaze for a long time, then turned to look at Ciwang. The old man dragging his bloodied, broken leg and with sparse white hair sticking to his wizened face was nothing like the arrogant man of times past. At his age, Ciwang should have been dandling a grandson on his knee in a warm tent, but because of the mistakes he made during that time long ago, he'd ended up in No Man's Land, alone and in a pitiful state.

Gongzha hesitated a moment, then slowly set down his gun. 'Get up,' he said.

Feng patted Gongzha comfortingly on the shoulder. Love and hate were choices: from the moment she'd chosen him, she'd not looked back.

Ciwang prostrated himself at Gongzha's feet in relief. Then two young disciples supported him as he limped over to Samu.

'They will help you home,' Samu said, waving his hand. 'We won't be able to save your leg, but if in exchange for your leg you are granted a life with a peaceful heart, Buddha will have been merciful.'

Ciwang wiped away his tears and hobbled off.

'Basang, take off your outer robe,' Master Zhamu said, passing the white conch shell to one of his disciples and turning to the elderly monk whose arms had been pinioned. 'The Medicine Buddha has returned, so you don't need to wrap yourself up any more. It just makes people even more suspicious of you.'

'Basang...? Basang from where?' Gongzha asked curiously.

'From your grassland. He said he came here on the instructions of Living Buddha Zhaduo, to take the Medicine Buddha back,' Zhamu said lightly.

'Cuoe Temple's Basang? Living Buddha Zhaduo's disciple?' Gongzha said in shock.

Zhamu nodded and motioned for the disciples to strip off Basang's head covering. They revealed a pasty face that looked very much like the old Basang of Cuoe Temple.

'In truth, I doubted you from the moment you arrived,' Zhamu said. 'Zhaduo came here himself a long time ago, when he got lost in a snowstorm and Samu saved him. He stayed for three months, studying Tantric initiation practices with me and traditional medicine with Samu. He was a good man, his heart was noble, and while he lived here he followed all of our rules. He knew the Medicine Buddha wasn't here, so why would he have sent you to get it?'

'Why didn't you expose me sooner?' Basang asked, a treacherous gleam in his eye.

'You'd not been in the Buddhist fold for long and I kept hoping you would see the light. The difference between a good thought and an evil thought is simply a matter of a change in direction.'

'"The difference between a good thought and an evil thought is simply a matter of a change in direction"?' Basang howled with laughter. 'You want me to be like you and spend my whole life reading scriptures, never looking at a woman? Do you even know what a car looks like or that you can fill your eyes with beautiful women if you have a TV? No, that's not the life for me. I don't want to live in the past – I want to enjoy the pleasures of now. Give me *baijiu* to drink and women to sleep with and I'll be just fine.'

Gongzha stepped in front of him and said accusingly, 'So you pretended to be Living Buddha Zhaduo's disciple because you wanted to find the statue he was protecting? I assume you were also involved in the theft of Cuoe Temple's ancient Buddhas – you and Luobudunzhu?'

'You want to know something? That Medicine Buddha statue was originally my family's.'

'Your family's…?'

'My great-grandfather took it from this place, but the old fart got confused and gave it to Cuoe Temple's living Buddha.'

'Your great-grandfather was that thieving herder Master Cinuo saved?'

'It takes skill to acquire the best things, but what would you know about that?' Basang threw Gongzha a scornful look. 'Do you really think I'd have made all that effort to pass myself off as a disciple of that crazy man just so I could get hold of an old statue? How much can it be worth?'

'Ah, I've got it now – you're after Princess Gesar's treasure!' Gongzha howled with laughter and his hearty guffaws echoed across the mountain wilderness. 'Everyone on the grassland knows the legend of King Gesar, but has anyone actually seen the princess's treasure? You really think those legends are true? What sort of grasslander are you – never getting your hands dirty, never doing an honest day's work, but focusing on bad things instead? You've had your eyes pecked out by vultures – you wouldn't recognise the treasure if it was right in front of you.'

'What do you know? If there was no treasure, why would these people live in a nest of scorpions?'

Master Zhamu, who'd been staring up at the mountains, turned and looked at Basang with pity. 'Do you want to see Princess Gesar's treasure?'

Basang opened his eyes wide. 'I've put so much effort into this – of course I do.'

'And the rest of you? Would you also like to see Princess Gesar's treasure?' Zhamu asked the ascetics behind him.

Most of the elders straightened their robes, lowered their heads, pressed their palms together and said, 'Master, it means nothing to us.'

Only a handful of younger ascetics looked at Zhamu with curiosity.

'Very well. Everyone come with me.' Zhamu walked towards his horse and two disciples rushed ahead and helped him up. He sped off through the valley, closely followed by everyone else. Basang was in the middle of the pack.

The sun hung over the mountain, its orange rays casting a rainbow of colours across the land, but the summit of Tajiapu remained wreathed in cloud; even five- and six-thousand-metre snow mountains seemed no bigger than hillocks alongside it.

A vast, barren plain of shattered black rocks stretched as far as the eye could see. The rock fragments were small, thin and sharp as knives: flowers couldn't poke their way through them, and any animal that travelled across the plain risked injuring its feet. Patches of the razor-sharp rocks gleamed in the sunlight, like the varnished black or bluish-black background to an oil painting.

The cloudless sky was a pure, clear blue and the rolling mountains, some capped with snow and some not, unfurled like a bridge beneath it. A troop of people dressed in crimson steered their horses into the setting sun, their shadows stretching long and low across the ground, creating strange patterns. Some of them walked with their heads up, scanning this new world to left and right, a spring in their step that caused the hems of their robes to flutter. Others kept their gaze lowered. Everyone wore a different expression, but they all kept spinning their prayer wheels, no matter how long or short their stride. The prayer wheels turned in a single direction, spinning to an easy, unhurried rhythm as natural as the heartbeats beneath those crimson robes.

Master Zhamu made his way to the front of the troop and a disciple held his horse steady. His face was deeply wrinkled, and perhaps because the sun was so strong, his eyes were narrowed. He had kept the secret of the treasure from the day he'd donned his crimson robes, and to protect it he'd sworn never to leave the valley. But to be standing there in peace, far removed from worldly matters and with his heart attuned to the Buddha, that was perhaps the greatest blessing of his life. Protecting the secret was not actually important.

When they reached the foot of the snow mountain, everyone raised their heads in unison to gaze up at the clouds gathered around Tajiapu's peak, stained gold by the evening sun. The white peak softened the fierceness of the sun and made it even more beautiful.

Zhamu sat cross-legged on the ground. Samu followed suit, then the others did likewise. Before them was the great snow mountain, which had waited for so many years. People had longed for this moment, dreamt of this moment: a swathe of crimson gathered at the foot of the mountain. As they looked up, the unexpected beauty of what they saw smote every one of their hearts. Even Basang, who had come for the treasure, lost the vicious look in his eye in the presence of such magnificence.

They began to chant the mantra of the Medicine Buddha, keeping to a gentle rhythm, neither too fast nor too slow, their intonations rising and falling in harmony as if they'd practised it thousands of time.

The seemingly endless chanting made Basang restless. He stamped his feet and occasionally kicked stones across the plain. He couldn't understand how, with the treasure right there in front of them, they could sit so calmly reciting scriptures. Eventually he could stand it no longer and he began to climb the mountain, impatient to get to the treasure.

Gongzha and Feng sat behind the others hand in hand, the brown horse standing beside them with its head down. For fifteen minutes, or perhaps a little longer, the monks' red robes swayed gently to left and right. Then they stood up and straightened their clothes, and a line of crimson dots began to move up towards the peak. Were they fulfilling something decided long ago, or were they brushing the dust from their hearts?

The setting sun slowly paled and the moon climbed towards the mountaintop. It was a sacred, timeless sight: the sun and moon in the sky together.

Suddenly they heard a crash and Gongzha and Feng turned to look. It was as if a patch of red flowers had come into full bloom on the rocky ground some twenty metres behind them. Basang, the man who dreamt of riches, lay in a rapidly expanding pool of blood, his hands and feet twitching.

Red figures came hurrying down the mountainside. Two young men crouched beside Basang, glanced at him and said, 'Master, he's already dead.'

Master Zhamu shook his head and sighed. 'Basang expected Princess Gesar's treasure room to be full of glittering jewels. But what he found was a series of frescoes depicting the twelve great vows of the Medicine Buddha. That is our treasure: the Medicine Buddha's wish that we be in possession of healthy minds, healthy bodies and healthy spirits. Basang could not accept that, so he jumped off the cliff.'

'If your heart and your mind are not healthy,' Samu said, 'then what good is it even if all the wealth in the world is piled in front of you? He never understood that.'

Early the next day, Feng and Gongzha stood in front of Master Zhamu's stone house saying goodbye to the old man.

Zhamu, and those who had hurried over at the news of their departure, escorted them to the mouth of the valley. Prayer flags fluttered between the two red cliff walls, the wind casting high into the air blessings that had gone unchanged for thousands of years. A clear spring rushed out of a fissure in one of the rocks, causing the prayer wheels set along its course to turn constantly. Mantras for peace and wellbeing sounded continually on the breeze.

Master Zhamu pulled out two *khatas* and placed them round Gongzha and Feng's necks. 'Noble children, may the Buddha bless you and grant you health and peace.'

Samu took their faces in his hands and pressed his forehead against theirs. He too placed a pure white *khata* around each of them. The rest of the community came forward and soon all anyone could see were *khatas* and prayer flags dancing in the air.

Gongzha walked over to Ciwang, who was being supported by two young monks because of his crippled leg. 'Yangji is not dead. She was recued in No Man's Land by Jijia.'

Ciwang raised his head and looked at Gongzha, tears glistening in his eyes. 'Thank you, thank you. Go back and tell your mother I am sorry.'

Gongzha nodded. He turned and mounted his horse, then reached down to help Feng up.

The same old horse and the same old gun; he was even still wearing the same old sheepskin *chuba*. They galloped off beneath the blue sky, their figures receding into the distance.

Under that blue sky there were just the two of them: the man rough and proud, the woman soft and sophisticated. The horse kept a steady pace and they passed the nameless lake again; its water rolled and rippled, and the waterfowl chased one another playfully.

'You know, Gongzha, my coming to Tibet and you being here almost as if you'd been waiting for me... it's as if everything was planned for us. That snowstorm that made me lose my way, maybe it was the Buddha who arranged for you to save me, so that no matter how hard I tried when I got back to Shanghai, I couldn't forget you and I had to come back.'

The blue sky is our priest, the great earth our witness; the cool wind carries our promise and prints it on the mountaintop. From this moment on, our hearts and bodies will stay as one and never part. Gongzha looked at Feng and was silent.

At the far end of the flat valley, a black dot suddenly appeared, and with it a voice travelled on the wind, yelling in accented Mandarin, 'Gongzha! Feng!'

'It's Sega,' Feng said to Gongzha. 'Let's go! Quick!' Then she shouted back, 'Sega...!'

'Feng, Gongzha, I've finally found you.' Sega galloped over on her horse. 'Come with me quickly, Yongxi... she... she won't be here long and she wants to see you. She's ill, seriously ill. The doctor's tried many different treatments, but it's no good. They say... they say... Auntie Yongxi might not... not last...'

'What's happened? She seemed fine when I was there,' Feng said, surprised.

'It's all Brother Jijia's fault. Do you remember the little antelopes you raised?'

Gongzha nodded.

'The one called Beibei wandered into Auntie Yongxi's pasture and never left. Jijia ordered his men to follow a herd of pregnant antelopes about to give birth, and they went to her pasture and... and... killed them all. Even Beibei was killed.'

'Poor Beibei, he was so trusting around people...' Feng's tears slid down her face and she buried her head in Gongzha's shoulder.

Gongzha patted her back and looked at Sega. 'And then...?'

'Yongxi's been sick ever since. She throws up everything she eats. Jijia made Qiangba bring her every medicine he has, but none of it's worked.'

'Let's go! Quick!' Gongzha kicked his horse's belly, Sega did the same, and they shot off like arrows to Yongxi's pasture.

29

Another side of Tajiapu Snow Mountain. The wilderness stretched into the far distance and across it a small river wound its way west. A black tent stood on the west-facing slope and a solitary dog lay beside it, staring out across the plain.

Jijia was pacing round and round the outside of the tent, looking more distressed than anyone had ever seen him.

The two horses sped up. The dog got to its feet and bared its teeth, but it didn't need to bark, because the new arrivals were familiar. It lay down again, gazed out at the wilderness and became lost in its thoughts.

When Jijia saw them, he stopped pacing. Gongzha, Feng and Sega dismounted, threw down their whips and followed him into the tent.

Yangji was wiping away her tears as she stood over the stove, stewing some meat, and her daughter Dawacuo sat miserably beside the couch, holding Tajiapu. Yongxi was lying on the couch, showing as little sign of life as a blade of grass in winter.

Sega hurried forward and called softly, 'Auntie, Brother Gongzha is here. Wake up...'

Yongxi finally opened her eyes. When she saw Gongzha and Feng, she tried to sit up but didn't have the strength, so Sega quickly helped her.

'Yongxi.' Gongzha walked over to the couch and Yangji passed him a stool. 'How come you're so sick?'

'Broth... brother, I heard... Feng... was hurt and I kept... worrying. It was all... all my... I brought you trouble, but now...

all is... well, you... have found peace. I can... be calm,' Yongxi said in fits and starts, looking from Gongzha to Feng.

Sega gave a quick translation.

Yongxi put her hand to her mouth and began to cough violently. She spewed out a river of vomit, throwing up all of the medicine she'd just taken. 'Feng, I... didn't protect... Beibei, he was shot... and killed. He...' Yongxi gasped. Her face flushed and she pointed at Jijia, who was standing behind Gongzha with his head bowed.

He didn't dare say anything.

Feng forced back the tears that were welling and lightly patted Yongxi's hand, which had got so thin her bones jutted out. 'That's okay, Sister Yongxi, Beibei has gone to Shambhala. That's a heaven for animals as well as people. He'll never be hurt again, so don't feel guilty, alright?'

'Bless you and Brother, you... you two are both... good people.'

'You're a good person too, Sister Yongxi,' Feng said. 'Without your directions, I might still be looking for him.' She glanced at Gongzha beside her, her eyes clouded with tears. Since coming back to the grassland, she'd been deeply moved by the kindness and sincerity of the grassland women: Yongxi herself, and Sega, who'd injured her and then saved her, and Yangji and Dawacuo.

Yongxi continued to gasp. Sega tried to get her to lie back down, but Yongxi waved her away. Once she'd caught her breath, she turned to Sega. 'Thank you, Sega. Tajiapu... Tajiapu...'

Dawacuo hurriedly brought the little boy over. 'He's here, Auntie. Tajiapu's here. Tajiapu, say something to your mother.'

'Ama...' he wailed.

Yongxi rubbed her son's head. Her eyes suddenly flashed and her words had force to them. 'Tajiapu, my son, Ama cannot take care of you any more. You must listen to Sister, and don't be naughty. When you've grown up, don't just go wandering about on the grassland – you have to go to school. Alright?'

Tajiapu didn't understand what she was saying, he just kept crying as he crawled onto her.

Jijia suddenly lifted his head. 'I'll send him to school, don't worry,' he said, tears dropping down his cheeks. 'I'll definitely send our son to school.' Watching the life of the woman he loved slowly slip away was enough to make even ruthless, bloodthirsty Jijia cry.

Yongxi didn't look at him; she didn't want to see him. Ever since he'd come into her life, she hadn't had a day's peace. But things would be better now; she would finally be released and she wouldn't have to worry any more. In her next life, she would marry a steady grassland man. She wouldn't care if their life was hard; as long as they lived out their days in peace, she would be content.

Jijia couldn't stand the sight of Yongxi's vacant stare. He knelt by the couch, grasped her hand and held it to his tear-streaked face. 'I'll disband the shadow hunters, woman. I'll disband them very soon, how's that? You get well, and I'll disband the shadow hunters.' Then he shouted out of the tent, 'Qiangba!'

Qiangba came in. 'Brother!'

'Disband the shadow hunters, give your auntie some peace. From now on, no one is allowed to kill antelopes. Do you hear me?'

'Brother...'

'Go! Tell everyone,' Jijia said fiercely. 'As of today, the shadow hunters are no longer.' He turned and spoke coaxingly to Yongxi. 'See, woman, I've put a stop to it. I won't kill any more antelopes, or wild yaks either. I'll just stay here with you and look after our son; we'll raise yaks and sheep.'

Yongxi looked at him, and there was a new calmness in her face. 'You owe the wilderness a huge blood debt, Jijia. Do you think the Buddha will let you off? If you really want to change, go and turn yourself in. Turn yourself in to the government.'

'Give myself up?' Jijia murmured. 'Go to jail?'

'You were never willing to stop the slaughter.' Yongxi averted her gaze. Her eyes swept over everyone in the tent and they were full of pain and longing. Then her head slumped to the side. She lay in Sega's arms and slowly closed her eyes.

'Woman…! Woman…!' Jijia lay down beside Yongxi's body and wailed.

The sky was suddenly thick with black clouds and hail came down in bursts. The dog continued sitting in front of the tent, staring fixedly at the snow mountain through the clouds. Then it let out a tortured howl and raced off into the wilderness.

A fortnight later, news circulated that the police had suddenly burst into the shadow hunters' base; it was said that some of the poachers had been arrested and others had escaped.

Yangji took her daughter Dawacuo back to the grassland and she had a little boy with her.

People said that Sega went back to Ganzi in Sichuan and took Qiangba, the shadow hunters' doctor, with her. No one knew what happened to Jijia.

Thanks to Feng's pleading, Gongzha finally agreed to give up trying to get his revenge on Kaguo. After all, Kaguo had only been acting in defence of her cub, just as he would have done anything to protect his Cuomu.

The mistiness that shrouds ancient legends eventually clears, and histories always have an ending. But when it comes to people…

> The stars in the sky
> Are like Brother's eyes
> Watching Sister's silhouette.
> The butter lamps ablaze all night
> Cannot see your eyes, Brother,
> As they fall inside the tent
> To light up Sister's heart.

Two figures that had seen a great deal were engraved into the eternal scroll of heaven and earth. Age-old songs lifted on the breeze and drifted in the deep blues of Cuoe Lake.

The woman smiled broadly, slipped her hand into the man's palm and rested against him. They gazed out across the grassland to where the jade-coloured grass met the sky. Up in the heavens, a great ball of fire hung gleaming and resplendent over Mount Chanaluo.

The two figures on the grassland stayed together, year upon year.

Translator's Note

Making decisions about the language used in *Love in No Man's Land*, a book written in Mandarin about Mandarin- and Tibetan-speaking characters, was no easy task.

In the hope that readers of this English translation will be equipped to find out more about the places and topics featured in the novel, I have tried to use commonly received place names and terms. Where none were readily available (primarily for character names, but also for some place names), I have used Mandarin Pinyin.

I have retained Tibetan and dialect family terms and translated Mandarin family terms into English.

– Hallie Treadway

Glossary

aba – father

ama – mother

baijiu – Chinese alcohol distilled from grain

bodhisattva – in Mahayana Buddhism, a person who delays entering nirvana in order to guide others along their spiritual path

bala – father

bola – grandfather

cham – Buddhist dance performed in masks and costumes at temples

chuba – traditional outer robe of Tibetan nomads, often made of sheepskin or leather with the fleece worn closest to the skin; it's fastened around the waist or hips and pulled up to create a spacious front pocket for carrying tools, food and other items; the sleeves are very long and one or both are usually shrugged off the shoulder and tied around the waist

fen – smallest unit of Chinese currency: one-tenth of one mao

Four Olds – the four elements of traditional Chinese culture – 'old ideas', 'old customs', 'old habits' and 'old culture' – that, according to the Cultural Revolution, needed to be smashed in order for China to progress

gela – teacher

Guxiula – an honorific for monks

khata – a ceremonial scarf, usually white, worn or presented on special occasions

living Buddha – reincarnate custodian and teacher of Buddhist doctrine; *tulku*

mao – unit of Chinese currency: one tenth of one RMB

mo – granny

momo – steamed meat dumpling

PLA – People's Liberation Army

production team – rural work unit in communist China

Shambhala – mythical Tibetan Buddhist utopia, Shangri-La or heavenly realm

struggle session – public meeting used during the Cultural Revolution to humiliate and forcibly extract confessions from anyone perceived to be a class enemy

tsampa – roasted barley or buckwheat flour: a staple food in Tibet, often mixed into hot tea

yuan – unit of Chinese currency: another term for RMB

Vajrapani – a bodhisattva and protector of the Buddha